BOOKS BY MARY ELSIE ROBERTSON

Family Life   1987

Speak, Angel   1983

The Clearing   1982

After Freud   1981

Jordan's Stormy Banks   1961

FAMILY LIFE

FAMILY LIFE

Mary Elsie Robertson

1987

New York

ATHENEUM

Sappho's poetry on page 49 is from Archilochos, Sappho, Alkman, *translated by Guy Davenport. © 1980 The Regents of the University of California. Reprinted by permission.*

ACKNOWLEDGMENTS   I want to thank the National Endowment for the Arts for the generous support which enabled me to write this novel.

Library of Congress Cataloging-in-Publication Data

Robertson, Mary Elsie, ———
    Family life.

    I. Title.
PS3568.02497F36   1987   813'.54   86-47925
ISBN 0-689-11890-2

Copyright © 1987 by Mary Elsie Robertson
All rights reserved
Published simultaneously in Canada by Collier Macmillan Canada, Inc.
Composition by Westchester Book Composition, Inc., Yorktown Heights, New York
Manufactured by Maple-Vail Manufacturing Group,
York, Pennsylvania
Designed by Laura Rohrer
First Edition

For my father, Tom Robertson, and in

memory of my mother, Esther Scherer Robertson

PART ONE

1

Waiting on the curb for the driver to take her bicycle from the luggage compartment, Chrissy heard wind—the breeze that comes near dawn when the darkness thins. Only the black shapes of the trees on the other side of the street loomed against the sky. It was too dark to see the leaves. She was the only one to get off the bus at Falmouth so early in the morning, and when the driver thrust the handlebars into her hands and swung back into the bus, closing the door behind him without looking back, she had a moment of regret for her seat by the window and for the sound of the big tires fanning the air into a faint sizzling sound.

She thought of her cot back in the camp in Maine, the pillow smooth as a seal's back. The others would find the note propped against the coffeepot when they got up—just now, in the darkness—to go out to the nesting sites with the traps.

"Family emergency," she had written. "Must go home immediately."

But the others would see the note only as further evidence that she was odd. Sneaking off was probably no more than they'd expected of her. Evidently she had been observed sitting on one of the boulders in the middle of the night, looking out to sea.

One day a girl with pale green eyes had asked when the two of them were standing behind the same rock waiting for the terns to rise from their nests, "Do you walk in your sleep?"

Chrissy shook her head.

"Somebody told me you did. They saw you out on the rocks for ages and ages. They say you're never in your bed." And the girl gave her a sudden, sharp look.

"I don't sleepwalk," was all Chrissy would tell her. She wouldn't try to explain that she couldn't rest in a roomful of sleeping girls—all those people breathing and rolling from side to side, whispering or grinding their teeth in the darkness.

But this was not the reason she'd left the camp the night before, pedaling away on her bicycle as soon as the others were in bed, heading for town and the bus stop. She'd left because of her mother's letters, every one of which had been so bland it was frightening. Estella's letters, into which she ordinarily poured her angers, frustrations, and joys, had become no more than a dull catalogue of events. "What's the matter with you?" Chris had written back, scared. "You sound like you've had a brain transplant."

Everything was fine, Estella wrote back. Just fine. She and Philip had gotten to Nantucket and unloaded the car and after that there seemed nothing to say. In the middle of a sheet of paper Estella's message took up five lines—and this from someone who usually wrote five or six pages with leftover sentences making a border up, down, and around.

So that was why Chrissy was pedaling down the streets of Falmouth through the dark tunnel the trees formed over her head, making her way like a snake knowing through warm, through cool, touch more precise than sight. She just shut her eyes and sailed. And then opened them in time to see the sign, picked out by the streetlight: *To the Islands*.

When she was little, she and Liddy used to watch for the *Islands* sign, sitting in the backseat of the car watching the trees move past like a reel of film. They would silently point when they saw it, pinching the thin skin along each other's wristbones while the little hairs rose along their arms, their faces turned to each other and their teeth clamped hard on lower lips to contain the glee. It was the best moment when they saw the sign. It was all there ahead of them—the sea, the ferry, the white sand under that intense sky. The four of them together for the summer.

As she passed the sign now, a ripple went up her backbone as though the back of a thumbnail were sliding upward touching every knob. It was the old childhood esctasy which she would hold on to no matter what. But Liddy, in London, had deserted. Having spent her junior year at

London University studying economics, she would spend the summer there too. But she had deserted Chrissy long before London, long before she went away to college, even. Now when Liddy wrote there was usually some unpleasantness attached to what she said. In reply to Chrissy's letter about being accepted, along with twenty other high school science students, to work at the camp in Maine banding terns—a letter in which Chrissy had attempted to be enthusiastic—Liddy had written back: "It's about time you got away from home, Chris. Seventeen, and you haven't even been to summer camp. But I guess it's never too late to learn." Chrissy now believed that even when they were children Liddy had often disapproved of her, though she hadn't noticed at the time.

Sailing down the low hills, under the trees still dark and stirred by strange murmurings, she came into Woods Hole and to the slip where two ferries waited, gray hulks in the darkness. Gliding past a long line of cars snaking up the slope waiting for standby passage, she could see people asleep inside, their necks lying crookedly along the headrests, their mouths open.

Then she was down the hill and coasting along the dock where the smell of salt had been waiting for her. Each time it was like being born all over again—that smell of salt, like ammonia, stinging her into awareness.

The silence except for the distant slap, slap of water against the pilings seemed uncanny, that invisible water with its sudden dropoffs into unimaginable depths—all that which was hidden by the morning fog.

On clear days when the sea lay deep blue under the sun it seemed a friendly, even magical element. But on cloudy days when it lay brooding and opaque, she was afraid of it. She could remember her father trying to pull her into the water on one of those cloudy days, telling her calmly and reasonably that the water had stored heat for weeks and it would be warmer than the air. But it wasn't the temperature of the water she cared about, and all the way across the sand she fought with such desperation to free her wrist from his hand that Estella intervened. "Have you set out to make Chrissy hate the ocean?" she said, her voice husky with disapproval. "Because that's what you're doing, Philip. Exactly what you're doing."

So her father turned her loose of her wrist just at the edge of the water, leaving her still shrieking and scrambling to get out of the way of the incoming wave into which he dived with such force.

* * *

Chrissy was riding back along the pier, heading once more for the ferries, when she heard the first birdsong. It was a robin, sounding tentative at first, maybe sleepy, the sound so pure and sweet it seemed never to have vibrated the air of this planet before. It could have been the first birdsong ever, from the throat of the first bird capable of uttering it.

For as long as a minute the first bird had the dawn to himself, and then his voice was lost among others. In Maine, Chrissy knew, the air would be full just then of the raucous cries of the terns. At first light, when they flew up from the rocks to fish, skimming over the water like a cloud, they covered the sky. But when they returned to their nests and were caught in the traps they grew quiet. As she fastened the bands around the terns' legs, they fixed her with their black eyes and she cawed back at them, pretending she was a tern, too. Their eyes, watching her, were like knowing blackberries or black doorknobs. Sometimes they clasped her finger tightly in their beaks, but their eyes never wavered from hers.

In the light that suddenly turned the sky pearly so the trees and roofs of houses were dark against it, the maw of the *Nantucketer* lay like the mouth of an enormous whale and a murmur of car engines began as drivers started to inch forward to what they thought would be good positions for entering the ferry. She had been in those lines many times and knew the whole routine. She and Liddy read as they sprawled on their backs in the station wagon, lurching from side to side as her father whipped right or left into a position that would give him three inches' advantage while her mother kept springing out to buy cups of coffee or to go to the edge of the ferry to look inside the cavernous space where the cars would soon be maneuvered. There appeared to be purpose in her striding, urgency in her speed, but it was only restlessness. She and Liddy read through it all, hardly bothering to look out the car window once the sun came up and the light grew ordinary. Once on the ferry they ran up and down the narrow stairs or went to the end of the deck to throw Fritos to the gulls. They were old hands and knew what was important and what wasn't.

That time, when she and Liddy sprawled in the back of the station wagon with their legs touching, was before Jasper was born. Now he loved to hear stories from that time; it was astonishing to him to know that they had managed without him. Even before he was born, he was sure, his presence must have been felt.

Among the Tungi, whom they had lived with for three years, Jasper would be a favored child, his mother's last, who would not have to give up her breasts to make way for the next baby. The last child is a lucky one. But Jasper missed out on Africa too—something he could never quite forgive the others for.

Chrissy had described many times the village with its round huts and the noises the hyenas made at night. "In the evenings Liddy and I could go anywhere we wanted to in the camp," she told him. "People would call us over and we'd go and visit. I was very happy when we lived there."

But when Chrissy told Jasper this a look of fury came over his face.

"You shouldn't have let me miss it!" he said to her accusingly. "All the good things."

People with bicycles were allowed to board first, and Chrissy entered the white mouth of the ferry and went as far as she could—until the front wheel of her bicycle nearly touched the end of the ship. Farther, farther, the men in work shirts waved. She pushed the bicycle forward a few inches and kicked down the stand. She would be the first off the ferry, bumping along the cobblestones before the cars even started to move.

While the rest of the bike riders established themselves in the best seats where they would be sheltered from the wind, Chrissy went directly to the deck and leaned over the rail. The fog still lay over the water, but she knew something about the weather on those coasts and was certain the fog would burn away as the sun rose higher; it would be a beautiful day with a sky of perfect purity.

Another woman chose to stand beside the railing too. She leaned over it, her elbows pressed into her sides. Chrissy watched the woman's sandals, the kind she associated with Greek children—sandals with heavy soles and wide bands of thick leather. The woman's hair fell forward covering her cheek so that Chrissy couldn't see her face. But the look Chrissy gave her was hostile. The woman was too near, had invaded her space, and Chrissy wanted to nudge her away with the sharp point of her elbow.

Yet when the woman half turned in her direction, Chrissy saw that she was smiling as she looked out over the water. The woman was happy, that was clear, and Chrissy was ashamed of her bad thoughts. For that reason she remained standing beside her so they were both at the railing when the ferry pulled out from the pier. They both saw the fog thin, and lighten, and the sun emerge suddenly from the wisps of broken cloud. For a moment Chrissy was dazed by the light and shut her eyes. What she felt was that old familiar sensation of sinking, hands and feet immensely heavy, what she knew of herself like a bowl rocking on the current.

(7)

Suddenly she felt the woman's hand, tight on her arm. "Watch out!" she said. "If you fall over the rail you'll be sucked under the blades."

Chrissy opened her eyes to see the woman's, watching her. But her feet rode the deck easily, her hands resting on the rail.

"It just got so bright all of a sudden," Chrissy said. "The sun's in my eyes."

"Mine too," the woman said. "For a minute all I could see was the sea, turning a dark purple."

When Chrissy opened her eyes again she saw that they had adjusted and the sea was blue-green and translucent after all; she was a little disappointed to see that the woman had moved toward the end of the boat where the gulls were swooping, looking for food.

2

Through the heavy white dust the narrow wheels of the bicycle slid. For a moment, like someone held in the frame of a photograph, Chrissy balanced, though the bicycle was held at an impossible angle and there was nothing she could do against whatever it was that would force her down into the dust. Into the bushes she sprawled, with one leg still over the bar of the bicycle, her attention caught by the glittering of the shadbush leaves above her head. Though she could feel no breeze, the shad leaves rocked on their stems, moving against all natural law.

She waited for the spirit to pass, waiting as she had learned from the Tungi. *Bad thing pass me by, he waiting for me.*

As she watched, the leaves of the shadbush stilled and hung as limply as the other leaves.

Only then did she pull the bicycle upright and push it to the top of the rise. When she reached the lane that sloped down to the house she lifted the chain barring the way and dragged the bicycle on its side. It was the easy part then, coasting through the dappled shade of the pine trees, the wheels silent on the thick needles.

Through the noon heat the only sound was the crack as the waves broke along the shore, though the heat waves quivering above the wild roses, the blackberry, shad, hawthorn, were surely a manifestation of sound.

All that life seemed to give off a kind of deep hum, a throbbing as from many beating hearts.

Faster and faster she came down the slope, fear suddenly taking her breath. She would find nothing when she rounded the bend but a pile of shingles and broken boards, a blackened shell gutted to the foundation.

But the house was safe, a gray the color of weathered granite, and there was the sea, a line of deep blue, and nearer, coming ever nearer, the crest of a wave that broke suddenly into startling white.

The bicycle bumped over the rough ground and came to rest against the deck railing. But though she stood, legs astride the bar, listening for voices, for Jenks's bark, there was no sound except that of the sea.

Cupping her hands around her face, she looked through the screen into the room, which seemed to have been abandoned only seconds before. There was the newspaper half unfolded, flung into one corner of the sofa, an apple core balanced precariously at the edge of the coffee table. Over the rectangle of floor, Jasper had made a pattern of rocks and shells—she knew how he had hunched, resting on knees and elbows, carefully placing each rock, each shell.

Very softly she opened the screen door and tiptoed into the room, picking her way between Jasper's stones. In the kitchen the breakfast dishes sat unwashed on the cabinet—dried egg caked on the plates, brown drops of coffee congealed on the sides of the cups. Slid onto the counter by careless or hasty hands, the cups lay on their sides in the saucers.

Inside her father's study, sunlight warmed his papers, which lay in neat stacks beside his typewriter, and on two walls the kinship charts hung as they had for years, drawn up in her father's small, beautiful hand. Their neatness and order comforted her. When she was a child she had often stood tracing her finger along the lines in the charts connecting family members. In her head she had seen them all clearly, sorted into families the way her paper dolls were in their boxes—there they were fixed forever no matter what had happened to the people since her father had captured them all there on the paper. Even death and dispersal changed nothing in the charts.

As she watched, the rose with its stem in a water glass suddenly released its petals onto the desk top, where they rocked gently from their fall. Chrissy whipped her head around to look at the door, listening for a footfall, before she ran through the kitchen, jumped the railing of the deck, and sprinted to the boathouse.

The boathouse had been turned years ago into a studio for Estella. One glance inside showed Chrissy that it was empty, but she ran through it anyway, hesitating only long enough to touch the squeezings of paint lying wet and gleaming on a piece of glass. Teal blue and vermilion stuck to her fingertips, and when she bent to look underneath the daybed she left dots of color on the spread.

The beach, too, was deserted, even the water abandoned. There was only the sizzling of the water as it emptied from the crabs' holes, only the shadows of the gulls sliding over the sand.

She was far along the beach before she looked down and saw the holes gouged by the heels of someone taking vigorous strides just at the water line. And then she saw, crisscrossing those, the prints of a dog.

It was Jenks's voice she heard first, far up the beach—the bass *arr, arr, arr* with a little wheeze at the end, the voice of an old dog. Then she could see him running to the foam dying in the sand, front and back legs working together the way a horse bucks.

One of Jenks's eyes was cloudy with cataract, and he was going deaf. Until Chrissy was very near he continued to bark, guarding the pair of jeans with the legs rolled up and the blue work shirt that Estella had dropped when she entered the water.

Chrissy crouched, telling Jenks good boy, good boy. When he was near enough to recognize her, he whined and pawed at her sneakers, and she patted him, though it was the pile of clothes she kept looking at, knowing just how Estella had stood with her eyes fixed far out on the water as she absently unbuttoned her shirt. She had unsnapped her jeans the same way, never once looking down as they fell into the sand. Straight out she had walked ignoring the cold, diving under the arching wave so its power had passed harmlessly over her head.

Shading her eyes, Chrissy searched for Estella's head bobbing beyond the point where the waves broke. But the sea was empty of everything except a small fishing boat, far out.

"Mom!" she called, her panic the old familiar one she had shared with Liddy so many times when they were children. How often they had danced up and down on the sand, straining to see Estella's head still bobbing in the water. "Come back!" they had cried, holding hands, forlorn, abandoned, at the water's edge. It was hard to see so small a thing as the human head among the waves, the sloughs, the sparkling of sunlight.

It had been Chrissy who had brought Liddy so many times to stare at Estella's chest as she lay with eyes shut in the hammock, Chrissy whispering, her fear contagious, "She isn't breathing. Is she, Liddy? Is she breathing?"

They had held their own breaths, hearts hammering, until they could see it unmistakably: Estella's chest rising and just as surely falling again.

Liddy's fury had broken then over Chrissy's head like a dark wave. "If you do this one more time, Chrissy, I'll pick up a rock and hit you with it. You hear me? I swear I'll hit you a good one." When Liddy was angry she danced up and down the way she would have stomped something small and deadly under her feet—a scorpion, say. What she hated most was being caught out; she detested revealing what she felt.

And it was true that Chrissy had liked to catch Liddy out; there were times when she was gratified to see that Liddy felt the same way she did, hard as she tried to hide it. Chrissy knew that Liddy had loved Estella as much as she had then, was as helpless in the strength of that love even though she wouldn't admit it.

When Chrissy looked at the water again it was to see a figure climbing heavily up the slope where the waves washed in and were drawn out—a figure dark against the sun with broad shoulders and powerful legs, the face shadowed so that Chrissy's breath caught.

And then the light shifted and she could see Estella walking slowly up the beach, every step made difficult by the power of the undertow. Her gray hair was slicked back by the sea so that her face emerged shining. Estella stocky and firm in her old green suit.

Over the noise of the waves Chrissy cried out, "I was afraid you'd drowned!"

On Estella's face Chrissy could clearly see surprise and pleasure.

"Where did *you* come from?" Estella said. And then, just as clearly, Chrissy could see Estella suddenly remember and the look of dismay replace that of pleasure as she lifted her hands, palms up. "Oh, Chrissy, I thought you liked it there," she said.

Chrissy looked down at her feet, embarrassed. Confronted with Estella's disappointed face it was impossible for her to explain why she had left the camp in Maine. Impossible to say, "I came back because I was afraid."

"I couldn't see you in the waves," Chrissy said, looking up to see the water streaming down Estella's body and falling into the sand. "I thought maybe you'd drowned."

"You had a vision up in Maine of me drowning and so you came down here to see? Oh, Chrissy, Chrissy! I thought you were staying through July." With her fists clenched, Estella thrust her hands into the sleeves of her shirt. "You were learning so much, that's what you wrote. I thought you were even enjoying it."

"Yes, well . . ." Chrissy said, but the words that would have told about her fear were impossible to say. "It's nearly Jasper's birthday," she said lamely.

Although Estella put her arms around her, Chrissy could feel Estella's disapproval through the stiffness of her shoulders.

"Aren't you even glad to see me?" Chrissy said, pulling away.

Estella threw her jeans over her shoulder and strode down the beach. "That's not the point, Chrissy. You know it's not."

Though her legs were longer than Estella's, Chrissy had to walk fast— had to trot, nearly—to keep up. As always in her mother's presence, she felt taken off balance.

"I hate it when you swim off by yourself like that," Chrissy said. "What if you got a cramp?"

"I'd drown, I suppose. And that would be that."

The note of bitterness that sometimes came into Estella's voice had always filled Chrissy with dismay.

"You didn't write," she said, tears coming to her eyes. "Nothing at all for days."

"Didn't I?" Estella said absently. "Maybe I didn't. I've had things on my mind."

Behind them Jenks wheezed, trying to keep up.

"What things?" Chrissy said.

"Why, your father," Estella said, turning on Chrissy a look of such hostility she felt her mouth drop open, though the words of objection would not come to her lips. And then she saw that Estella's eyes were distant after all and it was not to her the hostility was directed. "Who else could make me want to kill?"

As though it were a matter of the greatest importance, Chrissy lifted her wrist and studied the face of her watch.

"But he'll cook in his own juice, as your grandmother used to say," Estella said, holding Chrissy's hand so hard that it might have been caught in a trap she could find no release from. "Don't ever think he won't."

"Look!" Chrissy said, lifting her free hand. "The hawk, right there above those bushes. Hovering. See her?"

They were both in time to see the hawk swoop, and they waited, breaths held, for the shriek. There was none, yet when the hawk rose again from the bushes they could clearly see the body—something small and gray—in its talons.

3

It was that crowd of people, come in on the ferry, jostling each other around the postcard stands. He hated the way all those people pushed in, thinking they had some right, thinking just because they came in on the morning ferry and would leave on the evening one that they had made the place theirs. They thought they'd come into possession of the gray houses with white trim, the cobblestoned street lined with elm trees. But they hadn't. He'd been coming there from the time he was a baby and he knew of places those people would never discover.

Outside the stationer's the tall man with the beard, the one with the Newfoundland puppy on a new red leash, was sitting on a bench talking to a friend. Jasper had seen the puppy earlier when the man carried it inside the store.

Now the puppy danced on the end of its leash when it saw Jasper, hopping on its hind legs and falling down awkwardly on all four paws.

"Hello, dog," Jasper said, dropping to his knees on the sidewalk and putting the puppy's front paws on his shoulders. "Sweet dog, sweet dog." The puppy licked his chin and then, in a transport of joy or shyness, turned its head sideways and leaped on the end of the leash. Dogs always liked him. He talked to them the same way he did to people, and he knew he had an understanding with them the same way his sister Chrissy did.

The puppy rolled over on its back and waved its large, foolish feet in the air. Its small twig of a tail trembled soundlessly against the sidewalk. Jasper picked the puppy up and held it cradled in his arms, sitting cross-legged to make a lap for it to lie in. Through the puppy's loose skin he could feel it leap with happiness. Jasper's face, inches above its head, the only object in the world it cared about. Oh, to touch skin with tongue.

Benignly, Jasper lowered his chin so the puppy could reach it.

"He thinks you're an ice cream cone," the man with the beard said above Jasper's head. Jasper could feel attention from the man centering on him, though he kept his head lowered.

"Dino loves everybody," the man said above his head. "Don't you, silly puppy?"

"Dogs love me especially," Jasper said.

When the man leaned over Jasper's shoulder to scratch the puppy familiarly on the top of the head, asserting his rights of ownership, Jasper pushed the puppy into the man's hands and ran down the sidewalk without looking back. He hated it when he talked like that, acting as silly as that puppy, getting all friendly and excited, loving to have attention centered on him. Later it was embarrassing to think about.

He crossed the street, dodging the slow-moving cars, and headed for the wharf where the yachts were. He would have plenty of time before his father came looking for him.

Jasper ran along the wharf, watching his dazzlingly white sneakers—brand-new Nikes with blue streaks along the sides—as they maneuvered so cleverly along the wide planks, dodging other sneakers, sandals, hiking boots. Flash, they went. Oh, very very fast. Never a mistake. And even while he watched his sneakers he was also watching from the corners of his eyes the wonderful boats, the gleam of polished brass and waxed mahogany. The people who owned the boats sat on cushions reading newspapers, working crossword puzzles, or doing needlepoint, oblivious and indifferent to eyes watching them from the pier. They were rich. They didn't have to take any notice of eyes watching them. They paid no more attention to people than they did to the gulls sitting on the masts of the boats.

Jasper understood their indifference. If he'd been one of them sitting in his own boat, so white it hurt the eyes to look at, he wouldn't have bothered to look up, either. He was like those people on the boats himself, not like those others wandering up and down the wharf, staring. And he could prove it.

Quickly he found the most beautiful boat of all, the one with the tallest mast, the longest deck. Sitting on this boat, only a few feet away from where Jasper stood on the wharf, were a gray-haired man and woman. The woman was leaning over a book and the man was doing nothing at all as far as Jasper could tell. Perhaps he was asleep.

With the toes of his gleaming sneakers extending over the edge of the pier, Jasper crouched and squeezed his legs against his chest. Dreamily he let his eyes climb the mast and rise to study the sky. After a long time, when he let his gaze plunge downward again, it was directly into the blue eyes of the woman, who had lifted her head from her book. He had known, long before her eyes looked into his, that she was watching. Jasper turned his head to the side as though overcome with shyness, feeling his hair fan over his forehead. When he looked up again he was smiling.

It was always the smile that did it. When he smiled, as he well knew, dimples appeared at the corners of his mouth. There was a small gap between his two front teeth which many people found appealing. And his hair, in the sunlight, shone with the rich gleam of true gold. He knew he was beautiful, since people often told him so. And he could see for himself whenever he looked into a mirror.

"Does it feel like you're flying, when you're under full sail?" Jasper asked the woman quickly before she could turn away.

"Yes, I suppose it does, rather," the woman said. At the sound of her English accent Jasper smiled again in pure and easy pleasure. The English ones, especially the old English ones, were so easy for him.

"It must be wonderful to soar that way."

The woman was charmed, he saw immediately. "Would you like to come on board and have a look around?" she said, making up her mind quickly the way the rich always did. "I don't suppose your parents would mind?"

"I'm not supposed to make a nuisance of myself."

"I wouldn't have asked you if you were being tiresome. Come on, then. Give me your hand and jump."

At this moment the man woke from whatever dream he'd been having and rose from his chair. Jasper landed at his feet and extended his hand toward the man's stomach. He was a very tall man, and Jasper had to tip his head far back in order to look him in the eye. It was important to have a direct gaze and a loud voice. That kind of man admired directness and loudness.

"My name's Jasper Sloan," he said, giving the man's hand a good, firm shake.

It was hard to keep his attention on the man's bulgy eyes when there was the whole of the boat to look at, but he forced himself to do it.

The man and the woman were taken with him, competing for his attention. The man showed him the instrument panel and the small wheel, like a toy, that steered the boat. The woman took him into the cabin and showed him the pink roses and the bowl of pomegranates. They seemed unsure what would please him most and he pretended to enjoy it all. Perhaps he did enjoy it. It was hard for him to tell, because he could act so well. It was no trouble at all to let a simple, sweet look come over his face. Though he was nearly seven, he was small for his age, so people often thought he was no more than five. He let them think what they liked.

"I'd love to have a boat exactly like this one day," Jasper said. "When I'm grown up. I'll sail through the isles of Greece and around the Capes."

"You might do that," the man said approvingly. "But I don't advise you to take a yacht around the Capes. Greece is a different matter, though."

Before they helped him off the boat again, the woman gave Jasper a pomegranate and the man stuck a cap on his head. *St. Crispinian* was the name on it. The cap was too big, so the rim came down over his eyes. He smiled under its weight, and the man and woman laughed.

"How sweet he looks," the woman said. "Don't you think so, Giles?"

Jasper left the cap on until the man set him on the pier, and then he took it off to wave. The man and woman, standing side by side, didn't ask him to come back to their boat, but Jasper thought this was probably just an oversight. Perhaps they were going to be in Nantucket for only one day.

When he came to an alleyway leading from the wharf, out of sight of the boat, Jasper took the top off a garbage can and dropped the cap inside. It was too big and he was sure it made him look silly. He sniffed the pomegranate, but not even its smell was appealing, and he hated the way it was pink and had a grainy, mottled skin. So he threw it into the trash can too and dropped the lid in place with a clatter.

Unimpeded, he looked up at the sky. The sun was full in his face and the shadows had shrunk very small. It couldn't be much past noon.

As Jasper came up from the alley he could see one portion of Main Street ahead of him—a rectangle like a picture in a frame. And right there, in the middle of the picture, was his father standing under one of the elm trees. But his father wasn't alone. Beside him, so close their shoulders touched, there was a woman—one Jasper had never seen before. Their faces were turned together and they were looking straight into each other's eyes as he had tried to look at the man on the boat. His father's hand lifted and settled on the woman's back, the hand like an animal of some kind, doing what it wanted. Jasper could see it clearly, the fingers spread, covering as much of the woman's back as it could. And then the hand slipped downward slowly, as though it were thinking about that, too, and sailed off vaguely into the air just below the band of the woman's skirt.

Now the two of them—his father and the woman—were talking to each other. They were still looking straight into each other's eyes.

Suddenly Jasper ran across the street, defying Volvos and Datsuns, Jasper running fast, watching his sneakers.

Between the woman and his father he pushed his head. He put his arms around his father's legs and held on, swinging back and forth, his father's legs like a tree trunk.

His father held Jasper's head, pressing it into his stomach, so it was there through the cloth of his shirt that Jasper heard him laugh.

"Jasper," he was saying, and the words rumbled in his stomach. "My son, Jasper. Hey, Jasper, look up, will you? I want you to meet a friend of mine."

They knew a lot of people, his parents did. Some he liked and some he didn't and he knew quickly which way it was going to be. This time, even before he lifted his head and looked at the woman, he felt it wasn't going to be any good. Even before he looked at her he disliked her.

Sometimes when people met him they bent down on one knee as though he were royalty or a dog they intended to shake hands with. The woman didn't bend her knees but she lowered her head to look at him.

"Hello, Jasper," she said, but her eyes weren't open to his. Her smile was too careful.

Jasper pushed his head into his father's stomach. "I'm starving. Can't we go home?"

"Jasper, you're being rude," his father said sharply. "You haven't said hello to Jane."

Jasper turned his head so he could see the woman's cheek. "Hello," he said, giving her the benefit of one of his smiles. But she wasn't even looking at him.

"I really am starving," Jasper said again.

"So are we," his father said. "We're starved too. I thought we'd go to the Sweet Shoppe for lunch."

"I thought we were going home."

"So we can visit a little more with Jane. She's an old friend of mine. She's an anthropologist, too."

"Could I have a banana split all to myself?"

His father laughed, looking at Jane over the top of Jasper's head, trying to get her to laugh, too, but she walked on, pretending to be studying the trees they were passing under. "All right," his father said. "You drive a hard bargain, Jasper."

It wasn't the three of them together at all, though that was what his father wanted. It was the woman looking away and his father watching her. Jasper wasn't with either one of them.

He balked in the middle of the sidewalk, and when they walked on without him the space where he had been, between them, closed up immediately the way water flows into a hole. They might have gone on without him and not even have noticed, but he caught up, taking possession of his father's hand, the hand on the side away from Jane—holding the two middle fingers tightly in his fist the way he used to hold on to his father's hand when he was very small.

It might be worth it, letting them have their boring talk, if he could have a banana split all to himself, but it wouldn't be the way his father wanted it. If he had to sit at the same table with them he would, but it wasn't going to be the three of them together. There were the two of them and there was him. That's the way it was, and he saw that even if his father didn't.

4

It had been Philip's belief, one built up and in fact tested over time—one that he could find evidence for not only among the people he had grown up with, lived with, loved and worked with but among those he had studied, too—that we choose most of what happens to us. Even our deaths, he believed, we often choose. At least something inside us becomes profoundly tired of being alive and decides that enough is enough—though surely there were accidents that were accidental, and surely happy people did sometimes die. Of course they did.

And yet it was the other belief that he fell back on slyly, tenaciously, and even with secret satisfaction. We choose what happens to us.

When he considered the matter carefully, however—and he did consider it practically every time he found himself alone—he could not quite convince himself that he had chosen to fall in love with Jane McHenry. That some malevolent discontent had harbored in his unconscious just waiting to strike, choosing the moment he saw Jane standing by the reservation desk of the Sheraton Hotel in Boston, preparatory to checking into the same Northeastern Anthropology Conference he was attending, to make itself known.

He knew instantly, even in that first moment, that she reminded him of someone else in her tallness, with her hair thick and heavy like a horse's mane. But it wasn't until she felt him watching her and turned her head to look steadily back, studying his face, on the verge of speaking or so he thought, that something about her eyes—that steady directness but also the color, a deep blue-green—suddenly stirred his memory.

At first he couldn't remember the name, it was buried so far back in his past, but then it came to him—Allison Wade Jackson, the first woman he had ever been in love with. Allison, whose image had accompanied him nearly every waking minute the summer he was sixteen. He could still see perfectly, anytime he chose, that sweet sweep of Allison's body when she had teed off the ball and was following it through with her eyes, her golf club raised to the sky. Her fine straight nose and the astonishing thickness of her eyelashes, even the gold locket she wore around her neck and that he had longed to open with a thumbnail—all of this was indelibly impressed on his memory. And impressed, too, was the awful, thrilling pain of that summer when he had climbed out of bed in the mornings so full of love and desire it made his heart race and cavort in ways that scared him. He thought he might die of a heart attack before he was twenty. And for all that he'd gotten so little. Allison was four years older than he was, a college junior, and he had gotten to do no more than carry her golf clubs around the course on Tuesday and Saturday mornings for the whole long summer, their conversations consisting of discussion about which club she should use for a stroke.

He had little good reason to think well of Allison, yet for years he had been attracted to women who reminded him of her. Only Estella had broken the pattern with her sturdy compactness and wild hair. And the very fact that she had broken the pattern gave him confidence that he had chosen right—that what he felt for Estella was real and would be lasting. He'd never been sorry he'd married Estella; after twenty-two years of marriage they were still good friends. How many couples could say the same?

So he was taken by surprise to see that somehow without his even knowing it, Allison Wade Jackson had settled down in some remote corner of his mind and stayed there confidently occupying that elegant body of hers, shaking that long thick hair around her face.

The ridiculousness of the connection between Allison and the woman crossing the lobby of the Sheraton Hotel in Boston stopped him where he was, three-quarters of the way to the registration desk. Right there, in that moment, he had his warning. But evidently he made his choice too, since the warning did no more than make him hesitate for a moment with a startled look on his face. After that moment he didn't hesitate. If he didn't hurry he would lose her and have to search later. There would never be such a natural and easy time again.

Still, "ridiculous" was the word he used over and over for the rest of that afternoon to describe his plight.

It was ridiculous the way his heart hammered as he stood beside her, peering over her shoulder as she filled out the registration form. Ridiculous the way the sight of her left hand holding the paper in place—the beautiful way her fingers curved, the delicacy of her wrist, and even the beat of her blood swelling and subsiding in a thin blue vein—made his hand tremble with the desire to touch, to put his hand over hers where it lay—as it seemed to him so vulnerably—on the desk top.

And it was ridiculous too the happiness he felt after he had followed her from the reservation desk to the elevator, asking her during the walk if she would have a drink with him at five o'clock and she had said yes.

Fool, he told himself in the safety of his room. Crazy fool. You know what you're doing, don't you?

But his face, looking back at him from the bathroom mirror as he shaved for the second time that day, did nothing but smile an idiot smile. It was a joke, all right. It wasn't that he didn't know it.

But when he saw Jane coming toward him across the lobby a little later, her skirt swinging, the joke didn't seem funny any longer. His heart lurched in what could have been either pleasure or fear—their effect on the human body being remarkably similar.

It was impossible, he knew, to explain why one face caught the imagination, seemed filled with mystery and promise, while another, maybe even more beautiful, passed almost unnoticed. Why was he so attracted by those blue-green eyes, those high cheekbones, and that delicate mouth with the little bulge in the middle of the upper lip? He couldn't have said. Only that she had some natural elegance—and he liked even her uncertainty, a kind of awkwardness, as she walked ahead of him to a table in the bar. As they had drinks he noted the way she leaned back in her chair, watching him. Those eyes that looked so steadily into his—what did they see? They thrilled him in some deep, secret way, and he felt sure she saw in him things he did not even know about himself—that she saw in him something nobody else had ever seen.

What are you thinking? he longed to ask. What do you know about me, what secrets can you guess? But instead he talked of other, safe things, though he hardly listened to his words. His eyes kept meeting hers and then, startled, even frightened, looking quickly away.

He had forgotten how exciting it was to fall in love. Already he was burning to press his palms against those cool shoulders. Even then he could imagine her head thrown back in desire and could feel her hands gripping his arms.

But they did not make love that first night. They were both too reserved or too cautious. They would wait and see, would sleep on it and see how they felt in the morning. In that first evening they did not say anything to each other that could not have been listened to by the entire anthropology conference.

"It's because we really didn't intend to get involved with anybody," Jane said later, after all such reticence had been dissolved between them. "If you'd taken a poll of everybody signing in we would have been the *only* two, probably, who would've said that we had no intention whatsoever of becoming involved with any person coming to an anthropology conference."

They both regretted the loss of that first night, so few had been allotted them. By staying an extra twenty-four hours after the conference ended, they told themselves, they were making it up. But of course it couldn't be. That night was lost for good, and so they both remembered with sadness those restless and sleepless hours they had spent apart from each other. All unnecessary.

"Isn't it typical of us that we stew so over what can't be helped?" Jane said. A certain streak of puritanism in both their natures amused and yet comforted them. Dependable, hardworking, they encouraged each other to lay aside those very traits they had lived so much of their lives by.

They spent as much of the four days together as they could, but there were papers they had to hear, people they had to greet; it was a small world, the one they moved in, and both felt a need to guard their privacy. Their love was nobody else's business. They didn't want eyebrows raised when they came into a room together or knowing smiles to follow their backs when they left. So even those four days had been marred. Only the night, day, and final night had been time spent wholly with each other, and over those brief hours had lain melancholy. The time was so short.

The rush to the airport, as they arrived only barely in time for Jane to make her flight to Philadelphia, he remembered as nightmare. The way she had kissed him hurriedly on the lips and then had practically run to the door leading onto the plane, looking down at the carpet the whole time—it had surely been a goodbye kiss if he'd ever experienced one. As he watched her turn the corner in the tunnel connecting waiting room with plane he was full of anguish. It was only the self-restraint practiced over a lifetime that kept him from calling after her.

Then she was gone and it was no use standing and staring at the door through which she had disappeared. He looked at his watch and saw he had time for a drink before his flight to Providence would be called.

As he drank his bourbon he imagined Jane on the plane, her eyes lifting from the book in her lap to look out the window at the late-afternoon clouds the plane passed through. She would be thinking of him, he was sure. And later, when she opened the door of her empty apartment, she would be desolate. But it was impossible for him to imagine what she might do after that. He had no idea what her apartment would be like, and so as soon as he saw her turn the handle of the door he lost interest in the scene.

Instead he thought of his own homecoming. Almost slyly he thought of the dinner warm in the oven and the fire made of apple logs, of Estella's laughing face and Jasper, in pajamas, half asleep in the big chair.

Safe. That was the word that slipped into his mind, though it startled him. Yet as soon as the word came to him he knew it had been on the tip of his tongue ever since Jane went down the ramp to her plane without turning her head to look back. What he'd known as he watched her go was anguish, but now he saw that he had been relieved, too. It occurred to him that there had been things about Jane that he'd felt uneasy about; in four days it was impossible to learn all you needed to about someone else. For a few days a person could make almost any impression; it was what happened over time that really counted, surely.

So a kind of fevered cheerfulness came over him as he finished his bourbon, and it accompanied him through the short flight to Providence and the drive home in the car. He was a hunter returning home successful after the hunt with the satisfying weight of game on his shoulders.

It was only later, when he had come into full possession again of all he had thought about in anticipation—while he was eating in front of the fire with Jasper in his lap and Estella leaning against the mantel asking him what he'd seen and heard and done—that the sharp pangs of loss came, perversely, into full flowering and he felt strange and isolated from all he had thought he loved and cared about. An impostor—perhaps with evil intent—had set his suitcase by the door and put his arms around the woman smelling of turpentine and linseed oil, had scooped the boy into his arms and kissed his forehead and hair, had held the old dog's head between his hands and said good boy, Jenks. Good old boy.

* * *

Turning so he could see over the top of Jasper's head the elegant line of Jane's nose and chin, her hair covering her cheek as she turned to look at one of the trees lining the street, he longed to touch her, though he would not, with Jasper to see. When he'd seen her coming down the ferry ramp, carrying a large suitcase and a bag of books, her frailty and, yes, her bravery in coming there to be with him had thrilled him. Since he'd taken the suitcase and the bag of books from her hands it was only when they reached the car and were able to set everything down on the pavement that he put his arms around her as he had longed to do at the first moment. He couldn't bear for her to look uncertain, to say, "Look, I know it was crazy to come and if you think this is a terrible idea I can go back on the ferry tonight."

"No," he said. His arms were around her, and he knew instantly that his body had forgotten nothing at all of hers. Yet it was astonishment to feel under his hands the delicacy of her shoulder blades, the wonderful smoothness of her skin under her thin shirt.

But here they were only a short time later, and he was dismayed with her, striding along with her hands in the deep pockets of her skirt, paying no attention to Jasper. And Jasper had to be courted. Hadn't she known that if she came to the island she would have to share him with his children and yes, with Estella too? Nevertheless, there she was, pretending to take a great interest in the elm trees, totally hopeless at endearing herself to a child.

"Jasper would just about sell his soul for a banana split, wouldn't you, Jasper?" he said, looking at Jane as he spoke over the top of Jasper's head, trying to draw her in.

"It's my favorite," Jasper said.

"Why?" Jane asked, finally taking her attention from the elms.

"It's the biggest," Jasper said. "Plus, it costs the most."

"Don't let Jane see what a rotten kid you are," Philip said. "Materialist to the core."

But Jane didn't appear to be listening to the conversation. When Philip opened the door of the Sweet Shoppe she would have kept walking straight into the back if he hadn't called her. "Why don't we sit over here so we can look out at the street?" he said, and she turned and came back to slide into the booth beside him.

He could tell, by the stiffness of her shoulder against his, how uncomfortable she was with the two of them, and he felt sad for her at the same time that he was disappointed. It wasn't something he would have guessed—that children would make her so uneasy. But, then, what did he really know about her?

"I was an only child," Jane said, toying with her coffee spoon. She might almost have been reading his thoughts. "I never did get the hang of being with other children. They always seemed odd to me. Like foreigners of some kind. I don't think I ever knew what people were talking about when they said, 'Oh, that's the way it is to be a child!'"

"When you are a child you can't see yourself from the outside, I suppose," Philip said. "You might be the first person in the world ever to have felt a particular thing. No wonder you can't put a label on it." He realized, in the middle of the sentence, that what he was describing, accurately enough, was his own state at that moment as he sat with his leg just touching Jane's under the wooden table.

"I'm a child right now and I know exactly how I feel," Jasper said in disgust. "I probably know everything if I just think about it."

Under the table, Philip rubbed his knuckle along Jane's thigh, wanting to comfort her, but he could feel it even through the cloth of her skirt—how shut off from him she was.

Her lips just touching the rim of the coffee cup, her eyes with that sadness in their depths, moved him so much his breath caught and he coughed, with tears coming to his eyes.

Embarrassed, he used his coffee spoon to take a bit from the strawberry scoop of Jasper's banana split while Jasper watched, surprised, with his own spoon poised.

But Jasper decided to be gracious. He slid the dish across the table to Philip. "You can have one more bite if you want it, only not the chocolate, okay?" he said. "Not a giant bite, either."

Jane, looking out the window, didn't even smile.

5

Jane could have sworn that on the afternoon she went into Wanamaker's to buy a pair of silvery-gray stockings to wear to a dinner party that night she'd not been thinking about Philip. On the contrary, her head had been full of a great many nagging things she had to do—in the back of her car there was a stack of books to take back to the library, there was a list of groceries she should buy, she was intending to go to her office to pick up mail and water the plants. None of this was important—and she hated to waste her time on trivialities—but she was an orderly person who made lists every day of all she hoped to accomplish before nightfall. Yet no matter how many jobs she completed there were always others she hadn't found time for, so she was constantly troubled. And Philip, if she'd been forced into categorizing him at the moment she passed through Wanamaker's revolving doors, she'd have described as another of those troubling, disturbing parts of her life.

After the anthropology conference they telephoned each other a few times, dialing their school numbers, but these calls had been a trial to her and, she believed, to him. Neither liked speaking over the phone; an odd constraint got in their way and they were reduced to making small talk about their work, to making remarks about the weather. Neither was capable of saying into a plastic mouthpiece "I love you," or even "I miss you." They were better in letters, since they were people used to convincing themselves by what they read on pieces of paper. The letters they sent discreetly to campus addresses had contained passages, at least, of truthfulness. She wrote to him, "I feel a little dazed here without you. Our time together was so short." And he wrote to her one long, rambling letter about some woman named Allison and how, because of this woman, he had been bound to fall in love with her, Jane—a letter she pored over as though it had been written in code. Philip did, as a matter of information, write to tell her when he and his family were leaving for Nantucket, giving her his address and telephone number, but he did not—oh, she was well aware of this—ever say, even once, "Do you think you might come here, if just for a few days?"

So there was no reason for her eyes to go immediately to the racks of swimming suits when the revolving door deposited her inside Wanamaker's that day in early June. Yet her attention was caught by those bright blues and purples and pinks; she walked straight toward them without thinking, though it was clear to her, if nothing else was, that in her present state she could not think of swimming suits without thinking of the sea, and she couldn't think of the sea without Nantucket coming immediately to mind, and of course linked with the thought of Nantucket was Philip. Nevertheless, she went to the racks of swimming suits and began choosing possibilities to try on. Her old suit was faded from the New Mexico sun, and anyway, she'd had it for five years. She told herself that surely she was entitled to another after all that time.

Just touching the suits, their silkiness soft in her hands, brought into her mind unbelievably white sand, water the color of turquoise. A feeling of happiness, as intense as a shudder, passed through her.

In one of the little dressing rooms she hung the handful of suits on a hook and got to work. She was in the habit of giving mirrors sidelong glances, of sneaking up on them—evidently she feared that the old stoop-shouldered gawkiness of adolescence still lay in wait for her if she looked at herself straight on. But this time she looked fully and critically at herself with every suit she tried on; she was serious about it—finding one that flattered her.

She turned this way and that in front of the narrow mirror, frowning, trying to see herself from the outside the way someone else—a knowing stranger—might look at her, thinking, "What a good-looking woman!" or "Oh, look at that, would you? Whatever made that tall, thin woman think she could get by with a suit like that?"

It was hard for her to see herself objectively—to be aware of the figure she cut. There were days, on her way to teach a class, when she felt she looked terrible—her eyes puffy, her clothes disheveled somehow, as though they'd been put on by an incompetent person. And yet when she caught an unexpected glimpse of herself reflected from the glass of a doorway she was startled to see that none of the faults she feared were visible after all. But there were other days when she felt fine, even happy, when friends of hers would look into her face intently and say, "Did you have a bad night? You look tired. There're circles under your eyes. You haven't been crying, have you?" She was baffled by this disparity between inner and outer and troubled by it.

That had been the wonderful thing about the two years she'd spent with the Hopi—she'd forgotten about herself and had entered a new life altogether.

She'd been relieved to leave the cream-colored walls of her apartment in Philadelphia where the leaves of the maple tree made fluttering shadows—that apartment she had always associated with coolness somehow and with some faint air of melancholy—to have left all that for the blinding sun of the West. The shadows under that sun were as distinct as though they'd been drawn with a heavy line of charcoal, and she was dazed by the light, which, she'd thought at first, must reveal all of what lay in its path the same way a searchlight would. Though she'd found this wasn't true after all. Light could conceal just as well as darkness could.

In that place of rock and sky and sunsets which blazed into heights of color each evening like a performance of some kind, she lived as she supposed she had always wanted to; she lived in some ways very much as she had when she was a child and she could do what she wanted with her time. In jeans and sneakers with holes in the canvas she spent her time from sunup until sundown on the desert, at the edge of whatever it was the others were doing that day. She forgot about suntan lotion and didn't notice until much later how squint lines made little fans at the corners of her eyes, and since she didn't bother to wear a hat her hair faded a little in the sun, taking on a silvery look, like moleskin. She, who had been so mindful of time, careful to make a list of her chores for the day as she drank her breakfast coffee, filling her days so there would be no waste, sat on her heels in the dust for hours at a time as she listened to the women who sat in the shade shelling corn; she hoed beside them as they worked in their gardens; she sat at the edge of the corral where the men were buying and selling horses—her notebook in her hand, though she often forgot about it, too—and simply let the voices wash over her.

Sometimes she would suddenly look up at the sky stretching so immensely over her head and she would feel that her head was a balloon, released from the earth and floating there; what she wanted to take in and know about extended further and deeper than she had first had any inkling of; she was aware that although the people she lived among answered her questions graciously and sometimes even passionately, there was more still that they were not telling her.

Yet it was this that made her happy in the time she lived with the Hopis—that sense she had of going deeper and deeper into a hidden and secret world. It was all she cared about, a pursuit that absorbed her completely.

She ate when she was hungry and went to bed when she was tired; some nights she didn't sleep at all and on some days she forgot to eat until suddenly, at nearly sundown, she would realize that her legs had gone weak and she was ravenous. Then she would open a can of chili and eat it from the pot even while it was heating, leaning over the stove scooping the beans up with a spoon. As she slid into sleep each night she could hear the voices her day had been full of, the voices rising and falling, the old ones cracked and out of tune, the young ones quick and singsongy. They washed around her head the same way the air did and filled her dreams. By the time she'd been there a year she was even dreaming in Hopi.

After two years, when she loaded up her car and drove away from the reservation for the last time, she felt strange and yet elated by her life there. She thought the changes that had taken place in her were profound and would be permanent—surely she would be able to take back to Philadelphia that sense of the great, still skies under which she had sat so many times forgetful of whether it was morning or afternoon.

But in fact that world started fading as soon as she reached the thruway and was caught up in the traffic. By the time she reached St. Louis she felt jangled and a little crazy; already she could feel that old rhythm beginning. Long before she reached Philadelphia, she was making lists in her head of the innumerable jobs she must do instantly, as soon as she pulled up beside the curb of the apartment house where she lived.

Though it was July and there was a heat wave in Philadelphia, as soon as she entered the apartment and saw the leaves of the maple tree rustling just outside the windows, goosebumps sprang along the backs of her arms. "All alone" were the words that came immediately into her mind, though this seemed a ridiculous thought to have. After all, she had many friends in Philadelphia; there were three or four households where she could appear at the door that very afternoon to be greeted with delight. Surely she had been far more alone when she had lived with the Hopi, since she could never have been anything but an outsider. She was not an intimate friend with any of those people and couldn't have been. Yet this hadn't mattered. As long as she had been there she hadn't been lonely.

For days after she got back home she puzzled about this, until one morning, when she was lingering over her breakfast coffee, she suddenly realized that what she missed was herself the way she had been in the desert, listening with her notebook on her knees as a grandmother told a story to her grandchild—just Jane, listening, Jane as she had been when she was a child listening in the night to the voices of her parents as she went to sleep, not even the words mattering but only the sound.

It was this she'd felt, much later, after she'd made love with Philip for the first time and they were lying with their legs intertwined. There was nothing at all she wanted to say or even to listen to at that moment— if she floated, in that half-sleep, for long enough she would know all she needed to know about Philip without a word being spoken. If they were just quiet long enough.

But though she'd known this clearly, she nevertheless fell suddenly asleep and didn't wake until hours later when Philip was just opening the door to go downstairs for a newspaper. She woke with a sense of loss so acute that she nearly called out to him, though when he smiled at her from the doorway she smiled back, letting him go. There would be time later, or so she told herself. They would have another chance.

But, in fact, the rest of their time together at the conference was hectic; there had not been a moment of such peace and ease between them again.

It was her desire to recapture this feeling that led her like a sleepwalker to the racks of swimming suits in Wanamaker's and led her, very possibly, to buy the one she did—a blue suit with tropical flowers curling into unlikely bloom between hip and breast. After paying for the suit she went directly to the sportswear department and bought a blindingly white skirt that, she knew, would set off wonderfully the tan she intended to get.

All had been planned out—it appeared—in great detail behind her back.

She'd been to Nantucket once, on a day trip from Cape Cod, and remembered distinctly the gray houses and the long, flat beaches. It was a place that appealed to her, and so there was no reason why she shouldn't take a working vacation there if she wanted to; Nantucket would be a good place to finish the article she was writing—"Empowerment Among Females in the Hopi Tribes." She saw herself clearly on a wide, empty beach leaning against a rock with a yellow pad in her lap. Philip, perhaps, had nothing to do with it.

Of course she might, after she'd been there a week or so, happen to come across him buying haddock in the fish market or wine in the liquor store. She'd say very calmly, "Oh, hello, Philip. I'm here taking a vacation. Isn't it funny to come across each other this way?"

Or, maybe, three days before she was to leave the island she'd contrive to telephone, suggesting they might get together for a drink somewhere. They were friends, after all.

But even while all this was going through her head she was aware that some other more efficient and more ruthless part of herself was planning something very different.

It was *that* Jane who wrote Philip a note that night using official University of Pennsylvania stationery—doubtless he got letters from colleagues all around the country, as she did, and there would be nothing suspicious to anyone about this envelope with her surname, McHenry, typed in the upper left-hand corner. In the note she said that she would be arriving on the ten-o'clock ferry five days from then. And that was all she said. Whether or not he would meet the ferry was up to him.

When she dropped the note in the mail slot at the post office she felt relief; it was all out of her hands.

When the ferry began pulling into the dock at Nantucket she studied the people waiting, their faces becoming clearer and clearer as the boat drew into its slip. Her heart began to beat heavily and sickeningly; he wasn't there. But even as her distress grew she told herself that it served her right; the careless ease with which she'd written that note to Philip now seemed to her crazy, and she didn't know whether she was disturbed more by his failure to meet her or by her maneuverings to get him to see her again.

She'd turned away from the bow of the boat and was nearly to the stairs that would take her down to the gangplank when she saw him, standing beside a post, watching the people disembarking. "Philip!" she called. But the distance between them was too great, and he couldn't hear her. He continued staring at the passengers in that strained, frightened way, and the look of uncertainty and fear on his face so shocked her that if other people had not been pressing so closely around her she would have turned around right there on the stairs and fled back into the boat where he would not see her.

But he already had. He called to her, and she waved back. When she crossed the gangplank she went to him docilely enough, pretending that the man with the strained and anxious face was the same one she'd seen watching her cross the lobby in the Sheraton Hotel in Boston.

And by that pretense, as she handed her bags to him and gave him a hurried kiss, she knew that she had trapped herself. Already it was too late to turn back.

6

Of course it was too hot to be jogging, nobody should be out at mid-afternoon in the hottest part of the day, and Estella was no athlete anyway, never had been, so what did she think she was doing, a fifty-year-old woman with more weight on her than she should have, fighting her way up that long sloping hill with the heat shimmering in waves off the blacktop and nothing to fill the afternoon silence except the cicadas? If she shut her eyes she could have been back in Tennessee, a girl in those empty, sad, and endless afternoons.

"What are you doing that for now? Why in this heat?" Chrissy had wanted to know.

"Because," she had said angrily. "Because I feel like it. Just hold Jenks," she'd shouted over her shoulder. "He's too old to come and he doesn't know it."

She wouldn't give up and walk, not yet, because if she could make it to the top of the hill then she could catch her breath on the way down. She could keep moving. And it was important to keep moving. It was strange how pain in the soul could be eased by making the body struggle— a truth she'd never learned before because she'd never been very good at any sport and she didn't do for long anything she wasn't good at. A competent, steady swimmer—that was all she'd ever been. And now she was on the move much of the day. At night she got cramps in her legs and would spring up amazed on her cot in the boathouse. What pain! She would nearly cry out with it before hard rubbing with her knuckles eased the muscles. She'd never had to pay much attention to her body before—she just fed it when it was hungry, kept its face clean, put clothes on its back. Without more than a glance at a blouse or a dress in the mirror Estella would already be unbuttoning. "That'll do," she'd say. Or "No. I don't like this one."

Now here she was laboring up the hill like any of those health nuts worried about their hearts and the softness of their bellies—springing out of their houses before sunrise to compete with the deer and rabbits for right-of-way down the narrow roads. But it wasn't the state of her heart— not of heart muscles at least—that concerned her. She came of a long-lived family whose hearts were not affected by whiskey or pork untrimmed of its fat, or by any other rigors their hearts were subjected to.

It came as a surprise, since she'd never needed to know before, that if she ran until every movement was an act of will and yet she still continued to lift one foot and then the other, all other pains receded to the point of disappearance. And if she continued on through that dull, endless time while her breath came in painful spurts, she would have the sensation that her mind—and maybe heart, too, whatever the mysterious link was be-tween those entities—floated in some white, neutral place.

But that state of ease was still a long way off. Already her sides heaved like a sow's in the heat. She remembered from her childhood how hogs would run until they dropped. If they got out of their pen on a hot afternoon you might as well kiss your efforts goodbye; they'd be dead of heat stroke before you could catch a glimpse.

If she could just make it up the next hill where shade from the pine trees overshadowed the road, she'd walk. She'd take her ease in that place where the land flattened briefly before the curve—the place that reminded her of certain stretches of the Botswanian landscape. It was the low hills stretching to the horizon, broken by only a few widely spaced trees, dwarfed and twisted by the winds that blew in during the winter from the sea that reminded her of that other place.

Philip said it didn't look at all like Africa to him, but what did Philip know? Striding through any countryside he found himself in with his hands clasped behind his back, his eyes fixed on the sky, talking, talking as he walked—of course for Philip all landscapes probably looked alike.

They were backdrops merely for the drama of his important life. Only gross sensations of extreme cold or heat could impress themselves on Philip.

She was nearly to the top of the hill and could see the shade dappling the road in what appeared to be coolness when a car nosed around the curve, its grille glinting in the sun like teeth. Of course, even from that distance, she recognized the car.

"Damn you, Philip!" she said aloud, squandering that much of her scanty breath. Against all reason she felt he was doing it on purpose—choosing that moment to appear. And of course she'd rather fall over on her face there in the middle of the road than let him see that she was reduced to walking.

He *would* drive slowly, being careful because of the narrowness of the road, concerned, or so the slowness was meant to indicate, for the safety of bicyclers and joggers and rabbits. A man who took responsibility for others' safety.

But his concern didn't fool her. She wished him death, immediate and, if possible, painful.

For an interminable time they drew closer and closer like two objects moving irresistibly toward crashing ruin—both drawn along the thread of road with no place to turn aside unless it was into the nearly impenetrable jungle of bushes and vines.

She kept her eyes on the road, but when the car drew even, her head lifted of its own volition. Or perhaps it was his eyes that had drawn hers. Though she was sure that rage lay naked and unmistakable in her eyes, in his she was jolted by something else that left her feeling she had been skewered by an ice pick.

She caught only a glimpse of Jasper's blond hair, the crown of his head showing above the window frame, and then the car had passed, leaving a thin, almost imperceptible haze of dust and exhaust fumes behind it.

Into the shade she came then and fell abruptly onto the dry grass. Sweat gleamed on her arms and legs as though she were covered with oil.

How strange! To see Philip's face with the sharp acuity she might have seen a stranger's. For years, she realized now, she hadn't really seen Philip's face. Only, occasionally, a haircut had revealed a surprising starkness—Philip's face emerging as though in bas-relief with the trimming back of the concealing hair.

But seeing his face through the anxiety of that other, tremulous time when they had first known each other, she was shaken by what she saw. It wasn't the faint lines or the gray hair of age that surprised her—she'd not been oblivious of these changes, though they hadn't been the focus of her attention. But why had she never seen before that at their edges his lips were thin and could set irrevocably against her? She'd always supposed that no matter how fiercely they might fight, on some other, deeper level they could rely on each other.

It came to her suddenly—it had been a flicker of triumph that had passed across his eyes when he saw her in the road. That flicker of triumph like a mouse's tail disappearing into a hole.

How terrible she must have looked to have sparked that gleam—oh, it was clear to her what he had seen. A fat woman greasy with sweat, her hair in strings, starting, in all probability, to sprout a faint mustache. The humiliation that suffused her was so great that she groaned.

Yet as she sat in the shade, the drying sweat making her skin prickle, her thoughts turned easily to the wide, nearly treeless stretch of land she could see across the road. It was Botswana that came to her mind, and the dance Philip had insisted on joining when they lived with the Tungi. "Oh, Lord, you're not serious, are you?" she'd said. "Won't you look like an idiot out there brandishing a spear in the air and pretending to stalk lion or whatever it is they do?"

To her surprise he'd been offended. "Jima's been teaching me," he said. "I think I'll look all right. And anyway I want to experience what it's like."

"I thought you were just supposed to observe. I didn't know you were going to put on a breechcloth and go native."

But he'd turned haughty; his feelings were hurt. So of course he was determined to dance, if only to show her.

She dreaded his making a fool of himself—and dreaded watching him do it. But though she considered going into the hut and writing up notes while the dance was taking place, she didn't do it. She was curious, after all. And perhaps, she thought later, she had wanted to see Philip make himself ridiculous after all.

So she had sat among the other women and children and the old men too infirm to take part, watching as the lines of dancers snaked into the open space in the middle of the village. And when at first she had not seen Philip she'd been relieved, believing that he had dropped out at the last.

But then she saw him, just coming into view—unmistakable, of course, even if he had been as dark-skinned as the others. Whereas their movements were fluid and charged with authority, his were stiff and awkward, betraying with every gesture his lack of skill.

Yet what struck her with surprise and embarrassment was the look on Philip's face. It was the intensity—the rapture, even, as he was caught up in ecstasy. She had turned her head away, unable to watch.

"Well, how was it?" he asked later, coming into the hut where she was already half asleep. But she was aware he wasn't waiting for her reply; he was still caught up in that pleasure with himself and didn't doubt what her answer would be.

"You should join the Tungi," she told him, rolling over on her back so she could see him from one half-shut eye. "I mean it. You should ask if they'd let you join. You should live the rest of your life as a Tungi."

"You hate letting me think well of myself, don't you?" he said, bitterness in his voice.

She didn't think that was it at all, but she had let the silence speak for her.

From the direction where the Volvo had disappeared it now reappeared, cresting the low hill. Estella immediately got to her feet, heart pounding. Harried from a hiding place, that was how she felt. How dare he come back to gloat just because she was out of shape and short of wind!

But there he was, leaning out of the window of the car, smiling, calling to her. "I thought you might like a ride back. You looked like you were on your last legs when I passed."

"And you came back to see me lying in the dust. My, wouldn't that be lucky for you. Poor Estella dropping dead of a heart attack, leaving you free..."

"Stop it, Estella."

"Didn't it flash through your head for just a second? Admit it."

She saw that his face had turned pale with anger, and this pleased her immensely.

He pulled his head back inside the car, looking wary. "I don't hate you," he said.

"Do you get to feel sorry for me?" she said. "Is that the way it works?"

Now his mouth was drawing straight and his eyelids narrowing that space where his eyes glittered. "Be careful," he said. "Be careful what you say."

It was the way he had spoken to the children when they were small. "I wouldn't do that if I were you," he had said often, something steely in his voice warning them but daring them too.

"Why should I be careful?" she asked him. "Do you have somebody in there with you, crouching down in the floor, taping everything?"

"You're being so childish," he said, and a pained look of bafflement—also very familiar to her—came over his face; for a moment it was a boy's face, unable to believe that anyone would want to hurt *him*. "I'm surprised how childish you're being."

"That's where we're different, then," she said in satisfaction. "Nothing you can do will surprise me."

"Because you've always known I was bad? Come off it, Stell. You can get so self-righteous." In another moment he would laugh, his voice full of good humor.

He leaned over to open the car door—that gesture he'd made for her so many times. It would be so easy to get in the car with him, to let him reason with her and coax her out of her rage. But she needed her anger the way a cold man needs his coat.

"If you don't leave me alone, Philip, I'll stand here in the middle of the road and scream my lungs out. I promise you I will. If you don't leave me alone."

And of course he had to then, carefully turning the car around on the narrow road, driving back the way he had come.

7

In the evenings the light held over the sea for a long time. When they ate dinner sitting at the square table on the deck of the house the sun had sunk only halfway down the length of the pine trees and the light on the water was clear and rich, the color a deeper blue than it had been at noon. Soon the sky would turn pink and then the water would take on that shade of blue that looks artificial—the color of the sea on cheap postcards.

Chrissy sat in her old place, the one facing the water, the one she'd occupied since childhood. In those days it had been Liddy sitting across from her, but now it was Jasper, turning his head to watch the bucking sweeps of someone's kite against the pure sky. If she stretched her hands she could easily touch Jasper's across the table and Estella's at her side. When she was a child, that was the way their meals had begun—all of them clasping hands in a circle around the table and shutting their eyes. But she and Liddy usually cheated, squinting so they could watch each other between their lashes. Sometimes one or both of them would refuse to stretch out their hands and would curl them instead into claws, making faces to show their disgust.

And yet, though she had never admitted this to Liddy, she had liked the practice all the same. She'd liked to feel all of them united, the wagon train drawn up against danger. And though there had been nothing in the center of the table to hold all that attention—nothing except the flickering candle flame—she always felt that beyond her closed eyelids, her clasped hands, there was a mystery she could no more than sense, *something* that would be lost when she opened her eyes. It was remarkable to her that though she and Liddy did not look alike, in spite of the way they each had thoughts the others could know nothing about, there was a connection as invisible as the oxygen in the air that linked them together.

Yet as she had leaned into the table—holding Liddy's wiry hand on one side and on the other her mother's with the wedding band pressing hard against her palm—she had often felt rising panic. Were these four all? Surely there were others, momentarily forgotten? Four was such a pitiful number, not nearly enough to make a circle against danger.

Later on, after Jasper was born, she thought that maybe it had been him, a ghost child, she had been turning her head trying to glimpse. But even after Jasper was old enough to join them at the dinner table she had still felt the old, familiar panic. There weren't enough of them, and, she finally knew, never would be. What she yearned for was irrevocably lost— that earliest time when there had been so many faces around the cooking fire. In her first, dreamlike memories, she was surrounded by faces that shone a little in the light from the flames. So many laps to sit in, so many arms to hold. And above the darkness where the sparks flew the stars were milky, bearing down, glowing.

"Why did we stop doing that?" she asked, her eyes fixed on some point beyond Estella's head. "Don't you remember how we used to have Quaker grace before we ate? And then sometime, I don't remember when, we just stopped."

"I didn't think you ever liked it much," Estella said. "You and Liddy were always making a to-do. You never wanted to go to silent Meeting, either. Not that I blame you."

"But when did we stop? I can't even remember that. Did somebody just say, one night at supper, well, we aren't going to do *that* anymore? Is that what happened?"

"Probably when Jasper was a baby," Estella said. "I didn't have hands to spare. And then Liddy went off to college. Is that what you think, Philip?"

As she spoke, Estella leaned over her plate, elbows on the table, slipping the prongs of her fork into a tomato wedge.

Philip was sitting sideways, his crossed legs pointing out to sea.

"I don't think anything."

"That's unusual for you. Not to have any opinion. I thought you had opinions on everything."

"Let it go," Philip said, looking out toward the water. "Chrissy's just come home."

"But we've got nothing to hide from Chrissy, do we? Or from Jasper, either. Haven't we always made a point of discussing everything openly, in front of the children? Didn't we always say we wouldn't allow little secrets to mold in dark corners? Wasn't it you who always insisted on openness? Or am I wrong?"

"I'm tired, Estella. Don't push it."

There was a stiff, pained look on her father's face. Even the way he set his wineglass on the table was careful.

"Push you into a temper, you mean?" Estella said. "Lord, how I'd like to see that." With one slice of her knife Estella severed the tail from her fish. A little spot of grease on her chin caught the light, and Chrissy kept her eyes on it in dread. "Remember *I* never said I'd live my whole life in light of the Peace Testimony."

Philip placed his fork and knife gently on the edge of his plate. "If you want to make a scene you'll have to make it by yourself," he said in a stiff voice.

Even the scraping of his chair against the boards of the deck was quiet; if there had been a door to close behind him it would have shut with an almost imperceptible spring of the latch.

"Oh, yes," Estella said. "How could I forget? I'm the one who always has to make a scene, aren't I? I'm the vulgar one. You're the long-suffering one who never raises his voice. I can just hear everybody say, 'Oh, she drove him to it.' Can't you?"

From the bottom of the steps Philip half turned. "I'm going for a walk," he said, so quietly Chrissy could barely hear him.

"I knew you'd leave," Estella said. "I knew you'd run from a fight."

"Can I come too?" Jasper called, already leaving his chair.

Philip did not turn, but he held out one hand, offering it in advance for Jasper to take.

At the corner of the boathouse Jasper caught up and they walked out of sight behind it, hand in hand. When they reappeared, walking at the water's edge, they were small figures, plodding on in the direction of the point.

"So," Estella said, rubbing her finger along the rim of the wineglass until it gave off a pure, almost unearthly tone. "There they go. Father and son. Don't you think that's sweet?" Around and around the rim Estella's finger went, forcing that clear tone—like a small cry—from the glass. "But what I want to know," she said in a perfectly reasonable voice, "is whether or not he went off today to meet Jane in town. Did he or didn't he, Chrissy?"

"Are you *sure* about . . . what you were telling me?" Chrissy said, embarrassment making her head feel as heavy and as clumsy as though it were filled to the top with melted lead.

"Don't mistake me," Estella said, clamping her hand over the top of her wineglass so that the sound she'd coaxed from it was instantly stifled. "At first I thought maybe it was a joke. I just couldn't take it in, what he was saying. But then he was so serious, and anyway . . . oh, I never thought it was a joke. Can you imagine? Solemn Philip making up a joke like that? But there I was, stuck. Unable to get beyond the main point. There was somebody else. Is that what he said? He had somebody else, cared for somebody else, oh, however he put it. How could I have failed to know? That's what really sticks in my craw."

From the place where the sun had sunk below the trees and beyond, to the farthest edge of beach, a golden light still glowed, and in that still air the midges whirled in perpetual motion as though it were joy they felt and not just the last of the warmth before darkness fell.

"I don't know," Chrissy said, too miserable to meet Estella's eye. Now her arms had gone as heavy as her head and there was no way she could have lifted them and put them around Estella's shoulders though she knew Liddy would have done this with no trouble at all. At emergencies like this she failed.

Of course it must be Liddy that Estella was longing for at that moment—Liddy, who would have been able to give advice and make suggestions. Liddy wouldn't just sit there looking hopelessly at the pile of fish bones in the middle of her plate. And she knew how much she wanted Liddy too, whose presence she could almost call up, sitting there between them.

When Estella leaned over to take Chrissy's plate, to shake the wilted lettuce and fish bones into the salad bowl, Chrissy half expected to see her toss the whole thing over the railing into the sand—that was what the force of her gesture seemed to demand. Chrissy had noticed before than when Estella got angry she suddenly started acting the part of the tough mountain woman. If somebody had put a twist of tobacco into her hands at those times, she'd have cut a plug and chewed the hell out of it, spitting the juice between her front teeth, turning her head just enough to clear the deck railing. Estella would set up her ancestors anytime to Philip's genteel ones.

But all Estella did was carry the salad bowl into the kitchen and empty the wilted lettuce into the garbage pail.

When Chrissy stacked the plates and carried them into the kitchen, Estella was standing thoughtfully, looking into the twilight where Philip and Jasper had disappeared. "I know things like this embarrass you," she said without turning her head. "Oh, I know they do, sweetheart. I can still see you when you were just a little thing and your poor old Grandmother Sloan would hug you and cry when we went to visit. How one of your feet was always busy inching backward, trying to get away. Yes, you stood there all right. Maybe you even kissed her back—you always were a good child. But I could see your foot, scooting back and back the whole time, searching for some safe place to get to."

Between cottage and boathouse Chrissy set up her tent. It was a two-person backpacking tent and small, but all she needed was shelter in case of rain.

At her side, Philip bent over to pound the tent pegs into the sandy soil. "I don't know why you don't sleep in the house," he said. "In a hard rain these pegs might wash right out. The bed's made up."

"You know I've always liked to sleep outside."

"I remember you and Liddy the time when you thought you heard somebody walking around the tent. You came inside pretty fast."

"That was when I was ten, Daddy."

Surely he knew as well as she did: she was setting up her tent between his bed and her mother's, the position of her sleeping bag making a link between them.

Kneeling to pound in the last peg, Philip told her without turning around that she should dig a trench in case of rain.

There was something pitiful to her in the way he was kneeling, his head lowered over the peg.

But she was helpless to let him know this.

"It's not going to rain, Daddy," was all she could tell him. "Look at the sky. Absolutely clear."

He shook his head dolefully at her, a man too big to have ever looked comfortable sitting at a desk in a cramped academic office. He should have been a captain of ships or a farmer. "Don't you know Nantucket weather by now? How quickly the rain can blow in? I'll dig the trench for you if you don't want to bother."

"It's okay," she told him, but he was already heading for the house to get the shovel, and she didn't object. She'd gotten used to him being the authority, the indispensable one.

She noticed how carefully he bent over the shovel, cutting a trench with precision up one side of the tent, across the back, down the other side. He was always painstaking in whatever he did—even his handwriting was small and perfectly clear. And she supposed her own patience came from him—a trait if not inherited then picked up in some other, more mysterious way. It was Estella and Liddy who were quick, impatient, extravagant in their gestures. And Jasper too was one of them. She and Philip were the ones whose eyes were so often focused on the distance and who yet, paradoxically, considered carefully what was directly before them. With every gentle thunk of the spade through crusty soil Philip was showing her his steadiness. No matter what anybody might tell her, she could depend on him.

But his very humbleness before her, his silent need for her approval, drove her to wild impatience, and she forced the sections of the tent poles together recklessly. It was precisely because she *was* his daughter, the one most like him, that she could not say, as Liddy would have done, "What's the *matter* with you? It's ridiculous, you're making a fool of yourself."

The trench was complete, yet Philip stood at the corner of the tent that filled with air as Chrissy lifted the poles into place.

"Now if it rains, you won't get soaked at least," he said.

Still he would not leave. "Not like the time you and Liddy stayed out here during a storm. When you came in with your hair plastered to your heads and looking so pale? Freezing, poor little things."

It drove her crazy the way he stood there, waiting for something she couldn't give. It was awful to be reminded of those earlier times when she and Liddy had done everything together.

"Feel the sand?" she told him. "It'll hold the heat for a long time."

Still he stood, resting against his shovel.

Chrissy crawled inside the tent and zipped the fly.

They'd had many conversations about family and ancestors, about the mating habits of gulls and the social structure of orangutans. What they had never spoken of was love. What they had never said was, we are alike.

Inside the tent Chrissy hugged her knees to her chest and waited. After a while she heard him walk away, dragging the shovel behind him.

Through the netting she could see the stars, only the most brilliant blazing in that bright sky with the quarter moon rising high above the point. On the other side of the sky the Sankaty Head light flashed at intervals above the pine trees. The sweeping arc moved slowly as though there were something in the immensity of the sky that the finger of light was searching for.

The pad, pad of Jasper's feet sounded on the sand before his voice spoke, nearly in her ear. "Chrissy? Let me in. I want to get in, Chrissy."

When she turned her head she could see him outside the netting, squatting like a toad with his knees on a line with his shoulders. Behind him trailed his sleeping bag.

Even as she lifted the zipper upward he was pushing against it with his head, too impatient to wait.

Then he was inside, pulling the sleeping bag behind him while she rolled over, making room. He was quick and deft in laying his sleeping bag beside hers and sliding into it. He had always insisted on doing things for himself even when he was very small—a trait unusual in the youngest, the baby, the one they could not help watching in amazement. Each smile, each new sound, had been an astonishment.

"If you look over your shoulder you can see the Sankaty Head light, Jas," she told him.

Deliberately he pulled the hood of the sleeping bag over his eyes.

"I know it's there," he told her. "I don't have to look."

They were always telling him things, informing of wonders and dangers. No wonder the look often surprised on Jasper's face when he didn't know he was being watched was impatience.

"You came home for my birthday, didn't you?" Jasper said, pushing his feet against her legs through two layers of sleeping bag. "It's on Saturday."

"I know when your birthday is, Jas. You think that's why I came?"

"Sure. Plus you knew I didn't have anybody to do things with."

"What you need's another kid."

"You know I like being with grown-ups better."

"That's because you're stuck-up."

He laughed, butting his head into her shoulder. "You didn't like other kids when you were my age, either. You told me so."

"I had Liddy. For ages we were together all the time."

"Then what happened?"

"Liddy started giving me these looks."

"Like what?"

"Like I had some strange smell only she couldn't figure out just what. I think it took her a long time to see we were a whole lot different. *I* knew it, but I guess she didn't. Even when we were kids, walking home from school together, people would turn their heads to get a better look at her. They never did that to me."

"People stare at me."

"Can't help it, can they? The way you show off."

Jasper had pushed his face near hers and she could smell the faint sweetness of his skin—a smell that reminded her of the inside layer of orange skins. A tumultuous feeling rose in her, which it took her a while to recognize as sadness.

"I'll tell you a secret," Jasper whispered in her ear. "You're really my favorite sister, Chrissy. Only don't tell Liddy."

"Guess what?" she whispered back. "You're my favorite brother."

He giggled. "But I'm the only."

"That's right," she told him. "You're the only, Jasper. Jasper?"

But although she put her arms around him so she could feel the warmth of his body against hers, she could not tell him her fear. She could not tell him she had the strongest sensation that if they put their heads outside the tent flap and looked around they would see that both cottage and boathouse had disappeared, leaving nothing but terrifying fissures in the ground.

Jasper's toes trailed up her leg. "I love it here, don't you? I just love it."

"Yes," she told him, watching the finger of light pass over once more in its futile search. Behind their heads, very near it seemed, the waves rumbled and hissed over the sand.

What she remembered, sharp as a dream, was the cloud of terns rising from the ground in the early morning leaving behind their young among the rocks. And then, from the direction of the sea, the cloud returned once more as each young tern lifted its head and searched the sky for one particular shape, listening for one particular raucous cry distinguishable from any other.

"Are you asleep?" Jasper said, kicking her with his foot.

"Yes."

"No you're not."

"I promise. I'm even having a dream."

"What about?"

"There's a herd of elephants under some trees, fanning their ears back and forth..."

"Oh, Chrissy," he said in disgust.

"But that's what I'm dreaming," she told him. "We're standing there under the trees thinking about a water hole and how it would feel if we were standing in it up to our tails."

"Me too?"

"Sure. You're there too."

"I have tusks, then. I can butt things."

"There're some men coming with guns. You could come up behind them and stick them with your tusks."

"No there aren't. No men with guns."

"It's my dream, Jas."

"I won't be in it if I don't like it."

"Okay then. It's just us, standing under some trees, fanning our ears back and forth. There we'll be for the whole day and nothing at all will bother us."

"Something will," he said, "only it will be something very small and I'll chase it away, shaking my tusks at it."

"All right, Jas," she told him, brushing her hand over his hair—the only part of him outside the sleeping bag. "Nothing will get us and we'll live happily ever after."

8

From her cot in the boathouse Estella could also see the arc of light sweep over the tops of the pine trees, and in its regularity and dependability she was soothed. Every thirty seconds there it came again—she could count them off if she wanted to. Certainly it wasn't the light that disturbed her, nor the sound of the sea—that rise, swell, and sinking of the waves that was like the swoosh of blood regularly leaving the heart or the long sigh as air left her lungs. No. What she strained her ears for—and imagined she could hear—was the sound Philip made as he turned from side to side on the bed in the cottage, the bed she had shared with him until so recently. She hoped he did turn restlessly, heaving the bedclothes from his back as water falls from a whale's sides when it breaches in the sea.

The circles under Philip's eyes as he sat at the breakfast table told her he suffered, and she was glad to see it. But his suffering, as she well knew, might have a source very different from her own as she lay awake on her narrow cot, watching from the open door the light shift over the sea, thinking of those lines of Sappho's:

> *The moon has set, and the Pleiades.*
> *It is the middle of the night,*
> *Hour follows hour. I lie alone.*

Even those lines might more meaningfully be given to Philip, tossing, as he probably was, in the pain of deprivation, haunted by the full breasts and slender flanks—or that was how Estella supposed her to be—of the woman he pined for.

But this was something she couldn't bear to think about. After all those years—that was what she couldn't forgive him for. Not that she would have forgiven him in the beginning, either, when they were first married.

She was not a long-suffering person, never had been, and it was one of the things that made her family uneasy when she first told them she would marry Philip. "You're long-headed," her mother had reminded her. "You always did rush straight ahead like a mule wearing blinders, and he seems the slow type to me. One thing at a time. But maybe it is opposites that attract."

It was true that nothing ruffled Philip.

She could still see him perfectly clearly, sitting at the desk they'd made from a door and two filing cabinets when they were first married, his books and papers and the pipe he'd taken to smoking all laid out neatly under the white glare of the lamp, getting ready for his evening of study. There he settled himself down as carefully as a cat kneading a pillow in the one comfortable chair they had in the Quonset hut that had been provided by the university for married graduate students—sitting with his mug of coffee and his pipe, settled with his books, until well after midnight. It was amazing to her how sure of himself he was. How each night he could settle down the same way, prepared for five hours of study, working steadily through any kind of noise and disturbance.

When Liddy was born she would leave Philip to baby-sit while she went to the art building to paint after supper, coming back after four or five hours to find Liddy asleep on a hot-water bottle across Philip's legs while he held a book under the lamp, sitting at an angle so as not to disturb Liddy. Not even a colicky babe, Estella saw, could bother him, and his calm had seemed to her uncanny and a little frightening. Since she could not possibly have duplicated it, she was in awe of it, a little. She felt at a terrible disadvantage—standing there in front of him exhausted, with paint and charcoal on her hands and the bridge of her nose where she'd rubbed her fingers, feeling jangled from the coffee she had been drinking and high on excitement because she was pleased with the painting she was working on—to find Philip exactly where she had left him and Liddy asleep on her hot-water bottle, her thumb in her mouth.

Though she would never, never have admitted it to him, she'd thought

Philip's character—formed by all those New England teachers and law-
yers—was really better than hers. In her family there was at least one
outlaw who had had to disappear into the wilds of Missouri to save his
hide and there were numbers of quarrelsome backwoods people so proud
they'd rather die than take an insult. Part of the time she admired those
kin of hers and part of the time she saw they were merely disreputable
and wrongheaded—which was the way she sometimes regarded herself.
Even her looks—that broad face and wild hair—she felt were disreputable,
though Philip would not hear her say so. There had been time he had
pulled her, struggling and laughing in embarrassment, to a mirror, and
held her head between his hands, forcing her to look. "Just look," he'd
said. "Can't you see?"

She saw the wild, dark hair and the wide surprised eyes before she
looked away. For a moment she had seen what he, perhaps, saw in her
face. But she'd known, even then, that this didn't really have anything to
do with her—just as he would never know that deep in his chestnut eyes
there were little flecks of green, or that when he smiled one of his eyes
squinted more nearly shut than the other; these were her secrets about
him.

But of course, in time, it was bound to go sour on her—that air
Philip had of being right all the time. It still made her skin crawl to
remember the way he would pick his way across a floor strewn with toys
and teething rings and spilled orange juice—this was after Chrissy was
born too—making his way patiently, trying not to step on anything.

"Stell," he would say in that quiet, careful way of his, "don't you
think we might pick up this mess?"

He would help—that wasn't the point. He would get down on his
knees and reach under the sofa for plastic rings, books with their corners
nibbled, terry-cloth ducks and bears. He didn't blame her, exactly. Not in
any open way she could attack him for. It was just the pained, patient way
he kneeled on the floor resting himself on one elbow, breathing in the
dust while he groped under the sofa, that drove her crazy. Frantic, even,
to pick a fight, since she was certain that he thought her whole way of
living was wrong. She knew he thought this because she saw it in his eyes
sometimes—bewilderment and dismay—though he wouldn't admit it.

There was all this life going on—that was the way it seemed to her.
She set up her easel in the middle of the living room, where the light was
best, and it didn't bother her to have the babies playing at her feet; she
stepped over and around them without thinking about it—everything was

fine until Philip came home and looked around with that pained look on his face.

Africa, she was fond of saying later, had probably saved their marriage. There it was rarely possible to have order of even the most rudimentary sort, and Philip had had to get used to living in chaos and uncertainty. Like everybody else they lived in a hut with a dirt floor and carried water from the river, and though they set a door that could be closed in one wall and put up mosquito netting over the windows, they had almost no privacy. Even at night, unless they talked very softly, they could be overheard by somebody. And there was a constant din and clamor of birds, monkeys, insects, frogs—noises as unavoidable as the dust that coated everything in the dry season. It was a world that at first even she felt overwhelmed by, though she had recovered more quickly than Philip. After all, she had grown up in a place that was hot and sometimes very dry, where flies were shooed casually from food and where some people still boiled their clothes clean in an iron pot over a wood fire. Life in the village, for her, was close to being familiar.

But of course, in Africa, she and Philip had to depend on each other. And it was then that they became such good companions—such good friends. She helped Philip with his notes, and he, in turn, often played with the girls so that she had time to draw; they learned to depend on each other's resourcefulness and goodwill—though it was also true that, in their isolation, their faults were also magnified.

She became aware suddenly one day when they were eating that as he chewed, Philip's jaw made a faint little popping noise. It seemed amazing she'd never noticed this before because once she was aware of it the sound seemed to her maddening; she couldn't keep from listening to it even when she sat with one hand surreptitiously covering an ear. She inched her stool farther and farther away from his, talked loudly to the children as they ate, and resorted, during one meal, to humming to herself between bites. If she couldn't stop hearing that sound of Philip's jaw popping every time he chewed she'd have to kill him—it was as clear to her as that. But then he was gone for a day, accompanying a band of hunters into the bush, and when he got back it slipped her mind to listen for the popping noise. Its importance had faded.

When they got home again, they remained good campaigners—old battle-scarred generals used to relying on the other's good sense. Over breakfast they planned their day—who would be at home when the girls got off the school bus; who would buy the milk, bread, bananas, and the kind of dog food the puppy liked best; who would cook supper.

If anyone had asked her whether or not she was happy she would have said she was; it wouldn't have occurred to her to suppose that Philip wouldn't have answered the same way.

And so, the night Philip told her about Jane, she was totally unprepared. She'd just been telling him some mundane thing about the car—about the way it had stalled on her at the rotary coming into town so she'd had to sit there in the middle of the road as other cars made their way carefully around her until the Volvo was ready to start again. It had always been a temperamental car, and now that it was old it was more temperamental than ever. For some reason, it stalled more for her than it did for him.

"Estella," Philip said, breaking into her complaints about the car, "there's something I want to tell you."

Though until that moment she'd had no suspicions about Philip, as soon as he spoke she knew what he was going to say. This came to her with such surprise that she couldn't brace herself or, in fact, feel anything except amazement. While he told her about Jane, she sat leaning against the pillows, nodding her head seriously and conscientiously as though it were an ordinary conversation she was following.

"I feel terrible about all this," Philip said, looking into her eyes, which she hadn't, it seemed, the presence of mind to avert. "I know how it must sound. I can see it there in your eyes . . . contempt . . ."

But it had not been contempt—not just then. All she was doing at that moment was waiting for him to go on with the story so she could continue nodding her head and letting that look of understanding wisdom come over her face.

She felt nothing at all, as she probably would not have felt in those first moments any pain if both her legs had been struck from her body. But when she saw tears rolling down Philip's cheeks she felt a sympathetic rush of water into her own eyes, and so they had cried together, passing the box of Kleenex between them on the bed.

And then, oddly enough, she had fallen into a heavy sleep, lying beside Philip with her feet brushing against his as they had slept so many nights, their bodies, those slow learners, continuing on as before—nothing, it seemed, changed between them in spite of all Philip had said.

But in the night knowledge caught up with her, and she woke in the

(53)

morning furious. Even before she opened her eyes she kicked both feet hard at Philip's side of the bed. But he was up already—she could hear water running in the bathroom—and she had to hold her fury to herself as she pulled on her clothes and went into the kitchen.

As she set bread plates and bowls on the table, took milk and butter from the refrigerator, her anger grew. What she couldn't bear to think about was the sheeplike way she had sat listening to all Philip had to say, and then had cried with him like some weak, silly girl. In the clearness of the morning, she saw what those tears of his had meant, how, even at the moment he was telling her he was in love with another woman, he was being self-indulgent, wanting her sympathy.

That was bad enough, but what drove her to worse fury was the knowledge that she'd given it to him—she'd cried and held his hand— and she hated the Estella who would do that.

The moment Philip came into the kitchen she'd tell him what she thought; she'd tell him all the things she should have said the night before but had been too dazed to think, much less to say. His audacity—telling her about Jane with that sly, watchful look on his face. And then sleeping beside her all night as though nothing of importance had passed between them.

But when Philip did come into the kitchen and sat at his place at the table, she didn't say anything after all. It was the stubborn, sullen look on his face as he dropped bread into the toaster that made her see he had come armed: in spite of his tears the night before he was prepared to change nothing, to give up nothing. And anger, in the face of that sullenness, would put her at a disadvantage. They had, in fact, played through this scene before, though never over anything as important as Jane—she shouting at Philip, her voice cracking under the strain—while he sat calmly watching her, merely waiting for exhaustion and despair to weigh her into silence.

And so she said nothing as Philip lifted the bread from the toaster and laid it carefully on his plate.

Instead, she went directly to their bedroom where she gathered up pillows, extra blankets, sheets, the books she had brought to the island to read at night before she fell asleep. Her arms full and with the blankets trailing over her shoulders, she passed back through the kitchen, her eyes fixed defiantly on Philip. He, however, had a book pinned under his elbow and did not look up as she passed two feet away from him. His hand carried the toast spread with peach jam to his mouth, and he ate it without once letting his eyes rise from the page he was reading. She might have been invisible for all the notice he took.

Acid remarks she might make came to her lips, but she didn't say them. She passed through the kitchen as regally as she could, burdened as she was with bedclothes, and went straight out into the sunshine.

It was only there, stumbling across the sand, trying to avoid tripping on the blankets, that she felt for the first time bedraggled and abandoned. She couldn't believe that their years of friendship had come to this—the ridiculous separation that would force her to sleep on the narrow cot in the boathouse while Philip lay, probably sleepless, in the bed they had shared for so long.

But as she stretched the sheets over the narrow cot and beat the two pillows into softness, she saw that it was all in her hands after all. Anytime she chose to look straight at Philip and laugh the old conspiratorial laugh they had used between them many times and say, "Oh, come off it, Phil— I'm much better for you than anybody else could be, and you know it," then he would laugh too and agree that this was so. She was certain this was a power she held. But she would let him suffer some before she smiled that conspiratorial smile again.

Yet before she could do this something happened. Something so slight that had it happened in ordinary circumstances she might not have taken note. But in her present state anger and pain had sharpened her senses and she saw things she would not have before. A few days after she moved into the boathouse she was working, occasionally looking out the window to check on Jasper and to watch the sky and the pine trees that towered over the house. On the deck of the cottage Philip was reading. He had been there for hours with his legs stretched out in the sun, and it was by chance she happened to look up just as he put his book facedown on the deck and walked toward the sliding doors leading into the kitchen. But just before he reached them she saw him stop and lean forward a little, looking intently at something directly in front of him. As he straightened, pushed his shirt into his jeans with the palm of his hand, and bent forward once more, she realized that the glass, backed by the darker interior of the cottage, provided a dim mirror. As she watched, Philip brushed his fingers through his hair and tousled it carefully, shaking the strands a little between his fingers. Then he leaned into the glass once more to study the effect.

It was at that moment, watching Philip primp in front of the glass like a seventeen-year-old, that she was overcome by a rage so great she could have killed him; she would have liked to incinerate him on the

(55)

spot—a dragon plunging a stream of fire into his cloddish back. The arrogance! Of course it was his youthful face he was looking for, trying to entice it from the dim reaches of the glass.

As she watched, she beat on her thighs with her fists in anger. For twenty-five years she had been married to a shallow man—a peacock strutting his tail—and she hadn't known it before. Bitterness burned in her throat like acid—she who prided herself on knowing so much had clearly been totally blind. An imbecile.

Suffer, she told him as she watched the Sankaty Head light make another sweep through the room. Suffer. She felt the word covering the ground between them like one of those insignificant-looking but deadly African snakes that slide from holes not much bigger around than a thumb and glide off into the darkness leaving only the faintest wavy pattern in the dust to show where they have been. It would slip into Philip's heart and ream it to the walls. *Where I come from,* she told him, *we hold grudges forever. Snapping turtles locking their jaws so they'd rather die than turn loose.*

Now that she was awake and would be until dawn, she might as well work. That was a form of revenge still left to her—the collage she had been working on tacked to the wall, a composition made by rifling the family archive of photographs. She had used two—or rather fragments of two—photographs, running them off on silk screen. These fragments were used over and over again in different colors and sizes, and in spite of their lack of obvious connection their violent juxtaposition here forced them into some mysterious link.

On a beach, sitting in a row, there were a man, a woman, two little girls. One of the girls was sitting with her knees bent so her chin rested between the two knobby peaks; the other girl had her legs stretched straight in front of her, and though her hands were not visible, the position of her body showed that she was leaning back on them and was, probably, looking up at the sky. The man's legs were loosely crossed, his hands lying at ease between them, resting on sand. The woman's hands were occupied with holding a baby over her shoulder; all that could be seen of it was a kind of cocoon-shaped bundle. But though the figures seemed to be part of a family group, they could not be identified as particular people, since the upper part of their heads had been cut away and only the smiling lips were left intact.

The other photograph used in the collage was of a pair of hands— a man's hands, judging by their size and shape. One of the hands was above the other and the fingers of both were curved slightly toward the palms, the kind of gesture that might be made by a person trying to demonstrate the way to unscrew a lid from a large jar. Or perhaps the hands were preparing to wring a hen's neck. Or were reaching toward a human throat. It was impossible to say just what action the hands were preparing for, just as it was impossible to say what the relation was between the photograph of the hands and the one of the family on the beach.

The white glare from the lamp destroyed the mystery of the night. On the table in the middle of the room she could see the rollers, etching tools, tubes of paint sharing the space with a bottle of ketchup, a loaf of bread, a half-empty jar of pickles; since she'd moved to the boathouse its space had gradually become crowded with more and more objects. As she padded around the table barefooted, grinding the sand under the soles of her feet, she took satisfaction from the slight shudder that followed her the length of the floorboards from the heaviness of her tread. The boathouse was her lair and she was an irascible bear moving noisily within it, peering out the windows with red and angry eyes.

Squatting beside the cardboard box of photographs, the raw material of her art, Estella lifted them and let them fall, all those smiling faces, all those days of bright sun, all those moments of time which seemed never to have been. And hadn't. At least they had never been as the photographs seemed to show—all those perpetually happy people with simple-minded smiles. Only the babies' faces were artless.

Even though she knew it was not reality she was looking at, she was nevertheless pricked with pain. There were Chrissy and Liddy in their various guises—as infants, as plump-legged children, as slim little girls in pigtails. And now, in the most recent photographs, Jasper could be seen briefly in his guise as a six-year-old; already it was impossible for her to picture him as he had been at five or three. What day, what moment, could she capture of that earlier Jasper? All that was left to her of that time were a few unreliable flashes that passed themselves off as memories.

Memories, she was well aware, depended on selectivity and structure as much as any drawing did. Looked at that way, the family itself was a kind of art form, as carefully constructed as any other; she remembered clearly the first time she had seen it that way.

Liddy was ten and Chrissy seven and a half and she and Philip had left them at home for two days while they went to New York. Mrs. Blalock, who stayed with them, had been their sitter from the time they'd moved into the house, and so she hadn't worried about the girls. She hadn't even thought about them very much during those two days. She and Philip were enjoying themselves, and if the girls had been along they wouldn't have enjoyed themselves in the same way.

Though they were away from home for such a short time, as they came down the road to the house late in the afternoon, she saw it all with fresh eyes—the dark hills rising behind the house, the rock wall with the jonquils blooming beside it, the squat and solid house with beautifully spaced windows and a wide, inviting doorway. The house was old, not of their building, and yet they had made that place as they had somehow formed the two little girls who came running along the driveway to meet them. How fragile it all was! That was what frightened her suddenly. If she and Philip had been struck down on the highway by some drunk or crazy driver, both killed, then this little world they had made would have died with them even though the girls would have been raised by someone else, the house would have been lived in by other people.

But they had turned safely into the driveway, leaning out the windows to wave; Jenks, not much more than a puppy, had run up and down wildly, barking and catching at the girls' socks with his teeth. They had gotten out of the car and hugged the girls to them, had felt the beating of their hearts under their frail bones, and she had been foolish enough to think as she held them that something substantial was contained in her arms. It seemed a long time that they stood there, the four of them under the maple trees where the buds had swelled nearly to bursting, yet that time had passed as quickly as any other. Maybe as she hugged the girls under the maple trees she already knew that this time—the four of them together in the white house—would be as brief as that moment. And yet she was reluctant to let go. In all likelihood that was why she'd had Jasper. The play would continue, only with a slight change in cast.

What she could not have known before Jasper was born was that the time spent with such careless profligacy when Liddy and Chrissy were small—there would be no end it had seemed then of that time—would become, with Jasper, self-conscious. By the time Jasper was born she and Philip knew too much, and it was impossible to recapture that old ease. That time had passed. She and Philip had been through it all before and sometimes were bored by repeating themselves. Yet at the same time they were haunted by poignancy and a sense of loss with each stage that passed— the baby lying on the floor kicking its skinny legs into the air, the baby crawling across the kitchen chasing after the cat; the catalogue was endless, mundane, and banal. But this did not prevent the melancholy pain from being genuine.

Yet of course she loved Jasper. She'd loved Jasper even before he was born—with that idiot love that had sharpened and shaped itself on Liddy and Chrissy, prepared, by that time, to love whatever it was that emerged from between her thighs even if it was a monster with two heads. Love had nothing to do with it.

From the pile of photographs, Estella lifted one that showed all five of them linked by clasped hands. It had been taken the summer before at a wedding of two of Philip's students when everyone had finished up dancing in the grass—a line of dancers weaving this way and that. In the photograph Jasper was in the middle flanked by her and Philip; the girls were on the ends. The photographer had caught them that way when they were hurrying to catch up with the others, to join on the end of the line of dancers.

Holding it to the light, Estella carefully cut the photograph into five parts, amputating arms and clasped hands. In the design she would make, the figures would stretch out their arms but it would be impossible to tell whether they were reaching for or repelling the other figures. Whichever it was, connection between them was permanently broken.

9

Jane did not appear to see Philip as he drew near in the car, driving slowly down the narrow street, but he could see her very clearly in the light from the streetlamp, standing beside the doorway of her hotel, smoking a cigarette in quick, deep puffs. The sight of her in her white pants and ivory blouse made his heart beat heavily, and he knew that nothing would have stopped him coming to meet her, slipping quietly out of the house, keeping the car door open until he'd reached the lane—though of course Estella, if she was awake, would have heard the sound of the motor and could have guessed, perhaps, where he was going.

He'd been in a fever to get to town, and as he was slipping hastily out the door, his shirt was snagged by a nail that had worked its way a little free of the wood; he heard with dismay the rip and looked down to see the fingernail-shaped tear. Even the nails in his house, it occurred to him, had some message to give, some warning to make. He stood on the stoop looking stupidly down at his shirt, suddenly ashamed of what he was doing—sneaking away from his wife under cover of darkness. Yet nothing would stop him.

He pulled over to the curb and called to Jane through the open window. She looked up at the sound of his voice, but the seriousness of her face didn't change. Dropping her cigarette to the sidewalk, she mashed it with her toe before she came over to the car and climbed in. Her slimness in the white pants, the way her shoulders moved as she walked, caused fine tears of lust to come to his eyes, but he did nothing more than rest his hand for a moment on her thigh before he put it back on the steering wheel. He couldn't tell whether she was glad to see him or not.

"A drink somewhere, or would you rather walk?" he asked her.

"I've been sitting around all afternoon. Why don't we walk?"

He was glad. He didn't want to take her where there would be other people. And the night was so fine—the air warm, the quarter moon bright enough to make shadows under the trees—he didn't want to waste it.

"Is something wrong?" he asked finally when they had reached the outskirts of the town and she had still said nothing.

"Why should there be anything wrong?" she said. "Everything's just perfect. I'm going to have this fine vacation on Nantucket, lying on the beach all day, and then I will take my wonderful tan and my books back to Philadelphia and it will all be fine, won't it?"

It was to hide tears that she lit another cigarette; he could see the trembling of her lips as she held it between them.

"And it was just a great hit I made today with your son, too, wasn't it? Don't you think that went off splendidly?"

"Jasper's spoiled. The baby of the family. It'll be fine when you get to know each other better."

She was looking straight ahead where the car lights shone on the narrow road.

"You don't have to say anything," she said. "I know I shouldn't have come. I'll take the ferry back tomorrow."

She looked down at her hands resting in her lap—like a child, he thought. A child whose feelings have been hurt, being brave. It was only then that he acknowledged a resemblance he must have seen from the first—Liddy, in her pride and brave defiance. Of course Jane reminded him of Liddy.

"I'm glad you're here," he told her. "I'm very glad, Jane."

But she shook her head. "I misjudged things. I hadn't known how it was going to be with your family here. A failure of imagination."

He was full of dismay, hearing how reasonable she sounded. No doubt she was right—it would be better if she left the next day—but the thought filled him with a kind of wildness which he recognized as being perverse. The more she drew away from him the more he wanted her.

"It'll be all right," he said, knowing he sounded foolish. "It'll be all right, I promise you."

He was looking with some desperation for a place where he could pull his car to the shoulder—for one of those paths leading over the dunes to the water. He would be saved if he could find one quickly enough, if he could get out of the car with her and hold her.

But when he saw a path and pulled the car to the side she stayed where she was, her hands in her lap.

He opened the door for her and held out his hand. "I thought we were going for a walk," he said.

"I don't think that's a very good idea. If I'm going back tomorrow..."

"There's no reason why we shouldn't go for a walk tonight," he said. "Come on, Jane."

She climbed out of the car then, dutifully, and started walking down the path. Everything about her warned him not to touch her, and so he walked just at her heels, watching the way she picked her way rapidly over the rough ground, avoiding the runners the wild roses had sent across the sand.

"I'd forgotten you were wearing sandals," he said.

But as he watched the way her fast stride carried her away from him, his pity for her left him; she was hurrying to get it over with—to end that time alone with him.

She didn't need his help, or his concern—that was what she was making amply clear to him, and in his resentment he walked more slowly, letting her far outstrip him. The knowledge of all they were missing, and could have enjoyed—the empty dunes, the scent of wild roses, the moonlight on the water—filled him with a dull anger.

Far ahead, Jane scrambled down a dune. He saw her, near the bottom, and then suddenly she was sprawled in the sand. "Wait!" he called. "Jane." But she was up in a moment, dusting off her clothes, climbing the last dune, the tallest, that led to the sea.

If she wanted to be difficult, then let her. Now that he thought about it he was sure there had been other times when she had been overly dramatic—when she had acted a part and watched him, seeing how he would respond. That was not a quality he liked, though he could remember clearly Liddy, at eight or nine, her shoulders as rigid as a board, staring him down, every muscle in her body showing in what disdain she held him. And all this over some infraction so slight he could no longer remember what it had been—he'd promised to take her roller skating and had forgotten, something like that. Yet with Liddy he had been entranced—it was amazing to him that one so young should know her rights and stand up for them so forcefully. With Jane, however, he felt rebuffed and annoyed by her refusal to let him help—her refusal, even, to explain why she was hurrying on so quickly without him.

While he climbed the final and tallest dune, he could see Jane on the beach, walking across it toward the water.

It was easier to run down the dune than to walk, and it came back to Philip from childhood—that wild flight, his legs acting on their own. Until he reached the bottom he did not even think about Jane, but then he saw that she was still walking toward the water—had almost passed the point where the waves sank into the sand.

"You're going to get wet!" he called, knowing as he spoke that it sounded silly. Surely Jane could tell that she was in danger of being soaked to the thighs by the next wave. But she didn't appear to hear him. She reached the edge of the water and without hesitating walked straight into it; even before the wave reached her she was wet nearly to the waist.

Philip took off his shoes and rolled his trousers to his knees before he sprinted after her. "If you're going swimming, why the hell didn't you take off your clothes?"

At last she did turn her head, though what she said wasn't clear. "All right," was what he thought she said. "It's all right." Her voice sounded perfectly calm, and even the gesture she made, of pushing the palms of her hands back toward him, showed that he did not need to follow her; all she was doing was taking a walk.

And, indeed, he was tempted to let her remain solitary in her folly. He was too old to enjoy a dunking with all his clothes on; for her it might be fun, but for him it would just be a damn discomfort. He couldn't decide what he should do. Absurdly, he moved back with the waves and dashed forward again when the danger had passed.

But as she continued, farther and farther out, he became alarmed. He couldn't believe that she was considering anything so foolish as drowning herself. Apart from anything else, he had brought them to the sheltered side of the island, where the water remained shallow for a long way out; no, what was far more likely—and it drove him into a frenzy of annoyance just to think about it—was that she would do anything to get attention and sympathy and he had been stupid enough not to realize this before. The wise thing would probably be to ignore her completely—to go and lie down on a dry rock and wait for her to decide to come back. After all, he knew perfectly well that the best thing to do with a child having a tantrum was to go off in a corner and clip your fingernails or take a book from the shelf and begin reading. He'd had plenty of experience.

But when the water between waves had reached Jane's chest, he couldn't bear to stand there watching her any longer. For some reason that later made no sense to him, he took off his shirt and threw it far back on the beach but he left on his trousers, taking time only to roll the pants legs higher above his knees. They he sprinted as best he could through the water, leaping high, his arms raised.

"Jane!" he called to her.

She turned her head, but he was too far away to see her face clearly.

"Stop!" he told her. "Wait for me, Jane."

But she walked on and he couldn't tell whether she'd heard him or not.

"Is this your idea of a joke?" he said, unable to conceal his annoyance when he reached her. "What's the matter with you?" he said. "We're both soaked and it's cold."

"You shouldn't have followed me," she said, and he could see that she was crying. "I'm sorry you've gotten all wet, Philip."

"What was I supposed to do? Watch you walk out into the ocean until you disappeared? What's the matter with you? Tell me, dammit."

"I was just so unhappy," she said.

The look of misery on her face softened him toward her once more, and he held her arm tightly as he headed back for shore, forcing her to jump with him when a wave swept up behind them. When they climbed out of the water he led her to a rock at the base of the dune, moving slowly because their clothes were so weighted with seawater.

As they reached the rock, he put his arm around her and pulled her close; she was shivering, and he could feel, too, her shuddering as she cried. "I knew it was stupid but I didn't want to stop walking, even when I reached the water. I wanted to go on and on." She kept her face turned from his, and he knew she felt mortified.

"I don't suppose we'll get pneumonia," he told her.

He felt very tired—exhausted in fact—but the exhaustion made him feel peaceful. He was no longer angry; it was only pity he felt for Jane, shivering in her wet clothes. "Don't cry, sweet," he said. "You don't have to cry."

After a time she stopped, rubbing the backs of her hands across her eyelids as a child would do. Then he pulled her to her feet and retrieved his clothes. They hardly spoke on their way back across the dunes, but he held her hand, helping her climb in her sodden clothes, and she didn't object.

In the trunk of the car he found a beach towel and an old T-shirt and pair of shorts belonging to Estella—clothes she used to put on over her swimming suit when she needed to go into a grocery store on the way home from the beach. The irony of his handing these clothes to Jane was not lost on him, and he was glad that Jane said nothing about them even though she must have known they belonged to Estella.

It was still dark when Philip eased out of Jane's bed. The early-morning air was cold enough to make his skin prickle, and he dreaded the thought of pulling on his wet jeans, which would still be clammy, though he had hung them over the shower rail the night before in the vain hope that they would dry a little. He was tiptoeing to the bathroom to get them when Jane stirred behind him and clicked on the lamp.

"Do you have to go? It's still dark out, Phil."

"But Chrissy's up with the first light. So is Jasper sometimes."

He pulled his jeans off the railing, though he shivered already in anticipation.

"Oh good Lord," Jane said. "You can't go out in those. You'll die. Wait a minute. I've got a traveling iron."

He wrapped himself in a blanket and watched Jane stretch a towel on the carpet and lay his jeans over it. He was touched that she would do this for him, that she cared about his comfort.

"Dear Jane," he said, sliding his hand along her neck under the thick, heavy hair that was still a little damp from the shower they'd taken together when they got back from the beach.

"Will I see you today?" she asked as she bent over the iron.

Any possibility that she would leave on the morning ferry had slipped away during the night.

"I'll come into town at two o'clock if I can."

"What I hate is uncertainty. I can't stand feeling abandoned."

The look she gave him was sudden and piercing, trying to see, or so he guessed, the impact of her words on him. Did she sound already like a nag or a dependent bore?

"I'm not being evasive," he told her. "But crises do sometimes come up. I'll be here if I can."

She held the jeans up for him to take, and when he put them on, the warmth was comforting to him. For a moment he was transported into childhood, warmed in a blanket that had been held in front of the fire.

He had kissed her and was nearly to the door when she remembered Estella's shorts and shirt and ran to get them. "It wouldn't be a good idea to forget these," she said as she handed them over. "Wouldn't that be a terrible thing?"

Instead of answering he pulled Jane to him and kissed her once more. He could smell sleep on her skin and knew that underneath her robe her body was warm and lightly damp—their lovemaking of the night before lay over them both like a trance.

"Maybe I should stay," he said. "Just a little longer."

"But they'll wake up and you won't be there. It's easier to go now, Philip."

And so, dazed, his jeans rubbing unpleasantly on his thighs, clutching Estella's shirt and shorts in his hand, he came into the street at earliest light when the gulls were sailing high over the buildings, shapes so dim in the thinning darkness that they might have been spirits.

Chrissy's Animal Essays: Elephants

My earliest memories are of Botswana—of lying on my back on a blanket and reaching my arms to the sky. It seems within reach, that soft, luminous blue, and I am totally happy lying on my blanket, reaching my arms not only for the sky but for everything—the droning of the flies and the excited cries of monkeys in the bush. Maybe, because that is the first world I remember, that is why animals have always been so important to me.

Mother has told me about a time when I was not quite two and just starting to talk a lot, finding me sitting on the ground beside a low tree where a monkey sat. It was a gray monkey, one of those that we often saw just beyond the village, moving in a group from tree to tree. But this monkey was all alone, crouched on a low branch of the tree only a few feet from where I sat on the ground. We were talking together. Or that, at least, was what Mother thought we were doing. The sounds I made the monkey made back at me, and the sounds it made I imitated. We understood each other perfectly well—that's what Mother thought. She stood and watched us for quite a while.

I wish I could remember talking to the monkey, but that afternoon is gone without a trace. What I do remember is watching elephants walking in a line to get to a watering hole late one afternoon. Elephants did not live near us when we lived with the Tungi, but we went once to Chobe and it was there I saw the elephants. Perhaps it was because I saw them only twice or at most three times that they made such an impression on me, but I think it was more than this. It was everything about them— their huge size and the way they swayed as they walked; the soft pads of their feet and the way their trunks moved as they touched each other. All I know is that I was drawn to them from the first moment.

I often think about elephants at night when I am drifting off to sleep. I like to think about the way they live.

When an elephant is born its skin is pinkish and soft, like the skin of a baby pig. The baby elephant would be a good meal for many kinds of animals and it can do little to defend itself. But it's not often taken as prey because when it is very small it stays beside its mother's legs and its mother towers above it, an enormous bulk. It must be like having a house for a mother— a shade that moves with you. Under her the baby is safe from the fierce sun and from pounding rain, and it is safe, too, from a stalking lion, because its mother has a commanding view and sharp, curving tusks that are so strong that even after she is dead the tusks won't rot. I half wish I were a young elephant with a mother like that. It must be so satisfying to hear her roar, knowing she can make all that noise just to defend you.

I like to think about the lives of elephants, but the reason I know for sure that they are important to me is something that happened when I was five. It was the most important event of my life, though for that reason I never talk about it. Nevertheless, there is nothing about that afternoon that I have forgotten.

There were, first of all, the dancing waves of heat which blurred the tiled roof of the monkey house, and the rich, fetid smells of fur, feathers, droppings that lay heavy in the steamy air.

I wasn't there alone. Liddy and I were running, and although I don't remember turning my head to look, I knew that Mother and Granny were just behind us, walking more slowly. There were many people walking along the paths, many sandals and sneakers slapping along the hard ground. And of course there were the many voices that sounded very loud and odd in my ears. We hadn't been back from Africa long, and everything about this new world was strange to me; I was in a kind of wild confusion during those days that gave me a giddiness like the way I felt when I had a high fever.

Maybe that's why I saw everything so clearly—the antelope in their enclosure looking up at the puffy clouds, the bears lying in the mouth of their cave, panting. Emerging from behind a bush a peacock shrieked and opened out his tail so the iridescent eyes caught the light.

Behind us Granny called out, "See his tail, you girls? Look! See that?"

It must have been while the others were watching the peacock strut, his tail billowing up and down, that I left them pointing and found my way to the elephants' moat. I'd seen the elephants earlier but had been carried along past them before I'd had a chance to look all I wanted to. It wasn't any surprise to find myself back at the elephants' enclosure, although I don't think I planned it all out, exactly. I knew where I wanted to go and my feet took me there.

The red clay in the bottom of the elephants' moat was cracked like a riverbed in the dry season. I had no trouble at all sliding down its sloping bank and climbing up again on the other side, since I was wearing sneakers and their rough soles caught easily on the surface.

At the top of the moat there was a wall, but since I've always been able to climb anything I wanted, the wall didn't even slow me down. I climbed it easily and on the top I squatted, holding the toes of my sneakers in my hands.

A few feet away from my place on the wall there were the wrinkled, gray legs of an elephant.

All I could see was those knees, coated with red clay dust that made a paste in the crevasses of the wrinkles—they filled the sky. The heat was like a heavy hand on my head, and I felt a little sleepy. The voices in the distance and, nearer, the rasping of the cicadas made a strange, eerie music. I sat for a long time before I looked higher than the elephant's knees and saw the pale tip of her trunk swaying in the air only inches from my shoulder.

I had known all along that the elephant's eyes, small in her enormous face, were watching me.

The trunk moved lower, curving to fit my body even before it touched me. When it swung around my waist and I could feel it squeezing under my ribs, I was surprised by how warm it was. It was like being lifted by someone's strong arm when the elephant raised her trunk and I rose from the wall. I think I was reminded of the way it had been when I was a baby, held against someone's chest. I wasn't at all afraid.

Slowly the elephant lifted me into the air. My feet trod on nothing but air and yet I wanted to go on up and up, higher and higher. The clouds wouldn't have been too much. I remember perfectly how happy I was and the way I lifted my arms up, pretending I could touch the sky.

I was sure the elephant knew me and had chosen me above all the other people at the zoo. She knew who I was. She had probably known there was something special about me when she saw me earlier, being pulled along by one hand behind Liddy.

I was aware of the people around me, of the brightly colored clothes and balloons, of the sparkle and flash of sunlight through the leaves and the noise of the voices and the peacock shrieks, but at the same time all that seemed very far away. I wasn't interested in any of that. All I cared about was right in front of my eyes—the elephant's broad forehead and her eyes that were looking at me. At certain angles of the light the pupils of the elephant's eyes were funnels, going deeper and deeper.

If I looked long enough and hard enough I was certain I would know what the elephant knew—and she would know what I did. Maybe, for a second or two, I'd *be* the elephant. It seemed very close, if I half shut my eyes and floated. Held in her trunk I could have been in a bed; the gentle bobbing from side to side was soothing and very peaceful, and I could smell her musky smell and feel the softness of her weathered skin. I think we were both dreaming, the elephant and I, and it was the same dream we were having....

It seemed like a long time that I was held by the elephant, but eventually I felt myself being lowered. When my feet touched the wall again I was wildly disappointed. And as I watched the elephant move slowly away, swinging her tail, forgetting all about me, I could have cried. But she didn't look back, and there was nothing to be done except to climb down the wall again and cross over the dry moat.

Later, when Mother and Granny found me, I was both scolded and coddled. It was a miracle, so everyone said, that the elephant hadn't thrown me to the ground and trampled me under her feet.

"It was because she wasn't afraid," people kept saying, as though this answered everything. "How lucky she's too young to know what danger is."

But it wasn't true that I didn't know anything about danger. By the time I was five, I had spent three years in Botswana and my earliest memories are of that strange and sometimes desolate landscape; I knew there were snakes and scorpions to be wary of, knew of the places haunted by bad spirits. But I had not been afraid of the elephant because I knew I didn't have to be. And, too, I think I knew even then that some things are worth risking your life for.

10

From the open door of the boathouse Estella could see Chrissy and Jasper on the beach, building a large and elaborate sand castle—a sprawling structure with turrets and towers—and she stopped her work to watch them. It gave her pleasure to see their heads nearly touching as they bent over the castle, absorbed. In spite of the difference in their ages they were close, sweet and understanding with each other. And yet the sight of Chrissy and Jasper together was troubling, reminding her of an earlier time when it had been Chrissy and Liddy who had been inseparable.

Until Liddy was twelve she and Chrissy were constantly together. There was just a little more than two years difference in their ages, and they shared a room, toys, clothes; they had a secret language that only they understood; their games were elaborate, complicated, and difficult for others to join. It had probably been those three years in Botswana that had cemented the bond so closely between them, though they had played with the other children in the village much of the time. It wasn't that they had been thrown only on their own company, but on the days when she hadn't gone with the other women with her gathering basket over her shoulder the girls had stayed with her in the nearly deserted village, and there had been many days when they'd had only themselves for playmates. They played in the dirt at the edge of the hut while Philip typed up his notes and she sketched. Of course the four of them were together a great deal, even sleeping together in the one-room hut.

But after they come to Providence, back to their "ordinary" lives, the girls remained just as close. Perhaps after those three years in Africa they didn't fit in with the other children, or maybe they held their differences to them through a kind of pride. Whatever it was, the girls' closeness pleased Estella. It seemed a mark of her success as a mother that her children appeared never to quarrel and had such a satisfying secret life together.

Yet she had a premonition that this closeness wouldn't last. For one thing, Chrissy's and Liddy's personalities were very different. Perhaps because she was the older, Liddy was also the more openly bold, the one who made the decisions. It was Liddy who "did the talking," as the girls called it, while Chrissy had hung back, uncertain. Estella knew that sooner or later Liddy would use her power to draw other people to her, and she would find Chrissy's company lacking.

It was a little surprising to her, in fact, that the old, exclusive bonds held as long as they did—loosening only when Liddy went to junior high and the two of them no longer shared the same school. Then Liddy started having long telephone conversations with girls she'd met in her classes; on weekends she went to slumber parties and for bicycle rides in the country.

It was understandable, it was probably inevitable, and yet when it happened it filled Estella with pain to see how quiet Chrissy became, how she moved around the house like a ghost, watching Liddy with sad eyes. Estella would have preferred her to get angry, to storm around the house in a temper, but all Chrissy did was to become quieter. When the house was full of Liddy's friends, Chrissy shut herself up in the spare bedroom and nothing would be seen of her for hours.

Estella longed to interfere, to take Liddy on one side and give her a good talking to, but she knew she must refrain from doing this. What good would it do if Liddy, through guilt and pity, included Chrissy sometimes in the bicycle rides or the swimming parties? It would never work. Chrissy was too young and could never fit in with those older girls. And of course Liddy had a right to her own friends.

But then Jasper had been born, and Chrissy had been entranced with him. She was the big sister to rock Jasper to sleep in his swinging cot, the big sister who taught him to pat-a-cake, the one who was most patient in following him around the house when he learned to crawl, keeping him from falling down the stairs, from poisoning himself on toilet-bowl cleaner. It was Chrissy who taught Jasper his first words and held his hand while he made his first drunken steps from chair to sofa.

Standing at the window, watching Chrissy and Jasper bent over the walls of the sand castle, Estella was suddenly assailed by grief. This closeness between Chrissy and Jasper couldn't last, either; she knew it. Jasper would grow tall and gangly and secretive, would cut himself off from them all, and she dreaded this loss. What use was love if it was so easily destroyed?

Angrily she paced back and forth, slapping a drawing pen against her thigh. She'd heard the car leave—there was nothing Philip could do to silence the motor of a car, much as he would like to, and she was sure he'd gone into town to be with Jane. She'd felt it the whole time she'd watched Chrissy and Jasper build the sand castle—the emptiness of the house, abandoned behind her.

So furiously was she walking that she didn't see Chrissy and Jasper standing in the doorway watching her. But when she suddenly looked up and saw their stricken faces she was full of remorse.

It was Jasper who ran forward to grab her hand and pull her toward the door. "Come look at our castle," he said. "It's beautiful."

"Darling!" she said, holding him tightly against her side as though she needed his support to help her out of the room. It was sweet, his soft yielding to her, his cheek rubbing against her arm.

"It's the best one we ever made," he said.

"Show me," Estella said. "I want to see this wonderful castle."

A child on each side, her arms around them both, she walked between them.

Just above the high-tide mark the castle lay, a whole world at her feet, the sun sparking into flaming color the pieces of glass worn smooth by the sea that decorated the turrets and towers.

"It *is* beautiful," Estella said. "And what a lot of work it was. What a pity the sea will get it."

It was terrible, but she could feel the tears swell against her eyelids as she spoke. She must be in an even more fragile state than she'd known if she could cry over the fate of heaped sand and fragments of glass.

Suddenly, as though he had read some part of her thought hidden even from herself, Jasper pulled away from her hand and leaped into the middle of the castle, crushing the central tower underneath his feet.

"Oh, Jasper!" she said. "What a little heathen you are!"

And yet she could not deny that she was glad he'd done it quickly and decisively. Now she wouldn't have to dread looking out the window the next morning to see the sand washed smooth where the castle had been.

Chrissy picked out one of the pieces of glass and held it up to the sky. Through the red glass the sky appeared a rich purple.

"This one's worth keeping, Jas," she said. "You don't often find pieces of red this good."

"Where has your father gone?" Estella asked, sitting on a piece of driftwood. She felt weak. "Did he go to town?"

They wouldn't look at her.

"He took the car," Chrissy said at last. "Maybe he went to the bookstore. He can hang around there forever."

"I don't think he went to the bookstore," Estella said. On some beach or behind the drawn curtains in a hotel room, Philip was lying beside Jane, his arm around her shoulder, her hair brushing his cheek. Rage boiled up in her. "And he's left us stranded here. If one of you had cut your hand on a piece of that glass you'd just have bled to death."

"We could have called for help," Jasper said. "We could have run to the road and stopped the first car that came by."

"And in the meantime you could have gone ahead and died, too," Estella said, unrelenting.

But it wasn't the fault of the children, who were standing in front of her with their heads lowered as though they were the guilty ones, and she felt remorse for having made them miserable.

"We should start supper," she told them. "You can both come and help."

"It's very early," Chrissy said. "Isn't it early?"

But when she got up from her piece of driftwood and headed for the cottage they followed, subdued, behind her.

If she'd been there alone she wouldn't have bothered to eat at all or would have smeared peanut butter on bread and drunk milk out of the carton. But because of the children she boiled eggs and made mayonnaise. Yet all the time she moved through the kitchen and talked to the children, it was another time and place she was occupying—one called up by the late-afternoon light.

Late in the afternoon the women came up the path from the stream carrying foraging bags bulging with food. Very leisurely they came, the women and children, and the camp, after the heavy, drowsy heat of the day, became lively. The village was full of voices calling out and of laughter, and the smoke from the cooking fires spiraled upward in meager threads filling the air with its acrid smell. All of it—the smell of the smoke and the voices—seemed to come to her from a world she had occupied once in a dream or, as the Tungi might have said, when she was a spirit child Long Time Before when she had not yet been dreamed by her father or entered her mother's body.

On the coals of her own cooking fire she turned the yams where the little fish, no larger than her hand, were already spitting their juices onto the red embers.

It seemed to her she had been happy, sitting by the fire just at that time of day when the shadows grow long, and yet looking back she knew that melancholy had hung over that scene, too. She knew now, as she had not fully known then, why, among the Tungi, the worst thing that can happen to a person—a fate so terrible as to be almost unthinkable—is to be alone. To be cut off from one's kin and one's own land where the ancestors are. To be exiled is to be a dead person, though he may still walk and breathe.

"Alone, he isn't a fellow," Wausu once told her. "He's a spirit. A bad spirit."

And so in the darkness, when the sudden African night fell, the light giving way to the dark with a violent suddenness that was like the severing of a knife, she too shivered at strange calls and rustling in the bushes. She too feared the spirits turned evil and hungry in their dazzling solitude, watching from their tree or from their dank hollow where the spring bubbled.

Before the sun reached the top of the pine trees, Estella was sitting with Chrissy and Jasper at the table, squinting into that strong, late-afternoon light.

"It's too early," Jasper said. "I'm not hungry yet." Slowly and methodically he cut an egg into small pieces and pushed them to the edge of the plate.

"It's not early," she told him. "Not very."

"And Daddy's not here," Jasper said. "Why are we eating without Daddy?"

"Why isn't he here to eat with us? That's the question you ought to ask."

"He's gone to town," Chrissy said. "He's forgotten the time."

"So we might as well eat," Estella said, pouring the dressing over the salad. "Not everything depends on Philip and his comings and goings."

When she took up her fork and began eating they dutifully ate too, nibbling the crusts from slices of bread, eating the yolks from the eggs.

"It doesn't matter," she told them. "It doesn't matter about Philip."

But she knew, by the faraway looks in their eyes as they turned their heads to the water, that they knew what she said wasn't true. And so she too fell silent as her attention drifted over the water, as alone, she knew, as one of the spirits watching from the grove where the ferns grew.

Philip parked the car at the end of a trail, against the dunes, took a blanket from the backseat, and carried it folded over one arm the way an experienced waiter carries a fresh tablecloth. It seemed to Jane absurd, the way Philip carried the blanket, and yet the thought of lying on it in the hot sun, sheltered in a hollow of the dunes, made her languid with desire.

Philip caught her hand in his, and she permitted him to hold it, though she felt self-conscious holding hands. She didn't like the feeling of being *caught;* it was always so awkward, pulling her hand away.

After walking along the beach a long way, Philip spread the blanket on the sand. From the place he had chosen they could see a long way in both directions.

"Of course there are Coast Guard planes sometimes," he said. "But I'm willing to take the chance."

Even as she smiled at Philip, a feeling of unreality came over her. She had no connection with this isolated beach on an unfamiliar island, and there was only this man whom she knew so little—this man she was even then unbuttoning her shirt for.

She slid down on the blanket beside him, his body something she might take shelter against.

"You're cold!" he said, astonished, rubbing his hands up and down her arms as he might have brushed the goosebumps from Jasper's skin when he had stayed in the water too long.

Yet as soon as she lay flat, out of the wind, she felt the heat from the sand through the blanket and was suffused with warmth.

After they'd made love he remained lying so close, with one of his arms over her chest, that she felt a little crushed, though she didn't move away. She studied his face, lying so near her own, and followed the lines that marked the skin—the one that came down his forehead straight as a ruler until it made a squiggle along the bridge of his nose and two more that curved around his mouth and continued, but more faintly, diagonally up his cheeks.

Lazily he rolled over and smiled at her. "Why are you looking at me like that?"

"I just wanted to see you," she said. How could she tell him that she was studying his face to see if he could be trusted, to see who he *was* after all?

It was surprising, and frightening, that she who was usually so careful—always planning, looking ahead to anticipate difficulties and taking precautions—should, in this, have merely shut her eyes and stumbled into the dark.

He touched her lips with his finger. "Are you happy?" he said.

"Yes," she said, but it was an answer she gave to stave off further questions, not one that gave any clue to her true state.

"I love you, Jane," he said. "I love you so much." Far back in his eyes there was a soft, out-of-focus, adoring look that filled her with panic. Who did he think he was seeing when he looked into her face with those eyes?

"I've never liked anyone to say that to me," she said.

The look Philip gave her was indulgent rather than alarmed. "Why not?" he asked. "Why shouldn't you like to hear that someone loves you?"

"Because of my father, I suppose," she said. "Before my father left for good he and my mother had these terrible quarrels in the night. They tried to whisper because of me in the next room, but what it sounded like was two snakes hissing. He'd fallen out of love, my father said. He didn't love my mother anymore. There was somebody else he'd fallen in love with. It seemed dizzying to me, like being on one of those carnival rides where you're suddenly standing on your head while your feet hold the floor. Centrifugal force or something. You can't even tell whether you're

right side up or not—it's the same either way. But after my father left,
my mother seemed happier without him. She'd seen through him a long
time before, she told me. What that put in my mind was my father as a
transparent person, like a pane of glass. When you looked hard there'd be
nothing there."

"It must have been difficult for you," Philip said. "Growing up without a father."

She looked at him with surprise. "That's not what I was saying," she
said.

"I think you were. In a roundabout way."

She closed her eyes and put her hand on Philip's belly, feeling it rise
and fall with his breath. "Do you love your children the same or do you
have a favorite?"

"I'm crazy about my kids," he said quietly. "All of them. But I worry
about different things with each one. With Chrissy it's that she isn't tough
enough. She's too gentle and sweet-natured. And with Liddy it's that she
takes chances. She expects everything to go right for her, and the thing
is that it *does*. But it might not always, you see, and then I don't know
how she'd take it. With Jasper, well, I don't worry about Jasper. Not yet.
His most grievous faults won't become apparent until he's thirteen or so—
that awful age."

"And Estella?"

"And Estella what?"

She could feel him grow tense under her hand. But he needn't have
worried. What she wanted to ask she didn't dare. What would Estella
think of her? That was what she wanted to know. If they met under entirely
different circumstances, would they like each other?

"Is Estella a good mother?"

"Nobody could fault Estella as a mother. She's always gloried in it.
Been bigger than life. When the girls were little—just babies in diapers—
Estella set up her easel in the living room and went right on painting with
the girls right there at her feet. The chaos drove me crazy, but she wasn't
even fazed. Only Liddy, I think, is as single-minded and strong as Estella.
But it's too soon to tell about Jasper."

Philip smoothed the hair back from her forehead and brushed his lips
over her eyelids. "Why do you want to know all that?"

"From the time I was nine there was only my mother and me. So of
course it's always seemed mysterious—brothers and sisters and all that. A

tableful of people every night for dinner. I just don't know how that would be. I imagine myself sort of lost in the crowd, sitting there ignored or something. But it fascinates me."

"You need to have children of your own."

"No, no. You haven't heard what I've been saying. I'd be terrified, I think."

She moved closer to Philip, wanting his warmth.

"You'd never be able to move if you looked at everything that way. We're surrounded by danger."

But he didn't have to remind her of this. She knew it all too well. Even now, under her head, the dunes seemed to be moving as though the entire island were being lifted by the waves. But of course this was only an illusion caused by the clouds high in the sky, racing with a wind that could not touch her and Philip there in the hollow in the dunes.

12

"Balloons?" Chrissy asked. "Do you want balloons, Jas?"

"We always have balloons," Jasper said, looking around at her in surprise. "Don't you remember? We tie them to the deck before we eat breakfast."

Chrissy dropped two of the packages of balloons into their basket.

"Oh, and streamers," Jasper said. "The good-luck streamers. I'll get some."

"All different colors," she called after him.

Usually she enjoyed gathering up the things for Jasper's birthday party, but she didn't look forward to his party this year. She knew already how it would be—all of them pretending to be having fun, putting on an act for Jasper's benefit. Yet Jasper would not be fooled. On his birthday he would be only seven, a little boy who had not yet lost all his milk teeth, but he often seemed older and wiser than that because he'd been so much among grown-ups.

"Candles too," Jasper said, putting them on top of the steamers. "You won't forget to give me a kite, will you, Chris? I have to have a kite."

"You're such a ritualist, Jas. Are we going to have to do the same things every year for your birthday until you're grown up?"

"Yes," he said gleefully. "Exactly the same. For years and years and years."

But next summer, who knew where they would be? This might be the last time they would rent a dune buggy on Jasper's birthday and drive out to Great Point with a picnic.

"A Chinese dragon kite," Jasper said, reminding her.

But of course she knew. When Jasper was three, Liddy had given him a Chinese dragon kite, and now every year one had to sail above his celebration, looking far with its dragon eyes, charging furiously the currents of air, frightening off dangers that might be approaching from any of the four directions.

They retrieved their bicycles from the rack outside the five-and-dime and pushed off into the blinding light of noon.

"We have to go by the post office," Chrissy told Jasper, suddenly remembering. "I've written a letter to Liddy."

"About my birthday? Will she come?"

"Oh, Jas, she can't come from England. Not that fast. But if you can absolutely keep a secret I'll tell you one."

"I can keep it," Jasper said confidently. "I keep secrets all the time."

She looked at him sharply, wondering, but it was probably true.

"Maybe, later on in the summer, Liddy will come home," she told him. "But keep that under your hat. Maybe she won't come after all."

That morning Chrissy had written a letter on the thin blue paper. "Maybe you don't want to hear this since you're so far away and I know you're busy. But everything is falling apart here and you were always the one who did the talking, remember? You're the practical one they listen to. In the evening I go with Jasper down in the lane to catch fireflies in our hands and I feel it's just us two in the world. It's like being an orphan nearly. Maybe worse. You're the only one they might listen to."

"I hope she comes," Jasper said. "This summer isn't being as much fun as usual."

Chrissy was touched by how competently Jasper wheeled his bicycle along the crowded sidewalk; it was hard for her not to think of him as a baby who had to be guarded from dangers every minute.

"Don't go too fast," she kept calling to him; it was difficult, among all those tourists, to keep up.

They were just turning away from the post office, wheeling their bikes to the corner, when Jasper suddenly pointed. "Look at that woman over there, Chris. Daddy made me meet her."

"Which one, Jas?" Chrissy asked softly, taking instant warning. "Only don't point."

"There."

She followed his gaze and saw the dark-haired woman, her shoulder weighted down by a heavy bag of books, walking quickly down the sidewalk with her head lowered. There was something familiar about her sandals with the thick soles and the heavy bands of leather, something familiar too about her hair, the way she held her head to one side. And then Chrissy remembered the ferry and the woman warning her about falling under the blades. The memory, which was pleasant, was accompanied by disappointment. She had liked the woman on the ferry.

Chrissy pushed her bicycle in the same direction the woman was walking, keeping nearly parallel though the street lay between them.

"When was this?" she asked. "When you met the woman?"

"I don't know. Not long. Her name's Jane."

Even though the woman was weighted down with the bag of books she walked very fast. It was almost as though she thought she might be followed and was looking for cover.

"Don't stare right at her," Chrissy said sharply to Jasper.

"Why?"

"She'll feel your eyes and then she'll look up and see us."

Already too late. At that moment the woman lifted her head and turned sharply; there was no escape from her eyes looking directly into Chrissy's. And so she saw it clearly: first the recognition and the pleasure and then, as the woman's eyes turned to Jasper's, the realization and the flash of fear before she lowered her head again and hurried on down the sidewalk even faster than before.

Chrissy stood, her hands on the handlebars of her bicycle, watching the woman's back. So that was Jane. It was amazing to see that she was a very ordinary person after all—one uncertain and who could be made afraid. She wondered if Estella would like to know this.

"Whenever you look at somebody like that you're using magic on them," she told Jasper. "They feel it. That's why a person always looks up if you stare at him."

Balancing her bicycle with one hand, Chrissy spit into the palm of the other and thrust it for a moment in the direction the woman had disappeared.

"What're you doing?"

"It's what the Tungi do when they have to pass a place where bad spirits might be living."

"Is she a bad spirit?"

"Maybe."

Quickly Jasper spit in his palm also and held it out.

"Does Daddy know she's a bad spirit?"

"I don't know."

"Should I tell him?"

"No!" she said fiercely. "Don't you say a word, Jasper. Don't even say you saw the woman again."

"All right," he said easily. "I won't. But listen, Chris, how do you know that about spitting in your hand? I never knew that about bad spirits."

"I remember a lot of stuff from the Tungi that I don't go around talking about."

"I wish I'd gotten to go there. You and Liddy had all the good times, Chris."

At the edge of Main they mounted their bicycles, though the cobblestones were terrible to ride over. "But maybe you were around as a spirit child, Jas. You could have been in a frog or a fish. Maybe I even saw you, hopping around a pool."

It was what Jasper loved—talk about what the Tungi called the Old Time. Busy thinking about his possible life as a frog, he would probably forget all about the dark-haired woman hurrying down the sidewalk with her heavy bag.

13

It was the peaceful, contemplative time of the afternoon when the air had cooled a little and colors grew rich again. For a long time the light would hold, and then it would fade gradually to darkness before the moon rose.

"This is my favorite time of day," Jane told Philip. They were sitting on the small terrace of the hotel, where, under a pot of lavishingly blooming fuchsia, they were drinking chilled wine. "In the summer it's my favorite. Not in the winter."

"What's the best time in the winter?" Philip asked. He was leaning back in his chair with his legs stretched in front of him, as he would have sat in his own living room among friends. He looked prepared to remain a long time, his head bent sideways against the back of the chair, but she was aware of every sip he took from his glass, knowing when he finished he would leave.

"In the winter maybe what I like best is night, because that's what everything heads for in the winter anyway. It's a relief when it finally happens and that's that."

She looked away from Philip's face, aware that he might think she was describing her state at that moment—it would be almost a relief when he left, since then she wouldn't have to dread it.

"I saw Jasper and Chrissy in town today," she said. "At least I was sure the girl with Jasper was Chrissy."

"Did Jasper recognize you? What did he do?"

"They were across the street from me," she said.

It was impossible to tell him that their eyes fixed on her face had made her cheeks burn. She had, occasionally in her life, been disliked, but never hated before. Being neither arrogant nor wholly determined to have her own way, she wasn't the kind of person to arouse deep enmity. Only sometimes a student, angry because of a poor grade, stormed into her office ready for a fight, and though the student usually left her office somewhat mollified she would brood about the encounter for days afterward.

Because those angry encounters upset her so much, she took precautions to prevent them—working out carefully what percentages quizzes, tests, papers, and class participation were worth in her grading system. She was afraid of being "found out" and yet she couldn't have said exactly what it was she feared. She was diligent in preparing her classes, kept ample office hours, was accessible and, she thought, far more considerate of students than they were of her. And yet she feared exposure. Somehow it would be revealed—that she knew far less than she seemed to, that she hid dark secrets even from herself. Someday a stranger, passing her in the street, would fix eyes dark with malice on hers and hiss, "I know what you've done." Whatever it was, she wouldn't be able to deny it, would know the moment the stranger spoke that it was a terrible truth he was saying. And the piercing shame of that truth would paralyze her on the spot.

"Jasper didn't wave to you? Probably he didn't see you then."

"Philip, you can't expect your children to like me. Not right now anyway."

"No, no, I suppose not," he said, looking distracted.

Of course, he did hope for that—for some miracle whereby he could have Jane and yet lose nothing in return. It was impossible to tell him that his children's eyes on her face and jolted her out of herself; in their eyes she could recognize nothing of the self she'd lived with for thirty-four years. Surely she was no monster?

"I haven't done this before," she said, and immediately wondered what—what was it she hadn't done before. Be a monster? "A married man," she finished lamely. And it wasn't true, anyway. When she was a graduate student there had been Dr. Boles. Only she hadn't thought of him as married, since he never talked about his wife.

"I haven't done this before either," he said. "But do you think it would make a difference if we had?"

"No," she said, but she knew it wasn't only Estella that concerned her; Dr. Boles, after all, had not had children. It was all of it—that entire household on the other side of the island, aligned against her.

"What about your other daughter?" she asked. "The one I haven't seen. What does she look like?"

She didn't quite understand it herself, her fascination with his family, but when Philip took a photograph from his billfold and handed it across the table to her she held it eagerly to the light.

On a beach a girl wearing shorts and T-shirt stood with her hands on her hips, stood looking straight into the camera. She was beautiful, but there was something about the way she was standing, braced against a wind, looking straight, even defiantly, into the camera—nothing coy there—that made Jane think it didn't matter very much to this girl what she looked like. She had more important things on her mind.

"There's something about the shape of her face that looks like you," Jane said, handing the photograph back.

"Liddy gets that olive skin from Estella. She gets just about everything from Estella except her hair. Estella's goes frizzy in damp weather and Liddy's doesn't. It's Chrissy who looks more like me. And Jasper's just himself, I guess."

Carefully Philip put the photograph back in his billfold, a faint smile he was probably unaware of lingering on his face. She'd noticed before that he usually smiled that way when he was talking about his children.

He drank the last of his wine and gently set the glass on the table. She knew that in a moment he would put his hands down flat on the table, ease his chair backward, and stand up. But for a few seconds, indulging her perhaps, he remained where he was, looking up at the purple blossoms of the fuchsia plant as though he had all the time in the world.

"Does Estella," she said, "know about me?"

And knew, as soon as the words left her mouth, that this was not something she should have asked him—not, at any rate, if she wanted him to stay with her a little longer in that peaceful time of day.

"She knows you exist," he said carefully, pushing his chair away from the table in just the way she knew he would. "I'm so sorry, Jane, but I really do have to leave now. No need for you to move from here, though."

(87)

"I'm going for a walk," she told him, getting up too. "I love walking at this time of day."

She would not be left, watching him go, looking bereft and pitiful.

She walked to his car with him, waved to him as he pulled away from the curb, but as soon as he turned the corner and was lost to sight she felt dazed with loneliness. What she most terribly longed to do, she realized, was to go with him to the house where he lived, to be part, somehow, of his family. But what role could she occupy? Second wife? Oldest daughter? This was impossible to say. And yet it wasn't at all difficult for her to see herself sitting at the dinner table with the rest of them, safe and casually happy the way it might so easily be in a dream.

Chrissy's Animal Essays: Mountain Gorillas

Late in the afternoon mountain gorillas begin making the nests they will sleep in that night. Each evening they construct a nest of boughs and leaves in the same way that Eskimos used to make igloos cut from slabs of ice wherever their travels after walrus led them. Swinging high in the trees, those nests the gorillas make must be like hammocks—in them the gorillas lie, sprawled, legs and arms flung carelessly over the edge, taking their ease. Family groups sleep near one another—the silverback, his mates with their young, one or two young males who haven't yet moved away to make groups of their own. I'm sure they can all hear each other through the night, the leaves rustling under them like cornshuck-filled mattresses when they roll from side to side. If they get hungry in the night, they can take a leaf from their bed and eat it.

If they aren't killed by poachers and don't die of disease, gorillas have long lives. They can live to be forty or fifty; the young reach puberty at about ten. Even after they are grown and move away from the family, the gorilla mother recognizes her sons and daughters and greets them with excitement. They know her, too.

The eyes of gorillas, as they look out from the photographs I've seen, are as knowing as ours—but what they know makes them sad. Maybe this is because what they know comes from what the Tungi would call Long Time Before and it has not been diminished by being siphoned off into words and speech. What gorillas know must lie very heavy with them since they can't ease the burden of knowing by describing things or labeling. Their knowledge must fill them like water in one of those tarns in deep forest where the surface is always black and utterly still.

Yet on their mountaintops, in the deep shade of their jungle, the gorillas seem to enjoy themselves, eating leaves and fruit, the babies watching the world from their mothers' shoulders and the young ones playing with each other, tumbling over and over like clumsy children. I think of them taking their ease in the heat of the day, slowly eating leaves, the babies lying against their mothers' thick sides, the silverback watching from the edge of the group, ready to defend them against danger.

When the young males are old enough and strong enough, they want mates of their own, but the only way for them to do this is to take females from an already existing family. The young male hangs around the outskirts of a family group, trying to attract the attention of one of the females, showing her how handsome and strong he is. The silverback chases these young males away, yet they return again and again. And sometimes, especially if the silverback is getting old and tired, they may eventually lure one or two of the females away from him.

I don't like to think about what happens next. If the females that have been lured away have babies holding on to their backs, the young male will, in the next few days, grab the babies from their mothers and kill them by bashing their heads against a rock. Of course, the babies born after this will belong to the young male, and it's true that the new family will probably stay together for a long time. But I can't stand it anyway, this terrible thing that happens. If I were a mother gorilla I think I would surely defend my baby. I wouldn't just stand there while it was murdered in front of my eyes, and I wouldn't have anything to do with its murderer afterward, either.

There is something about all this that makes the fear slide along the wall of my stomach—it feels like a little snake lives there, gliding around and around. That murder of the baby gorillas is terrible, but there's something worse about the story. I think so, anyhow. What's worse is that the mothers have new babies and the new babies seem to make up for the loss of the old. They forget. Or seem to. And this is the thing I can't stand. This is the thing that is so scary.

14

Days passed when Estella hardly saw Philip. They were so used to arranging schedules, to working out agreements between them, that this, too, they might have arranged between them.

She had always gotten up before Philip, getting breakfast on the table before he came into the kitchen. So now nothing had to be changed in their habits if she and Philip wanted to avoid each other in the mornings. She, Chrissy, and Jasper ate early while the light still lay pearly over the water. They moved around the kitchen quietly, talking in low voices, though Estella was sure that Philip was sleeping so heavily they'd have to bang on pots with spoons to wake him. She'd heard, too many times, the sound of the car in the lane after dark and heard it again hours later when the darkness was thinning. Philip had taken to keeping Liddy's hours, getting up at ten when the best part of the day, as far as she was concerned, had already passed. It was a kind of revenge for her—to leave Philip's plate set at the table with the neat array of jams and cereals arranged in front of it.

While she and the children ate lunch out on the deck, Philip remained in his study. Sometimes she could hear the whirring of his typewriter, sometimes nothing at all. She suspected he took naps, shoring up his energy for Jane.

Dinner was the only meal they still ate together, the four of them under the pink sky—for the children's sakes, Estella said, but it was more complicated than that. Later on, in the night, Philip might go off to Jane, but for this time she could keep him there with them—through guilt he would stay. But she also kept him because she knew he suffered during those dinners, although he tried hard to hide this by playing games with Jasper and, as they carried the dishes into the kitchen after they ate, by singing with Chrissy the songs they had sung together when she was small—"You Are My Sunshine" and the one about the rabbit, "Hey, Mr. Rabbit, your fur mighty white...Yes indeed, I'm quite a si-ght..."

She and Philip didn't often say anything to each other, but when they did they were very polite. There was a cool irony in her politeness, but Philip's was a kind of patient gentleness—as though she were sick and her bad temper had to be ignored—that drove her wild. It was amazing how easy it was to fill in silences with some totally banal remark. "I got three ticks off Jenks today. You've got to remember to spray him if you take him on a walk. You know he runs back in the bushes." Probably they had always talked like that, but before conversation had flowed naturally— whatever came into their heads they would say—and now it was made-up and stiff. At any moment she could turn on Philip—it was never far below the surface, her anger—or she could let it ride. It was in her control whether she allowed her anger to flare or not. And Philip knew this as well as she did. It was the reason he sat so guardedly at his plate, tension evident even in the way he sat so straight, pressing hard against the boards of the deck through the toes of his jogging shoes.

Only over the use of the car did they openly quarrel; for Philip to say he needed the car was for her to fight him every inch. She needed to go to the post office, she had to buy milk, Boston lettuce, tarragon vinegar; she'd promised to take Jasper to Cisco Beach. There were always places she must go and reasons she had to have the car. So it wasn't surprising, exactly, that Philip started taking the car without telling her he was going to. The first time he did this she was surprised—it was unlike Philip, after all—but following the surprise her feeling had been less of anger than of a kind of sly triumph. Philip too could act badly. Just give him some trouble in his life and he could act as badly as anyone else.

So she didn't bother to say anything to him about the car. She didn't have to. It was clear enough the way he forced his eyes to meet hers across the dinner table, guilt and defiance there for her to see. He knew as well as she did that he was acting in a way he didn't approve of himself; he who hated sneakiness was now driven to it.

It had been so long since they'd had a real conversation that the afternoon Estella looked up from her work and saw Philip standing in the doorway of her studio her heart leaped in fear. It was treacherous of him to take her by surprise that way; she didn't even know how long he might have been standing there watching her while she was too absorbed to take notice. Without thinking, she ran her fingers through her hair as though that gesture might have tamed it, but it was too late for any such gesture to do any good. Of course, she hadn't combed her hair since early morning; of course, she was wearing an old paint-spattered shirt with most of the buttons missing and baggy sweatpants, grimy around the bottom. Though Philip had seen her at work hundreds of times and she'd thought nothing of it, now she wouldn't have chosen for him to see her... "unprotected" was the word that came to her mind. Nevertheless there he was, bending down a little in the doorway, looking into the room.

"Can I come in for a minute, Stell?" he said as though it were the most natural thing in the world. It didn't occur to her to refuse him. She shrugged her shoulders and pushed aside her work as though to get it out of the direct line of fire.

He entered quietly, looking around that space where he had been so many times. But now he looked a little dazed, not knowing, having passed through the door, where he should go next. Yet it seemed absurd to offer him a chair as though he were some distant acquaintance paying an unexpected visit. As she debated, he went over to the wall to look more closely at the collages she'd thumbtacked there, making his way slowly from one to the next the way he would have done if he'd been in an art gallery. And as she watched she grew increasingly nervous, wondering what he thought of those collages; even in their changed and mutilated state he could surely recognize the members of his own family. Besides this, Philip had always been a good judge of her work.

But he turned away from these pieces without saying a word, and in spite of herself she was disappointed and full of anxiety. Perhaps this latest work of hers was so bad that it deserved no comment at all?

But then as Philip continued walking around her studio, picking up the shells and rocks she'd brought from the beach, she realized that perhaps his preoccupation was so great he hadn't even seen the collages, as he certainly didn't see the shells and rocks he caressed between his fingers. And her irritation and anxiety immediately attached itself to something else; now she couldn't bear to see him touching those objects that belonged to her with the same fingers—the nails neatly cut, the fine golden hairs sprouting thickly below the knuckles—that must have caressed Jane's skin.

"What is it, Philip?" she asked sharply; she would scream if he didn't stop pacing up and down and put those stones back on the table where he'd found them. "You must have had some reason to come out here."

At last he sat uneasily on the edge of the only other chair in the room—a straight-backed kitchen chair that she usually used to prop her feet on. "I thought we should talk to each other," he said. "We can't just go on pretending nothing's happened, can we?"

In spite of herself she laughed; it was so absurd. "Is that what we're doing?" she said. "Pretending nothing's happened? You sure could have fooled me."

He smiled wanly, knowing exactly what she found so funny.

"I've been wondering how you are," he said. "How you are really. I don't suppose you'll believe this, Stell, but I never intended to hurt you in all this."

He spoke very earnestly, for the first time looking her full in the face. Of course it would please him—showing concern. That was a role he was used to. But she wouldn't let him get away with it.

"What *did* you intend to do then, Philip?" she asked almost sweetly.

"Nothing that would hurt you. I certainly didn't plan to fall in love with Jane. Never intended anything like that."

"It just happened," she said. "A bolt from the blue."

"Yes," he said with dignity. "I know how that sounds, but it's true all the same. For your sake I'm truly sorry it happened, Stell."

"And for yours?" she said cruelly. She wouldn't let him have his good opinion of himself.

"I'm in love with her," he said. "I can't deny that. What else can I say?"

"Sacred love. What can I put up against that? Oh, only paltry things. The children, I suppose..."

"No," he said, and she could see that she had finally stirred his anger; he always grew very quiet at such times, his face turning pale. "Not a word about the children."

"I don't very well see how we can leave them out of it. Do you? But you've always romanticized them so. The Children, the Children."

Almost, she was enjoying herself.

"There are times, Estella, when I want to kill you."

"In spite of the Peace Testimony?" she asked. He didn't seem to find this as funny as she did.

"Why do you have to make this all so impossible?"

It was that note of reasonableness in his voice that suddenly made her feel utterly exhausted, and perhaps he sensed this tiredness in her.

"Have you considered," he said, his eyes resting somewhere near her breastbone, "going back to Providence for the rest of the summer?"

For a moment she merely stared at him, unable to believe he had actually said such a thing, had played into her hands so completely.

"Noooo," she said. "Among the many possibilities that is not one that ever entered my head."

"It might be easier. Less terrible for everyone. It's you I'm thinking about too, Stell."

"Oh, I'm sure you are," she said.

It was odd that she could speak so calmly when she was so furious; she could feel that satisfying flush of her anger radiate out even into her skin.

"I should leave you a clean field, shouldn't I? Crawl back to the farmhouse and lick my wounds. I'm sure that would be easier for you."

"It's not me I'm talking about. It's you."

"Then I can put your mind at rest. Aren't you glad? It might be, as you say, easier if I went back home, but I certainly won't do it. I have work to do, I'm set up for the summer, and nothing will make me move. So to hell with you."

Philip sat perfectly still, his eyes fixed on the window. "I wanted to spare us both grief," he said.

"It's your grief you'd better worry about then. You'll lose Jasper, you know. Have you thought about that yet?"

The more murderously angry Philip became the more quiet and polite he grew; Estella saw all the signs as Philip carefully got up from his chair and set it back gently in exactly the same spot it had occupied before he came into the boathouse. "Let's leave Jasper out of this," he said. "We're not ready to talk about that or, it seems, anything else."

"Just remember this," she said. "I'd see you dead before I'd let you have Jasper."

Philip, heading for the door, was so angry and affronted that he limped slightly as he walked.

She watched him cross the space to the cottage, climb the steps to the deck, and disappear through the sliding door. Not once did he turn his head.

15

Sitting in his study, staring at but not seeing the kinship charts on the walls, Philip was so angry—both with himself and with Estella—that he wanted to do something violent—pound his knuckles against the table, thrust his hand through the window. He didn't understand what had happened exactly in that talk with Estella, how it had ended up as it had. Estella thought she knew so much, knew him so well, and yet this time she'd missed seeing what to him had been perfectly clear. If she'd seen the truth she would hold him in more contempt, perhaps, but less hatred. And for two cents he'd go back there, stand in the doorway, and say, "Guess what, Estella. You think you know people so well, but you didn't understand the first thing about why I came to the boathouse to talk to you. It went right over your head."

It would have been satisfying to say that even though he knew he should be relieved that Estella had not known what was in his mind when he appeared in her doorway. Because his act of going there—looking at her like a stray dog venturing near a place that emanated a strong smell of food—had not been the act of an honorable man. Honorable men thought their way through to a decision with caution and deliberation. They came to decisions slowly, not taking their finger from the chess piece until all possible dangers had been taken into account. But after they reached their decision they acted consistently and firmly. They did not depend on others to do this work for them.

And the shameful truth was that he'd gone to Estella in the pain of indecision. Estella was the only person he knew who could ask question after question, forcing him to consider this possibility and that, until he would see, with sudden clarity, the truth. This had happened in the past— it was part of their old comradeship together—and this was what he had wanted from her, though he had known, even before he went to her door, that he could hardly say to her, "Estella, what shall I do? I can't bear being in this painful state any longer." Of course he couldn't say that. And yet he'd thought that somehow, once they began talking, she would under- stand what he wanted and would use this to strengthen the old bonds between them. She would be patient with his dilemma.

So when she looked at him with contempt and even hatred, he could not possibly let any surprise show on his face; that sharp stab of dismay had to flatten itself against the steadiness of his bones. Not by a blink would he betray himself.

And perhaps he had provoked the response from Estella that he had wanted after all—the response that would make his decision easier. He could not go on being so fair-handed, could not continue saying to himself, "Well, there is this . . . but on the other hand there is that . . ."

His profession had prepared him well for ambiguity but not for certainty. In his teaching he delighted in laying out one train of argument, step by step, watching his class become more and more convinced and sure. How wonderful! This was the answer, then. What pleasure to know, to have doubt eliminated. At this point the students would begin squirming in their chairs—all right, all right, he had made the point, he had convinced them and now they could turn their attention to something else.

He always paused then, aware of the importance of drama in teaching. He would lower his hand from the blackboard, pull down his cuffs, and half turn toward the book lying open on his desk—the book he used as prop only, since he had already moved far beyond what was put forth there—he would take a half-turn before he pivoted on his heel and headed for a clear expanse of blackboard. There he would begin to write very rapidly arguments against every one of the points he had just made— arguments based on the same data and made with the same authority.

How his students hated it! He could feel their dismay mount until, by the time he had finished, the frustration would have turned into anger.

"So what are we supposed to believe, then?" some student would be sure to ask belligerently. "Which is right?"

"You ask me which is right?" he would retort, waving his arm toward both portions of blackboard. "You evidently haven't been listening to me closely, have you? Sitting there taking notes like a diligent monkey, hoping that will get you through the final. Ah, but I won't let you off so lightly. I will force you actually to think. A hardship, isn't it? Painful. I won't tell you the *answers*. How awful of me. Makes you hate my guts, doesn't it? If you learn nothing else in this class, I want you to know this: data can be interpreted in different ways. Simplicity is never the answer. Complexity will never be complex enough. Beyond what you can know there will always be more that you don't. Truth will elude you. *That* you can all write at the top of your papers. Truth will elude you in spite of your best efforts."

And they would, indeed, bend over their notes, scribbling furiously and underlining. In some form or another this would be on the final; that was a truth they'd practically bet their lives on.

How would it go if he were laying out for himself, on the blackboard of a classroom, the complex impasse his own life had reached? What points were to be made for each possible way his life could go?

He had been married to Estella for twenty-five years and had never seriously regretted marrying her. For a moment he saw her clearly—that girl with the frizzy hair and the clear blue eyes, a child riding each hip. Nothing fazed her, nothing bothered her. It had been amazing to him to see her in front of a big canvas, humming to herself as she worked while the girls—babies really—rolled toy trucks over her bare feet. That was Estella at her best, maybe, and he knew it and admired it even while he felt overwhelmed by the chaos and annoyed with her because of his discomfort. She had not bored him; she had never bored him, and that counted for a lot. Quick-tempered, fiery, she seemed to him somehow always a step or two ahead of him, impatient with his care and caution. As long as they were on the same side they were good companions. But their very differences had always seemed to him one of their strengths. There were times when he caught her face when she didn't know she was being watched—guileless and open, that was the way she looked—and he was wrung with a kind of pleasurable pain—he was moved. He loved especially that open clarity at her center.

Oh God, he thought. And with one stroke wiped away all those ridiculous statements. They were true, but they said nothing about his condition.

Because if the sight of Estella's face could sometimes wring from him that drop of feeling as unselfish as any he could rise to, then Jane could do this to him nearly every time he saw her. Her mouth only, with that pouty upper lip, that swelling bud exactly in the center that made him want to press it against his own as though by pressing some sweet juice could be extracted—just Jane's lips, without considering the rest of her body, could make his breath catch... that sadness in the back of her eyes which he could not bear... it was all that love fanned helplessly by each of his children, a tenderness he felt he might die from... it was all this that Jane aroused in him. He could never have loved her at twenty-five the way he did at fifty-one.

He sat at his desk looking out at the sunlight glinting from the needles of the pine trees and saw that nothing he knew could help him. He was like one stumbling down a dark and unfamiliar hallway with nothing but his fingertips against the wall to guide him.

16

When they had been living with the Tungi for seven or eight months, there began to be talk of a women's dance to make love magic. Among the Tungi, events never took place quickly, and so Estella had almost forgotten about the dance when the day for it was finally set.

"They'll let you go along with them, won't they?" Philip asked. "Men aren't allowed, and it would be a great help to me to have a description."

"Oh, maybe I'll go," Estella said offhandedly.

In fact she had every intention of going, but there was something about Philip's attitude that put her back up. If she went it would be because she wanted to go; it would be because some of the women, Wausu in particular, were her friends, and she would join them in the dance as she joined them for foraging—because she wanted to be with them. She would not be going for the good of science.

For some time she and the girls had been going out in the mornings when the other women left with their foraging bags, and she had become as good as any of them at digging for yams and tubers. But she could rarely catch a fish and was ignorant still of many of the seeds and roots the other women could identify in a moment. Her ignorance was amusing to them—a grown woman with babies of her own who still did not know what was good to eat and what wasn't. But although they liked to tease her—"That one's not a good wife. Her husband goes hungry and will find him a better woman"—they liked to teach her what they knew. And Liddy and Chrissy they treated with the patience they showed their own children, pointing out the foods they could pick along the way and pop into their mouths at once.

Though Estella did not say this to Philip, she was sure she was accepted much more readily by the women than he was by the men. The presence of the two little girls had something to do with this. She was a mother and so knew the life of the women—not so very different except in details from the life she led at home. But not much in Philip's life had prepared him to spend the day racing over the hills after antelope with a spear in his hand.

The morning of the dance the women were excited, drawing together in little groups, laughing more than usual, obviously pleased that the men seemed subdued. Nevertheless it took a long time for the women to finally move off from the camp and head for the dancing circle two miles away. Nothing the Tungi did was ever in haste. The day was long and what had to be done during the course of it would be done.

When they reached the dancing circle, it was the old women who took the grease and paints from their foraging bags and began drawing the designs on the bodies of the younger women. The old ones remembered best the proper designs for the different clans—for crane, eagle, kite—but some of the younger women joined in tentatively; they needed to learn the designs against the time when the old women would have died.

At first, Estella sat to one side under the shade and watched as the designs were drawn on the bodies of other women—the thick band of black charcoal across the breasts and the lines of red ocher above and below the black, the inverted halfmoon just below the breasts with a straight line in black leading from the apex of the arc down, all the way over the soft mound of the belly. That was the design for those in the crane clan—for those in eagle or kite there were variations.

It was pleasurable smelling the odor of the grease the women rubbed their bodies with, listening to the voices of the women as they talked and laughed among themselves, their voices softer here, less strident than when they were in the village.

When it came Wausu's turn to have the designs painted on her body, Estella moved closer, laughing with the others when Wausu made a face at the first touch of the charcoal on her skin. Wausu was the first who had befriended her when they came to live with the Tungi—her two children were the same ages as Liddy and Chrissy, and this was one of the things, though not the only one, that had drawn them together. Whatever the other was remained mysterious, as was always the case with an attraction. Wausu was, as Estella came to see, a little bit feared by some of the other women because she was loudmouthed and bossy—even the men listened to what she had to say. But Estella wasn't intimidated by Wausu, and perhaps this was one of the reasons Wausu had sought her out. It took boldness to come up to a strange white woman and say on her third day in the camp, "Come and look for yams with me. I will show you where to dig."

And now it was Wausu, her body gleaming with grease and transformed by the red lines across her cheeks and the heavy white, black, and red bands, who came up to Estella and said, "Now it's your turn to make the love dance."

Some of the other women laughed, doing a step or two, shaking their shoulders and their hips. The Tungi loved to tease, and Estella thought this was all that Wausu meant—a joke for the others to laugh at.

"I can't," Estella said, smiling to show that the joke was okay; she didn't mind. "I don't know the dance."

Wausu made a gesture of unbuttoning. She had made fun of Estella's shirts before—it was silly, she clearly thought, to wear them at all.

Estella unbuttoned her shirt, though she expected the others to laugh, showing it was all just a joke. But she was willing to take the risk. She wanted to be decorated as the others had been. She wanted to take part in the dance.

And when she was bare from the waist up, no one laughed. When Wausu motioned for her to come, she sat in the dust with the others who were being daubed with clay and ocher.

While she rubbed the fat along her skin she could hear Wausu and some of the others carrying on a heated discussion too rapid for her to follow. At first she thought the others were objecting to including her in the dance, but then she heard the words for crane and kite and guessed that they were arguing about which clan design she should be given.

After a time the dispute was apparently ended, and Wausu, under the supervision of one of the old women, squatted in front of her and began making the charcoal lines above and below her breasts. The others, she was aware, were watching, curious, and Wausu clearly enjoyed being the center of attention. She worked very slowly and carefully, concentrating so intently on the designs that she did not look up into Estella's face. It gave Estella a strange feeling, as though her body had little to do with her, though she could feel Wausu's fingers moving across its surface and could feel the skin draw a little as the clay dried. Sometimes the others watching pointed and gave advice, though nothing broke Wausu's concentration. And Estella sat, a little removed from all that was happening, already worried because she had never been quick at picking up dance steps and would probably make a fool of herself.

Liddy, who had been playing with the other children, suddenly noticed what was going on and came running up. "I don't like that," she said. "Take it off."

"I'm just going to look like the others," Estella said. "Don't you think they look pretty?"

"No," Liddy said. "They look like bad spirits."

"It's to have fun," Estella said. "It's to play."

But of course it was not play. It was magic. She would dance the secret love dance which only the women knew, the dance that would arouse your husband to more fervent desire if you danced the dance for him, or would draw the desire of some young man for a lover if that was the charm you made.

As Estella sat, drowsy, feeling Wausu's fingers move slowly but without hesitation over her breasts and belly, something more than the ocher and the clay seemed to her to be passed from Wausu's fingers to her skin. There was power in those lines; she could feel it. Although she could not see the design that Wausu drew on her back or on her cheeks, and though she could view her breasts and belly only imperfectly, she nevertheless knew that by those designs she was transformed.

When Wausu finished and stood back one last time to admire her work, Estella was afraid to move for fear she would smear the designs; at first she was stiff in her awkwardness. But as she got up from the ground and moved around with the others she could feel herself grow more and more used to the drawing of her skin under the drying clay, more and more used to her startling, decorated body. It was impossible to smile or to open her mouth without being reminded by the puckering of the skin under the heavy bands of paint that her body was different from the way it had been.

Now some of the women began the singing, their feet stamping out the rhythm so that the red dust rose and swirled lazily over their ankles; in their hands the women carried sticks, which they clicked together — sticks painted red and invested with magic; sometimes the sticks were jabbed sharply in the air, sometimes they slid sinuously through before and behind the dancers, the movement of a snake through grass.

The women sang the man's penis—the words a charm that made it grow. In the words of the song the man's penis grows and grows long so that the man is sick with desire; he is dizzy and staggers like a spear-struck antelope and cannot walk anymore. He falls into the dust and lies, unable to get up, his desire so great he cannot move.

Then the women rubbed the red sticks between their legs, singing their own genitals long, singing them powerful magic. The man lying on the ground sees them and cries out; over to him the woman dances and falls down beside him. The man cries out with joy when he enters her, their souls soar from their bodies in bliss, like eagles mating on the mountaintops.

"Come on then," Wausu said. "Come and dance the love charm. I will show you."

Estella wanted to join the others, but she felt shy. The steps wouldn't go right, the words would sound strange from her lips, the magic wouldn't touch her.

But she went to the circle, timidly shuffling her feet forward and back, swaying from the hips. Wausu saw that she did not have any sticks—the red sticks painted with magic—and she danced her way out of the ring and came back with two that she put into Estella's hands.

It was even more awkward, holding the sticks, though she watched the others and tried to imitate them. Step, step, step forward, step back, sway right, sway left, swing from the hips in a circle—and the words, which she spoke so softly at first that they could not have been heard inches from her mouth.

The sun blazing down on the red earth was hot, the dust rose to her ankles, her thighs, blurring the movements of her feet. In time the words became in her ears sound only, devoid of meaning—her head grew dizzy with the heat, the swirling movement, the shrill song.

She forgot herself and forgot to be afraid of making mistakes. Now she no longer watched the others' feet or the sway of their bodies—she was her feet stamping the ground, the song coming from her mouth. She danced and sang for a long time, though she had no sense of time passing. Perhaps it was a kind of light trance she was in, made by heat and movement and song. She wasn't tired, wasn't even aware of her body except in its movement.

When she noticed, finally, that some of the women had broken from the dance and were sitting in the shade under the trees, she became aware of herself and sat down with them. Sweat mixed with oil rolled from her armpits and from the crooks of her knees, yet she didn't feel tired. The dance had eased her body, had released it, and she was full of the pleasure that comes after exertion.

But she was surprised to see the shadows lying long over the ground, surprised to see Liddy and Chrissy, their bodies streaked with dust, lying asleep with the other children. All coated with the red dust, they looked like children made of stone.

She was very thirsty—her throat dry, her skin burning—yet her spirit was rested. She thought about nothing as she sat and watched her sweat make pocks in the dust.

But finally the others began to get slowly to their feet, to stand and shake themselves, to gather up the sticks which the men must not see, to wake the children from their sleep. And she stood also and waked Liddy and Chrissy, taking Chrissy on her shoulders as other women were lifting their children.

It was with a kind of swagger that they all walked back into the camp, arms swinging, bodies easy, a distant light in their eyes.

When the men called out, "Did you sing good magic?" they laughed and rolled their eyes, trying to make a joke. Nevertheless the men watched the women uneasily. The women had made magic all day and its power was still on them; the men felt this strongly.

When Estella reached her hut, with Chrissy riding on her shoulders and Liddy holding her hand, Philip looked up from his notebook and what came into his eyes was first amazement, then horror.

"My God, Stell!" he said.

It was only then that she realized she had walked through the camp as naked as Wausu and the others, that from the waist up she was clothed only in paint.

"I danced," she said, lowering Chrissy from her shoulders.

"So I see. I hope you took notes."

She looked at him and laughed.

"Then I hope you have a wonderful memory," he said in a tight voice. "Nobody has collected this material before, and I think you know how important it is."

"My memory is fine," she told him, sitting gingerly on one of the camp stools. She had left her shirt lying back there in the dust near the dancing circle, but this did not trouble her in the least.

Philip went into the hut, and came back with one of his shirts in his hand. "I don't know what you were thinking," he said as he handed it to her. "It might be all right to go around naked with the other women, but the men won't like it. Western women aren't supposed to do that."

She put the shirt lightly around her shoulders but did not button it. It was the designs on her body she was concerned about; she didn't want them smeared.

"You look terrible," Philip said. "Do you have any idea? Look here." The little shaving mirror he thrust into her lap held no interest for her; she didn't bother to pick it up.

"Don't you think these designs are interesting?" she asked him. "Wausu's adopted me into the crane clan."

"I'll make a note of them before you take a bath," Philip said. But she could tell that merely looking at her decorated body was distasteful to him.

She watched with amusement as she ran her fingers lightly over the red streaks crossing her cheeks. It wasn't anthropology he was thinking about at all; she knew this. Until she took a bath he was going to be uneasy in his soul, and it wasn't his fear of the men's displeasure in her nakedness, either, that troubled him. Though he would never, ever admit it, what made him uneasy was the question he would not ask: who had she made the love charm for?

Yet he needn't have feared. The love charm she had sung that day was for him and not for some lithe-limbed boy. But this was a secret she would keep. She knew already—she felt it in the languidness of her body—that their lovemaking that night would be fierce and sweet. The lover she had danced that day would embrace the woman whose skin had been emblazoned with the red and white and black.

But not even then, in the middle of lovemaking, would she tell him the true words of the love chants—the secret words which only the women knew. Those words she would keep for herself and perhaps for her daughters in time to come. Why should she give up power like that?

Chrissy's Animal Essays: Wolves

A pair of wolves stay together a long time, usually for life. Though they mate only once a year, the two live together in ease and affection; when the female has pups, the male brings her food, and when she is able to hunt again they both bring food back to the babies. So, often, do other pack members—the pack being made up of offspring from earlier litters who choose to stay within the home territory. And so a wolf pack is a family made up mostly of blood kin. When they are separated from each other, pack members keep in touch by howling, since all the wolves in a pack know the voices of the others. When they are all together, they howl sometimes just because they're so glad to be back in the family once again.

If a pack member gets far separated from the rest it seems to know where the others are even though they are too far away to hear howling. The lost member knows where the others are because he needs to know—because the bond among the pack members is powerful. They love each other, of course.

When they are running together on the hunt, wolves think in the same way. They know how to lay out an ambush, how to trick a deer or moose into turning one way or the other so that other pack members can attack.

Wolves know that to look hard and long at another animal is a threat; that is the way they look at prey. And so wolves will look into the far distance when a strange animal approaches or they will turn their gaze to one side—those tawny eyes that see so much.

It isn't surprising that there are tales of human infants being raised by wolves; it would be ecstasy to lie in the warmth of the den against that thick silvery fur. And what joy it would be to live in that world of crackling ice, to run silently over the snow, running with the pack in cunning and silent speed, baring teeth to bring down the kill, learning those stratagems of survival worked out over ages of time.

Brothers and sisters, we are one.

On the morning of Jasper's birthday, Chrissy was the first to wake, opening her eyes at first light, when, in Maine, she would have pulled on her jeans and shirt and stumbled with the others into the kitchen of the camp to drink hot chocolate before she went to the blind to watch the terns lift from their nests, a white cloud flying low over the water.

She knew, even before she opened her eyes, that the light on this morning was dull. When she unzipped the flap of the tent and crawled outside she wasn't surprised to see fog dimming even the boathouse a few yards away; the water was blotted out altogether.

Behind her, Jasper pushed against her arm until he could see out the tent flap. "I want sun," he said in disgust. "I want it to be bright the way it always is for my birthday."

It was true that Jasper's birthday was ordinarily fine—a day of brilliant light with sea and sky richly blue.

"You know how it is here," she told him. "The sun usually burns the fog away by the middle of the morning."

"You think it will?"

"You're lucky, aren't you? For you the sun may come through."

She knew exactly the way it was on days when the fog grew brighter until it was a bubble reaching greater and greater luminosity and then there was a rent and a slit of blue sky became visible. Those days could be the best of all, when the dampness left by the fog made the air as fresh at midmorning as at first light—when drops glittered on every leaf and fell from the tips of the pine needles. That was the kind of day it could be if they had any luck.

From far away there came the mournful call of a foghorn, a sound Chrissy had always found immeasurably sad.

"I'm getting back in my sleeping bag," she told Jasper. "It's still cold."

Beside her Jasper climbed into his sleeping bag too and scooted, wormlike, over the floor of the tent until he was pressed against Chrissy's side.

"Tell me about when I was born," he said.

"You know that story backwards and forwards, Jas."

"Yes, but I like it."

So she told him again how it had been on the morning he was born.

She and Liddy had still been asleep when Philip came into their bedroom to say he was taking Estella to the hospital; the baby was going to be born. They ran into the bedroom to see Estella and were relieved to find her doing ordinary things—putting her toothbrush and paste into her overnight bag, looking for the book she was in the middle of reading. She looked the way she always did, only sometimes she would stop what she was doing, shut her eyes, and hang on to the edge of the dresser.

"Does it hurt?" Liddy asked timidly. They were both afraid, holding hands in the doorway.

"Sure it hurts," Estella said, and her cheerfulness seemed to them weird. "But the sooner it starts the sooner it's over. Anyway, I want to see what this baby looks like. Don't you?"

They nodded their heads, but it wasn't the baby they were thinking about. It was Estella they were entranced by; she was touched with mystery on that morning—imagination could not carry them through the miracle of one person becoming two.

Although Estella hugged them and said she'd talk to them as soon as she could after the baby was born, they felt her withdrawal; not even the words she used or the tone of her voice sounded the way they should, and they were afraid because they did not know the means to bring her back to them in the old way.

As soon as she left in the car, waving to them from the window, they didn't know what to do with themselves. It was impossible to concentrate on books or television or cards, and impossible to go outside in case the telephone should ring. They walked around and around from kitchen to dining room, one and then the other stopping suddenly and saying, "Shhhhh. Was that the telephone ringing?"

"And then Liddy remembered how it had been with the Tungi when a woman had a baby," Chrissy told Jasper. "How she went off to this little hut back in the bush and some other women went with her. Liddy never got to see inside, because she was too little when we lived there, but she'd seen women making a dance that would cut the pain for the woman having the baby. So that's what we did too. We danced so mother would have you with no trouble."

"And it worked," Jasper said. "At nine-thirty I came out and looked around."

"And cried because it was nicer where you'd come from."

"And then Mother held me and I felt better."

"You just lay there squinting up at the faces as if you already knew who they were."

"I remember the light and everybody smiling."

"And mother named you."

"Jasper. Because I was so beautiful."

"That's what *she* thought. When Liddy and I got to see you we thought you were funny-looking. Daddy agreed, but he said it was just because you were so new. All babies look a little crumpled."

"But I held on to your finger, that very first time."

"And I said, 'Oh look! He even has eyelashes,' and everybody laughed."

"When I got to come home you and Liddy argued about who was going to hold me next."

"Sometimes we did. Mostly we were good about taking turns. You got passed back and forth like a doll. Mostly you just slept, but every once in a while your face would scrunch up and you'd jump. It was like holding a rabbit."

"Well, that's how it was," Jasper said. "And now I'm seven."

He rolled over to lift the flap of the tent. "Fog's still there," he said. "We'll just have to wait."

"You're supposed to tie the streamers on the deck before breakfast," he said accusingly.

"After a while," she said. "Not now."

All the other years, Liddy and she had tied the streamers on the deck together. They had set the breakfast table and piled Jasper's presents around his plate, keeping him away until everything was ready.

"Do you think Daddy will eat breakfast with the rest of us today?"

"I suppose so."

"I hope so. What do you think?"

"It won't work," she said with her eyes closed. "You might as well know the truth, Jas. It's not going to be any good."

"Yes it will," he said, furious, kicking her through his sleeping bag. "Say it will, Chris. Say it's going to be like always."

But she wouldn't. She rolled over to face the back of the tent, and after a while Jasper got tired of kicking her and lay still too.

18

Estella understood that if they were going to give Jasper the celebration he wanted, it would be necessary for her and Philip to go into town together so one of them could drive the dune buggy back to the house—only a vehicle with four-wheel drive would get them to Great Point—and she was full of dread as they climbed into the car. For twenty minutes they would be cooped up without the children as a buffer.

"Isn't it strange the way the fog lies just on our side of the island?" Philip said as he pulled out into the narrow road. "The rest of Nantucket can be in bright sun and here we are, under a cloud."

Estella, her head turned toward the window, said nothing. She wished, absurdly, that she'd taken time to put on a little lipstick and had worn the blue shirt that Philip had once told her matched her eyes so well. Before they set out in the car she had considered making these changes but then had refused out of defiance. Philip knew what she looked like in all her guises, and she wouldn't demean herself by playing the girl again; she'd always made a point of being simply herself.

For a long time they rode in silence, but at the top of the hill where they should have been able to look down and see part of Nantucket town lying in the curve of the harbor, they both caught their breaths. All they could see was the fog and the trees that rose above it like islands in a swirling white.

"What rotten luck," Philip said. "I can't remember another time when it's been like this for Jasper's birthday, can you?"

"No," she said, still looking out the window.

Not only her body, sitting pressing against the door, but her very thoughts were stiff and careful. Where there had been ease and freedom—with Philip she had always said simply what came into her head, certain of his interest—there was now watchfulness. Not for anything would she show weakness to Philip or play into his hands.

The worst of it was that she saw, with bitterness, that her ease had betrayed her before. She knew now that Philip had watched her—who knew how long?—with critical eyes, had found her irritating or disgusting perhaps, had been bored even when he appeared attentive and amused. It made her cringe to think of herself in that earlier, unaware time. The fact that she couldn't guess how long Philip had played a part with her was the worst of her humiliation.

"Do you remember," Philip said, his voice lively, a good copy of what it had been so many times before, "on Jasper's first birthday when he put his hands down in the cake icing and then patted his cheeks? Chocolate icing? What a mess."

In spite of herself, she looked at him amazed. "I don't want to talk about that," she said.

"I wasn't thinking," he said.

If he'd felt the kind of pain she did he couldn't have spoken so casually about the past, when they had been, as far as she knew, happy. And if he didn't feel pain it was because, bolstered by Jane's love, he was protected from it.

"Listen, Philip," she said, her voice hard and calm. "We'll carry through this day together because of Jasper, but let's not have any bullshit. We aren't friends any longer, so why pretend we are?"

"All right," Philip said, and now his voice was grim. "We'll make it as miserable as we can for each other. Is that what you want?"

"You've always managed to pervert what I say."

"Always?" he said. "I've always heard you wrong?"

"How would I know? It's clear you've always kept a lot of things from me."

"Like what?" he said. "Just like what?"

But now it was her turn to keep quiet, her lips pressed hard together, and they drove through the fog-shrouded streets.

* * *

(*114*)

"Why don't we take the kite with us?" Estella called to Chrissy and Philip, who were gamely running up and down the beach with the dragon kite trailing limply behind them. Now, at midmorning, the fog lay pearly over the island and the air was too still to lift the kite.

"We should go off with the picnic if we're going to," she called once more. This time Philip began rolling up the kite string onto the stick. She had already put the picnic and blankets into the back of the dune buggy— also the swimming suits and towels and the boat that Jasper had just gotten for a present, a replica of a clipper ship with sails that could be unfurled and rolled up again. Everything for their pleasure that it was possible to take had been packed.

Estella climbed into the dune buggy, into her usual place, and waited for the others. It was always like that; she was the one who did the necessary jobs while the others played. "Somebody will have to lift Jenks into the back," she told them. "He's too old to jump up so far."

"I want my beach ball," Jasper said just as he started climbing into the back of the dune buggy, so of course they had to go back to the cottage to look for it. Almost, Estella thought, it could have been any of their family outings, that confusion and slowness in gathering was so familiar.

They had reached the narrow road where the wet branches slapped against the sides of the dune buggy when Estella looked back and saw Jenks running behind, his tongue hanging out, head thrust forward desperately as the distance between him and the car increased.

"I *told* you, dammit! There's Jenks running behind us and he's at his last gasp, he's too old..."

The sight of Jenks trying so gallantly to keep up rent her heart. It was horrible to be responsible for that need, that love—horrible to have made a helpless animal dependent on them when they couldn't even take care of themselves.

The moment Philip stopped the car she opened the door and was in the road calling to Jenks, showing him they would wait. When he reached the car, his sides heaving, she helped Chrissy lift him into the back.

"I told you, goddammit," she said to Philip as she climbed back into her seat. "Why don't you listen to me? He could have died out there. He's an old dog and he can't run anymore."

She was shaking with anger, and tears of fury came into her eyes.

"I thought the kids had gotten him in," Philip said stiffly.

"You thought, you thought. Open your eyes and look. Or can't you do that anymore, with all those other things on your mind?"

"Estella," he said warningly, and she shut her mouth on all the rest she would have said, aware of the quietness behind her where Jasper and Chrissy sat with their heads turned away.

The road petered out onto a rough trail, onto a narrow spit of land with water on both sides. On this trail, which was nearly washed out in places, Philip had to drive slowly, easing the wheels through the ruts. Wild roses had sent trailers across their path; birds rose from the undergrowth as they passed. Land disappeared behind them, and in the whiteness of the fog they could see no more than a few yards ahead. It was eerie moving through that land enclosed in a small, luminous space. If they were suddenly swallowed up, who would know? The land before them might have been unexplored territory; transformed by the fog it took on the strange quality of a dream landscape.

They all grew very quiet. Hidden in that whiteness, *something* that wished them ill could have been listening.

A dark shape emerged from the mist, just clearing the bushes ahead of them. It appeared so suddenly that Estella cried out, startled, before she saw the heavy wings beating, the long slender legs stretched straight.

"A heron!" she was able to say before it disappeared again, swallowed up.

They could not see, but they could tell that the land had narrowed because the sound of the sea became louder, rolling and booming from both left and right.

Estella felt disoriented by the noise. The low bubbling as the waves rolled toward the shore, the silence as they rose, crested, and then roared crashing onto the sand. Because she could not see its source the sound took on an exaggerated, terrifying quality; what she kept imagining was an enormous wall of water of the kind that had pursued her more than once in dreams, a dark wall she would not see until it rose, rearing to fantastic heights above her head.

As they drew nearer the lighthouse, the noise of the foghorn grew louder and Philip drew the dune buggy uncertainly to a halt just where the tangle of bushes and undergrowth gave way to open sand.

"This is far enough," he told them. "Close enough to the Point in this fog."

Though they all climbed out of the dune buggy and stood in the sand they were reluctant at first to move far from it.

"Since we've brought the picnic all the way out here I guess we'd better eat," Estella said.

But the place frightened her. She hated the subdued light and the sounds rising from it; she hated the sense she had that they—the four of them and a dog—were the only survivors of some unspeakable catastrophe, that they would see, when the fog lifted, that they were surrounded by a blasted, lifeless landscape.

But she was comforted, a little, taking the red blanket from the back of the dune buggy and lifting to the ground the heavy picnic basket, the same one they had taken with them for years.

The landscape that frightened her seemed to excite the others. She looked up just in time to see Chrissy and Jasper, holding hands, their figures dimmed by the fog, walking back the way they had come.

"Be careful," she called out, alarmed.

"We're following the tracks of the dune buggy," Chrissy said. "We won't go far."

"It's like Hansel and Gretel in the woods," Jasper called back. "It's so spooky I like it."

"Don't you think they should stay here?" Estella said, in her distress slipping without thought into the old habit of collusion with Philip.

"They'll be okay, Stell," he said, kneeling on the blanket to lift food from the basket. "If they call we can hear them."

She supposed he was right. There were no serious dangers she knew of that might befall them as long as they stayed together, yet she was afraid when she saw how easily the fog swallowed them up.

She watched Philip lift the tomatoes from the basket and the sack of pears, setting them carefully on the blanket, his movements slow and even restful. The way he lowered the sack of pears gently to the cloth was very familiar to her; she knew so well all his movements.

"If I'd known it was so foggy out here I wouldn't have been in favor of coming," he said.

"I know," Estella said, and as soon as she spoke she felt an immense though uneasy pleasure at being able to agree with him again, even on a matter so insignificant.

"Of course, I just wanted to give Jasper what he wanted, and what Jasper wants is the ritual—the same every time."

"But it can't be the same this birthday," Estella said, and then could have bitten her tongue. "I mean because of the fog," she said lamely. "And of course Liddy isn't here."

But they both knew what she meant.

As they set out the plates and glasses on the blanket they grew silent, and Estella saw that Philip, too, kept looking over his shoulder at the place where the children had disappeared. In an earlier time, she would have put her arm around his waist and they would have waited together, sharing their anxiety. But now Philip sat on his side of the blanket and she sat on hers, their backs to each other.

She heard rather than saw Philip scramble to his feet and looked to see the dim shapes of the children emerging from the mist.

They were so beautiful—that was what she would have liked to exclaim over. The dampness had made ringlets around Chrissy's face, and the beads of fine mist caught in Jasper's hair had turned it the color of old silver. But because Philip had hurried to them she remained where she was on the blanket, watching jealously as he hugged them and their voices, indistinct, excited, carried back to her.

She felt left out and alone watching the three of them, excluded from the circle.

As they ate, huddled together near the center of the blanket, she noted how much difference the sun made. Other times, sitting almost exactly where they were now, there had been the wonderful blue of sky and the sparkle of light on the water; those days had been buoyant with happiness. But she wondered how much of the pleasure had come from the light, from the warmth of sun on their skin. Happiness was so fickle, after all.

They'd eaten the deviled eggs, the cheese and freshly baked bread, were just getting to the pears, when Jasper suddenly pointed above their heads. "It's thinning," he said.

It was true. Above their heads they could see a patch of milky blue sky.

"Come on, sun!" Philip said, stretching his arms wide. "All together now. If we all say 'Come on, sun!' as loud as we can it'll come."

"Oh, Daddy," Jasper said, exasperated. But when Philip said *one, two, three, now!* he shouted the loudest.

By the time they got to cake and strawberries, the sun shone palely on their heads and their world had expanded to the edge of the water.

And then even that became visible.

"See?" Philip said, laughing, spreading his hands as though all the world they could see was under his power. "What did I tell you?"

Jasper swooped down to the water and came back, holding a piece of cake in his hand. "Let's call the sun again!" he cried.

Chrissy was laughing too, calling out when Philip and Jasper did.

Only Estella was left alone on the edge of the blanket while the others laughed.

She turned her back, looking out at the water where she could see the dim shape of a boat just emerging from the fog.

Though she would not join one of Philip's games, she knew very well that she was the one made to seem churlish. And it seemed to her, too, that Philip was fully aware of the position he'd put her in; it wasn't her imagination, that note of triumphant glee she heard in his voice.

19

There was a glut of bicycles in the rental shop, black, green, blue, three-speed, ten-speed—her choice. Who else would rent a bicycle on a foggy day when, it appeared, all of the island was enshrouded in white?

"You just taking it around town?" the man in the shop asked Jane as he made out the slip for the bicycle.

"Unless the fog lifts," she told him, wondering if he'd let her have the bike if he knew her real intentions.

Leaving the shop, she pushed the bike down the sidewalk, afraid to mount it within sight of the man who'd rented it to her. She hadn't been on a bicycle in fifteen years; if she was going to wobble uncertainly she wanted to do it unobserved.

In her pocket was a map of the island with the way marked in pencil, the line winding along the roads like a snake's track in the sand.

When she first mounted the bicycle the front wheel wobbled and she lurched along uncertainly, but by the time she reached the edge of town she felt more confident. It was exhilarating, in fact—the rhythm of her legs pumping up and down, the quickness of her breathing.

She was halfway to the turning from the main road before it occurred to her that because of the fog Philip and his family might not go on a picnic after all. What if she rode into the yard and there they all were, watching from the deck? She would be the specter at the feast, that was certain. What could Philip possibly say to explain her presence as she made a wide circle of the house and rode off again into the fog? Though it made her laugh as she pumped the pedals hard, leaning forward to take a long hill, she knew that if it happened as she imagined the scene would give her anxiety dreams for years to come.

But she'd always enjoyed secretiveness. Perhaps being an only child had something to do with this.

It had thrilled her to tiptoe into her parents' bedroom when they had gone shopping or to the library, to quietly slide open drawers and the doors of closets, to touch her father's pipe and rub the cloth of her mother's nightgown over her lips. Although she realized later that the secret of sex no doubt had something to do with the way her heart hammered as she touched those objects belonging to her parents, she knew too that wasn't the only secret—nor even the most important one—she groped her way toward on those afternoons when the house settled around her with its gentle creakings and she could hear the sound of a robin singing, piercingly, just outside the window. It was the very mystery of her parents' lives that she longed to plumb. To know *everything*—to be at the center of knowledge. The arrogance—she knew this—of the only child who observed the world from an elevated position.

She could remember thinking, when she was ten, that children knew more than grown-ups and the reason they knew more was that they didn't feel compelled to put everything into words. Curled up in the back of her parents' closet taking in the smells—cloying and stale—of tobacco and perfume, of street dust and sweat, she was surrounded by the unhappiness of their lives together. She knew, then, how her mother was thwarted and her father overbearing.

When she'd gone to St. David's some of the other girls had seen through her quickly. "Jane's a sneak," they said. "Don't trust Jane." But that was only in her first year. After that she became much cleverer in assuming the apparent openness and guilelessness that had gotten her through the rest of her years there. She became popular, in fact, and her room the center for after-hours gatherings.

There were secrets by this time about her family and not just about herself that she kept from the others. Her father had left her mother, and her mother grew distant and sometimes careless of her; there were school holidays she spent with her aunt. But these were not stories she told the other girls, not even to the ones who considered her an intimate friend. She would remain the one the others depended on—the treasurer of others' secrets.

The first boy she was attracted to she stalked as a hunter might stalk a deer. It was the summer she was fifteen, and Brock was two years older, spending a month with his grandparents while his parents were in Europe. He drove a red Corvette around the town—a car that was unmistakable even before she memorized the license number, and it had been easy to find where he was in the town, playing tennis or drinking a milkshake. On her bicycle she followed him to the house where he lived, only five blocks from her own, and many times a day she rode past the house, never turning her head to stare or seeming to take any notice, though she knew when he became aware of her, when he watched for her passing. And so one thing had rapidly led to another and she was soon occupying the seat beside him in the Corvette, riding beside him through the town and along the winding, aimless little back roads down by the river where Brock would park the car and they would kiss until their lips were tender and lightly bruised. But long before the summer was over she was bored with Brock, with the way he always carefully took off his glasses before he kissed her and then, before he put them back on, polished them with a cloth he kept in the glove compartment of his car. He no longer fascinated her, and it was hard to remember why she had ever pedaled up one street and down another looking for his car, feeling her heart leap when she spotted it.

The fog she pedaled through now blotted out much of the world. Paths led to invisible houses; bushes white with blossom emerged alarmingly from the mist. Even those trees and bushes seemed to her full of meaning and portent.

If she had not been watching for it, she would have missed seeing the mailbox with *Sloan* painted in black letters. But her eyes were drawn to it as she came up the rise.

When she lifted the heavy chain barring entrance to the lane and stooped to walk the bicycle underneath, she could see clearly the tracks of a car in the damp sand—tracks so fresh and clear they might have been made only minutes before. She was already gliding down the lane under the pine trees when she remembered that she was leaving the tracks of her bicycle wheels behind her, and when she looked back she could see them clearly—a narrow band of fine lines overlaying the heavier, thicker tracks left by a dune buggy. It bothered her to leave such obvious evidence, but Philip's family, she supposed, would not notice. Others were not as devious as she was.

At the bottom of the lane the house loomed in the mist, a house with deck facing the sea, the shingles weathered to a silvery gray nearly the color of the fog itself.

Someone had tied brightly colored streamers to the railing of the deck, and they hung there limp and forlorn. Over the weathered boards of the deck a pearly luster lay, a sheen marred by her footsteps. Cupping her hands, she looked through the sliding doors into the kitchen, where the breakfast dishes were still stacked beside the sink.

Someone had left wet sneakers in front of the refrigerator, the dog's dish sat just inside the door. Even these familiar objects held fascination for her. If she stood there long enough studying the cereal bowls, the child's drawings attached by magnets to the refrigerator door, the tea towel lying in a heap on the cabinet, she would understand the mystery of the people who had so recently occupied the room.

When she pushed the sliding door she wasn't surprised to feel it opening easily; this was the kind of family who would consider it a little vulgar to be too self-protecting. And at the end of their sheltered lane they would consider themselves safe from intruders.

In the middle of the kitchen there was a round table, cleared of dishes and with the chairs pushed into place. Estella, Jane decided, sat in the chair nearest the stove and Philip took the one with his back to the doorway; Chrissy and Jasper would sit between them.

When she left the kitchen and entered the hallway she saw immediately the bedroom that Philip—or Philip and Estella?—occupied. The bed was unmade, though someone had drawn the bedclothes up roughly to the pillow; the ridges and troughs left in the blanket could have concealed a body under their disorder. The rumpled bed, the pillow which still held the faint indentation of a head, drew her and made her feel sleepy. What she wanted was to crawl under those blankets to lie where Philip and Estella had lain, to see the window from the angle they would see it every morning when they first opened their eyes and were still made vulnerable by their dreams...just to sink down on that bed under the soft blue blanket, to stretch out there with her hands at her sides. The strength of the desire was so compelling that she was suddenly afraid. What if she really did do it—really did lie down on the bed and fall asleep to be found later by the entire family, like Goldilocks in the house of the three bears? The fact that she could even have such a bizarre fantasy made her distrust herself—if she could climb into the unmade bed of her lover and stay there for hours, then what other things might she be capable of?

Books on anthropology, psychology, lay scattered around the bed, but there were no books that she would have assumed to be Estella's, nor were any of the clothes or objects in the room hers. Gray sweatpants were folded and lying in a chair, sneakers sat side by side underneath. A penknife, a package of cigarettes, a half-empty roll of breath mints were lined up on the dresser; a man's robe hung on a hook on the door. If Philip slept alone in this room, then where did Estella sleep? The other bedrooms clearly belonged to children.

She wandered through the cottage, walking slowly and contemplatively as she would have made her way through a museum, stopping sometimes to study artifacts. It was all very ordinary, really—in the living room there were the same kind of wicker chairs and the coffee table with water rings marring its surface that could be found in any number of summer houses. And it was inevitable that there would be souvenirs from the years in Botswana; she could have predicted the foraging bag hung on a nail, the zebra skin tacked to the wall. After all, her own apartment was full of Hopi jars and rugs. Somebody was reading *The Hobbit*. Somebody else was halfway through Tinbergen's *Animal Societies*. The fireplace had not been cleaned for a long time, and a faint smell of woodsmoke remained in the air.

After a time she slid back the doors onto the deck and went outside. She'd seen, when she first arrived at the cottage, that there was a second building—an old boathouse, though it was clear to her because of the deck that had been built along the side facing the water that the boathouse had been converted to another purpose, and she supposed that it was now a guest house. It didn't occur to her until she pushed the door open and stepped inside the room that this was Estella's studio—Estella's lair.

She was struck from the first moment—assailed, really—by energy, anger, pain. Photographs and portions of photographs covered the tables, were tacked carelessly to the walls, were scattered over the floor. Wastepaper baskets were crammed and had spilled over; the daybed had been yanked into the middle of the room so it partly blocked one of the doors. Jane had an image of Estella dragging the bed around with her from place to place during the night, not able to sleep anywhere. She knew exactly how that would be.

When she studied the collages covering the worktable and recognized even in their mutilated state the family members, Jane understood just as certainly Estella's intention. The juxtaposition of images was grotesque, the severing of family members one from the other brutal—they were ripped, torn from one another's grasp. And in the middle of all that outrage the smiles showed an idiot, mindless happiness, sinister in its ignorance.

As she walked from collage to collage, Jane felt the muscles in her hands tense as though they had held the scissors that had severed those heads and detached one clasped hand from another; what she saw was herself, hands outstretched to hold father on one side, mother on the other, standing in a line against trees, or perhaps it was a hedge, smiling in that old dream of perfectly unity, of all-encompassing love....

How odd to have remembered that.

She'd forgotten she had ever felt anything other than Jane alone lying under the white sheet, watching the moonlight shift across the floor of her bedroom as the leaves of the maple tree swung forward, back, dipping in the breeze.

Even in the mutilated photographs Estella's strength was evident. The way she stood, firmly, shoulders straight, her bulk an indication of her power. Although Jane could not see the scene in which she and Estella might confront each other directly, she could imagine them in some disembodied dream state in which every word spoken and even those left unsaid would vibrate between them with meaning. They would understand each other as sisters would, able to read signs that others would miss.

Feeling suddenly weak, Jane sat on Estella's bed and looked at the tabletop piled with tubes of paint, brushes, pencils, jars of pickles and ketchup, a half-gone loaf of bread—the wrapper lying limp as the sleeve of a man with an amputated arm—and at the jeans lying where Estella had stepped from them, a shirt, dirty socks, swimming suit sticky with sand; all lay where they had been thrown to the floor or against the wall, violence in their very postures.

It was this energy, the fierce heat and wild rage, that pinned Jane to the battered cot bereft, almost, of her own will.

How could such violence be brought about through such a simple thing as love?

When Jane finally got up from the cot, she smoothed the blanket behind her. Not even a slight hollow on the bed would she leave. Nothing, not even her knowledge of this room, must be allowed to linger in the air, since Estella would be as alert as a shaman to any intrusion.

Suddenly afraid—terrified even—of being caught in that place belonging to Estella, Jane ran from the boathouse, past the tent—a red splotch in the fog—where she suddenly knew the children slept between the house of the mother and the house of the father, the balancing pole in between.

When she reached her bicycle she yanked it upright, hurriedly put her leg across the bar, and began pedaling furiously through the thick sand. She had pillaged, plundered, but what she took away with her was in no way what she had come for.

20

Estella's dream oddly enough was strangely peaceful—was in fact bliss-fully happy. She'd just given birth to a baby and it lay against her side so that she could feel the sweet urgency of its body. Even in the dream she marveled. It seemed she had not known she was going to have a baby, but there, suddenly and miraculously, it was. And she was overcome with that old familiar love, the one she thought she had forgotten, the love a mother feels for a newborn baby. Never had she loved anything so deeply in all her life, and it was this love that she felt lifting in her wondrously as the priest lifts the chalice so that the miracle can occur, the magic act made once more. She could smell the baby's skin, the smell of the womb, and she was bending down to sniff the new baby's head as she had those of her other children when they were born....

"Estella!" someone was saying. "Estella!"

She opened her eyes to pearly whiteness, to a kind of milky blue, the color of the sea when something white moves beneath the surface. She was lying the wrong way around, in danger from the waves washing very near.

"Philip," she said, sitting up, ashamed that he should have seen her asleep, with her mouth open perhaps. Maybe snoring.

"Look," he said, kneeling on the blanket beside her as grown-ups sometimes kneel so their eyes will be level with a child's. "I'm sure it's nothing to worry about. But I don't quite know where Jasper's gotten to. He was here just a minute ago and now he's disappeared."

"What do you mean, disappeared?" she cried, getting instantly to her feet. In that split second she had seen the pale body lying face down in the water and knew that Philip had done this with his stupid carelessness, with his crass self-absorption.

"He has to be somewhere near," Philip said. "He has his boat with him. Chrissy's gone to look for him."

"Why weren't you watching?" she said, her voice steely. "What were you doing?"

"I was sitting on the blanket, he was playing right over there in the sand, and then when I looked around he'd disappeared."

"You were sitting there thinking about Jane," Estella said. "Like some sixteen-year-old boy. Weren't you? Well, weren't you?"

"For God's sake," Philip said. He turned pale but would not meet her eye. "I'll go this way," he said, pointing toward the dune buggy. "You go the other direction, toward the lighthouse."

"I'll go wherever I damn well please," Estella said. "You're getting very efficient all of a sudden. After you've lost him."

"And while we're standing here shouting at each other he could be in trouble," Philip said, his voice grim.

"Drowned, you mean. Go ahead and say it. He could already be dead."

That alarm, always set on a hair trigger, was easily released. As Estella ran toward the lighthouse through what appeared to be an opening in the clouds with the sun shining through it palely, all those other times she had been mortally afraid for one of the children came with her. The sudden fevers in the night, the time she thought Liddy might have eaten the mothballs, the time at a state fair when Chrissy had been lost for over an hour. Always, each time, she had been convinced of the direst possibilities. Always there had been warnings overlooked, precautions not taken. And now too she was half convinced that no matter how loudly she called his name, Jasper was in a state past hearing her voice.

Yet even as she ran with fear accompanying every step, some inner voice amazing in its coldness took satisfaction; if Jasper was drowned, then Philip would blame himself for the rest of his life. He would suffer terribly, waking in the middle of the night bathed in sweat and full of irredeemable loss. Because he had been sitting on a blanket daydreaming about the woman he was in love with, thinking about her breasts under his hand, because he was thinking those thoughts and had grown careless, his son was dead. He would never be able to forgive himself. The inner voice said quite calmly and clearly, It might be worth it.

She was running down the road, back the way they'd come, when she heard a child's laugh on her left, somewhere out in the tangle of bushes and vines.

"Jasper?" she called.

He didn't answer, and she was forced to turn from the road to fight her way through the bushes, where the wild roses pulled at her shirt and vines caught her feet.

Then, just ahead, she saw him, crouched on his heels beside a little pool, blowing on the sails of his boat to make it careen lopsidedly over the water. The sight of him, so solid and familiar, filled her with such relief that she stopped and caught her breath before she called to him.

"We were looking all over for you," she told him. "Didn't you hear us calling?"

"I had to find a sheltered place for my boat," he said, ignoring her question. "It would get smashed in the ocean."

"Get it and come back now, Jasper. Everybody's worried about you."

He was in no hurry, lingering long enough to send the boat once more around the pool before he drew it in and stood up.

It wasn't until she held out her hand to him that the poignancy of his body in all its familiarity—the scrape across one knee that had left a white streak on the tanned skin, the faint pale lilac shadows in the pit of his eyes—struck her with the shame and horror of what she had so recently been thinking. Now that she held him in her arms she knew that nothing could ever have made up for his loss, and she didn't understand how she could have held such terrible thoughts and desires, what madness had consumed her.

"Here, Jas," she said. "Let me see if I can still lift you."

He raised his arms and she swung him up onto her hip, where he clung. She walked heavily through the bushes with one of his arms around her neck, the other holding his boat against his chest. With one hand she stroked his leg, and the love she felt for him brought tears to her eyes. Her beautiful child, the trophy she was bringing back to the others.

She was nearly to the blanket before she called out, "I've found him. He's here."

Even after Philip reached them she kept Jasper on her hip. "He had his boat with him," she told Philip coldly. "He might have gone straight to the water and tried to wade out with it."

She saw the lingering traces of fear in Philip's eyes, but she would not relent.

On the way back to the cottage she held Jasper in her lap with his head on her shoulder, his legs lying along hers. He still liked that some-times—to be held and rocked like a baby. "You're a lapful," she told him, but she wanted him there all the same. With her arms encircling him she leaned forward to blow into his hair so it parted at her breath and lay back in a circle.

From the corner of her eye she could see Philip turn his head to watch, over and over turning his head as though he were compelled to do so. In that quick intensity of gaze there was the kind of unbearable yearning a child has sometimes to touch velvet or fur which is worn by a stranger.

Once he put his hand on Jasper's knee, but she abruptly and delib-erately moved Jasper's leg away so that Philip's hand had to fall back. The rest of the way home she sat near the door and Philip used both hands to steer the dune buggy down the bumpy trail.

21

He'd put on a good show—they expected that and would be terribly disappointed if he didn't enjoy himself—but it hadn't been the way he'd wanted. Nothing had been exactly right, and his mother and father were angry about something, so he'd had to work at entertaining them, had to say, "But why won't the kite go up? Why won't it?" though he knew very well why not, and he'd made a mess of blowing out his candles so they'd laugh. He got very tired of it sometimes, being the one they all watched expectantly.

He liked lying against his mother, her shoulder the perfect place to rest his head, and he didn't mind that the fog had blown in again so that it was all white outside the windshield of the dune buggy like dragon's breath. It was the mystery he liked; anything could rise up out of that fog and bolt across the road—even a hippopotamus maybe. He rolled his head back and forth on his mother's shoulder, in the hollow made by her shoulder blade; he liked seeing everything in a blur.

"Oh, you're wriggly," his mother said in his ear. "Can't keep still half a minute, can you?" But there was love in her voice; she had her arms around him because she'd had a fright. He'd seen that in her eyes when she found him by the pool with his boat. She really thought he might have waded out in the ocean and been swept away. And that would be sad. If that happened he didn't know what they would do or how they could possibly live without him; they might never laugh or even smile again without him there to entertain them. They would die of sadness. But it was all right, because he would never go out in the ocean alone. He knew very well what was safe and what wasn't and nothing bad was going to happen to him.

He reached his hand up and touched his mother's cheek.

When she bent down to kiss his head he could feel her taking a long breath—it went from her throat to her chest and all the way down into her stomach. And all the while his father kept looking over, little quick looks as if he weren't really doing it. His father felt left out and later on he'd probably have to sit in his father's lap for a little while to cheer him up.

Chrissy, sitting in the back with Jenks, was patting him slowly over and over between the ears, though Jenks had gone to sleep with his head on his paws. What Chrissy wanted was for Liddy to be home. She wanted all of them together sitting out on the deck watching the sun go down and then the little sparkles where the fireflies lit their lamps.

"Was it a good birthday, Jas?" his father said with that yearning in his voice.

"Oh sure," Jasper said. "Maybe not *quite* as good as last year but I liked it."

The truth was that disappointing things had happened from the very moment he opened his eyes that morning, but he wanted to be gracious about it. They all wanted him to enjoy himself. And so over and over again he had to think, Is this the way a happy child laughs? Is it?

"You don't have to put on an act," Chrissy said.

"I *did* enjoy it," he insisted. "I even liked the fog. Everything looks so different."

All ruined. That was what Chrissy was thinking.

"Let's sing something," he said. "It's my birthday, so you have to."

And for the rest of the way back to the house he made them sing "Old MacDonald Had a Farm," which was the very first song he'd learned— the animal noises at least. It sounded all right, all of them singing together, if you didn't listen for what was underneath. So he wouldn't. He didn't always want to know things all the time.

22

Philip entered the house in a frenzy to leave it again—to escape. How dare Estella treat him that way, as somebody who counted for nothing at all in the family? He couldn't get it out of his head—the way it had been with all of them shut up inside the dune buggy so he'd felt their very thoughts trapped in there with them too—electrical charges with nothing to ground themselves on. It filled him with horror. And the way Estella had cut herself off completely from him; he hadn't known before how much she wanted to make him suffer. There she had sat with Jasper on her lap, as heavy and dark and unapproachable as some late-medieval Madonna, her Child seated on her lap as on a broad and uncomfortable throne. He could not even run his hand down the smooth sweetness of Jasper's leg, though he had burned to do this; every time he had turned toward Jasper she had pulled him away. Philip had been excluded and isolated—an exclusion that filled him with a wild anger and agitation.

His hands trembled as he laid the stacks of clothes into the suitcase he'd opened out on the bed, cramming socks and shorts into the crevices between the shirts. All he could think about was getting out of the house; it was impossible to understand how he had slept there so many other nights when he had laid himself down on the bed like a man stretched on a rack—Jane on his left hand, Estella on his right. Between them he had felt the heavy, poisoned darkness where Estella brooded and had known the tremulous anxiety tempered with joy that emanated from Jane. It was amazing he had rested at all there in the middle, had been able to close his eyes on whatever dreams had risen underneath his eyelids.

As he raked shaving cream, toothbrush, razor, pills into his bag, he caught a glimpse of his face in the bathroom mirror and turned away instantly in fright from those wild, untrustworthy eyes. There was no understanding the fear—it went far beyond what was reasonable and out into some ancient guilt and childhood terror. If Estella came into the house and caught him packing his belongings, he would stutter like a trapped boy choking on the frantic beating of his heart.

When he had shut the suitcase on the clothes, he was tempted to leave with just that. But he knew he had to take his work with him; the thought of casting himself adrift from that anchor panicked him more than did the prospect of taking another thirty minutes to get out of the house. He'd lived his entire adult life with discipline, and he couldn't go without taking the manuscript of his book and his notes with him.

He would drive directly to Jane's hotel and ask her to go with him— he could see himself coming wild-eyed through the door of her room and her rising slowly from her chair, scared in that first moment. But she would come with him; why shouldn't she? Without him she had no reason to stay on the island. It was to her apartment in Philadelphia they would go—it was the obvious place—and there he could get his bearings and decide what he wanted to do next.

Nothing in his past life had prepared him for what he was doing; he had always been dependable—even, he often feared, tending a little to dullness. Yet each person, he knew, shared a skin with various strangers, some of whom could behave in surprising ways, and since he'd fallen in love with Jane he did not know from one day to the next what he might find himself doing. No wonder his face in the bathroom mirror scared him; it was for all he knew the face of a maniac, of someone who had lost the thread of his life and was headed for . . . perdition.

The old-fashionedness of the word made him smile even in his frantic state. It was a word his father might have used—his father sitting with the other elders at Meeting, his heavily lidded eyes looking across all the heads to some far distant point.

But it was Estella's word he feared more applied to himself—"trifling." Of no account, shifty, undependable, without weight or substance. A man not to be taken seriously after all.

When the car was loaded he stood hesitating, his hand on the door handle. If he did what he wanted he would get into the car that moment and drive away, his foot heavy on the gas, fleeing. But this—much as he would have liked it—he saw was impossible. He could not leave without a note of some kind. For the children's sakes he must do this.

And so he went back inside the house and bent over his desk, smoothing a piece of paper under his hand. "Must go away for a while," he wrote, hearing the words in his head, abbreviated as though it were a telegram he was writing and each word were costing him money. "Have to spend some time in a good library. Leaving the car at the airport, keys in the usual place. In touch later."

It was a crazy note—he knew that even as he was writing it—but Estella would read between the lines and understand what he was really saying. And the children could believe that about the library if they wanted to; at least he was giving them that possibility.

He left the paper in the middle of his now clean desk, anchored with his stapler, and walked to the door. Now that he knew he would make his escape easily his panic left him and he felt very calm. Long ago he'd passed the point where anyone might have called out to him, "Stop!"

PART II

1

Even before Philip opened his eyes he could hear the gurgling of the pigeons as they strutted stiffly over the slate roof. Rome, he thought. I'm back in Rome. He was amazed by this and full of pleasure, but uncertain too. How had he gotten there? He couldn't remember that detail...the apartment with the slanting ceilings and the little windows out over the street. Daverio, wasn't it? The place where he and Estella and the girls had stayed for a month the summer after they came back from Africa.

When he opened his eyes and saw the tall windows, lightly shadowed by the leaves of a large maple tree, he felt confused. The windows had been bare, there had been no tree. But then, like the pieces of a puzzle sliding neatly into place, one room fitted into another and he knew it wasn't Rome after all but Jane's apartment in Philadelphia, two blocks from Rittenhouse Square—a place which held no history for him after all. Five days he'd been there. That was all. And each morning he had waked happy—the feeling he had when he was on vacation, cut free from ordinary life.

In the kitchen Jane was making coffee. A spoon touched glass and rang a pure, sweet note; the refrigerator door clicked open and gently slammed again. Hearing Jane humming, he too smiled, sharing her happiness. He could imagine her clearly—those pale circles under her eyes when she woke, the shadow of sleep that disappeared when she came more fully awake, standing with her hands deep in the pockets of her old flannel robe as she rested her head against the window frame, looking down at the courtyard where the maple tree grew, moving in a kind of dream.

In her own place, with the objects she had assembled in those rooms, she moved with an assurance she had lacked on Nantucket. Sometimes he caught glimpses of an earlier, younger Jane. Once, seeing her curled in an armchair with her feet under her, fitting into that space like a cat, he'd seen Jane at ten with a sweet, lazy attentiveness on her face.

When she had first brought him into the apartment and shown him through it she had been nervous, hoping he would like what he saw. And he did like the high-ceilinged, well-proportioned rooms. High up, under the roof, they seemed peaceful and removed from the world. But they were austere. In truth the rooms, which were too austere for his taste, disturbed him a little, though he was careful to hide his feelings from her. The bedroom where he lay—a cool room with the shadows of the maple leaves moving over the wall—contained nothing except a bed, two bedside tables on thin legs, a chest of drawers, a straight-backed chair. It was not a room to lounge in, to take your ease in.

"I don't like a lot of things around getting in the way," she had told him with a hint of apology in her voice. Perhaps she did sense that he didn't like those rooms as much as he pretended to. But he had agreed that he didn't care for rooms crammed with furniture either; he too was a very neat person. It was her desire to please that touched him and yet made his heart sink; it would be easy to hurt her.

When Jane came into the bedroom, carrying two mugs of coffee and walking gingerly so she wouldn't slosh any over her feet, he drew back the sheet for her and quickly puffed the pillow. Though it was too early for the sunlight to reach the wall where the shadows from the maple leaves moved, he could tell by the rectangle of sky he could see—a faint, luminous pink—that it would be another fair day.

"I thought," Jane said, when she'd climbed into bed again, "that today we might go out to Meridian Station and spend some time in the Barnes Museum. There's a wonderful collection of Renoirs, and you know that painting by Seurat? The one with the people in the park all looking in the direction of a little lake? Well, that painting is in the Barnes."

As she spoke a feeling of mild dismay came over him. Each day since they'd been in Philadelphia, Jane had had an itinerary worked out for them. They had gone to secondhand bookstores, to the Museum of Art, to the Rodin Museum; they had walked along the river and had gone to favorite restaurants of hers. She was afraid, it seemed, that if she didn't take him to places of interest, if she didn't entertain him, he might be bored. Or, more disturbing, she was afraid that if they didn't have definite things to do an awkward silence would fall between them; they'd have nothing more to say to one another.

"We don't have to do anything special, Jane," he said to her gently. "We could just spend the morning in bed reading the newspaper. You shouldn't feel you have to entertain me."

"Is that what you'd rather do?" she asked, giving him a look that was both uncertain and unhappy.

"No, not especially," he said quickly. "Whatever you want to do is fine. Only don't feel you have to take me places."

"It's just that I think you'll really enjoy the Barnes. It's in this beautiful old house—estate, really. Ordinarily you have to write in advance, asking for tickets for a particular day, but one of my students is working there this summer. He's the gatekeeper and he'd let us in with no problem."

"Fine," he said, putting his hand over hers where it lay on the sheet. "That's what we'll do then. But sometime this morning, I have to telephone home. I've been putting it off, but today I must."

She frowned, a fine line between her eyebrows. "Of course you can telephone from here," she said. "Anytime you want to."

She would rather not be reminded—he saw that—of his family. He too dreaded speaking to his children, hearing reproach in their voices.

Still, after breakfast while Jane was dressing, he made the call, sitting at the table surrounded by toast crumbs which he crushed under his thumbnail as he listened to the ringing of the phone. He could see it so clearly hanging on the kitchen wall in the cottage that it seemed to him the very vividness of the picture would draw someone to answer. The sound of the ringing filled him with both terrible dread and anticipation, so that he couldn't have said at that moment which he wanted more— for the phone to be answered or not answered—but when after six rings he put the receiver back on the hook, he realized he was flooded with relief.

"They're at the beach or the pond," he called to Jane. "Nobody in."

His relief, in fact, carried him through the trip on the train to Meridian Station and the walk to the museum. It was a beautiful day, and his spirits lightened. He took Jane's hand in his as they walked, and he knew by the way other people looked on them benignly as they passed that the two of them must have looked happy and open to the world.

(141)

Jane took him into the room where the Seurat hung, and he stood looking at it for some time, marveling at the sheer industry that had impelled the painter to place all those tiny dots of color on the canvas. But it was wonderful the almost magic way those dots—unrelated, it seemed, when he stood very near the canvas—were transformed into order as soon as he stepped away. The shimmering veil of light that was this world—how easily it was dissolved. Reach out to touch, and there was nothing there after all.

When Philip turned away from the Seurat, he saw that Jane had moved on to another room, and so he followed what seemed the general movement of the crowd. In the next room he was surrounded by Impressionist paintings—painting after painting of summer in its fragile beauty. He'd never paid much attention to the Impressionists before—their bright colors had pleased him, that was all—but now, surrounded by all those depictions of summer lushness, gloom suddenly came over him.

Trying to escape it, he moved on and came to the Renoirs. It became clear to Philip, as he made his way around the room, that Renoir had used his own family as models—the same woman and the same children appeared over and over, doing ordinary things. A mother and daughter sat at a table with a book between them, a brother and sister—their hair the same shade of reddish gold—stood side by side holding hoops in their hands. He looked at these paintings for a long time, unwilling to move on. In spite of himself he was moved by those ordinary scenes of family life which, the longer he looked, assumed for him a kind of monumentality. It seemed to him that the solidity of those paintings—the captured and transformed moment in time—should have given him pleasure and re-assurance. But it didn't. Instead he felt such pain, looking into those faces, that he had to turn away and tears came to his eyes.

Of course, it was his own loss he grieved for. He knew that. It had nothing to do with the family depicted on canvas.

Lowering his head, he left the Renoirs and came into the hallway. He was ashamed to have been moved the way he was, and he kept his eyes averted from the people moving past him. Glancing at his watch, he saw that it was eleven o'clock and if he wanted to telephone the cottage while Estella was still in her studio, he should do it. A guard told him where to find a pay phone, and he followed the directions into the basement.

It was dread he felt, listening to the ringing, and after five rings—when he was just lifting the receiver from his ear preparatory to putting it back in the cradle—Chrissy's voice, sounding very far away, said hello.

He came close to pretending he hadn't heard after all. What he wanted was to ease the receiver back onto the hook. But instead he took a deep breath and answered. "Chrissy, it's Dad," he said.

For three seconds, four, Chrissy said nothing at all as he waited in fear that rose to panic. He knew how she was standing, leaning against the kitchen wall, wrapping the telephone cord around her fingers.

"Chris?" he said, nearly shouting.

"Do you want me to get Mom?" she said, and he said no, no, *she* was the one he wanted.

"I'm in Philadelphia," he told her, speaking very quickly. "I have to be here for a little while"—he wondered what Estella had told Chrissy and Jasper, but knowing Estella, he knew she had probably told the truth, sparing him nothing—"and I want you to have my address and telephone number in case you need to reach me. Do you have a pencil, Chris?"

"I'll write it down," she said, "but I don't think we'll need to call you."

"You might," he said, trying to be reasonable. Sometimes that otherworldliness of Chrissy's was hard to take. He knew she was perfectly capable of writing his telephone number on some tiny slip of paper that would immediately get lost. "And listen, Chrissy, how are you? How're things there?" He tried to keep his voice steady, even hearty, though he could hear its tremor.

"Okay," she said. "Jasper's down at the beach or I'd call him. One of his front teeth came out, so he's got a gap. You can see the new tooth, though, coming in. And Jenks stepped on a nettle or something and is going around on three paws."

But do you miss me? he longed to ask. Are you miserable without me?

"I miss you, Chrissy," he said, anxiety making his voice stiff. He hated himself for his inability to be easier, warmer somehow.

Over the line, silence. Chrissy saying nothing at all. Was she waiting for him to say more? Or was there something she was gathering herself to tell him?

It grew longer and longer, that silence, until he was frantic with it.

"Chris?" he said. But at the moment he spoke, she did too. "Bye," she said to him and instantly hung up the receiver the way a three-year-old might have done.

"Dammit," he said as he put the phone back in the cradle. "Dammit, Chris."

(143)

But his anger was only a shield for his agitation. Chrissy said so little of what she felt; it drove him wild, that reticence of hers. He'd have gotten more out of Jasper—far more, probably. Jasper was much more direct.

At the top of the stairs he found Jane looking at a tapestry, but when she saw his face she turned her attention to him. "Did you call the cottage?" she asked.

"For all the good it did me," he said in despair. "You can't get anything out of Chrissy. I had this feeling there was something important she wanted to say but couldn't. Or wouldn't. It's impossible to tell with her, and it's so difficult, dammit."

When they were outside again, walking down the path to the gate, Jane said—carefully, as though this were something she'd thought about saying for some time and had only been waiting for the right moment— "You know, I really couldn't blame Chrissy for being angry with you. I would have been angry too if you'd been my father."

"But she wasn't angry," he said. "Maybe she should have been angry, but she wasn't. I don't know what she felt."

"Other people's anger makes me go weak at the knees," Jane said. "I want to crawl into a hole."

And so they talked about anger, and this led to other topics. The other—his concern for and annoyance with Chrissy—slipped from his mind.

But that night, when Jane had gone to sleep, curled on her side with one arm lying like a shield above her head, those anxieties overwhelmed him at a time when he couldn't protect himself.

He had done a terrible thing to his children—this was blindingly clear to him as he lay looking at the darkness. Abandoning them and leaving them defenseless. A son too young to be able to fully explain himself, and a daughter who was too sensitive—who suffered over the slightest things. He'd brought them into the world, had loved them more than anything—or that's what he'd always said—and then had gone off and left them when they still needed him. Because of his own misery and pleasure he'd done this. It was no use pretending anything else. Not at three in the morning—that cold clear time when thoughts are unimpeded by other distractions. At three in the morning it's the truth that makes itself known. He'd always believed that. And so there was no escape from what he knew: he'd done a terrible thing.

For a long time he lay awake, turning fitfully from side to side, and by early light, when he'd gotten up and was making coffee, he acknowledged the decision he'd come to in the night. He knew what he had to do, though he dreaded telling Jane, who was already awake, smiling at him from the pillow.

"How nice to just lie here listening to you in the kitchen," she said when he set the coffee cups on the bedside table. "Most of the time I like to be the one to get up early, but I like this too. Being waited on."

He slid into bed beside her and pulled the blanket up.

"I could feel in the night that you were awake," she said. "And I kept intending to wake up too and keep you company, but I couldn't seem to do that. I kept dreaming I was back in New Mexico, listening to that wind that rises on the desert just before daylight. 'Just a minute,' I kept thinking. 'I'll wake up in just a minute.'"

"I'm glad you slept," he said, cupping the mug of coffee carefully in his hands. "I liked looking over and seeing you sleeping. It made me feel more rested just to watch you."

"You were worrying about something," she said, keeping her eyes on her hands. "Even in my sleep I could feel you worrying."

He put his mug of coffee back on the bedside table as though by doing so he was clearing the way for what he had to say next.

"I decided in the night," he said carefully, "that I have to go back to Nantucket. No, not to the cottage," he said quickly. "That's not what I'm saying. I want to rent a place somewhere there. Just so I can be near the children if they need me."

She sat very still, looking down at her hands, her breath barely stirring her gown.

"I want you to come with me."

Jane didn't answer right away, and he began to fear she wouldn't—that in another minute she would get out of bed and offer him a second cup of coffee, sparing them both from making any comment on a proposal so mad.

"I do want you with me," he said again. "More than anything."

"More than *almost* anything," she said carefully. There was no rancor in her voice, but she wanted it to be clear, what he was asking.

"All right," he said. "I do want you and I do want to be near the children. Both things."

Jane took the mug of coffee in her hands and looked inside it, but she didn't lift it to her lips. Instead she began clicking one of her fingernails against the handle—an erratic clicking as though it were a message in code she was sending to herself.

"I don't know if I can take that," she said. "Going back. I was so glad to leave that island. I dreaded coming upon your children by accident in town, and I felt so, oh, I don't know...odd."

"But it won't be the same this time. We'll rent a house on the far side of the island—quite a long way from the cottage. And we'll be together. It won't be at all the same as it was before."

"Even if you do go back, are you certain you'll see your children?"

"I'll be there in case they need me. It would make all the difference in how I feel. And it's only two months, Jane."

He was close to begging her, though he could not quite do that. She would have to decide freely.

She sat still, clicking her thumbnail against the handle of the coffee mug, her face averted from him in her unhappiness. He tried to steel himself, knowing that if she couldn't look into his face she couldn't say yes, either. He would have to learn to live without her, though the thought filled him with desolation.

"The truth is, Philip," she said at last, "I don't think I should do this. Anybody I know would tell me it's crazy, and I think it is too. I'll regret doing it. I feel that. But there's something else too..."

She set her coffee mug on the bedside table and looked up at him so that he had to see the misery in her face.

"I'm not ready to let you go," she said. "I can't do that."

And he was stroking her hair then and her cool, lovely shoulders, and he felt such a wave of tenderness for her that his throat swelled with it and his eyes pricked.

He would have done anything at that moment for love of her.

2

It was just light enough to show her the clouds above the roofs of the houses.

"Have you ever noticed how the clouds sag here?" Liddy asked Nigel, who was keeping his eyes straight ahead, on the highway. "Like old men's drawers," she added, and grinned at Nigel's cheek.

"That's not very funny, Liddy," he said stiffly, taking on that superior tone he knew she couldn't stand. Clearly he was still upset about the night before.

Liddy shrugged her shoulders and looked out her window at the London suburb they were passing through—Ealing, she thought it was. She wrinkled her nose at the semidetached houses with their small, neat gardens—everything diminished somehow, even the cramped little Mini she was riding in, though it wasn't that she objected to exactly. It was some more general cramping of the spirit.

"I'm sorry I had to be by myself last night," she said, turning on Nigel a look suddenly and carefully serious. "But it wouldn't have been any good if you'd stayed. You know how it is when people hang around at the airport when there's nothing left to *say*. It would have been like that."

"There were things we could have said." Nigel's face had that set look it got when he was hurt. "Things I wanted to say."

"You could tell them to me now," she told him, leaning forward, trying to coax his eyes just for a second away from the road. "It'll take us an hour to get to Heathrow, Nigel. You can say a lot in an hour."

"Oh, for God's sake," he said, exasperated. But he couldn't keep it up, his bad temper. When he smiled—against his will, she could tell—she smiled encouragingly back.

"Even when I have every reason to be angry with you I can't keep it up," he said.

"I know."

"It isn't good for you, getting your way all the time."

"It's fine for me," she said. "It's other people who don't like it."

Given her druthers, as her Grandmother Harrison had been fond of saying, she would part with Nigel on good terms; they'd had fun together and she liked him. But if he was going to try to make her feel guilty—and she could feel this hovering underneath all he said to her—then something would slip out before she could stop herself. It always did.

As though to get the trip over with as quickly as possible, Nigel drove faster and faster until the little Mini was making a loud thrumming noise; Liddy lowered her window so that the damp air blew straight into her face, lightly numbing her skin in a way she found pleasant.

On his side of the car, Nigel shouted to her for some time before she leaned far enough away from the window to catch the words. "...see you?" he was saying. "Will I see you when I come to New York in the spring?"

"Why not?" she said, her eyes narrowed against the stream of air that blew through the car.

"Because with you it's so hard to tell," he said, and his voice had taken on that plaintive note she disliked so much. "You may decide you have to be alone, the way you did last night. Nothing's easier than not answering letters."

"All right, Nigel," she said. "You may be right. Once I leave here you may never hear from me again. That's a possibility, isn't it?"

The look he gave her was unmistakably furious. With her hands deep in the pockets of her raincoat, she looked down at her lap. After a moment she took a deep breath and sighed.

"I didn't say you *wouldn't* hear from me," she said. "I only said it was a possibility. A chance you take."

"Why am I the one who always has to take a chance?"

Because you're the one in love, Liddy thought, but did not say.

"And of course you may be the one who never writes to me," she said reasonably. "Of course that's always a possibility, too."

"I hate it when you're like this," Nigel said, using the plaintive, little-boy voice that came out when he was hurt. "The way you make clear how ridiculous you find it. How I feel. Sometimes I wonder if you really love anyone."

What was the point in saying, But I'm just not in love with *you?* Within an hour she would have said goodbye to Nigel, and there was no point in allowing herself to get in a fight.

"I've always thought that falling in love was pretty much a solitary entertainment," she said. "Even if the other person is in love with you, you're still on your own. That's always been clear to me."

Nigel was either too upset or too furious with her to answer. He drove with his sandal pressing the accelerator nearly to the floorboard.

"You know, I could catch a taxi or a bus," she told him. "You don't have to take me to the airport if you're going to be so angry."

"Don't be ridiculous," Nigel said. "How could I just leave you standing by the side of the road?"

"I'd manage."

"Oh yes, you'd manage, all right," Nigel said bitterly.

In spite of his bluster she saw that he was more hurt than angry, and she felt herself relenting toward him. She could afford to now that she had made it clear that he had no little hooks in her—no little hooks at all. What he felt for her gave him no rights.

"I'm glad you're driving me to the airport," she told him.

In spite of the earliness of the hour, the traffic at Heathrow was heavy, but Nigel insisted on taking her all the way inside. She would need help with her bags, he said. She would have preferred to say goodbye to him in front of the door to the TWA terminal, but she hadn't the heart to insist on it. She'd already been horrible enough to him that morning.

Nigel insisted on carrying her two heavy bags himself, his shoulders sagging with the weight, while behind him she carried her overnight bag and her camera. Inside the camera, she remembered, on the roll of film she had yet to get developed, there were shots of her and Nigel in one of the Regent's Park boats. They had passed the camera back and forth, taking each other's pictures, and near the end of the roll they had started acting silly, crossing their eyes and sticking out their tongues. There was one shot, she remembered, of her pretending to throw up over the side of the little boat.

The line for checking baggage was a long one, and she was sorry, after all, that she'd let him come inside the terminal with her. There they were, with nothing to do except nudge the heavy suitcases forward every few minutes.

Nigel cleared his throat and popped the knuckle on his left ring finger. Something serious was coming.

"I hope you find things all right when you get home," he said, cutting his eyes sideways at her. "I'm sorry about... all that."

She should have been touched by his concern, but instead she was annoyed that he had reminded her of why she was going home early. She was sorry she'd told him about Chrissy's letter.

It was when she was first getting to know Nigel that she'd talked so much about her family; she'd felt lighthearted then and had wanted to amuse him. But later he'd used that knowledge in his attempts to become more intimate with her, and she'd regretted telling him so much.

"I'm sure it'll all blow over," she told him, not encouraging further discussion. She hated mess—all that embarrassing mess.

They reached the counter, her bags were taken away, and suddenly she and Nigel were set free.

"Time for one last cup of real English tea," Nigel said, smiling at her coaxingly. How much he wanted everything to end on a good note. But she couldn't take any more of this prolonged leavetaking.

"Nothing's worse than waiting for people to leave when they have one foot out the door," she told him. "I want you to go home and dry out. And I'll imagine you sitting in front of the fire, having a hot cup of tea, as cozy as a cat."

"I'll be depressed, driving back alone." He looked at her sorrowfully.

"But you'll write to me and I'll write to you," she told him, carried along on a last-minute current of good feeling. "In the spring you'll come over to visit and I'll show you around New York. You're not to be depressed."

And then, when she resolutely set her bag on the floor and put her arms around Nigel to kiss him goodbye, she did feel sorry, after all. He *would* miss her, would go around for days feeling melancholy, and she hated all that. She much preferred people to be happy.

She kissed him on the lips, grabbed her bag, and rushed down the corridor to her gate. Though she knew he was watching her, hoping she would turn back once to wave, she rushed on. And then, even if she had looked back, she couldn't have seen Nigel any longer; the corridor made a turn, and there was only the plane ahead. Already, England seemed far behind her.

3

"Will you stop running up and down?" Chrissy said to Jasper, who was careening through the little waiting room of the airport. It was a Wednesday and not many people were waiting for the Boston plane. But those who were frowned at Jasper, who was swooping, one arm up and the other down, clearly being a plane or a gull.

"I'm too excited," he said.

When Jasper was very small he would whirl around and around when he reached a certain pitch of wildness and then he would throw himself on the floor and drum with his feet and scream. He didn't do that any longer, but he could still be embarrassing.

"Let's go outside and wait, Jas," Chrissy called, and he swooped past her, through a side door, and into a space enclosed by high mesh fence. She followed him into the bright sunlight.

"Do you think maybe I won't even recognize Liddy when she gets off the plane?" he asked.

"Don't be silly. She can't have changed that much."

But though she wouldn't admit it to Jasper, this was Chrissy's fear too, exactly. What if Liddy no longer seemed the same person she had been? What if, for instance, she'd picked up an English accent and sounded strange?

Behind the closed door of the bedroom, Chrissy had changed clothes three times that morning after she got the phone call from Liddy, though she'd known all along what she would wear—the old khaki shorts and the T-shirt emblazoned with the picture of a whale and the words "Gentle Giant." All her clothes were alike anyway; she didn't possess anything that Liddy would consider remotely grown-up. And even if she'd had many possibilities to choose from she didn't know what impression she wanted to make. She only wanted something to happen, some magic to occur. And so she had pulled one shirt and then another over her head before she gave each one a despairing glance in the mirror and yanked it off again.

So now she stood looking down at the holes in her sneakers, lifting the hair from her neck to let it cool, not bothering with a comb, since it couldn't make any difference—there she'd be when Liddy arrived, skinny, her hair cut in that same blunt, plain way she'd worn it since she was eight, and Liddy would think, Well, there's Chrissy, same as ever.

"Chrissy!" Jasper was saying. "Come over here, Chrissy, and look at this cat."

The cat was in the shade against the side of the building in a portable cage; it was lying on its side panting, its tongue very pink, and small drops of water fell from the tip of its tongue, making dark circles in the bottom of the cage.

"Poor pussy," Jasper said, trying to put his finger through the wire of the cage. The cat hissed, but without much conviction.

"Leave her alone," Chrissy said. "She's miserable enough as it is."

"I just wanted to pat her with my finger," Jasper said. "I thought she might be lonesome."

There was the noise of an airplane nearing the airport, and Chrissy's stomach fluttered.

"I'll bet that's it," Jasper said, leaping to his feet and running to the fence.

The cat was panting hard, her eyes half shut. Her sides went in and out like a lizard's on a rock, the drops of water falling from the curled tip of her tongue. "Sweet cat," Chrissy said. "Sweet cat."

"This is the one, Chrissy, isn't it?" Jasper called. "Aren't you going to come and watch, Chris?"

The plane was at the far end of the runway, touching the ground and then bouncing into the air again, leaping toward them.

Chrissy got to her feet and joined Jasper at the fence. Jasper's hands were so small he could put them between the mesh links, and he stretched out his arms—begging, it could have been. She curled her fingers around the mesh and held tight.

The plane came to a stop near them, though it was impossible to see inside the little windows. Then the door was swinging open and the steps were pushed into place.

"I'll bet she's the first one off," Jasper said.

But Liddy was not the first off. Every time a new person came through the doorway of the plane Chrissy's heart leaped, but none of them was Liddy.

"Maybe she's not on it," Jasper said. "Maybe she missed it."

"I don't think so," Chrissy said, though she, too, was beginning to doubt. She watched some of the women passengers all the way down the steps, thinking that one of them might turn out to be Liddy after all; she would be standing there looking foolish when somebody she'd taken to be a stranger came over to the fence and said, "Well, don't you know me?"

But then there she was. Coming through the door of the plane and starting down the steps, carrying a bag and a camera, swinging down the steps quickly, as Liddy always moved, not looking up until she reached the ground.

"Liddy! Liddy!" Jasper called.

Of course it was Liddy, even the way she walked was unmistakable, yet everything about her was dazzling to Chrissy, so that even though she stared she couldn't take her in. Liddy was wearing tan slacks and a peach-colored blouse—clothes Chrissy hadn't seen before—and her shoes, too, with wedge heels, they were also new. She'd let her hair grow and it was to her shoulders—that dark, thick hair—how brown she was! Surely there wasn't that much sun in England? And had her face grown thinner, or had Chrissy forgotten the exact shape of her sister's face?

Overcome with that old familiar sickness of anticipation and anxiety, Chrissy did not run back through the door with Jasper, back inside where they could meet Liddy. Suddenly shy, she would have taken flight if there had been anywhere to run. But the only place she could go was through the door Jasper had already entered, and so she slipped back through it and stood watching Jasper hug Liddy and the way she bent down and kissed him. Chrissy held her breath, waiting for Liddy to look up. And then she did, looking at Chrissy and grinning, her almond-shaped eyes shutting to slits.

They were coming toward her, their arms around each other, and

Liddy was laughing about something Jasper had said—she was setting down her bag and coming to meet Chrissy.

She put her arm around Liddy's shoulder, feeling the silky blouse smooth under her hand. Liddy wasn't bony the way she knew she was, leaning awkwardly on one leg.

"How's it going, Chris?" Liddy said, picking up her bag again, and that distance came into her eyes—Liddy thinking of ten things at once.

"You've bought a new watch," Chrissy said, and instantly felt foolish, since it wasn't the watch, of course, as it wasn't the new shoes or the clothes that were important.

"Oh, that," Liddy said, looking down at her arm as though the watch were a surprise to her, too. "The other one stopped running."

The luggage hadn't been brought in from the plane yet, but Liddy couldn't stand quietly and wait for it; she had to pace up and down, going to the glass doors to look out, taking a schedule of flights from the desk and sticking it into her pocket—everything she did appearing to be purposeful even though, as Chrissy knew, it was really just impatience, an excess of energy. How well she knew that pacing, that straining forward as though it were only force of will that kept Liddy from going to the plane and dragging her luggage out herself. Jasper was just the same, dancing along with Liddy wherever she went, asking questions he never waited to hear answered. She stood with Liddy's other bag and the camera at her feet, watching Jasper and Liddy run up and down. They were so certain, so quick, the way they charmed others to their will. For them doors opened, strangers hailed cabs—they were like royalty, passing through. When she was drawn in with them she was pleased, dazzled—just being in their presence was enough—but when she was left apart she saw through their charm and thought it cheap.

She stood aside, watching them heap the luggage onto a cart, both working in that fast, efficient way, tugging the bags into place, quick, quick, so not a moment would be wasted.

And then in the dizzying heat the three of them were loading the car and Liddy was saying, "Why don't you let me drive, Chris? I haven't gotten to drive a car in a long time."

So of course she gave Liddy the key and Jasper climbed into the front seat, leaving her to sit in the back, to share the seat with two of Liddy's bags.

Liddy rolled down the window and her elbow jutted out into the sun; she'd always driven fast, with one hand on the wheel.

(155)

"Guess what?" Jasper said, unable to wait any longer to tell. "Daddy isn't at home. He left a note telling about a book, but what it really is is Jane. He's somewhere with Jane."

"Philadelphia," Chrissy said from the backseat. She looked out at the heat waves shimmering above the bushes and stunted trees. "I told you that, Jasper."

"What I'd like to know is when he's coming back," Jasper said. "That's what I want to know."

Chrissy lifted her eyes to the car mirror, and there, in the glass, Liddy looked back at her. For three seconds, four, their eyes held the way they'd done when they were children in the back of the station wagon, listening to the grown-up talk Estella and Philip didn't know they were listening to. Looking deep into each other's eyes, they followed all that was said and traded questions back and forth.

"Mom's sleeping in the boathouse," Jasper said. "Chrissy and me are sleeping in the tent."

Liddy snorted. "Well, I intend to sleep in the house. In my own bed. Am I going to have the place to myself?"

"Yep," Jasper said. "Everybody else's gone somewhere different."

Chrissy leaned her head against the seat back and watched the golf course go by in a blur. They were going down the long hill where the Sankaty Head light stood, but Liddy wasn't slowing at all. It was exciting going so fast. It made her giddy, having Liddy there with them again.

"We saw Jane in town one day," she said. "She's not all that pretty, Lid."

"We did this," Jasper said, spitting into his hand and holding it, palm up, out the window. "Chrissy said she might be a bad spirit."

"Do you really do that in the middle of Nantucket town, Chris?" Liddy said, sounding delighted. "They'll lock you up."

"Maybe she is a bad spirit," Chrissy said. "Don't you remember that dark place, the one under the trees where the spirits lived?"

"Of course I remember it," Liddy said. "I was older than you were when we lived there. But I never saw a spirit. I always looked but I never saw anything. I don't think I ever believed all that as much as you did. What did Jane look like?"

"Tall. Long dark hair."

Suddenly Chrissy pushed herself from the backseat and leaned over so her head was between Liddy's and Jasper's. "You really want to know who she looks like? If you really want to know, I'll tell you. The person she looks most like is you, Lid."

"After you just got through saying she wasn't good-looking," Liddy said, making a face.

"You're prettier, but there is something that reminds me of you."

"I don't think she looks like you at all," Jasper said.

"She does, though, all the same," Chrissy said.

She wanted the car ride to go on and on, to never end, just the three of them together. But already they were to the lane and Jasper was climbing out of the car to open the chain.

"Mother'll go wild when she sees you, Liddy," Chrissy said. "We kept it a secret so you'd be a surprise. We wanted to come and get you ourselves."

"I was up even before daylight," Liddy said. "And now I'm just floating along. I don't know who I am or where I am..."

"Can't you smell the pine trees and the roses?" Chrissy said. "I'd know this place even if I was dead. Even if I was a ghost I'd know where I was, here."

"My head's floating," Liddy said. "I don't belong anywhere."

4

When the car stopped beside the house and Jasper came running to the door of her studio saying they had a surprise, a very big surprise, and she had to come that minute, Estella felt her knees go weak. What first came into her mind—it was the old childhood hope, never outgrown, that the gift would turn out to be heart's dearest desire—was that she would go to the car to find Philip climbing out smiling sheepishly, Philip as he had been before he ever met Jane.

But it was only that first moment when she thought it might be Philip waiting for her. Long before she reached the car, she had steeled herself against disappointment, and so she was totally unprepared to see Liddy climb out of the driver's seat and look up squinting into the sun. "Liddy!" she said, and tears came to her eyes. She hadn't known how much she'd wanted Liddy until she saw her coming across the driveway. How straight her shoulders were and how direct her gaze! How sure of herself she was! She'd always been like that, Estella realized, watching Liddy cross the driveway, but Estella had forgotten. Now her elegance awed Estella a little and she was suddenly aware of her own uncombed hair, of the sweatshirt smeared with paint.

But then her arms were around Liddy, Liddy was holding her tightly, and she saw it was needless after all to be awed. There was still the familiar child Liddy had been concealed in this grown-up woman, something of the old childhood intensity in the way she held on—Liddy afraid. And then she stepped back and her eyes, still looking into Estella's, drew back, too. Even that was familiar.

When she was a child, that had been the way Liddy was—the giving and then the stepping back. Estella remembered Liddy at three or four afraid of the darkness in her closet, afraid of the empty shoes standing in a row, the darkness inside the toes concealing maybe hordes of spiders. Liddy had buried her face in Estella's lap, her shoulders shaking. But then, very soon, she'd sat up, almost pushing Estella away in her hurry to draw her hand over her eyes and say, "I'm not scared anymore. You can go back now."

But Estella had been too wise for that. She'd put her hand into each shoe in Liddy's closet so that any spider lurking there would make itself known by biting her finger. She had understood Liddy very well when she was a child.

Estella kept her arm around Liddy's shoulders as they walked together to the trunk of the car, where Chrissy was lifting the suitcases to the ground. She wanted to take Liddy off to her studio right away, to sit her on the bed—the one comfortable place—put a cup of coffee in her hands, and talk. But that would have to wait.

"I know you're exhausted, sweetheart," Estella said, and even Liddy's fragility was precious to her; she felt that great riches had just been put into her hands. "But now you're home you can sleep for a week."

"No, I'm fine," Liddy said, drawing away to carry one of her bags to the house, and Estella remembered *that* about Liddy too—her stubbornness, her dislike of being interfered with.

So during the afternoon, while Liddy unpacked and went to the pond with Chrissy and Jasper, Estella watched and said nothing though it was clear to her that Liddy was in that state of exhaustion when rest seems inconceivable—in that delicate state of euphoria.

It was nearly dark when Estella started dinner since she'd taken the time to go to town to buy fresh sole and good wine. This dinner would be a celebration in spite of Philip's absence.

She'd just turned on the lights in the kitchen when Liddy came in and leaned against the cabinet, watching her unwrap the fish. It was the time she'd been waiting for, when she would have Liddy to herself, but this very knowledge made her self-conscious. Liddy was like some exotic animal that moved just beyond the shadow of the forest, an animal she wanted to hold there by the calmness of her gestures.

(159)

She slid the bottle of wine from the brown paper and put it into Liddy's hands. "You can open this," she said. "We might as well have a glass of wine while we cook."

Estella noted how expertly Liddy opened the wine, and this fact, mundane as it was, seemed to her worthy of remembering. After Liddy's year away there were so many gaps to be filled in.

"Tell me about England," Estella said. "You were dutiful about writing, Liddy, but your letters never said very much. 'Went to Hampton Court and saw the maze.' Things like that."

When Estella lifted the romaine and the spinach from the refrigerator, Liddy took them from her to wash. Estella had forgotten how easily and well she and Liddy moved together in a kitchen—of the children it had always been Liddy who cared most about cooking. When she was twelve she'd started making the mayonnaise and baking the cakes. Now, without saying anything, she'd taken over the salad making.

"Well, I did go to Hampton Court and I did see the maze," Liddy said. "That was more interesting than saying, 'Went to classes. Studied.' Wasn't it?"

"Yes, but don't be so skimpy. I want to know everything, Liddy. Tell me about the people. There were all those names in the letters, but there seemed to be a lot of coming and going. Nobody around for long."

"I knew a lot of people."

"There was Nigel," Estella said, "and Dennis, and wasn't there a Patrick?"

Liddy shrugged her shoulders. Into a bowl she dropped the broken pieces of romaine. "Nigel took me to the plane this morning. It seems about a hundred years ago but it was just this morning. Nigel hated to see me go. It was depressing."

"And you?" Estella said. "Did you hate to say goodbye to him?"

"He'd started being a pain," Liddy said. "Wanting to see more of me than I wanted to see of him. I wasn't sorry to say goodbye."

"So your heart wasn't broken in England," Estella said lightly as she set the plates on the table and laid out the cutlery; it had grown too dark to eat outside on the deck.

The look Liddy gave her was steady and a little contemptuous. "My heart's never been broken anywhere, Mother," she said. "You know that. I doubt if it ever will be."

Estella thought this was very likely. Liddy would never be hurt as Chrissy, she was certain, would be. But on the other hand, Liddy's coolness and certainty troubled her. Was Liddy just the most sensible of her children, or was there something hard about her?

"I've got more important things to think about," Liddy said, and the way she set her shoulders as she bent over the salad let Estella know that this was a topic she had better drop if she wanted Liddy's company.

Though she remembered very well the good times with Liddy when they had talked and talked, lingering over the dishes far longer than they needed to, each reluctant to move away from the other, she had chosen to forget the times when Liddy had been secretive, had fallen silent or changed the subject. But of course she should have known all about that—it was the way she'd been with her own mother. It had taken Liddy's birth to change things—through the colic and teething she and her mother had suddenly become good friends and had laughed together so much when her mother came to visit that Philip had looked back and forth between them with a prissy look on his face. But when Liddy was ten her grandmother had died and so that was the end of that.

All afternoon while Liddy had been unpacking, she had longed to join her, to say casually as she hung Liddy's blouses on hangers, "So what do you think about Philip's leaving, Lid? Doesn't it seem unbelievable?"

But now, when she had Liddy to herself and a silence had fallen between them, she felt something like shyness make her hesitate.

"You haven't said a word about Philip," she said at last. "Not a word, Liddy. But you must have been thinking plenty."

Into a pitcher, Liddy measured the wine vinegar, holding it up to the light; her concentration made her seem distant.

"I didn't know until I got here that he'd moved out," she said when she'd lowered the bottle of vinegar to the cabinet top. "I keep expecting to hear him walking across the deck."

"But were you *surprised?*" Estella said, turning so she could look straight at Liddy. It was this she'd most wanted to ask.

"Surprised about what exactly?" Liddy asked, refusing to look up.

"Surprised that he moved out," Estella said impatiently. "Surprised that he found Jane in the first place."

"Yes," Liddy said. "I was surprised."

"Really?" Estella said, leaning back against the table. "Because, you know, I'd about decided I was crazy and maybe it was very obvious to other people."

"But the thing is," Liddy said, as though Estella hadn't spoken, "I'm surprised you didn't pick up clues. Dad's never been good at keeping secrets as far as I know. You could always tell what he was thinking, even when he played poker."

"Obviously he was better at keeping a secret than I thought he was."

"You really didn't notice anything at all? Nothing different?"

"I just said so, Liddy," Estella said sharply. "And you said you were surprised, too. So why is it so hard to believe I was in the dark?"

But the moment she spoke she saw by the way Liddy kept her back turned she was showing her disbelief—or if not that, then her disapproval. Liddy, it was clear to her, supposed you were deceived only if you wanted to be, if you were weak and spineless. And in Liddy's disapproval she felt suddenly diminished and wounded.

"But I haven't even been here for a year," Liddy said. "And if I had been... well, I'm not married to him, Mom. You couldn't really expect..."

"Of course not," Estella said, but she felt hurt all the same. Liddy, she'd thought, would understand better than anyone how she felt.

There was a cool detachment in Liddy which she was more aware of than ever. Probably it *would* be impossible for Liddy to be deceived. And if she ever were, she would detach herself immediately from an unfaithful man as decisively as a surgeon making that first deep cut through layers of skin. She admired this in Liddy, but it lay as a division between them too. Because of it she couldn't appeal to Liddy, couldn't say, "Liddy, Liddy, what do you know that I don't?" The young are so certain, so cruel in their knowledge.

"Of course," Estella said, "you always did admire him, Liddy. That old flirting around between fathers and daughters."

"When I was little, I suppose," Liddy said, shrugging her shoulders.

"Though of course now you see through us," Estella couldn't stop herself from saying. "You see how foolish we really are." There was an edge of bitterness in her voice that she would have instantly retracted if she could. She saw it unmistakably, that step backward into herself that Liddy took—that shutting of a door—and she could have bitten her tongue.

"I'm sorry, Liddy," she said. "I was just too anxious to have you to talk to. And you haven't even had a chance to rest."

Liddy bent over the bread, cutting it, Estella noted, just the way she'd taught her years ago—sawing back and forth lightly. Liddy *was* her daughter, flesh of her flesh, and most like her in spirit, too, though maybe Liddy wouldn't recognize this for years.

Impulsively Estella put her arms around Liddy, squeezed her hard, and just as quickly let her go again. Perhaps because she was the oldest of the children and had always been so quick and competent, she had expected too much of her.

"Tomorrow you'll feel better, sweetheart," she said. "After a good night's sleep. You always did sleep like a stone here, you know. Hours and hours."

"Yes," Liddy said. "I always did."

5

The airplane was still in full sunlight, high up where it was, but below, Jane could see that the island was already in shadow. Yet the light was so clear that she could see perfectly the stretches of beach ringed with white where the waves were breaking into foam. Beyond that, the water was a deep blue-green, almost tropical in its intensity. It was there below them, the entire island—so small from that height that she suddenly felt terrified. Much better to arrive by ferry, to see the land slowly become distinct from the water. Seen that way, it seemed much more substantial than it did from above.

"That's Madaket," Philip said, leaning across her so he could see out the window. "The house we're renting is there somewhere. But we'll swing south before the plane comes in to land."

She could feel his excitement through the tenseness of his body and drew back from it. His excitement, which she didn't share, was distasteful to her. And there was something else too—the way he had so easily accepted the fact that she would return to the island with him; he'd never doubted it, really.

That easy acceptance of what had been for her so difficult made her feel lonely. He didn't understand her after all.

"The island looks terribly small from up here," she said, drawing back from the window, giving him the room he seemed determined to take anyway. But she could see, even from the corner of her eye, that it was no longer true that the island looked so small. The plane was descending fast.

"But beautiful," Philip said. "You can't deny it's beautiful, Jane."

She didn't deny it.

The plane had descended low enough for her to see distinctly the dark expanses of scrub—a jungle down there below them. It could have been, almost, an uninhabited island they were drawing near, one still capable of concealing mystery.

"I hadn't known so much of the island was overgrown like that," she said, leaning forward to see.

But then they had passed over the heart of the island and as the "No Smoking" sign flashed on they were again near enough to see the water; she could see distinctly the houses and the roads.

They sank beyond the point where the rays of the sun could reach and were instantly in shadow.

As the runway lights came into view and the wheels clunked down from their storage compartment, Jane shivered.

"In three minutes we'll be on the ground," Philip said, taking her hand. "I didn't know planes made you so nervous."

"They don't always," she said.

"It'll be all right," he said, squeezing her hand. "You don't have to worry about anything."

How can you possibly know that? she would have asked him if she could. But the wheels of the plane had touched the ground and the roar of the engines, going into reverse, would have drowned out anything she might have said.

6

Clinging to the long blade of coarse sea grass, the large moth trembled slightly, its wings pulsating with . . . what? Chrissy wondered. It was a huge moth, nearly as large as Jasper's hand, the color of ivory with pale green blotches on its wings. Fine hair made its body fuzzy, and its wings, too, were covered with down.

In the dust Chrissy and Jasper bent over the moth, watching. It seemed to glimmer; the faint trembling of its body could have been giving off light—a ghost moth, the ivory of its wings the same color as the sand in that pale light.

Jasper's finger reached out—Chrissy could see it point—longing to stroke.

"Don't touch," she whispered.

To make sure, she took his hand in hers and held on.

"I just want to see what it feels like."

In her hand, his tugged.

Though she was squatting in the sand with Jasper, her face turned toward the moth, she was aware of the lighted windows behind them and of the muted clinking of a pan against the stove, of the voices rising and falling.

"What?" Estella said once, clearly, and then there came her laugh, that rich, full laugh that Chrissy hadn't heard for a long time.

She was wild to hear what Estella and Liddy were saying—she'd forgotten the way they talked to each other when they were together, discussing things that Estella never discussed with her. Even before Liddy went away to college Estella had talked to her as she would to any grown-up. And Chrissy knew the way Estella had watched Liddy that afternoon with a hungry look on her face. Only Liddy, it seemed, could give her what she wanted.

What would it be like, to be the one Estella looked at in that hungry way? Just once, Chrissy wished that Estella would look at her like that, and yet if she ever did, Chrissy feared she would turn out to be a failure. She wouldn't be able to give Estella what she needed.

The moth climbed the slender stalk of sea grass, slowly and, it seemed, painfully.

"If you weren't here I might put my hand down..." Jasper said.

"You don't have any right, just because you don't like something."

"Yes I do," Jasper said with certainty. "I have a right."

Behind them the voices rose and fell the way the waves crested and broke.

The moth reached the tip of the blade of wiry grass, which, too frail for its weight, slowly tipped. One moment the moth still clung to the blade, swinging upside down, and the next it was flying, fluttering its big wings, dipping up and down over the dunes. Jasper followed the moth and Chrissy followed Jasper. Behind them Jenks trailed, his nose to the ground.

Over their right shoulders the moon was just rising above the water. It looked enormous, a bright, coppery pink. Chrissy saw it first and called to Jasper, "The moon, Jas! Look!"

Far over the water it cast its pink light, making a path for itself.

On the beach they lost sight of the moth. By the water, away from the house lights, there was only the moonlight, strong enough to cast dark shadows, almost bright enough to read a book by.

Jasper stood where the waves broke into foam, letting the water wash up to his knees.

Beside him Chrissy felt the sand and small rocks being sucked from under her feet as the water swept back down to the sea. It made her dizzy, that sweeping of water, and to steady herself she put her hand on Jasper's shoulder.

"If you shut your eyes," Jasper said, "it makes you feel like you're being carried right out into the ocean. *Scary!*"

"Then don't shut your eyes, silly."

"But I like it. I like being scared."

It gave her the creeps to think how, just behind the shelf of rocks near the shore, the water fell away into terrible depths. Not even the sheen of moonlight could altogether hide that darkness underneath.

Leaving Jasper behind, Chrissy ran up the beach to the dry sand, where she stood holding her elbows in her hands, shaking from the cold.

Jasper followed her, as she knew he would.

"Ever since Liddy came you've acted funny," he said, trailing his toes through the sand and leaving a wavy pattern behind.

"How have I acted funny?"

"You just have. Don't you like having Liddy back?"

"Of course I like having her back. Why shouldn't I?"

"I'd forgotten how much I love her. I'm just crazy about Liddy, to tell the truth. Her hair shines like a cat's."

"So why are you hanging around with me if you're so crazy about Liddy?" she said sharply. There were times when Jasper got on her nerves terribly. "You don't have to stay here with me."

Lifting his arms from his sides, Jasper turned around and around in the sand, his version of whirling.

"You're hanging around with meee," he said. "I came out here first. I was the one chasing the moth. You followed along behind me."

"Just stay out here by yourself for all I care," Chrissy said angrily, walking away from him, taking big strides, her heels digging smooth holes in the sand. "Maybe a big wave will come and wash you away."

"You'd feel bad if it did. You'd feel terrrrible."

Jasper stepped into the prints she'd left in the sand, stretching his legs wide trying to fit his heels into the dents hers had made.

"Stop following me, Jasper," she told him without turning around. "Leave me alone."

It was the unfairness of it that made her furious and hurt her feelings. If it hadn't been for Jasper she would have been all alone where she wanted to be, sitting on the bottom step of the deck, listening to Estella and Liddy talk in the kitchen.

"Chrissy's jea-lous," Jasper said behind her, making a singsong of the words.

"Why?" she demanded, whirling on him. "Why should I be jealous?"

"You are," he said, stopping too, his legs spread wide so he tottered and then fell on one knee into the sand. "You're jealous of Liddy."

(168)

"I am not!" she said, tears of hurt and rage coming to her eyes. "What do you know about it, anyway? Before you were born Liddy and I were together all the time. I know things about Liddy you'll never know. So who needed you, anyway? You shouldn't have been born is what I think. You shouldn't even have *been*."

Tears pricked her eyelids and she turned around blinking furiously, not wanting Jasper to see. For a long way she ran heavily through the sand without looking back; when she did she saw Jasper was just the way she'd seen him last, sprawled in the sand with one leg in front of him and the other behind. His head was bowed and not once did he look up.

She stopped where she was, looking back at him. "We wouldn't have missed you, either," she said. But her rage was ebbing and in its place came desolation. In all their lives together she'd never said such a terrible thing to him.

For a time she waited, looking back at Jasper unmoving on the sand, before she called to him.

But still he sat without lifting his head, too crushed, his shoulders said and his bowed head, to rise from the ground. He would stay there forever until he died or the sea washed him away.

Even when he did finally get to his feet and trailed behind her he would not look up or come close.

The distance remained between them.

"I thought you loved me," he said finally when they had reached the beach in front of the house.

"That's what I thought about you, too," she said, the hardness of her voice a surprise to her.

"I was only teasing," he said. "But you weren't. You meant it, what you said."

"You meant it too, Jas," she said, and it was sadness that exhausted her suddenly.

7

In the middle of the night, Chrissy came abruptly awake, listening for a repetition of the sound she thought she must have heard—furtive footsteps over the sunbaked ground. But though she listened, shutting her eyes to concentrate, she could hear nothing at all except the faint stirring of a breeze that made the tent shiver slightly as a cat moves with the hand that strokes it. It was the moonlight, she saw when she opened her eyes, that was the presence—the moon had crossed the highest part of the sky and was in the west now, shining between the needles of the pine trees; she could see the shadows moving across the ridge of the tent.

It was because of the moonlight that she sat on her heels in the opening of the tent, looking out at the brightness. Even in her sleep some part of her had been aware, had not wanted her to miss seeing that strange world.

She'd been looking for some time before she lifted her eyes to the deck and saw Liddy sitting at the top of the steps, gazing in the direction of the water. Liddy wearing the old cotton pajamas she'd used for years at the cottage—Liddy with her hands around one knee, leaning back with her face to the moon, though even from that distance Chrissy could tell that her eyes were closed. She was smiling.

In the pearly light, Liddy was touched with mystery—lifted out of the ordinary in spite of her bare feet, the rough cotton pajamas, the tangled hair pushed back from her face. And Chrissy felt shy with her as she had that afternoon when Liddy climbed down the steps of the plane—Liddy in all her familiarity but yet a Liddy transformed.

With her heart beating fast, Chrissy crossed the hard ground and climbed the first two steps. Liddy's eyes were still closed, her head tipped back.

"Lid?" Chrissy said.

But perhaps Liddy had heard her coming after all, because she scooted a little way across the step, making room.

Chrissy sat, her thigh touching Liddy's. She remembered their old game of pressing so closely against each other that one would be pushed off balance and have to give way. But she was content this time to remain quietly in Liddy's warm place.

"What're you looking at?" she said, though the question, she knew, was a foolish one.

"The moon," Liddy said. "Just the moon."

"With your eyes shut?"

"Yes," Liddy said, laughing. "With my eyes shut." But as soon as she spoke she opened her eyes and looked at Chrissy, smiling. Chrissy had half forgotten that slight upward tilt at the outer corners of Liddy's eyes. There was something dreamy in Liddy's voice, as though she were talking in her sleep.

"I didn't think you'd wake up until noon tomorrow probably," Chrissy said. "Aren't you tired?"

"The moon woke me up. And anyway, time goes haywire when you travel so quickly. It's hard to believe I really am here. If *here* exists."

"I could pinch you," Chrissy said. "You'd know then."

It was an old joke between them, trying to talk the other one into realizing that the world as they saw it existed nowhere except in their imaginations. They'd scared themselves more than once that way. But it was another game Chrissy was reminded of.

"You remember when I'd tell you to shut your eyes and then I'd give you bites of something to eat?" she said. "Mashed bananas or little bits of hard-boiled egg and you'd have to guess what it was? How hard it was to do?"

"Practically impossible if you held your nose. There was that time you gave me a mouthful of Grape Nuts and I spit them all over the floor, certain you'd given me puppy kibble. Remember that?"

"Nothing had any taste, one thing blending into another."

"And don't you remember how we always got suspicious playing that game? We were always afraid we'd be given something horrible to eat and wouldn't know until too late? We never expected to be given good things. Isn't that odd?"

Chrissy looked over at Liddy quickly, wondering what she was thinking, but it was impossible to tell. A kind of dreaminess lay over Liddy's face like a glaze, though it was probably only a reflection of the disembodied state that comes with exhaustion.

"Liddy?" Chrissy said, her voice catching on uncertainty, although anything, it seemed, might be said at that moment. "What were you and Mom talking about before supper? I could hear you laughing."

"She wanted to know about England," Liddy said. "All about it. But I wasn't ready to be asked. And it all seems distant now. Not very important."

Liddy moved her hand back and forth over the crown of her head, back and forth the way she had done from childhood when she had more to say but was being close-lipped.

"Did she say any more?" Chrissy asked. "Anything about Dad?"

"She wanted to know if I was surprised. You know, about his leaving."

"Well, were you?"

Chrissy cradled her feet in her hands and looked down at them. She sat hunched as though she were cold.

"Everybody seems to think I should know whether this was something he'd do or not. Well, how could I know? The way I look at it is, he's *done* it. It's an accomplished fact. I don't see any point in going over it and over it."

"I think," Chrissy said uncertainly, "that Mom feels like she's got to understand why. I mean, you trust people and then they let you down. *I* don't understand it myself. How he could do that..."

"But it's *done*," Liddy said impatiently. "And now they should get on with their lives."

The division between them made Chrissy suddenly sad. Liddy had another life altogether which she never talked much about; she didn't want to be troubled about the rest of them.

"Do you know the thing that makes me feel most strange?" Chrissy said.

Liddy shook her head.

"It's that Dad could have more children. A whole new set. Maybe even two girls and a boy again. I just thought of that the other day, and it gave me the strangest feeling." As she spoke, a shiver went up her backbone, the words pulling her into a long, whirling tunnel. At the other end was a mirror world.

"Silly," Liddy said. "They wouldn't be us, Chris, no matter how many more he had."

But Chrissy saw that the world in the moonlight quivered, the light shimmering on the water, all insubstantial.

"Don't hang on to things so," Liddy said. "Things never stay the same, anyhow."

Liddy spoke the same way she had when she was a child, insisting that the two of them make their play house behind the sofa instead of outside beside the rock wall the way Chrissy wanted. Liddy always sounded so sure of herself, paying no attention to what other people wanted.

It filled Chrissy with despair, the way Liddy couldn't be pinned down— the way she wouldn't really listen. She knew it wouldn't do any good to grab Liddy's arm and hang on tight; there was no way she could grab hold of what Liddy was thinking and hold her there. Liddy would just slip away, detaching herself from any kind of strife. She couldn't be depended on.

8

It was easy enough for Liddy to slip back into the habits of childhood. In her chest of drawers there were faded shorts and T-shirts that had been there since she was fifteen; in the closet there was a tennis racket, outgrown running shoes, a Mick Jagger poster she'd thumbtacked on the far wall, boxes of puzzles and other things that had never been opened.

The room had been her father's when he was a child; he'd told them stories about throwing firecrackers out the window on the early morning of the Fourth of July—a lighted string that would keep exploding for a long time. He'd been an only and indulged child.

But she and Chrissy had shared the room for as far back as she could remember—her side strewn with old sneakers and dirty socks, Chrissy's side perfectly neat, the poster of the Peaceable Kingdom on the wall in between, separating the two halves of the room.

Every summer she resolved that she would go through the closet and chest of drawers and bookcases, ruthlessly cleaning out the things she no longer wore, played with, or read, but though she'd left her room in the farmhouse nearly as empty as a nun's cell when she went away to college, she had never taken the time to clean out her portion of the room on Nantucket.

And the clothes were useful. It was easy when she woke in the mornings to put on an old pair of shorts and a T-shirt, to run her fingers through her hair and go off barefooted and half asleep to the kitchen to pour a cup of coffee from the pot Estella left plugged in for her. The others had eaten long before, leaving behind their cereal bowls and coffee cups in the sink. Even when she was a child she'd usually had her breakfast alone, sitting on the deck in the sunshine, watching the boats on the water and thinking idly of the dreams her night had been full of. The others felt sorry for her eating on the deck by herself hours after they had been up, and she knew they considered her mildly afflicted to take so long to wake up; when they were most full of energy there she was sitting in the sun drooped over her cereal bowl like a sick cat. But she had liked that— watching the world, each object hard-edged and distinct, slowly reaffirm itself.

These mornings she carried her coffee to the deck and sat on the steps where she'd always liked to sit, her eyes fixed on the weathered boards, scratching a mosquito bite absently with a thumbnail. It seemed unnaturally quiet. Even Jasper, playing down by the water, seldom raised his voice. But perhaps she was wrong and little had changed after all from those earlier summers when Philip had spent the morning in his study, his typewriter softly whirring. Maybe she had just forgotten.

Ordinarily, by the time she'd gotten her bowl of cereal and brought it to the deck he would come out of his study, stretching, doing limbering exercises, and drink a cup of coffee with her. "Well, Beauty," he'd say, "what's up with you?" Since she'd been very small and had made him read "Beauty and the Beast" over and over to her, he'd sometimes called her Beauty. What he'd not understood, however, was that it had been the Beast's house that had intrigued her—that house which magically catered to every whim, and the garden where roses bloomed even in the winter. Beauty herself, with her too exquisite sense of right and wrong, Liddy had never liked very much. But she had never bothered to enlighten her father, since she knew it gave him pleasure to think of her as Beauty— the woman willing to give up her own life, if necessary, so her father might live. Why disillusion him? She'd learned early that people saw her the way they wanted to, that they made up stories to suit themselves. She grew used to watching with cool eyes and letting people think what they liked. As long as she knew the truth it didn't matter what anyone else thought, though she was sometimes struck with a sudden loneliness of the kind that kings and queens must often have felt, cut off from ordinary life.

She remembered clearly how it had been when she was very small, curled up in the corner of the sofa, propped on pillows with a picture book opened over her knees, her father looking down at her for a long time before he said in that hushed, urgent voice, as though he were afraid somebody else might be listening, "You're my girl, Liddy, aren't you? Aren't you my sweetheart?"

And she'd lifted her eyes to see him standing there very tall, with the sunlight shining through his hair, his mouth smiling—rather like a tree she had thought him, or like the highboy in Grandmother Sloan's house where the sunlight brought out a glow in the wood that was like embers. She hadn't agreed or disagreed that she was his girl; it was enough to lift her eyes to his face for a moment before looking back at her book. Above her head he could go on, say anything he liked. Later, when she looked up again, he would have disappeared.

But her mother would scoop her up from the sofa, slide her onto her hip, and jiggle her up and down. Her mother's face was like a moon but with her hair jagging around it the way Liddy made the light zigzag out from the sun when she drew a picture. Her mother laughing, saying for all the world to hear, "You're my baby, aren't you, Liddy? And look! You've got my nose right there in the middle of your face. See that? Maybe I should take my nose back." And her mother would play the game of taking away her nose—thumb caught between fingers—until Liddy laughed, demanding to have her nose again. With her mother everything was easy.

For two and a half years she had filled all the spaces a child might occupy. "Liddy is standoffish but loving," her parents told the relatives. "She feels more than other children, only she won't show it. She's smart, quick, limber as an eel, can carry a tune, is fascinated by numbers, friendly but self-possessed..." There was no quality lacking in Liddy, it seemed, to hear her parents tell it. Considering what a paragon they found her, it was perhaps surprising they had bothered to have another child.

"But you need a playmate," they said. "You need a little brother or sister so you will have someone to play with." They didn't want her to grow up lonely.

So, for her convenience, Chrissy had been born. That was the way she had understood it. And because her parents had gone to a lot of trouble to provide this sister, this companion, she had viewed Chrissy hopefully from the beginning. Though to start with Chrissy had been a failure as a companion, Liddy had tried to overlook this. She was patient with Chrissy's first efforts—the way she gurgled and kicked her legs in ecstasy when Liddy sent the birds, balanced on their fine wires, whirling above Chrissy's cot. Even better was playing pat-a-cake when Chrissy could sit up, regally, her back straight, her legs in front of her. Yet it was clear to Liddy that Chrissy was hopelessly behind; even the room where Chrissy sat with her back so straight was Liddy's room, and most of Chrissy's toys had once belonged to Liddy and would have still if she'd wanted them. So she was aware early on—as far back as she could remember—that since she had appropriated everything else for herself, what Chrissy should have was...her.

Of course, Chrissy looked up to her and thought she was wonderful. Why shouldn't she? Everything Chrissy learned, Liddy had learned before. Naturally Chrissy admired her and followed her around; she laughed at Liddy's jokes and played the games Liddy thought up. Chrissy, Liddy thought for a long time, was just like her only a little behind and slower with everything. She was used to having Chrissy look up to her and thought that was right.

Only there were times when Liddy didn't want to play—when she had to be by herself. When that happened, Chrissy would get upset and cry, but Liddy couldn't help it. Most of the time she was gracious and let people admire her or whatever else they wanted to do, but when it got tiresome and boring she would just slip away; she had to disappear for a while. People should have the sense to let her do this when she needed to; she didn't *choose* to be cruel and rarely was. Only when people expected too much.

That was what she'd liked so much when she first went to England— she hadn't known anybody. For a little while nobody expected anything at all of her. But of course that couldn't last. She had met people, and those friends had led to others; soon there were so many she'd felt crowded by them all. And eventually, too, there had been Nigel, his face illuminated by the light of the candle that sat between them on the table in the little Soho restaurant, his eyes looking everywhere except into hers as he said, "I wish you would tell me why...."

But of course he didn't want to be told why at all. He didn't want to hear the reasons why she wasn't in love with him even if she could have given them. What he wanted was to use his pain to make her suffer too so that she would change her mind about him. What he *said* was meaningless.

And all she had been able to do was to sit looking into the candle flame, trying to keep that patient and understanding look on her face while all the time she was thinking how tiresome it all was—people wanting, wanting, getting themselves into humiliating states, all over something they'd made up themselves to start with.

"Liddy?" Chrissy said.

Liddy had not heard Chrissy cross the deck, but she hadn't been listening. Leaning over her coffee cup so that the warmth of the sun would fall on her shoulders, her thoughts had gone elsewhere.

Without waiting for a reply, Chrissy sat beside her and leaned back against the wall of the house. "I just got this letter," she said. "Just now in the mail."

The white envelope dangled between her thumb and forefinger; it might have been a mouse she was holding gingerly by the tail.

"Yes?" Liddy said absently. For days she had felt sleepy at odd times, as though to make up for that first day and night when she had not been able to sleep.

"It's from Dad," Chrissy said. "He and Jane are back on Nantucket and he's given me his address. He wants to see me and Jasper."

Liddy glanced through the short note and put it back in the envelope. The note was typewritten—which she thought was typical of Philip—but it was his neat signature at the bottom of the page that held her eye, that small, self-contained writing, each letter carefully and even beautifully formed.

"I don't want to see him," Chrissy said. "There wouldn't be anything to say. It would just be embarrassing."

"Then don't see him," Liddy said sharply. "He can't always have what he wants."

It was disgustingly weak of Philip to come back after he'd left. Pride, if nothing else, should have made him firm in what he'd decided to do. It made Liddy furious to be forced to see him that way—as some wishy-washy person who couldn't make up his own mind.

She'd been annoyed sometimes when he came out on the deck saying to her, "Well, Beauty?" But she had waited for him all the same and had been disappointed when he didn't come out of his study. He wasn't wrong in thinking there was a special bond between them—the older daughter he'd taken time to teach things he wouldn't see the necessity of teaching any later child—but what he hadn't known, it seemed, was that for her to feel that special link between them she had to admire him. An admiration she wouldn't have admitted, even if someone had asked her, but one she assumed he knew of anyway. Hadn't the look that passed between them

(178)

sometimes—that look of secret amusement and love—been evidence he understood?

What he had not known was that her patience with him was on a short leash. If he'd thought he could depend on her to feel the same way about him no matter what, then he was wrong. Admiration is a dangerous thing to lose.

"Come with me to show Mom, will you?" Chrissy said, and so Liddy followed Chrissy across the deck.

Estella leaned against the wall while she read the letter, holding it into the light, refusing to wear the reading glasses she probably needed. As she read, her face grew more and more stern; when she'd finished, it was formidable.

"He seems to think that without him we'll crumble into some pitiful little heap," she said, her voice tight and hard. "Did you ever hear of such arrogance? Without him to watch over us with that lordly, godlike eye of his, nothing will go right, disasters will happen. Obviously it's never entered his head that he might not *be* the center of this family. Isn't that funny? Well, almost pitiable if you look at it in a purely detached way."

Her eyes were fixed on them, but Liddy knew it wasn't them she was thinking about as she slapped the envelope containing Philip's letter back and forth on her thigh.

"I wouldn't pay any attention," Liddy said. "I'd ignore it."

"But as you said yourself, Liddy," Estella said, the distant look still on her face, *"you're* not the one married to him. There are things you can't understand."

When Liddy looked back as she was going out the door, she saw that Estella's face had gone desolate, even haggard. For a moment, she looked old.

9

She would not write him a note, Estella decided. She would give him no warning at all. And she rather hoped Jane would be there too in the house—"trapped" was the word that came to her mind. She saw herself swooping down on the two of them the way, in her childhood, she had seen a setting hen, feathers puffed out from the ruff around her neck, wings flapping menacingly, attack cats, toads, her father's boots, the small round eyes fixed madly, the beak open, ready to peck.

It gave her pleasure to think about.

There was never any question in her mind what she would wear to conduct this attack—her paint-smeared jeans and khaki workshirt, sleeves rolled to the elbows, tail free and flapping around her thighs. These were her working clothes and therefore her fighting outfit. But she did imagine, for her own entertainment, other possibilities. The ceremonial robe she'd brought back from Botswana—an orange-and-red affair reaching to the tops of her feet. Or perhaps her white linen suit with the emerald-green silk blouse and the string of old pearls left to her by her grandmother. At ten in the morning if she came up the walk of his house dressed in that outfit, Philip would think she'd lost her mind.

It might almost be worth it to give Philip the shock of seeing her in the family pearls, but she did not want to conduct this confrontation wearing anything that might get in her way or crimp her style.

"Keep an eye on Jasper," she shouted to Chrissy as she shut the door of her studio behind her and headed for the car. "I've got to go out for a while."

Chrissy didn't ask where she was going, though she watched until Estella climbed into the car.

It was, Estella noted as she drove down the lane, beautiful and clear, and she felt another jolt of anger against Philip, who was making her waste this perfect working day.

Her anger and resolve carried her through town and onto the Madaket Road, but there her hands grew slick against the steering wheel, so she had to keep wiping them on her jeans. So she was nervous after all, she saw with dismay. But of what? Everything was on her side.

She recognized the house, even from a distance, and she was sure it was the right one even before she was able to read the name on the mailbox. The house had nothing to shelter behind, so she could see the entire front, though she couldn't see the western deck until she'd driven three-quarters of the way up the drive. And there was Philip, stretched out on a chaise longue. At the same moment she saw him he evidently recognized the car, because he sat up and rose quickly to his feet.

Well, well, she thought. So there he is. And immediately a great calmness came over her so that she knew that the other—her nervousness and sweaty palms—had been nothing but stage fright. Now, when she was on the point of giving her performance, her fear left her and her hands were altogether steady.

By the time she'd climbed the steps, Philip had moved away from the chair and was standing at the edge of the deck, with his back to the moors.

She came straight forward, stopping only a couple of feet from him— so near, she knew, that she was invading his space.

"I hoped Jane would be here too," she said. "But I see she isn't."

"She's gone swimming," Philip said in a stiff voice.

She could see it clearly on his face—the dilemma he was in. Should he offer her coffee and a chair to sit in, trying to make of this visit a social occasion? Or should he turn haughty and cold immediately, falling back behind his line of defense?

"Still, Jane doesn't interest me one way or the other and never has, much," Estella said, her arms crossed in front of her chest, looking him straight in the eye though she knew that what she'd just said was a lie. "What I want to know is why you're back here, circling like a vulture.

You don't think we can possibly survive without you around? Is that what you think? Or did you just want to come back here to torment me? Which is it?"

He drew himself up—on his dignity, she could see.

"I came back for only one reason," he said. "I wanted to be near the children. I thought they might feel I was abandoning them, the way I left so abruptly."

"You did abandon them!" she said. "When you left the house you deserted me and abandoned them. Any lawyer could tell you that."

"It's not the law I'm talking about, Estella," he said—oh, she could hear how hard he was trying to be reasonable. "Let's not have that nonsense between us. You know what I mean as well as I do. It was for the sake of the children themselves. I wanted them to know I was nearby if they needed me."

"Don't try playing that good-father stuff with me. Trying to worm your way back into their good graces."

"Say what you want to," he told her, lifting his gaze upward, to the side of the house. "But you know I put the children first."

"How dare you say that! How can you stand there and say you put the children first, the way you left here!"

"That's why I came back," he said, and she realized suddenly that all those years of teaching stood him in good stead. No matter how impossible the student, no matter how he was wronged, he would keep his dignity, he could bring down like manna from heaven that patient-sounding voice. "It wasn't easy to come back. I knew I would be letting myself in for scenes exactly like this one. But I felt I had to do it."

"Fine," she said. "You're back. You and your woman. But you keep on your side of the island and we'll keep to ours. I will not let you see Jasper. I will not let you set foot in the cottage. And you'd better understand me, Philip."

"You didn't have to come charging over here to tell me that," he said, and she saw that his resolve to stay calm and cool was beginning to crumble after all. It wasn't easy to arouse Philip's temper, but once it had been roused, it would simmer for a long time, giving him heartburn and sleepless nights.

"Oh yes I did," she said. "I knew exactly what you would do next. The telephone calls. The letters. The assignations with Chrissy and Jasper. The terrible need you have to plead your case. To be understood and forgiven. Don't think I don't *know* all that, Philip."

"I think," Philip said, and she saw that look of sly triumph slide over his face, "that you don't understand me as well as you always thought you did."

She hated him for looking at her like that—so detached and cold. But it hurt her too.

"Certain things," she said, "you're teaching me right now."

Philip lowered his eyes. "Estella," he said, "couldn't we talk like reasonable people?"

"I knew that was coming," she said. "The appeal to reasonableness. To my understanding as a wife and mother. After all—isn't this what you were going to say?—we've *lived* together for twenty-two years. And mostly in harmony. Doesn't that count for anything? Isn't there credit accruing after all that time?"

Now she saw it for sure, the pallor that always came over Philip's face when he was furious.

"Do you really hate me so much?" he said, and there was something in his voice that distressed her and she felt her resolve wavering. She'd wanted to hurt him, but now that she'd done it she felt remorse after all. In another moment she might have reached out her hand to him, but he had misread her silence and turned abruptly away.

"Of course," he said, "I always knew you had a vindictive streak, Estella. You like it, don't you, feeling you have the upper hand?"

After that she didn't care how much he suffered. She hoped he did.

Crossing the deck in three strides, she jumped into the sand and got into the car. Only when she'd started the motor did she consider sticking her head out the window and saying, "Liddy's back from England. You didn't know that, did you? But she doesn't want to see you."

She preferred to keep that knowledge as secret power; there was no reason she should let him know. And so she did nothing but turn the car around and drive back down the driveway, refusing even to look in the rearview mirror for a last glimpse of Philip standing on the deck.

10

Jane knew, as soon as she came onto the deck in her wet suit, with a damp towel around her neck, that something was wrong with Philip. He was standing on the edge of the deck staring out across the moors with a stony look on his face. He didn't even turn toward her when she came up behind him—he seemed unaware that she was there at all—and fear caught in her throat. What had she done that he would have turned so implacably against her? When she left to go swimming he had been in good spirits, only he said he didn't feel in the mood to swim. While she was gone had he found out something about her, some terrible thing?

"Philip?" she said, stopping before she reached him.

When he turned around she saw that there was a set, rigid look on his face.

"You look so pale..." she said in alarm.

"Estella just came here," he said. "She made me so furious I could have killed her."

Jane felt her stomach lurch. "What did she say?"

"I don't want to talk about it," he said. "I'd just be furious again."

Jane tugged the towel back and forth, swaying it against the nape of her neck. "But what was it about?" she said.

Me? she wanted to ask. Was it about me? She felt weak with relief that she had not been at the house. In a confrontation with Estella she would shrivel to nothing; she would be paralyzed on the spot, unable to move a muscle.

"The children, of course," he said. "She says she won't let me see them, but she can't very well stop me. Now that they know where I am they'll come looking for me. She can't stop that."

Jane was half afraid he might follow her into the house and up to the bathroom, telling her everything Estella had said and everything he had replied to her, supplying all this information she didn't want to have.

Though she reached the bathroom without Philip following her, she locked the door behind her in case he changed his mind. She would fill the tub and sit in it a long time. When she came out the danger would have passed.

It made her shudder as she knelt beside the tub with the steam rising into her face—if she'd waited just a few more minutes before she went swimming, if she'd sat over one more cup of coffee at breakfast, nothing could have saved her. All the vague unspecified guilt she'd ever felt—that guilt always ready to overwhelm her if, indeed, the stranger in the street did hiss to her someday, "I know what you've done"—all that would have submerged her with one look from Estella.

She stripped and climbed into the tub, settling back in the water until it reached her chin.

It was a mess she'd gotten herself into; there was no question in her mind about that. Though she'd never intended to injure Estella—had harbored, in fact, no bad feelings against Estella at all—she could not pretend that she was above the chaos or uninvolved in it. Yet it seemed unfair that she should be in that bad position of doing injury when she hadn't intended it or wanted to—she who so hated being disapproved of.

It made her face burn with shame when she thought about being disliked. Even, perhaps, hated.

It was unfair and cruel of Philip to have brought her back to this island where she could be so easily humiliated and held up to scorn. If he truly cared for her or had her welfare at heart he wouldn't have done it. Of course, he couldn't have forced her to come back there with him, but he had exerted his power over her all the same, and in an underhanded way, as she now saw it.

Because of his children, he had said. But she was no longer altogether convinced that this was the truth. Or the whole truth. Many other things were involved that she hadn't realized at the time. She knew how much he hated to be left out, to feel he was inconsequential. And, too, he had wanted to get back at Estella.

He'd known perfectly well she'd never wanted to return to the island, but he had set up the terms so that she either had to return with him or give him up—that was what it amounted to—and she hadn't been able to give him up then, so quickly. In that, too, he had played on her feelings cruelly—leading her to fall in love with him, leading her to think that he was a man she could depend on, one she didn't have to be on guard against. It had never been her feelings he thought about; he'd never considered how it would be for her there on the island with Estella and his children.

She climbed out of the tub and drew a towel rapidly across her shoulders and down her back. Walking softly, as though she were afraid he might hear her, she went to the window and looked down at the deck. But Philip was still there with his feet propped up against a chair, a book held resolutely in front of his face.

Steathily she finished drying, in great haste, and ran into the bedroom, where she put on a blouse, a skirt, sandals. In less than fifteen minutes she could pack her suitcase and with it in hand she could make her way down the stairs, through the living room, out the front door, and then...

But the picture at this point became absurd. Climbing onto one of the mopeds, she would have to hold the suitcase balanced across her knees, would have to travel that way to either ferry or airport, and of course Philip would hear the motor of the moped start up; he would come after her.

She'd taken her suitcase from the closet and opened it on the bed, but now she sat beside it, uncertain.

She was still sitting there when Philip came up the stairs, and she saw on his face instantly that he understood all she'd been thinking, as though the open suitcase and her brooding there on the bed had been a dumb show planned especially to inform him of her true feelings.

"Oh, Jane," he said, hurrying across the room to her, and she was sure she didn't mistake the sorrow and the pity in his face. "It is terrible for you, isn't it? You can see yourself pounced on, any moment."

He sat on the bed and put his arms around her, and what she felt then was remorse for all those suspicions she'd had about him. Surely they couldn't be true after all if Philip could look so pained on her behalf.

"I thought how awful it would be if I'd been here when Estella came," she said, looking down at her hands. "What could I have said? I would have wanted to die."

"But she won't come back. She's said what she had to say. And anyway, you know, it's me she's furious with. Not you so much."

"But I hate being in this position. You have put me in a terrible position, Philip."

"It won't always be like this," he said. "I don't want you to worry about it, Jane."

He took her hands in his, and she allowed him to hold them and to comfort her. She wanted to believe him. Yet she knew that doubt had come into her mind all the same, and it would not entirely disappear.

11

Because it was bright outside and much darker inside the pharmacy, Liddy took off her sunglasses when she came through the door. Nevertheless, she was half blinded and lowered her eyes, watching her feet as they moved down the narrow aisle, heading for the back where she would get the prescription for her birth-control pills refilled. She was already halfway through the store when something gave her warning and she looked up to see Philip standing near the cash register with a bottle of after-shave lotion in his hand.

It was clear he hadn't seen her, and she stopped where she was, in the middle of the aisle, feeling her heart pound in her throat. Taking a quick look backward toward the door, she weighed her chances of easing to it before Philip saw her, but she was paralyzed with uncertainty and so she simply stood, staring at him.

Philip had grown slimmer than he'd been the last time she'd seen him, and he was very tan. There was something different about his hair, too—the way it was cut. Always a handsome man, he had grown even better-looking.

As she walked toward him slowly, the way she might haved approached a high-strung horse, he remained in a brown study, staring unblinking in the direction of the hairbrushes.

It was uncanny, how oblivious he was. She was near enough to have reached out and touched his shoulder if she'd wanted to before she said, "Hello, Dad."

Philip's eyes, rising instantly to hers, looked so startled that for a moment she thought he might bolt from the store. But a step backward only brought him to rest against the glass case holding watches; his hand, lying beside the tray of lipsticks, trembled.

"I thought you were in England," he said, his face so pale that it might have been a ghost he thought he was seeing. Still, even in his agitation, he lowered his voice. Never for a moment did either of them forget they were in a public place.

"I've come back home." This seemed to her instantly a foolish thing to say, since it was, after all, obvious, but everything except the obvious seemed to have deserted her.

"I thought you were staying until fall," Philip said, his eyes fixed on her in intensity and dread.

"It seemed I should come back early."

Instead of looking away, Philip bent more intently to her face, rooting out her thoughts. And then he suddenly straightened as a fleeting look of anger passed over him. "They should have left you alone to finish out the summer," he said.

"I was ready to leave anyhow."

She could see that his mood grew lighter now that his shock had passed, and he took her arm just above the elbow, intending to steer her out of the store.

"I *am* glad you're back, Lid," he said. "The only one who can talk sense. Let's go somewhere quiet. Jane's at home, so we can be by ourselves."

But she was stubborn, refusing to move along with him, to be steered by one elbow anywhere.

"Not now," she said. "No."

"Why not?" he wanted to know.

"I just can't," she said again, irritated with him for trying to force her, for assuming that only what he wanted was really important.

"I have to see you, Liddy," he said. "It's been so long. Couldn't you meet me tomorrow, then, if you can't stay now?"

She didn't want to give in too quickly—a trace of her irritation remained—but the urgency in his voice swept her along and she said she would meet him the next morning at ten o'clock.

"The Sweet Shoppe?"

She nodded her head and pushed past him without looking back, heading down the aisle to get her prescription filled.

As soon as Liddy came into the Sweet Shoppe the next morning she saw Philip in the back, in a far booth; she would have been surprised if he had not gotten there before her. He was watching the door and waved to her as she came in—a wave she did not return. Though he smiled when she slid into the seat opposite him, the tenseness around his eyes gave him away.

"Have you eaten?" he asked. "Or is it just coffee?"

Liddy caught the eye of the waitress. "Tea," she told her. "With milk."

"Become very English, have you?" Philip said. "You're looking very well. Whatever it is you've done with your hair suits you."

"Yours suits you, too," she told him.

Because of Jane he had become more aware of women, she realized—of their hair and clothes and the texture of their skin. And she was aware, too, as she wouldn't have been before, of the way his pale blue shirt matched his eyes, of the scent of his cologne. Just as she had picked up a kind of sexiness in what he wore, in the way he walked, in the way he looked appraisingly at women, so he had picked up the same thing in her—the men she had slept with had left some impression after all.

"I just remembered how you used to bring me here sometimes for breakfast," she said, slipping to the safety of the past. "I'd just be getting up when you were ready to come to town to buy a newspaper. We'd sneak off while everybody else was busy and you'd let me order anything at all. A bowl of chowder and a vanilla soda—anything."

For a moment, as she looked down at her teacup and the fat little pitcher of milk, Philip became the daddy of her childhood, and it came back to her how he had held her between his hands in the water as she learned to swim, the way he had trotted along beside her bicycle the day he took off the training wheels, keeping one hand outstretched and ready to grab the handlebar if she wobbled. She had been certain then that she was his favorite.

Stirring his cup of coffee idly, around and around, Philip seemed lost in thought. "How long have you been back?" he finally asked.

"Ten days."

"And you weren't going to see me?"

Philip's eyes searching her face looked injured; even his skin had turned pale under the tan.

It was the old ploy of pain and guilt, but she wouldn't be drawn in.

"Probably not," she said.

Still he stirred his coffee, a gesture she was beginning to find maddening.

"If you want to see me suffer," he said, "it's not hard."

"*I'm* the one I don't want to suffer," she said, leaning over the table, jabbing her thumb against her chest. "Me! Whatever you and Mother do you can do it on your own time, all right?"

"Just then you sounded exactly like her," he said, and his voice took on a bitter note. "I never could bear it when Estella turned self-righteous. That superiority."

Liddy threw herself against the booth with such abruptness that she might have cracked her backbone. Almost, she could have laughed. "You don't know the first thing about it if that's what you think. That I'm sitting here feeling superior. You think I don't *understand* how you could fall in love and all the rest?"

But she saw by the look of relief that came over Philip's face that she had made a mistake. He'd taken contempt and converted it into understanding.

"Liddy, you know I didn't intend for all this to happen," he said, leaning forward across the table so she could see clearly that distant glitter in his eyes—that greediness to tell everything. "You're the only one of the family who could understand about Jane. You don't know how much I've missed you. I didn't even know it myself until I saw you yesterday, just miraculously there in the pharmacy. You know I didn't intend to fall in love with Jane, and it wasn't a rejection of Estella. Not in the beginning, it wasn't that at all. It was just that Jane is, well, very special."

It was the faint, involuntary smile that Philip couldn't suppress when he said Jane's name that steeled Liddy finally against him. It was foolish, that smile, and she couldn't abide foolishness in him.

"What you're saying hasn't got anything to do with me," Liddy said. "Not a thing."

Against the back of the booth she pressed her shoulders. What she couldn't stand another second was Philip's self-absorption, the way he never doubted that she wanted to hear his story, that she found it as engrossing as he clearly did himself. Not once did he say, "But tell me,

Liddy. Tell me what it was like for you in England," though she could have told him plenty.

She was sliding to the end of the booth, on the point of leaving, when Philip grabbed her arm.

"Liddy, wait," he said. "Maybe it was crass of me to try to talk to you about Jane. I'm sorry if it was. But there's something else. Just hear me out for a few minutes."

It was his old authority that held her where she was and made her sit back again, waiting. She had never been a dutiful child in the obvious ways, and yet she had never been as indifferent as she had seemed.

"The thing is," Philip said, "that I've got to see Jasper. Estella won't let me—it's her way of punishing me—and I must talk to him. I've got to explain things to him in my own way."

"Is this the only reason you wanted to see me?" Liddy said, speaking slowly and distinctly as though Philip were a foreigner who understood the language imperfectly. "Because of Jasper?"

"Liddy," he said, and his eyes looked into hers. "Don't you know how much I love you and always have?"

"Yes," she said. "But I don't want to hear about it. Not right now I don't want to hear about it."

If he said the word "love" again she would hit him.

"All right," he said, looking away. "This is terrible for all of us. But I need your help, Lid. You really are the only one who can help me in this."

"In what?" she said sullenly.

"In seeing Jasper. He's only a little boy, Liddy. He must wonder why I've disappeared the way I seem to have done."

"He knows more than you think. Jasper's a stunted adult. You know that. But what can I do about it anyway?"

"Bring him to town with you and let me meet you."

"What makes you think I care whether you see Jasper or not?"

"Don't be so hard, Liddy," he said. "God, it hurts me when you say things like that."

It was his wounded, betrayed look that finally she could not say no to, though she could have thrown what was left of her tea in his face, she was so angry.

"One time," she said. "Just one time I'll do it. And after that you can get Chrissy to do your dirty work for you."

"I can't ask Chrissy," he said. "You know that."

"So why do you think you can ask me?"

"Because," he said, taking the check from the table and standing up, "you're old enough to understand things Chris can't."

But what makes you so sure I want to know? she wanted to yell in his face. What makes you so sure about that?

At the cash register, Philip's attention was taken up with paying the bill. "Day after tomorrow?" he said. "In front of the A&P at two?"

"If I can't make it, I can't make it," she said, heading for the door. "You'll know soon enough."

"Wait, Liddy," he said. "I'll come out with you."

But she was already through the door, sprinting down the sidewalk to the place where she'd left the car. She knew very well that he wanted to give her the hug he'd not yet had the chance to give her. That he wanted to kiss her on the cheek and say, "Well, Beauty, I missed you. Know that?" But she wouldn't give him the satisfaction.

12

The moment Liddy asked Jasper if he wanted to go to town with her, Chrissy took warning and looked up from her book. But Liddy's face gave nothing away.

"I'm only going for groceries," Liddy said. "But you like coming to town, Jas."

"Okay, I'll come," Jasper said, getting up from the floor where he'd been playing with his action men.

Chrissy knew, by the way Liddy kept her face averted, that she didn't intend to ask her too, though she kept hoping Liddy would turn around and say, "Of course I'd like you to come too, Chris."

They had already passed through the doorway, the screen had slammed behind them, when Chrissy suddenly ran to the door and called after them, "Wait! I think I'll come too."

Liddy looked back, exasperated. "You know you get bored trailing around supermarkets," she said. "And I've got lots of stops to make, Chris. The A&P, the Grand Union, Cumberland Farms, the fish shop, the liquor store..."

In the doorway Chrissy hesitated. It was clear that Liddy didn't want her to come.

But if she made up her mind to do it, she could run to the car, open the back door, and climb inside before Liddy could say anything. It would be embarrassing to do that—to insist on being included—but she could do it anyway if she chose.

While she stood in the doorway, poised between staying or running after them, Liddy and Jasper got in the car and Liddy started the motor.

It was only when the car was disappearing around the bend that Chrissy couldn't hear it any longer and ran after them, calling out, "Wait! Wait!" though she knew very well they couldn't hear her and even if they had Liddy might not have stopped. But if she was able to catch up with them at the end of the lane that would be a sign—one that showed she was doing the right thing—and so she ran as fast as she could through the dust.

But at the end of the lane, she saw the car already moving down the road, so far ahead now that she knew it was no use running after it. She watched until it went down the rise and was lost to sight.

Jenks was asleep in the shade of the house, lying in a shallow hole he'd dug for himself, searching for cool, and she sat beside him, reaching over to pat him between the ears. He was heavily asleep and didn't wake. Only his skin rippled along his backbone, a discouragement to flies.

"Jenks," she said. "Wake up, Jenks." She took one of his front paws in her hands and moved it back and forth, the way he would move if he were running. But he only raised the loose skin above his eyes and went on sleeping. He was an old dog who spent more and more of his time asleep; he wasn't as much concerned about all of them as he had been when he was younger. Then he'd wanted to be with one of them all the time.

Leaving Jenks, she walked over to the boathouse and went inside. She didn't bother to knock first, since Estella didn't mind when one of them came into her studio; most of the time she didn't seem to notice, as she didn't this time. Sitting on a stool in front of her table, wearing an old shirt of Philip's and ragged jeans, she continued with her work. But this was what Chrissy liked about coming to Estella's studio—it wasn't necessary to talk. Estella accepted another person in her studio the same way she accepted a piece of furniture or the noise of the waves against the beach—her attention swept past all that and continued out to a place where she couldn't be followed.

Chrissy lay on Estella's cot and looked up at the rafters of the boathouse, as she had done on many other summer afternoons. It had always been restful, listening to those sounds of pen on paper or brush on canvas.

When Chrissy was young she had brought toy animals with her in her pockets, animals she would play with as she lay on her stomach on the cot. Her lips would move as she made up stories about them and sometimes she forgot to whisper and said the stories out loud, but it hadn't mattered, because Estella was too lost in her own dream to listen. Sometimes Estella talked out loud to herself, too, asking herself where she'd put the scissors or the glue. Sometimes she scolded herself as she looked down at her drawing or collage. "That looks like the horse's ass," she said just before she wadded up the paper.

On those occasions when Chrissy had gone to sleep lying on Estella's cot she would find, when she woke up, that nothing had changed while she was asleep except the light, which would either have intensified toward noon or diminished toward evening. It had always been comforting to her—that dependability.

"Liddy and Jasper went off to town," Chrissy said, looking at the rafters. "They didn't want me to go with them."

"Liddy had a lot of shopping to do," Estella said, not looking up. "You get impatient doing things like that."

"I don't think that's the reason," Chrissy said. "There was something else."

As she spoke, the true reason Liddy hadn't wanted her to go with them suddenly came to her. Perfectly clearly she saw Liddy, Jasper, and Philip, sitting in a row on the wharf, dangling their legs over the edge, their arms around each other's waists, all laughing together. Maybe they had done this before; maybe it was a regular arrangement, Liddy and Jasper keeping their father to themselves. Each time they would say, "Oh, Chrissy doesn't want to come. She doesn't want to see you."

"They've gone to meet Daddy," Chrissy said. She lifted her arm and looked at the rafters from between her fingers.

"Liddy wouldn't sneak off that way," Estella said sharply. "She'd have told me."

"No," Chrissy said. "It's what they're doing."

Estella sat leaning on her elbows, tapping the end of the drawing pen against her teeth.

"I'll never forgive Philip for coming back here," she said. "He's like one of those vultures we used to see in Africa. That's the way he is, hovering out there. He couldn't stand it—that we might get along perfectly all right without him."

Chrissy saw her father with that pursed look of concern on his face, overseeing the loading of the station wagon, caulking the cracks around the windows against the winter wind. He was the only one who could do those jobs as they should be done; without him, he had often implied, the rest of them would be unable to deal with the most rudimentary jobs of everyday life.

"But you're wrong about Liddy, Chris," Estella said. "She would have told me if she were going to see Philip. Liddy's very honest."

It was surprising to Chrissy that Estella seemed so sure. What gave her the confidence to speak with such certainty about what Liddy would or wouldn't do? After all, there had been a time when she'd known Liddy better than anyone else—a time when she thought she knew nearly everything about her, though she knew now that wasn't true. You never knew anyone except just a little. Just a few things. That was why she watched them all so closely, studying all that could be observed. Clues were everywhere—in the way a person moved a hand or averted a glance. But the difficulty was in reading all those clues, in sorting them out. There were so many things to consider.

"But you didn't know about Dad. Did you?" Chrissy said.

"I suppose I didn't," Estella said.

"But why? *Why* didn't you know?"

"Maybe I didn't want to see," Estella said, looking down at the sheet of paper she was resting her elbow on. "There are times when you don't want to."

But it was terrible to think of not knowing. It seemed to Chrissy that there were some things you had to depend on, to know for sure about. If there was nothing at all you could depend on, then you were totally, totally lost. So you had to believe that you knew certain things about the people you loved—that there were things you could be sure about if you read the clues the right way. It was like making your way through dangerous country with just a map to show the way.

Maybe it was no wonder she paid so much attention to trees and rocks and the sea, which might look different from hour to hour and even from moment to moment but still didn't change the way people did. It was with people you were most lost.

13

On the way to town, Liddy drove so fast that on the curves the wheels made a squealing noise. Even so it wasn't fast enough to suit Jasper. "Go faster, Liddy," he told her, watching the speedometer greedily. She was up nearly to seventy, but he wanted to see the needle touch eighty. He leaned into the wind blowing into the car window, blowing so hard he had to squint his eyes, and the sound of it, rushing past his ears, was like water when a wave crashed over his head. "Hit eighty, Liddy," he said. "Just once."

But already Liddy was easing her foot from the accelerator.

"You want to kill us?" she said. "This is a narrow road, Jas."

"I don't care," he said. "I love to go like the wind."

"You can't have everything you want," Liddy said, sounding mad about something.

Coming into the A&P parking lot, Liddy had to slow to practically nothing. There were a lot of people pushing grocery carts and carrying sacks, heading for their cars.

"There's a parking place," Jasper told her, but she drove right past it.

Up ahead there was a man standing in the shade under some trees.

"That looks like Dad," Jasper said.

Liddy stopped the car so suddenly, just beside the man, that it shook a little.

"Dad!" Jasper called, leaning out the window, waving, and his father left the shade of the tree and came over to the car. He opened the door for Jasper and stood aside for him to scoot out.

"Jasper, Jasper," his father said, and there in the parking lot he picked him up and kissed him. It was embarrassing to be held like that in a place where anybody could see, and Jasper wriggled to free himself, but his father held on until he was ready to let him slide down to the pavement. "You're coming with me for a while, Jas," his father said. "I haven't seen you in a month of Sundays."

"I was going shopping with Liddy," he said, but his father ignored him. He bent down and looked at Liddy through the car window. "Back here in a couple of hours?" he said.

"Hour and a half," Liddy said, sounding madder than ever.

"Liddy," his father said, and he sounded unhappy. "Don't hold this against me, Liddy."

But Liddy pushed her foot hard on the accelerator and the car spurted away. She didn't look back.

Jasper stood beside his father as Liddy drove away. He would have preferred it if she'd stayed with them. It was strange to meet his father in the A&P parking lot, and he looked different than Jasper remembered. He'd gotten very brown, for one thing, and his hair was cut in a new way so it was longer than usual over his forehead and ears. His watch had slipped down his wrist from its old place so a sliver of white showed on his father's arm like a new moon.

"Ice cream maybe?"

Jasper could tell that his father wouldn't let him have any time to himself—he wouldn't be able to run down to the wharf where the yachts were, though this was what he would have most liked. But since he couldn't do that he might as well run a hard bargain.

"The five-and-dime store," he said. "And then an ice cream after that."

His father had never liked taking him to the five-and-dime because he lingered there too long and his father got bored, but Jasper knew that on that day his father would do whatever he asked.

"Twenty minutes in the five-and-dime," his father said, giving in as Jasper knew he would. "But no longer, Jas."

His father let him buy a boomerang, a family-size packet of Kit Kats, and two action men—a good haul for twenty minutes. But his father tailed behind him impatiently, wanting to get him outside again so he could have him to himself. As soon as the door shut behind them his father started asking questions. How were things going at home? Was Chrissy unhappy? Was he?

Jasper walked along stubbing the toes of his sneakers against the sidewalk, pulling back on his father's hand. "Why aren't you at home with us anymore?" he asked.

And his father, as he knew he would, forgot about the questions he'd just asked in his distress at being asked this one.

"I'm living in another house, with Jane, on the other side of the island," his father said carefully in that way that meant he would go on and on for a long time explaining things.

"I know *that*," Jasper said quickly. "But why do you like living with her better than with us?"

"No, no, it's not like that," his father said, getting upset the way grown-ups so easily did. "It's complicated. But whatever happens between your mother and me, just know I'll always feel the same about you, Jasper. And about Chrissy and Liddy, too. Will you remember that?" His father held his hand tightly, looking down trying to see his face.

But Jasper turned his face away. He knew a lot of kids who lived with their mother part of the time and with their father part of the time, he knew about things like that, and he didn't want to have to listen to his father explain, on and on.

With one yank he pulled his hand free of his father's and ran down the sidewalk. "Race you," he called back. "And if I get there first I get three scoops. With sprinkles."

His father only play-acted running, which was what he knew would happen. Of course, he won and was already sitting on one of the benches kicking his legs back and forth and licking around and around the three scoops so the top one wouldn't fall off by the time his father got his ice cream and sat down too. His father sat in silence, which was a bad sign, since it showed that he was turning serious again, getting lost in thoughts of his own.

"Mom's finished reading *The Hobbit* to me," Jasper told his father quickly. "Now we've started on *The Lord of the Rings*. Mom bought me a copy the other day. And she let me use her camera to take a whole roll of film."

His father just went on taking big bites of his ice cream, trying to finish it off as soon as possible. He ate his own slowly, turning the cone around while he nibbled a little from one side and then the other.

His father finished, wiped his fingers on a napkin, and started talking.

He was explaining something at great length, which Jasper didn't bother to listen to. Whenever he did tune in for a second, there his father was, still going on: "... want you to live with me," his father said, "like Jane ..."

Now his father's voice rose a little and grew silent. There was a question Jasper was supposed to answer.

"I'll stay with Mom," he said, breaking off a tiny bite of cone between his front teeth—so small a bite that it melted in his mouth and he didn't even have to chew. "I'll come visit you on weekends."

"You weren't listening," his father said, and he started explaining all over again. "New York," his father was saying. "If you go with your mother you'll have to live in New York. Maybe not right away, but soon. You'll have to change schools and it'll be all new kids. And you hate making new friends, Jasper. You'd be all cramped in a little apartment somewhere and you couldn't play outside. Or at least you'd have to go to a park where there'd be a lot of other children, never by yourself the way you like to play, out under the trees, climbing over the wall."

"No, I won't have to move," Jasper said. He'd eaten past the ice cream now and was down to nothing but cone.

"Your mother never really liked Providence," his father said. "And now she'll do what she wants to do. You can be sure of that, Jasper. And you could still see her, you know. You'd see her during vacations."

Jasper said nothing as he put the last part of the cone in his mouth and fitted his lips around it—a round disk. He thought about playing astronauts and aliens with Bruce and Evan under the ginkgo trees at the far edge of the playground, and he thought about waking up very early in the morning, in his room under the eaves, and kneeling by the window to watch the sun come up very big and red, just that first slit of red like a knife tearing through something soft.

Looking at his father, he opened and shut his lips around the bottom of the cone, making a face like a fish.

"Think about it, will you, Jas?" his father said. "I want you to stay with me so you won't have to move away from everything you care about."

Jasper suddenly crunched the cone between his teeth, and it splintered into many little pieces.

He did not intend to move from his house and he didn't intend to live with his father if Jane was going to be around too. He would go on living in his room under the eaves, only he wouldn't tell his father he was there. In the middle of the night, when his father and Jane were asleep, he'd go down the stairs to the kitchen and gather up the best food to take to his room. Chrissy might come down with him if she stayed on in her old room. If he wasn't mad at Chrissy he'd let her come too. But the only other person who'd know where he was would be his mother. Maybe she would even stay in his room with him if she and his father were going to get divorced. There was plenty of room for another bed. But if, in spite of everything, she did go off somewhere else to live, then he'd go to visit her whenever he could. When he came to visit he'd bring a big sack of all the things his mother liked best to eat—Gorgonzola cheese and croissants and strawberry jam made from wild strawberries—and his mother would be thrilled to see him. Probably when he came to visit she'd be so glad to see him she'd buy him anything he asked for, even if it cost a great deal of money. But when he went away again she'd be very sad and he'd have to make her laugh to cheer her up.

"I don't think you should tell your mother you saw me today," his father said. They were walking back to the parking lot, and his father was holding his hand. "She'd be very angry and wouldn't like it that Liddy brought you to see me. You can keep a secret, can't you?"

"Sure," he said.

"Okay," his father said. "If you can keep a secret, you can keep this." He took a five-dollar bill out of his wallet and handed it to Jasper. Jasper took the money, but inside one of his pockets his fingers were crossed. He didn't believe in making promises you couldn't get out of—it was dangerous doing that. It was important to make it so that no matter what happened you had a way out.

14

Estella was listening for the sound of the car's motor as Liddy drove back down the lane. When she heard it she laid aside the piece of charcoal she'd been drawing with and went out to help carry in the sacks of groceries. That was her excuse, at least, for coming out to meet Liddy as soon as the car came to a stop beside the tall pine tree at the corner of the house. The truth was she wanted to look closely into Liddy's face. She'd always prided herself on being able to read her children's thoughts—picking up what she needed to know by the gaze held too rigidly steady, by the stiffness of a mouth, by a false note in a voice.

And she saw this time, with a sinking heart, the startled look Liddy gave as she brought the car to a stop and turned off the motor. A startled look too quickly smoothed over.

"We can bring in the groceries," Liddy told her. "You don't have to take the time."

"It seems hard to make you do everything when you've taken the time to go shopping," Estella said.

It was her own eyes that she lowered, not looking at Liddy as she opened the back of the Volvo and lifted two sacks of groceries from the well behind the seats. She hated duplicity and resolved to have no part of it. Later on, at some time when she had Liddy alone, she would ask her outright; she would risk making a fool of herself. Anything was better than sneaking, than trying to catch Liddy out in an unguarded moment when her face might reveal more than she'd intended.

She was resolved to look with suspicion on neither Jasper nor Liddy. But when she had the last sack of groceries in her arms and was glancing into the backseat to see if anything had been left there, she saw a small sack with a boomerang extending from its mouth. And knew instantly where the sack had come from and who had bought the boomerang for Jasper. She could see it clearly, the way Philip had followed Jasper around in the five-and-dime, watching him with hungry, anxious eyes. She might have been there with them, two steps behind Philip, she saw it all so clearly, and the sight filled her with dismay and anger.

Devious. Her children were devious, turning on her their bland and seemingly guileless eyes.

She watched Liddy as they put away the food together, moving carefully through the kitchen trying not to get in one another's way. It was like an intricate dance the way they stood side by side putting cans and boxes into the upper shelves of the cabinet without once ever quite touching, not elbows nor thighs nor even feet. Estella was aware, since she knew at least this much about Liddy, that the way she tossed her head so that her hair lifted from the back of her neck and fell farther down on her shoulders was a self-conscious gesture. Liddy pretending ease and innocence.

But she said nothing to her, choosing to bide her time.

It wasn't until much later, after dinner, that Estella saw from the deck Liddy walking alone along the beach in the direction of the point and knew that she wouldn't have a better opportunity to talk to Liddy alone. She jumped into the sand and hurried after her, though she dreaded confronting her with what she knew.

Liddy didn't wait, but she was walking slowly, looking out over the water, which had turned glassy in the late-afternoon light, and it wasn't difficult to catch up.

"When you went to town this afternoon you met Philip, didn't you?" she said.

Startled, Liddy couldn't keep from looking once into her mother's face—a glance so quick and abrupt it was almost like being struck.

When she spoke it was to the water she seemed to be aiming her answer.

"I didn't exactly meet him," she said.

(204)

"What's that supposed to mean?" Estella said. "You either met him or you didn't."

"I hardly saw him at all," Liddy said. "I didn't say more than three words to him. It was Jasper I took to town to meet him."

Estella halted where she was, in the sand, not trusting herself to speak. "I see," she said finally.

Liddy had walked on, but now she stopped too and half turned around. "No you don't," she said. "You don't see at all."

There was an unexpected bleakness in Liddy's voice that curbed Estella's anger, and she walked on slowly.

"If you hadn't felt sneaky about what you were doing, you'd have told me, Liddy. Don't you agree? You'd have said you were going to meet Philip in town and you were taking Jasper with you."

"And if I had done that? What would have happened if I'd done that? Tell me. What would you have said?"

"You know exactly what I would have said. I'd have told you that if you wanted to see Philip then that was your business. You're grown up and can do what you want to. But I wouldn't have let you take Jasper."

"You see?" Liddy said though she didn't sound triumphant. "I knew you'd say no if I asked you about Jasper, so there was nothing to do except sneak."

"It was Philip who made that arrangement, wasn't it?" Estella said, knowing suddenly how it had all been worked out.

"Yes," Liddy said sullenly.

"How did he know you were back?"

"We saw each other by chance, in town one day."

"And he talked you into taking Jasper to meet him. All that elaborate setup about going to town to buy groceries. I hate the thought that I can't trust you, Liddy."

"But what do you expect of me?" Liddy said passionately. "Both of you. I don't want anything to do with it. I want to be left out, left alone, but you can't do that, can you? I'm trapped between the two of you."

"Liddy," Estella said firmly, "do you seriously think he should have everything his own way? That he should see Jasper whenever he wants to? Whatever he wants? Do you really think that?"

"No," Liddy said. "I *hated* seeing him again. Don't you know that? I hated the whole thing. But you can't really be surprised I didn't tell you I was taking Jasper to meet Dad. I'd have been crazy to do that."

"If you'd told me, you couldn't have done it, could you?" Estella said. "Admit that too, Liddy. Your promise to him was more important than telling me he was asking you to do it."

"All right, I promised him," Liddy said, her voice rising. "I told you I promised him. Okay? So I'm guilty. What do you want? My head?"

"Don't be melodramatic," Estella said. "He put you in an awful position. I do see that, Liddy."

It was on the tip of her tongue to say, But you could have said no. Would that have been too much to ask? Just to say no? But she bit these words back. What she wanted—terribly—was to have Liddy on her side. To have Liddy unequivocally on her side.

"I don't want to have anything to do with it," Liddy said, the way she would have asked, when she was a child, to be allowed to stay at home while the rest of them went somewhere in the car.

"Who does want anything to do with it?" Estella said. "Do I? But I wasn't given a choice in the matter. And I'm afraid you don't have a choice either, Liddy. Pretending it doesn't exist won't change anything."

But Liddy, her hands deep in her pockets, her shoulders stiff, was hurrying down the beach, determined, Estella could see, to get away.

"Liddy!" she called. "Don't go away in a huff."

But Liddy rushed on, a figure growing smaller and smaller, until not even a shout could have drawn her back.

15

Liddy woke angry the next morning, and everything she saw when she opened her eyes was altered by her anger—even the sunlight on the pine trees she could see from her window. Of course, the house was silent; the rest of them had eaten breakfast a long time before.

Impatiently she got out of bed and made a cup of tea in the kitchen. Standing with it in her hands, looking out past the deck to the water, she knew she didn't want to go outside, didn't want to stay in the kitchen, didn't want to do anything. After a time she wandered back to the bedroom and sat on the edge of the bed.

Feeling helpless was what she couldn't stand—the way she'd let her father maneuver her into a corner that had necessarily gotten her into trouble with Estella—getting flung this way and that like the person on the end of the line in crack-the-whip.

Angrily she got up from the bed and walked up and down the room, sloshing tea over her bare feet. It was herself she couldn't stand for allowing it all to happen, for letting herself slip into the swamp where the others were already floundering. She remembered thinking while she was still in England that she could stay above it all; she would be the one standing impartially above, telling the others what they should do. But now it was herself she was discontent with, and this feeling tainted everything she saw or touched—the unmade bed, the rumpled rug at her feet. The half-open door of her closet, revealing the mess inside, seemed to her particularly intolerable.

She strode across the floor, flung the door wide, and squatted on her heels, looking with loathing at those outgrown sneakers, those socks wadded into balls.

On her hands and knees, pawing like a dog digging a hole, Liddy began covering the floor behind her with debris. In her anger she would be ruthless, throwing out everything.

At first it was easy, since there was no reason whatever to continue keeping shoes she could no longer wear, socks without mates, tennis balls that had lost their bounce, hunks of modeling clay that had grown furry with dust in the dim reaches of the closet. But as she moved deeper in and came to the boxes stacked against the walls, dismay came over her. It was here that she'd put out of sight all those boxes of games, puzzles, kits for making potholders, Indian beadwork, leather billfolds, and moccasins—all those things that Estella and Philip had given her at one time or another for birthdays, or to liven a rainy day.

All those evidences of their love. It was because of this that she had kept those presents she'd never liked and had stacked them against the back wall of her closet. When she was a child, presents often made her feel guilty, because so few of them gave her pleasure; when she'd put them out of sight in her closet she'd thought she wouldn't have to think about them anymore. It had seemed cruel not to appreciate other people's attempts to give her joy, and she'd never wanted to be reminded of this.

But now, holding back the rack of clothes so she could see those stacks of boxes, those furled kites, and even a doll, wrapped in a blanket, she saw them differently. Pleas for *her* love, she suddenly knew. That's what they really were, all those presents. Not so much to give her pleasure as to buy her love; *that* was why she'd never felt free to throw away those things she didn't want—it had been simpler to put the whole thing out of her mind by stacking the boxes in the back of her closet.

It was this way of thinking, she could see clearly enough now when it was too late, that had made her say to Philip that just once she would bring Jasper to town to meet him.

It occurred to her as she held back her clothes with one arm, straining her eyes to see in the dim light, that what she'd been accused of sometimes by friends—being cool and inaccessible—was entirely wrong. The truth was she was too easily made to feel guilty. The real trouble was she hadn't been ruthless enough.

In a rage she pulled a stack of boxes toward her and began tossing them out of the closet, scattering them over the floor behind her. She'd keep nothing, would make her life as clean as that closet when she'd finished with it. The thought eased her.

With her head pushed under the clothes, she heard Jasper's voice behind her. "What are you doing, Lid?" he said, pulling on one of her heels.

"Can't you see what I'm doing?" she said. "Cleaning my closet. Throwing everything out."

"Everything?" he said. "Can I have anything you don't want, then?"

She crawled from the closet to see Jasper crouching on the floor sorting through boxes and Chrissy sitting behind him, her arms around her knees.

"I'm trying to get some work done," she said. "Can't you see that? And you're not going to help any, either one of you."

"If you're throwing all this stuff out, can't I take whatever I want?" Jasper said again.

"No."

He looked at her indignantly. "Some of the boxes haven't even been opened," he said. "They're brand-new. It would be a terrible waste."

"You won't do anything with them either," she told him. "It's nothing but greed."

Jasper had picked up one of the boxes and was running his fingernail through the cellophane that encased it. "Let me have this one anyway, Lid," he said. "It's a belt with Indian beads on it, and I need a belt."

"All right," she said reluctantly. "That one thing. But no more, Jasper. That's it."

"I need a billfold, too," Jasper said, drawing one of the other boxes to him. "And here's some moccasins to stitch together, just my size, I think."

"No!" Liddy said. "Can't you understand the English language? Are you deaf? I said no. No. No. No."

"But that doesn't make any sense," Jasper said, his eyes growing wide. "You're just going to throw these things out to get buried or burned or something. And I can *use* them. You're being mean for no reason at all."

"The point is," she said in an icy voice, "I'm trying to get rid of this stuff. If you carry it all off to your room it's just been moved from one closet to another. That isn't getting rid of it."

"It is as far as you're concerned," Jasper said, holding three of the boxes on his lap.

"I don't need this trouble from you," Liddy said. "It's hard enough as it is."

Between two of the boxes Chrissy found a folded piece of drawing paper and opened it out on the floor. "I'd forgotten about this," she said. "I made it for you once, Lid. Remember?"

Liddy looked at the drawing, which showed animals—lions and elephants and monkeys—standing in front of piles of squiggly shapes she knew were supposed to represent food. The animals had their tongues out of their mouths to show that they were licking their chops. "Yeah," Liddy said. "Animal Heaven. Sure, I remember that."

"If you don't want it, I'll take it," Chrissy said.

"I didn't know it was in the pile," Liddy said. "I didn't mean to throw it away."

"You don't have to keep it. I'll take it if you want to clear everything out of your closet."

"I *said* I wanted to keep it, dammit," Liddy said, taking the drawing out of Chrissy's hands and tossing it onto the bed.

"You don't have to."

"I *want* it," Liddy said. "What do I have to say? I want it to pass down to my children and my children's children. A treasure we'll keep in the family forever."

"You don't have to make a joke about it," Chrissy said, hurt.

"Goddammit!" Liddy said. "Can't you both just go? Leave me in peace? Let me clean out my goddam *closet?*"

With great dignity, their eyes averted from her face, Jasper and Chrissy got up from the floor and went toward the door. They could have been tiptoeing for all the noise they made.

"Look," Liddy said. "I'm sorry I screamed at you. But it was aggravating. You must see that."

Jasper walked past her, his hands empty.

"I thought you wanted that Indian belt," she said to him. "You could take it. I said I didn't care."

He shook his head before he opened the door and passed through it. Behind him he closed it gently.

"Listen, Jasper," she called through the door to him. "I'm going to put all this stuff in a garbage bag and set it out on the deck. You can take anything you want to out of it, but I don't want to know about it. All right?"

He didn't reply. All she could hear was the faint sounds of their footsteps in the hallway. She knew how their heads were hanging, how sad their faces looked.

Sitting down beside the closet door, she put her head down on her bent knees. "Shit," she said. "Just shit."

It was no good even finishing with the closet, since now that remorse had overtaken her it would be impossible to be ruthless. She couldn't even do a thing as simple as cleaning out a closet.

As she bent over with her eyes closed, she suddenly saw the quadrangle under the yellow-and-orange leaves and herself walking there under them, fast, her knapsack of books on her back and her Cambridge scarf around her neck, the ends stuck into the pockets of her jacket. And she was filled with the urgency to be there, to be hurrying to a class, happy. But it didn't seem possible that this would ever happen—that she would ever walk again under those trees, her head as empty and pure as the sky. It seemed as remote as being grown up had done when she was six. A lifetime away.

16

Every time Estella went into town she half expected it would be the time she'd see Philip and Jane together coming out of the post office or turning the postcard stand idly around and around inside the stationer's—the meeting she knew was bound to take place sooner or later, since the island was small, after all. And for a time she'd avoided going into town, sending Liddy or Chrissy instead, wanting to avoid that meeting in public when surprise, if nothing else, would make her heart beat wildly and her hands tremble.

But after Philip's meeting with Jasper, anger was like a current running through her, giving her strength. She wanted to meet them, would welcome the chance to tell Philip what she thought of him. "You're nothing but a cheap little liar, using your children to do your dirty work for you," she would tell him. "Did you know that's the kind of man you're getting?" she'd say to Jane. "A man like that?"

They would be more surprised than she would, she told herself. They'd be the ones looking for escape routes.

And yet, the afternoon when she did see them, she was taken by surprise after all. The odd thing was that on that particular afternoon she hadn't been thinking about them and hadn't bothered looking down the sidewalk trying to pick Philip's face out of the crowd. She was in a hurry and had just come to town to buy printing paper—to dash in and out buying that one thing and not even bothering to stop at a grocery store.

The car was parked down a side street and she was heading for it, the unwieldy roll of paper under her arm, a roll so long that she had to be careful not to knock people with it as she passed them on the sidewalk. It was that she was thinking about—the paper and the crowded sidewalk and whether she'd put the car keys in the pocket of her jacket or in her purse. Her head full of all these things, she looked up, by chance it seemed, to the top of the steps leading down from the old Friends' Meeting House— quite a distance away—and saw, as though through magnification, even her eyes behaving strangely, Philip and a dark-haired woman just turning away from the door and heading for the steps.

Estella stood absolutely still in the middle of the sidewalk, forgetting altogether that this was an awkward thing to do, especially since she was holding the roll of paper, which extended in front and behind her. The only thing that existed for her in those seconds was Philip's head tipped toward Jane and Jane's, lowered, turned toward him. Instantly she'd taken in everything, even noting that Philip was wearing the blue-and-white shirt she'd helped him pick out at Saks on one of their trips to New York, but it was Jane she couldn't take her eyes from, though Jane's hair, falling over one cheek, hid her face. Tall, slim (oh, she would be slim, Estella thought bitterly), wearing a pale green knit top and gray slacks, nothing remarkable there at all, not the clothes of someone who cared a great deal, shoulders a little hunched, or maybe that was because she was listening so intently to Philip as the two of them slowly descended the steps. Older than Estella had thought. No girl. In looks—she noted it at once—a little like Liddy, but a less certain Liddy, one who moved more cautiously. But if anything that resemblance was a relief to her. At least it was proof that it was still the familiar Philip preferred; he had not fallen in love with a honey-haired girl with skin like milk.

There was definitely something, oh, scrunched-up about Jane, she thought. That stiff way she held her arms, that way she had of tipping her head in Philip's direction. Jane was someone who would hang on to every word. *That* kind of woman, not at all her own sort. But he *would* go for that—being put on a pedestal, spoiled the way academics so often were, getting used to being made little tin gods. How much it revealed about him—and the thought gave her satisfaction—seeing the woman he'd gone out of his way to fall in love with.

(213)

They were almost to the bottom of the steps, and she knew that when they did reach the bottom they'd be certain to lift their heads if only to see the sidewalk in front of them. They'd see her standing as unavoidably solid as a rock, since with her roll of paper she took up most of the space between building and sidewalk.

It was without thought or consideration that she looked around in sudden panic, seeking cover; when she saw an alleyway just behind her—she must have passed it a minute before but hadn't noticed—she slid into it as urgently as a fish into water, all thoughts of confrontation having left her. She told herself it was the surprise—she needed to prepare herself to carry off the scene she'd planned—but she knew it was more than this. In her favor, she knew she wanted to see more, to watch Philip and Jane when they were unaware, but she also knew that the fear that had made her take cover was unexpected and even baffling.

Pressing her shoulders against the building behind her, she looked around the corner and saw that Philip and Jane had reached the sidewalk, still walking slowly, coming toward her. Philip was gesticulating with his hands, intent on what he was saying. It was utterly familiar to her, that way he had of gesticulating, though it was odd seeing it from the outside, from a distance. Jane was looking down, looking away, her head inclined in Philip's direction, thoughtful, or that was what she appeared to be, a stance also familiar since Estella recognized it as one she'd assumed many times herself. Only she'd not been so submissive-looking, surely? And much of the time when she'd leaned her head to Philip she hadn't been listening to him after all. She'd be noticing the pattern stains had made on the bricks or the odd way the shadow of an awning fell against a building—not hearing a word Philip was saying.

But in spite of that she knew all the same what Philip was telling Jane as they slowly approached. Since they'd just come from the Friends' Meeting House, Estella was certain that the story Philip was telling was one she knew by heart and could easily have told Jane herself. It was the story of the small boy Philip being taken to silent Meeting at his grand-parents' house Sunday after Sunday—all the family gathering in that staid and stiff parlor, unable to attend a larger and possibly more interesting Meeting because the old grandmother had had a stroke and was unable to leave the house. So they all came over every Sunday to sit on chairs lined up facing the heavily laden bookshelves. How interminable and melancholy it had all seemed to Philip, with his legs pricking against the cushions of the mohair sofa, listening to the solemn sound of the old clock in the corner going slowly tick...tock...tick...tock like the very sound of eternity itself. "Even to this day I can't abide hearing the ticking of a clock," he was probably saying at that moment to Jane. "I could easily be driven *mad* by that sound, if anyone wanted to torture me."

So Estella had been the one to suffer by taking the children to Meeting when they were small, though, as she was fond of saying to Philip, she wasn't the birthright Quaker and had never cared for churchgoing of any kind. In the very meetinghouse Philip and Jane had just left, Estella had sat on the hard, straight-backed pews and tried to hush the children's restlessness by taking pencils and paper furtively from her purse and passing them out. Philip, when he had accompanied them at all, had sat with his head lowered, a look of patient stoicism on his face. He was the one who had already suffered too much in that silence and could not be expected to do anything further now that he was finally grown up and free to leave it behind. Of course, she'd felt sorry for him, as she supposed Jane did now, hearing the story for the first time—the too sensitive little boy being forced to sit still for what seemed an eternity in the old house where the curtains had been drawn against the sunlight and the solemn ticking of the clock filled the silence. She should know, if anybody did, Philip's power to impress his story on another person.

They were so close now, still walking in that slow, almost detached way, showing how engrossed they were, that Estella drew back into the alleyway. She'd propped the roll of paper against the wall and so was unencumbered; there was nothing to stop her from striding from her cover, planting herself firmly in the middle of the sidewalk, and barring their way like an avenging angel, her eyes fixed on Philip's face. "Liddy told me about the way you talked her into bringing Jasper to meet you," she would say in a resounding voice. "Did you think I wouldn't find out? You should be ashamed, forcing your own daughter into lying and conniving." How he would hate that private scene made public on a Nantucket street! Vulgar he would think it, though he wouldn't say so; all he'd want would be escape and balm for his humiliation. There would be something immensely dramatic and satisfying about her sudden appearance in front of them—almost as though she had descended from the sky for the purpose.

And yet she stood where she was, feeling the seconds slip by. Maybe it was the deliberation that held her against the wall—she needed the shock of acting on the moment—or perhaps she was waiting until she saw the toes of their shoes and a portion of their legs revealed not more than two feet away from where she stood.

But when she did see the toes of their shoes—Philip's boating sneaker and Jane's sandal—and then their legs and Jane's hand resting on her shoulder bag come into view, she still didn't move. It was something else that held her.

She could see perfectly the rough skin around Jane's thumbnail—clear evidence that in moments of doubt she still chewed her fingernails—and the somehow feeble thinness of her arm, held so carefully against her side. Jane had lifted her head so that her hair had fallen back from her cheek, and to Estella's eyes there was something pinched about that cheek, the muscles too tightly held. An ordinary person, and not at all the way she'd pictured her before. Philip, with his head still turned toward Jane, was talking so that she could hear the murmur of his voice and even a string of perfectly enunciated words—"I couldn't stop myself," he was saying—as he passed by. How trivial he sounded! Yet how seriously they both took themselves, with their intent faces and the careful way they walked, allowing their shoulders just to touch. Relief came over Estella as she watched—they were so inconsequential, both of them.

She watched them pass from her view, and then they were gone. Not even the sound of Philip's voice carried back to her.

Only then did she spring to the opening of the alleyway and stand, totally vulnerable if one of them had chanced to look back. But she knew neither of them would. And it was of the greatest importance that she watch them as long as possible, confirming what she'd known as she watched them pass in front of the alley.

From the shadow of the buildings they emerged, far down the street, and came out into sunlight—for a moment Jane raised her hand to shield her eyes—and then they turned right so that the glare of the sun fell on the tops of their heads and not on their faces. At the curb Philip took Jane's arm—that old-fashioned gesture she knew so well that it was on her own arm she felt his fingers.

And with that remembered touch she felt a pang of pain take her by surprise so that she gasped and dug her knuckles into her ribs—though that wasn't the location of the pain, exactly. It was so unfair, that sharp pang, as though something inside herself had given way with a little lurch, just when she was sure she was beyond all that.

Watching them cross the street, because she couldn't help herself, she saw them pass out of sight beyond the next block of buildings, and still she stood, looking at the place where she'd last seen them. Illogically enough, it was loss she felt—loss and disappointment. If she could have, she would have followed their progress down the street, as near to them as the heels of their shoes, a presence they couldn't shake.

After she'd recovered her roll of paper from the alley, she made her way to the car, feeling as she had when she was a girl emerging into the blazing sun after two hours in cool darkness watching a movie matinee— disoriented and melancholy. When she reached the car she fell back against the seat, grateful even for the heat that made her head buzz. If she'd been running for an hour she couldn't have been more exhausted—so exhausted, in fact, that she was past caring about anything. That was all she knew about her state as she took the key from her pocket and turned on the ignition.

17

It wasn't just because of that afternoon Liddy and Jasper spent together with Philip—that afternoon only confirmed something Chrissy knew anyway: Liddy and Jasper had a secret understanding between them. She, who had been close first to Liddy and then to Jasper, was the one left out, the one hanging around the edges.

In the evening she watched them as Liddy and Jasper sat side by side on the deck at dusk, dangling their legs under the railing, looking at the fireflies flickering in the heavier darkness under the trees and talking softly the way two people do who are so close they can practically share thoughts. Behind them, Chrissy sat with her back against the wall of the house watching every move they made; if they turned around they could see her, staring at their backs. But they didn't turn around. They knew she was sitting behind them—the very fact that they never once turned around showed her that. They thought if they ignored her bad temper it would go away and they wouldn't have to trouble themselves.

Estella came out on the deck from the kitchen, and under her buttocks Chrissy could feel the boards tremble with her tread.

"Do you want to walk down to the water with me?" she asked. "Chrissy? Do you want to come?"

But Chrissy shook her head no, and her eyes, fixed on the space where Liddy's and Jasper's shoulders touched, did not waver. What she was holding herself back from doing was pushing Liddy and Jasper sprawling into the sand. Spitting sand out of their mouths, they would have to take note of her, that was for sure. But it was more than this she wanted.

"Why don't you come for a walk?" Estella said. "Keep me company for a while."

It was that coaxing note in her mother's voice that annoyed Chrissy so much—Estella speaking to her the same way she had when Chrissy was four. "No," she said. "I don't want to go for a walk. All I want is to be left alone."

"All she wants," Liddy said without turning her head, "is to make everybody miserable."

Chrissy got up, brushed past Estella, and went inside the house. There was nowhere else to go, since she had just said she didn't want to go for a walk—nothing to do except go into the room she shared with Liddy and close the door. If she listened, she could still hear the voices of the others on the deck, but she didn't choose to listen. She lay down in darkness on the bed where she had not slept for so long, and looked up at the ceiling.

It was all ruined. Everything, everything was ruined.

The only question was whether or not this ruin would still have come about even if Philip had not gone off to live with Jane. Sometimes she thought it wouldn't have made any difference—it would all have happened anyway, only perhaps not as quickly. But other times she was sure that if Philip were still there things would be all right. If he were there Liddy and Jasper wouldn't be so thick, for one thing; if he were there they'd both be spending time with him, and so of course the balance would be different. That was the way she saw her family—like the Wallendas making a human pyramid suspended in air on nothing but a fine rope. Naturally if something happened to one of them the whole thing would collapse and they'd all be flung out into the air—that was so obvious it didn't even need remarking on. And where Philip had once been there was now a big blank. A nothing.

She wondered if Philip had talked about her when he met Liddy and Jasper that day. Had he been disappointed because she hadn't come along too? Did he think about her, in that other life of his? But she'd never know, since she'd never ask Liddy or Jasper; she'd rather die than ask either of them.

But of course she *could* go and see him for herself. That wouldn't be hard to do. In fact, it would be very easy. All she'd have to do would be what Liddy had done—offer to go to town to do the shopping. And then once she was in the car, she could keep going—Madaket wasn't so far. And she remembered very well the instructions her father had given in the letter he'd sent her. The house would be easy to find.

If she wanted to see him, she could.

She lay on her bed with her hands in the pockets of her shorts, looking up at the ceiling and thinking about whether she did or didn't want to see Philip. But perhaps she should see him if only to let him know that he couldn't believe every word Liddy and Jasper told him. She should do that much at least.

Yet the next day she wasn't certain she'd go to Madaket to see Philip—not even after she'd told Estella that she'd go into town to buy milk and fruit. She didn't decide until she was driving away from the Grand Union and had to make the decision—one direction or the other. Even then it didn't feel like a decision exactly; she just turned right instead of left, that was all. At any point she could change her mind—even when she was halfway down the Madaket Road she could still turn around. Even when she saw the house loom, exactly as her father had described, and came close enough to the mailbox to read the name.

No one was on the deck, but she studied the two beach towels hanging over its rail, looking at them as though they might hold some message.

Beside the mailbox, she came to a stop.

No one moved behind the glass in any of the windows, but this did not keep her from having a sudden vision: behind the bare windows of the house which looked out only on sky, her father and Jane lay together, their legs intertwined, their faces nearly touching.

Never, she realized then, could she go up to that house where, when she knocked, she would hear after a silence that soft padding of her father's feet in the hallway before he opened the door and she would see him standing in his robe, pulling the ends of the belt tightly around his waist. "Yes?" he would say.

Suddenly Chrissy pressed so hard on the accelerator that small stones were flung upward from the back tires. It wasn't until she was far down the road, to the place where the dunes led to the sea, that she stopped. There she climbed out of the car, uncertain what to do next.

Near the water there were a man and two little boys, the man walking in the middle holding a child's hand on either side, but there was no one else in sight. There seemed no particular reason to turn in either direction, but it was to the left Chrissy turned finally—into the sun.

As she walked she looked over the water where the light glinted. When she turned away to the beach again she could still see the colors—deep purple and blue—the afterimage of all that light. Strange to see the world so easily transformed and made as eerie as the objects on a film negative. Of course it had always been there, that dark afterimage—all you had to do was look closely and then you knew. The bright was always followed by the dark.

Because the sun was so much in her eyes that she had to squint, she did not see Philip and Jane until she was only yards away, too close to turn and run. Side by side they sat in the hollow between two low dunes, their hands clasped around their knees. Something about the way they were sitting with their hands so carefully held, the right over the left, brought home to her their intimacy together—it was the same posture, exactly, each of them held as they looked up and saw her.

She came to an instant halt and immediately felt enormous standing there—an object too big to move quickly away or to hide. If she could have, she would have canceled herself out as she stood rooted there on the sand.

In that moment when Philip first lifted his head and could hide nothing, she saw surprise in his face and just the faintest flicker of fear. But then he was getting to his feet, pulling Jane up with him, and his face smoothed over so it was impossible to read as he called out loudly to her and hurried across the sand.

She stood very still when he put his arms around her, hugging too tightly, and when he let her go she looked down at the rounded rubber tips of her sneakers.

"I'm so glad to see you, Chris," he said. "I was afraid you'd never come to see me. Come over here and meet Jane."

He grabbed her hand before she could move and pulled her along the same way he had done when she was a child, hauling her down to the slate-colored waves on a cloudy day when she was afraid of the water. Then she had fought him, had kicked and squatted low to the ground, had struggled and shouted until—just where the waves broke and foamed hissing into the crabs' holes—he had let her go.

But this time she had to allow herself to be pulled along until her father said, "This is Jane," and she shook the hand that was extended to her. Not to have done that much would have been terribly rude.

"You were on the ferry when I came over," Jane said. "Do you remember? You were leaning over the railing so far I was afraid you'd fall in the water."

"No," Chrissy said. "I don't remember that."

But she had to lower her eyes as she spoke, because it was a lie; of course she remembered.

"I *knew* Chris would come to see me," her father said triumphantly to Jane. "Didn't I say that?"

"Yes," Jane said, but she looked hurt.

Chrissy turned to her father, and it seemed to her that his jaw had grown broader than she remembered. All summer he seemed to have been eating food too rich to be good for him, and there was a sleekness about him that hadn't been there before.

It was awkward, the way they were standing, her father with his arm heavily across her shoulders as though he were afraid she might run away.

"I'm going to take a long walk down the beach, Philip," Jane said. "I'll see you back at the house."

Her father didn't object, but Chrissy could feel him grow quiet. He'd wanted to keep Jane there with them.

A kind of shyness fell between them when Jane had gone, and neither could think of anything to say. Chrissy remembered that it had always been like that when they were alone together, though before it hadn't mattered, since they'd known well enough what the other was thinking. Now things had happened between them that made the old connection hard to reach. That man with the broad, sleek jaw didn't seem like her father to Chrissy; a stranger had slipped into his body.

"Tell me how things are going," he said at last.

They were walking along the beach, retracing the way she had come, and he left his arm over her shoulders like a heavy bar. It was hard to walk that way, so close together—they were walking in different rhythms, it seemed, and their legs kept bumping. But he didn't want to take his arm from her shoulders. Or, now that he'd started walking that way, he felt awkward about lifting his arm away—she might think that he didn't want to have his arm around her after all.

There were so many things to tell him, but she didn't know how to start, which thread to pull.

"Liddy and Jasper are together a lot," she said.

"Jasper probably missed Liddy," he said, his attention elsewhere. "Are you still sleeping in the tent? You and Jasper?"

She nodded her head. "Liddy's the only one sleeping in the house."

"Finished reading Tinbergen?"

"I've finished *Animal Societies*," she told him. "I'm reading Konrad Lorenz now."

Their conversations had always been like this as they walked slowly toward the point late in the afternoons; he had waited for her when she stopped to pick up a rock or to lift, for a moment, a cluster of sea grapes from the sand before she let them drop again. "There was a higher tide than usual last night," he would say. "See how far up the water came?" Or he would point out a bird call to her and make her listen closely. "Hear that little marsh wren?" he would ask. "Rare to hear one of those here."

But they hadn't needed to say any more. This was the pattern of their talk. It was only to her he would have pointed out the marsh wren; to the others he talked of different things. And it had never occurred to her to wonder, before, if he enjoyed talking to Liddy or Jasper more than he did to her. She had always been sure that what they shared was special and important. But now, as she walked awkwardly beside him, trying to adjust her stride to his, she wondered if perhaps when he was with her he talked of birds and baboons and whales because there was something lacking in her—something that made any other kind of conversation impossible. Maybe with Liddy and Jasper he felt much more at ease. She didn't know.

"Have you taken the Sunfish out much?" he asked.

She told him no. Only Liddy had taken it out a couple of times on the pond.

"You know I was teaching Jasper to sail," he said. "I thought maybe you'd taken over."

"Jasper's been busy doing other things. He never liked going out on the boat with me very much."

Surely her father knew that Jasper didn't like going on the Sunfish with her because he feared she was unreliable in water. It was something he'd once known, only now perhaps he'd forgotten all those details of his old life.

All along there must have been something about living with them that her father hadn't liked. For a long time, maybe, he'd only pretended to be happy. How could she know? She couldn't tell that any more than she could tell whether or not it was true that she shared something special with him that was theirs alone.

"Look," he said suddenly, pulling her around and pointing out over the water. "Do you see that? Someone's dragon kite carried away by the wind. The string must have snapped."

There it was, rippling along, too high up to have any connection with the ground.

"Jasper would have a fit," she said. "If it was his we'd have to go out and buy him another one."

She'd spoken before she remembered that it was the night of Jasper's birthday that her father had left, and she gave him a quick, uneasy look. But he seemed to have noticed nothing.

In the distance she could see the path leading from the beach to the place where she had left the car. If she didn't speak now, she'd never be able to tell him how things were falling apart. She'd never be able to ask him if he was happy living with Jane. But her tongue pressed against the roof of her mouth and remained silent.

She had a sudden picture of her father walking along a beach—this beach, perhaps, or some other—holding by the hand a child, another little girl, so young she would fall if he did not hold on. How carefully he would fit his steps to hers, showing her the crabs' holes, showing her the terns wheeling above their nests. All over again, with a new child, he would point out the world. But she could not say to him, What about *us*? Your old family?

They turned away from the beach and followed the footpath to the car sitting up ahead.

"I'll bet nobody's checked the oil since I left," he said. "None of you thinks about anything like that."

So she had to wait while he lifted the hood and wiped the rod from the oil tank between his fingers and then checked the oil level. She longed to leave, but she had to wait for him.

"Tell Estella the oil's getting a little low," he told her. "Remember that, Chris. Best-grade detergent."

Before she could get inside the car, he put his arms around her again and she hugged him back, hard, and quickly let go.

When she was inside the car he leaned down to the lowered window. "Now that you know where I am, Chris," he said, "you must come back to see me."

She was busy fitting the key into the ignition and didn't look up.

"Will you, Chris?" he said again, and she heard the pleading in his voice.

The motor caught just then, and her father moved away from the window.

It wasn't until she was nearly to the road that she looked back and waved and saw that he was still watching her. He lifted his arm too and slowly lowered it. Until she stopped looking into the rearview mirror she could still see him standing the way she'd left him, his arm held stiffly as though he thought he might lift it and wave again.

Chrissy's Animal Essays: Garter Snakes

Even when I was very little I would put my hand on the ground and hold it still for what Liddy and I called a grass snake—one of those little brown-and-rust-and-gold-colored snakes, as slender as a pencil and with large, gentle eyes—to ride over. And if I sat long enough without moving the snake would do this. It would tap my thumb once with its blunt head and then would slide on across, thinking maybe that my hand was nothing more than a little mound pushed up in the dirt by a mole. Or maybe it knew all along that the little mound was a hand. Anyway, if I was quiet enough, it would accept my hand as being some part of the natural world and would ride over, a touch like being licked by a cat's tongue. If the snake had been lying in the spring sun it would be so warm I would want to close my fingers over it and bring it up to my face, to touch my cheek. I could easily imagine that warm, shy touch along my skin and longed to feel it, but I didn't want to scare the snake by moving suddenly. So I sat very still and the snake would pass over my hand and on into the grass, pushing aside the blades with its small, oval head.

They were always alone when I would see them in the summers, those little snakes, though I knew that several often hibernated together under the rock wall at the end of our yard. Once I saw two of them emerge from a crack between rocks in the spring and climb onto the wall to lie in the sun. Once they came out of hibernation they went their own way along the wall and under the dried leaves under the trees on the other side. Except for mating they wouldn't come together again until the late fall, when they might slide again through the same crack in the wall and curl up under the rock. It wasn't company they were looking for when they did congregate under the wall, since all winter they would just sleep. But the space there under the wall was a perfect place to spend the winter, and the snakes all knew this.

Once I came across a garter snake which had just had babies. Or at least I was in time to see the little snakes—no bigger than worms—crawling under the dry leaves of a maple tree. First I saw the cluster of snakes all moving away from each other. And then I saw what I guessed was the mother. She was already several feet away, crawling off in the direction of our pond. Certainly she wasn't paying any attention to the baby snakes. If every one of them had been eaten by a crow fifteen minutes later, she wouldn't have known anything about it. And she wouldn't have cared, anyway.

But the little snakes didn't need her. Already as I watched they were taking cover and moving through the leaves as though sunlight and leaves were things they had known about always. They seemed to know immediately what to do in the strange place they suddenly found themselves in.

Snakes, I think, can never feel lonely. They have no craving to be stroked or nuzzled the way mammals do; they don't love each other, I don't think. They're free of all that.

And yet they enjoy themselves. When they have just eaten a beetle or a baby mouse, they like lying on a warm rock in the morning sun. They lie still with their eyes dulled in sleep, and they have a content look about them.

Since their world is made up of sight and touch and smell, they have to be very alert to detect through reverberations what is usually detected by sound. And that must be exciting—to have the world come to you through your skin.

It would be a good way to live, and sometimes I half wish I were a snake. I'd like never needing anyone except myself and to never feel hungry for something I couldn't have. Why wouldn't anybody choose that if the choice was ever offered?

18

In the house Philip and Jane rented together, the house that stood alone among the moors like the prow of a ship sunk in sand, Jane was jolted each morning when she opened her eyes to the pearly light of earliest day. Each time she tried to transform the room with the bare windows that looked out over the dunes into another room out of her past—her childhood bedroom in Baltimore, where the blue flowers trailed their leaves in regular progression up and down the walls, or the room in New Mexico, where she had waked in the mornings to see the walls of adobe stained with streaks of smoke. Each morning she was panicked—what was she doing in that strange room?—until she felt Philip's warm back under her hand and heard his breathing, deep and slow, the silence between breaths her anchor there in that room under the milky sky. Listening to the gulls calling as they flew lazily overhead, to the raucous cries of the terns rising from their nests, she eased the covers from her legs and slid carefully out of bed.

As she walked from window to window, padding through the house barefooted, standing for minutes with her hands deep in the pockets of her robe and looking out over that strangely bleak landscape—at the trees stunted and twisted by the winds that blew in from the sea in the winters, at that wide expanse of sky—she noted how, in its simplicity, the landscape reminded her of the desert. And she clung to that sense of familiarity, slight though it was.

Coming into the kitchen, opening the doors onto the deck, smelling the warm, salty air as she squeezed oranges and filled the coffeepot with water, she did feel pleasure after all—pleasure coaxed into being each morning as though it were an act of magic that she performed. It pleased her to set out the white plates on the red mats, to find the blue-and-white bowls stacked in a far corner of a cabinet, to find the silver candlesticks behind the double boiler. The people who owned the house had a strange sense of order, but they had good taste. And she liked the resonance that came from those other lives as she used the objects that belonged to them.

As she put the linen napkins under the forks, she heard Philip's feet hitting the floor in the bedroom above the kitchen. Next the door of the bathroom closed and there was the rushing noise of the shower. Just as she lifted the coffeepot from its stand he came into the kitchen smelling of soap, a big man with graying hair, wearing an old T-shirt and shorts, clothes that did not altogether suit him.

Sitting across the table from Philip, watching him stir milk into his coffee, she noticed how golden the hairs were that lay smoothly over his arms, how the bones in his feet made knobs under the skin, and these things—which he was unaware of himself—were moving to her, indications of his vulnerability. She knew things about him he didn't know about himself—the way, for instance, his stubby blond eyelashes grew thickly along his eyelid so that the lid seemed weighted a little and never fully opened. Though it was the slick smoothness of the coffee cup she held in her hands, it was the prickly tension of his eyelashes she could feel on her fingertips. She watched him—she was aware of this—with such care that she might have been memorizing him for some test she would later have to take.

Philip, suddenly aware of her eyes on him, shifted uncomfortably in his chair. "Do I look wild?" he said, running his hand backward over his hair, his eyes looking swiftly and sharply into hers.

"No," she said, embarrassed, dropping her eyes to his chest and then lower still to his hands. Surely it was safe to look at his hands.

"When you look at me that way I get the feeling you can see my thoughts."

"You have that half-awake look that means you're probably still thinking about dreams," she told him evasively.

In fact she knew well enough what he was thinking as he looked over the open and nearly empty land.

The day he came across Liddy in town unexpectedly—when he thought she was still in England—he had been badly shaken, still so agitated when he reached the house that for a long time he couldn't carry on a conversation about anything else. A faraway look came into his eyes and he forgot in the middle of a sentence what he had been about to say.

"I just can't believe she didn't try to get in touch with me," he said. "It was such a shock meeting her that way I could feel my legs turn weak. I couldn't *believe* it was Liddy, right there in the pharmacy on Main Street."

Maybe it was some perversity in her, but Jane felt more sympathy with Liddy's position than with Philip's. She could understand his surprise and shock, but she could feel Liddy's resentment even more sharply. Dragged into a mess—that was the way Liddy must have felt.

When they were still in Philadelphia, Jane had known that Philip should have written Liddy explaining everything. But Philip had put it off. He hated to commit feelings to paper—hated to commit feelings to words at all. And besides that, he wanted too much to keep Liddy's good opinion and was afraid of saying the wrong thing. Liddy wasn't one to be sympathetic to weakness; Jane had seen that clearly enough in her face even in the one photograph Philip had shown her. Liddy wasn't one to compromise or beat around the bush.

So of course Philip was nervous about that meeting with Liddy. Jane would have been terrified of it herself. Yet by the time he left the house to go and meet her he had convinced himself that all would be well; there was even something jaunty about the way he rode his moped down the driveway, waving back to her.

Still, Jane knew it was a false optimism that was carrying him to town—one he'd talked himself into—and so she wasn't surprised when he came back later subdued and a little angry.

He didn't tell her all that had passed between him and Liddy, but she gathered that Liddy had held herself aloof, had refused to be sympathetic. Philip had been left dissatisfied and therefore annoyed.

"I went to all this trouble just to be near them," he said, "and what do they care? They won't trouble themselves."

But Jane knew better than to agree with him, because he would resent it later if she did. Although he might talk to her about his children, he would consider it presumptuous of her if she tried to interpret them to him. So she kept quiet.

But she knew, all the same, that if she had been one of his children she too would have resented being thrown into the middle of all that difficulty and pain. She'd seen it clearly enough in Chrissy's face the day she'd come to the beach and found them together. Jane knew that Chrissy had recogized her as being the woman on the ferry even though she'd denied it. She even understood why Chrissy had pretended not to know her, though she'd been hurt all the same. Of Philip's children, Chrissy was the only one she felt she might have liked. She understood certain things about Chrissy.

She could have told Philip a lot if he'd ever asked her, since she remembered clearly how it had been for her when her father left her mother. She'd known how it had been for her mother, too, even though her mother had kept her feelings to herself and had not burdened Jane with them. The loss of her husband was of no importance—that was the attitude her mother took; she'd told Jane that she'd known for a long time that he couldn't be depended on. Or that was what she implied. But Jane had heard her mother walking up and down in her bedroom in the middle of the night, had seen the dark circles under her eyes in the mornings, and she had known that her mother was both furious and miserable. They just hadn't talked about it.

And Jane had pretended to notice nothing. Had pretended, in fact, to be almost wholly oblivious to her father's absence. When she and her mother sat alone at the dinner table a strange ebullience had come over her and she had talked and talked, telling stories about school and her friends, explaining the plot of the book she was reading, telling about the dreams she'd had the night before—a stream of words had come from her mouth so that later she felt tired and dismayed, as if she'd been visited by a fit of some kind.

Her father left home when she was eight, but they'd never been close. She feared she bored her father, who never seemed to listen with more than the vaguest attention to whatever she told him, and as a result she never felt at ease in his company, nor safe somehow. He might take her somewhere and then forget she was with him, leaving her behind in a department store or in the restroom of a filling station.

So when he left the house and didn't come back, she wasn't aware of missing him, exactly. On the whole she found it a relief not to have to endure the unease she'd felt in his company. Yet she'd also been aware that her mother missed him far more than she pretended to—that she was in fact devastated by his rejection, though not once did she ever say this to Jane. And Jane gave no sign that she understood, hiding instead behind a barrage of words. To listen to them talk when they were alone it would seem that Jane's father had sunk into oblivion leaving no trace.

And so it was not at all difficult for Jane to guess what Philip's children were feeling on the far side of the island. She understood them well enough even though Philip—it seemed clear to her—bore no resemblance to her own father. Philip did take pains. He had played with his children and listened to them and had been in all the obvious ways a good father. And it was this, she knew, that had drawn her to him in the first place. Here was a man, she was sure, who would not let her down. If he would go to such trouble to remain a good father to his children, surely he would remain dependable for her too.

That was what she had thought in the beginning, at least.

At night when he held her tightly to him she could see in his eyes a feverish intensity as he said, "I love you, Jane. God, how I love you." Something trembled inside her then, and she wanted to let go and be submerged in that intensity. Wasn't that what she had always wanted?

And yet she couldn't do it.

Even as she lay half lost in Philip's arms, something in her also drew back and watched from a distance. It was this clear-eyed, dispassionate self that distrusted him after all. It wasn't, she was nearly sure, really she that he saw when he looked at her with such intensity—his eyes, in their depths, focused on something beyond her, something that left her out.

It was at those times, when she looked on Philip with that kind of clarity, that she knew it wasn't necessarily love that had brought him back to the island and his children, just as it might not have been love she could see in his eyes when he held her close. Perhaps it was something more controlling and willful than love was supposed to be.

So she studied him across the breakfast table as she studied him at night when they lay together.

She lifted her mug of coffee to her lips, but set it down again without drinking. "If you want to know what I think," she said, "it's that children don't tell either parent the truth. There's the grown-up world and there's the world of children, and the two are completely separate. I remember that from when I was eight."

But Philip was not listening to her. He was merely waiting until she finished talking so he could say something else.

"But of course," she said stiffly, "I don't have children of my own, and maybe I was just strange when I was a child. I'm sure I was, in fact."

It was impossible for her to explain to him what she felt—not when he was looking at her in that absentminded way. And she suddenly wondered if her own father, after he left home, had ever talked to a woman friend of his the way Philip talked to her—if her father had concerned himself with the daughter he had left behind, even to the extent of wondering what Jane thought about him. She was almost certain he hadn't. If he had been withdrawn when he was with her, wouldn't he have put her out of his mind altogether when he never saw her anymore?

But no one could accuse Philip of ignoring his children or forgetting them, either, no matter what it was that had drawn him back to the island. Certainly he hadn't turned his back on them as her father had done on her.

Suddenly she felt a sharp stab of jealousy toward Philip's children, who could afford such casualness about him. They could afford indifference, after all, because they were so sure of him—a certainty she had never had in her life.

"Why should you bend over backward to court your children all the time?" she said to Philip. "Let them come to you."

"Old habits," he said, looking unhappy.

"They would respect you more," she said. "Why should you cater to them all the time?"

"I don't think I *cater* to them, exactly, Jane."

"Oh, of course you do," she said in irritation, getting up from the table. "All the time. Don't you know that?"

And because he didn't like to admit that there was anything about personal relationships he didn't know, he said that, yes, she was probably right.

"If things come too easily to you," she said as she disappeared into the kitchen, "you don't appreciate them." She heard the bitter note in her voice, but it was too late to draw it back.

Nothing, she knew, had ever come easily to her, and besides that she'd always felt in danger of losing what she did have. Why should she waste sympathy on Philip's children, who had so much?

19

The sweet fragile green of June passed, and the clear skies of July. In the heavy air of August the leaves drooped on their stems and the air was full of the pungent smell of blackberries as they ripened and fell softly, one by one, from the thorny branches of the blackberry bushes. The leaves on the oak trees turned a deeper green, the water a deeper blue. Darkness gathered under the pine trees and slid, each day, a little earlier over the sand as the sun sank behind the Sankaty Head light.

Always, in the summers they had spent at the cottage, it had been the same—the summer an eternal time, it seemed—the days long and even monotonous with their warm sun and blue sky only occasionally spread over with the pearly fog that rolled in from the sea. Time suspended. And then, some day in August, they became suddenly aware. The days were getting shorter. Time was passing.

Estella, working in her studio, felt that pressure, and it was like a fever in her head to get images onto paper. She knew that the series she was working on had to be completed there, in her studio on the island, where she had begun it. Later, in the fall, in a different place, and with all the turmoil the fall was going to bring, it would be impossible. Time was drawing in.

Sometimes in the middle of the morning she would look up from her work to see that Jasper and Chrissy had come into the studio when she was so absorbed she hadn't noticed. They would be sitting cross-legged on the floor, looking out the door toward the sea like half-wild animals, stretching out their legs into the patches of sunlight the way stray cats, left behind on the island by irresponsible people, sometimes slipped onto the deck of the house and sat uncertainly watching the door, remembering another door where they had not been barred entry, another door they had passed through easily to the bowl full of food and the cushion under the window.

Estella would be brought up short, turning her attention from her work to see them there.

"Did you eat breakfast?" she would ask them. "Are you hungry again?" But they would shake their heads, looking out at the sunlight glittering on the water.

Then when she turned back to her work she would forget them again. Much later, when she looked up, they would have gone.

But at some point late in the afternoon when the shadows from the pine trees had grown long across the ground, Estella would push her stool back from her workbench and stand up. She was finished for the day. The mood broken, exhaustion taking its toll. She would not even look again at the sheets of paper tacked to her workbench, would not glance back as she walked, slowly and a little unsteadily, toward the door. For a little while she was finished with those drawings and would not think of them again.

Because she had been absorbed all day, she would become acutely aware of everything she saw as soon as she closed the door of the studio behind her and walked up to the house. The pink clouds floating above the pine trees, the wild daisies that Jasper had picked and stuck into a water glass and set in the middle of the table—everything she saw would strike her as remarkable and she would be filled with wonder, as she would have been if she'd been sick for a long time and had just been allowed back into the sunlight.

She would call to the children and set them jobs to do—once more she was the general marshaling the troops—and she knew they were relieved each day when she returned to them again. They had missed her even though they could see her anytime they wanted to, bent over her work in the studio. But she wasn't really with them at those times, and they knew it. She was dimly aware, even as she worked through the day, that a kind of melancholy lay over the cottage.

So as she sliced the eggplant into rounds, handed Jasper the napkins to put at the plates, kept an eye on the vegetables Chrissy was sautéing, she would fill the kitchen with her energy and try to pass it to her children. For a little while, as they worked together filling the kitchen with their noise, the sadness would lift. There they were, all together in that comfortable kitchen full of the pleasant smells of cooking food. A heady joy would come over Estella. Things would be all right; happiness was still possible.

But a little later as they ate under the pale yellow sky the way they had done when Philip still lived with them, silence would fall, and Estella would look around the table uneasily at her children's faces. She could see it clearly in their eyes—a faraway look.

She would urge more food on them, piling their plates with eggplant parmesan and chicken cooked with lemon. "You must keep up your strength," she would tell them. Of course she feared it was Philip they pined for, though they did not say this and she didn't ask. If they missed Philip she didn't want to know, since there was nothing she could do to ease their loss.

"What I wish is that we could go back to Africa," Jasper said one night. "Only this time I'd be there too."

But Estella only shook her head.

"The village we lived in doesn't exist any longer," she told him. "The men work as herders now and they don't live in the bush, so it's gone. We knew at the time we were seeing the last days of that way of life, and that was one of the reasons we stayed as long as we did. We knew there wouldn't be a second chance. And we were right. Maybe sometimes the old women still go into the bush to gather when they get hungry for wild food. I hope they do. But that's all. That way of life is gone."

"If we went back we could find another place, then," Jasper said. "We'd find a jungle nobody knows anything about, and in the middle of it, where nobody ever comes, there'd be a village..."

"I'm sorry, sweetheart," she told him. "There isn't such a place."

"Then it isn't fair," Jasper said. "Why should I miss all the good things? Why is it too late for everything?"

"Not everything."

"Yes it is too," he said, and she was pained to see tears in his eyes.

20

Jasper nudged Chrissy with his toe, making sure she was awake. "Chris?" he said. "Stay awake and talk to me."

"No," she said, drawing her knees up to her chest with her back to Jasper.

"You don't ever want to do anything anymore," he complained.

"Maybe I don't feel like it."

"Everybody feels bad because of Dad. Is that what it is?"

"I don't know. Maybe."

"It's all that Jane's fault. I hate her."

"Don't be dumb, Jas," she told him. "Don't you know that Dad wouldn't be staying with Jane if he didn't want to? Nobody made him. He's the one you ought to have it in for."

"Don't go to sleep, Chris," he begged. "Stay awake and talk to me."

She heard him climb out of his sleeping bag and felt him kneeling beside her head. Then his fingers touched her eyelids, pressing them back so she'd have to look at him. It was an old game between them, going back to the time when Jasper was two and she'd been a little afraid he might poke her in the eye when he pressed the lid back. But he'd always been sure with his fingers.

"Well?" she said.

He bent over her and smiled his most winning smile, the one that made old women cluck at him.

She studied his face in the dim light, and as always when she looked at Jasper her heart drew in on itself in a little quiver of pain. Her beautiful little brother.

Earlier, when he had smiled at her like that she'd given in. But now something in her hardened against him. She knew there was something too calculating about that smile—something too practiced about the way he stroked her arm with two fingers as he might have patted the ridge of a cat's backbone.

Now when she looked at Jasper she couldn't be sure any longer. Once doubt crept in it could never be entirely erased.

"You'd better go to sleep," she told him. "Can't you sleep?"

"Tell me a story, and then I could."

"No story," she said, lifting his hands from her face and shutting her eyes again.

After a while she heard him crawl back to his sleeping bag.

"You could roll over and sleep right next to me," he said, but when she lay still without responding, he sighed and lay still too.

It was at that moment, when he gave up, that she was most softened toward him, was close to reaching out her hand to him after all. But she waited too long, the moment passed, and they went to sleep far apart from each other, pressing against the sides of the tent.

21

In the shade of the house, lying in a deck chair, Jasper slept with his head rolled to one side, his fingers lying loosely over the comic book that lay on his stomach.

Liddy lifted a finger to her lips as she quietly slid open the door into the kitchen and motioned for Chrissy to follow. "Want to go swimming?" she said. "Tom Nevers Head? I haven't been out there yet this summer, and I want to go. I'll leave a note for Mom telling her where we've gone."

Chrissy looked at Liddy in surprise. For days now when she and Liddy had gone to the pond or had swum in the ocean in front of the house they hadn't been very friendly with each other. She had watched Liddy from a distance, and Liddy had pretended not to care—or even to notice. But now, for no reason that she could see, Liddy seemed to have forgotten all about that. Because Liddy was tired of that suspiciousness, she would make it disappear; it was as simple as that. But of course it had always been Liddy who set the terms for their being together—she saw that more clearly all the time. Even now, as though it were all decided, Liddy headed for the bedroom unbuttoning her shirt as she went.

In the kitchen doorway, Chrissy balked. "I don't think I want to come," she said.

"Yes you do," Liddy said from the bedroom. "We don't have to stay long, Chris."

"My suit's wet from this morning."

"I've got an extra," Liddy said. "But that's so silly, Chris. Why don't you get a second one?"

"I can never remember things like swimming suits."

Trying to appear uninterested, she followed Liddy into the bedroom and watched her rummage through her drawers.

But when Liddy tossed her an old suit that had faded with much wear, she caught it in her hand. Unable to keep a smile of pleasure from her lips, she yanked her T-shirt over her head. It had been a long time since she and Liddy had been out to Tom Nevers together, and she wanted very much to go; she'd known that all along.

Estella had told Liddy and Chrissy when they were children that they must never go swimming alone. "If one of you gets into trouble the other can always manage to get her up to the shallow water," she told them, her voice full of assurance, though Chrissy had always known that what Estella really meant was that *she* would have been capable of pulling a drowning person to shore. And perhaps, if she had to, Liddy could have performed this feat too. But Chrissy also knew that if Liddy disappeared under the water all she could do would be to shout as she frantically treaded water and searched the swells for Liddy's dark head. She could never have gotten her back to shore.

So when they went swimming together she had begged Liddy to stay close. Every time a swell lifted them high before it crashed beyond the shelf of rock that extended out from the shore, she would watch to see that Liddy wasn't carried away. "Stay right here, Lid," she would beg. "Don't go away."

But because Chris wanted her to stay near, Liddy couldn't resist swimming away on her own sometimes, leaving Chrissy to run up and down the shore with her heart fluttering wildly in her chest. When Liddy climbed out of the water looking a little shamefaced, Chrissy was too relieved to hold her defection against her. Though later, when she'd forgotten how scared she'd been, she'd be cool with Liddy. It was mean to make her suffer so much.

Liddy rode her bicycle just ahead of Chrissy's, setting the pace, and Chrissy settled back to ride behind her. She was used to that position, since it was the one she'd always assumed with Liddy, who took the lead without question.

But as they climbed the long hill leading to the lighthouse, Chrissy realized that she could overtake Liddy easily if she chose; she had to hold herself back and shift her bicycle into a higher gear in order to remain behind. Though she tried to hide it, Liddy's breathing grew ragged. In London, it seemed, she had not gotten as much exercise as she might have. But even before she went away, Chrissy had known that her stamina was greater than Liddy's. In this she took after Philip; Estella had never been much of an athlete. But it disturbed Chrissy to know how easily she could have passed Liddy if she'd chosen.

Only on the last part of the ride, when they'd turned off the bike path and were heading down the road to the cliff, did Chrissy come up even with Liddy and pedal beside her. And that was just for companionship.

At the top of the cliff where once Nantucketers had watched for the spouting of whales, they could see only the smooth, almost oily surface of the water, with a few fishing boats moving slowly over it. The whales had long since been killed from those waters.

After they climbed down the cliff and reached the beach, they turned to the right without consulting each other. They always went beyond the beach nearest the foot of the cliff where most people stretched their towels on the sand. By walking on they could find an expanse of beach all to themselves.

"Of course, you know what Dad would say if he knew we were here," Liddy said. "You know exactly."

"There's a bad undertow here, girls," Chrissy said, imitating Philip's careful way of talking. "You always need to use caution on this beach."

Liddy laughed.

"Well, we will," she said. "We'll use caution. After all, we're swimming together, the way Mom always insisted."

Liddy dropped her towel on the ground and began pulling her T-shirt over her head. "This is a good place," she said, her voice muffled, and Chrissy saw no reason to disagree.

For a short way out the water came only to their knees, but then there was a trough that sank them immediately to their waists. And on the other side of the trough, the shore sloped downward.

"Oh God, look at that," Liddy said when they were in the trough. "That wave's going to kill us."

Always, in the beginning when they first entered the water, the waves seemed to tower like mountains, and they both shrieked as the swell lifted them and passed harmlessly by.

(241)

But the next wave suddenly broke almost directly above their heads, and there was no escaping that one. The noise of the water pounded in Chrissy's ears as she struggled, kicking, overcome with a panic she had never outgrown when a wave crashed over her head. It was the roaring and the sense of her own helplessness that was terrifying.

"Let go," her father had said. "Don't fight it. Kick your legs and you'll rise to the surface, Chris." But all she'd ever managed to do was to curb the panic a little; it was always there.

And yet, when they'd fought their way beyond the breakers to where the water rose only into gentle swells, it was very peaceful.

Here they lay on their backs and floated, their hands extended in the water nearly touching. When they had been much younger they had often held hands as they floated, their fingers pressed so hard together that the knuckles turned white. Together they would ride out any wave that stirred underneath then, roiling like a huge body turning over and over.

Nothing seemed to exist in the world except what they could see— the green water they floated on and the sky, a pale blue dome above their heads.

Chrissy turned to see Liddy, lying easy with her eyes closed, smiling.

What was she thinking? It was the same smile she'd seen on Liddy's face many times when she didn't know she was being watched. It was a smile she kept only for herself.

"Liddy?" she said. "What are you thinking about? You have a very contented look on your face."

"I was just thinking...well, I don't know what I was thinking. It went out of my head as soon as you asked me. Maybe my head was as empty as a gourd."

It was what they'd once said of other girls, back in the time when they'd looked on other children from a distance, secure in the understanding they had with each other. "I'll bet her head's as empty as a gourd," they'd say of this girl or that.

Chrissy wondered if this was something Liddy remembered or if the phrase had just slipped out. Sometimes it was dangerous to remind Liddy of that earlier time—a distant, absent look would come into her eyes and she wouldn't appear to have heard.

"You know, we could be lying here wriggling our toes while all along we're being carried out to sea," Liddy said. "When we open our eyes we'll be so far out the land will just be a little speck. A little speck that disappears even as we watch."

"And then we'll float on and on until we come to this South Sea island," Chrissy said, continuing the game. "It will be an island with breadfruit and coconuts and fresh water and we'll have nothing to do all day but sit by the edge of the sea and comb out our long hair and sing sweet mermaid songs."

"Until, one day, this horrible monster rises up out of the sea and heads straight for our beach with its teeth flashing and its claws reaching. Hungry monster, yummy mermaids, and gulp! There we go."

Chrissy laughed, joy suddenly making her so light she could have floated on nothing but foam.

It was her exuberance and the pleasure she took in the old games she and Liddy used to play that made Chrissy remember another of them. She rolled over in the water and slipped under its surface carefully, barely disturbing the water. In this game, stealth was important. Kicking her legs, she swam underneath Liddy so that when she looked up she could see her, a dark shape in all that translucent green with a halo surrounding her—Liddy's body gathering the light to itself and intensifying it.

"Shark," they'd called this game, and also "Snapping Turtle," though they'd known there could be neither shark nor turtle in those cool waters.

Coming up underneath Liddy, Chrissy made little pinches along the nape of her neck and the backs of her legs, and even under the water she could hear Liddy's shrieks of surprise. Though Liddy knew those pinches didn't come from a jellyfish brushing against her skin, even though she knew perfectly well it was Chrissy under the water pinching her legs with her fingers, she was still afraid.

"I'll kill you, Chris," Liddy said, thrashing the water into foam, and Chrissy laughed when she came up for air. When they were children, this had been the end of the game. Since surprise was the most important element, it wasn't a game that could be played very often. But this time Chrissy wasn't willing to give it up. She filled her lungs with air and again dived under the water.

She hadn't planned in advance what she would do—all she knew was that she wanted to continue the game.

But when she saw one of Liddy's feet kicking back and forth just in front of her nose, she closed her hand around it and kept diving, pulling Liddy under with her. "Carried Away by a Whale into the Kingdoms of the Sea"—perhaps this was the game, invented in the moment.

Chrissy could tell by the wild thrashing of her legs how furious Liddy was, and how surprised, but it wasn't hard to hold on to her foot. As they sank deeper, she didn't know whether she was pulling Liddy or whether Liddy was pushing her, but what she did know was that the light was growing dimmer. Below them the depths fell away into darkness.

If she had dived that deeply into the water alone, Chrissy would have been terrified. And yet she was the one who forced them to sink deeper. She knew she could hold her breath a long time.

At first Liddy kicked wildly so that Chrissy had to hold on tightly as she moved her legs back and forth, back and forth, fighting against the upward surge that would have pushed them where she was not ready to return.

And then Liddy grew cunning, as she always did in the games Chrissy played with her. She grew very still in the water, waiting Chrissy out, so that the two of them remained that way, perfectly suspended.

Chrissy knew it was time to let go, to tend the game. In another second . . . and yet she held on. It wasn't a game after all, and through Liddy's sudden frenzied kicking Chrissy knew that her sister realized this too. For the first time in her life, she had Liddy at her mercy. It was she who would decide to turn Liddy loose in her own good time . . . or not. Liddy was in her power.

Yet it wasn't that which made Chrissy go on holding Liddy's foot. Or not altogether that. It was because the two of them were there together with the rest of the world so far away. There was only Liddy's foot between her hands and the pounding in her ears as Liddy fought to rise to the surface—a pounding that was, she thought, perhaps Liddy's heart. She knew Liddy's fear, even her thoughts. In another second, or two, or three, she would be able to slip through whatever frail division there was between them into Liddy's very skin, and it would be through Liddy's green eyes that she would see the water. Already, whatever it was that separated the two of them had grown thin as a membrane—she was on the point of slipping free to go where she wanted to go . . . if she could just hold on.

She didn't remember, afterward, releasing Liddy's foot, nor did she remember shooting upward through the water, propelled by arms that had grown suddenly weak.

All she knew was that her head exploded with light; red suns spiraled over the milky sky and the sound of the water gathered as it rose from the shelf of rock far below and filled her ears with a roar.

In the pain of that light her eyes sharply teared, and through the tears she saw she had been returned to a place where water and sky blurred and merged together.

It was only then as she gasped for breath, her arms flailing, that she realized the water around her was empty. She turned around wildly, but could see nobody. All along she had known that Liddy couldn't hold her breath as long as she could, and yet she had held her there under the water even when Liddy grew quiet. "Liddy!" she cried.

Not until that moment did the thought of where she had just been— so far down in the water that the light had grown dim—suddenly terrified her, and for a few seconds all she knew was panic.

And then, just beside her, Liddy coughed, and she saw her face.

"Are you all right?" she cried.

Liddy could not answer, though her mouth opened and shut, gulping air.

Her eyes, though they were fixed on Chrissy's, didn't appear to see her. "I thought I was going to *drown*, Chris," she said, and to Chrissy's horror, Liddy's eyes filled with tears.

"I'm sorry, Lid," she said.

"No, you aren't," Liddy said, kicking away furiously, but Chrissy saw that it was to hide her tears that Liddy broke away so angrily, and it was Liddy's tears that made it impossible for her to explain what she'd felt, holding Liddy under the water with her. There was nothing she could say.

It was only then, following behind Liddy, that she looked up and saw how far out they'd been carried. The beach lying full in the sun, where a boy ran with a dog and a man struggled to lift a kite into the air, was so far distant it might have been another world.

"Liddy!" she called, but Liddy was swimming on, furiously, her fear having transformed itself into anger, and so Chrissy followed her lead, concentrating on her strokes.

She could not see that they were making headway, though each time she looked up she could see that the expanse of beach in front of them had changed; they were being swept parallel to the shore but were not drawing any closer.

"Liddy," she said, "we're not getting anywhere."

Liddy treaded water with her as she studied the shore. "We have to catch the swells, and we will do that if we just go on steadily. Stay right with me."

Chrissy was relieved to see that Liddy's anger had been swallowed up in this new danger. Now it was Liddy taking charge again, explaining what had to be done, slipping back into that old familiar role.

For a long time they swam, shifting from the crawl to the backstroke and to the crawl again, but gradually Chrissy saw that they were making headway after all; they were catching the swells, just as Liddy had said they would, and she could tell that they were being carried forward more strongly with each wave.

Still, by the time they were able to feel the ground under them once more and had struggled out of the water onto a part of the beach where only two people sat on a blanket, throwing a green tennis ball for a golden Labrador to chase, they were so spent that they lay down in the sand and looked up at the sky, which was the same milky blue it had been when they were floating and nothing had seemed to exist except that lucent dome and the green water. But this world they had returned to seemed foreign to them as they lay on the sand and listened to the shouts of people far up the beach.

Chrissy lay shivering, and not even the sun could warm her.

"We've got to go get our clothes," she told Liddy. "It seems miles back, though."

"That's because it is miles," Liddy said sullenly, getting to her feet and brushing at the sand that clung to her shoulders and thighs.

Even the long walk up the beach couldn't warm them, and when they finally reached their towels and the heap of clothes, Chrissy saw that Liddy's face was so pale with cold it looked faintly blue.

"I'm going to do a beach change even if I have to stand here naked," Liddy said. "I won't wear this wet suit another second."

Chrissy held the beach towel for Liddy to change behind and then Liddy held it for her, but even when they'd gotten on their dry clothes they still shivered, and their fingers were so stiff with cold they could hardly tie their shoelaces.

"Liddy," Chrissy said, leaning over her shoes and looking down at them, "I'm sorry about scaring you out there."

"I don't want to talk about it," Liddy said. She'd finished with her shoes, and she stood up with her towel draped over her shoulders.

"It was just a game," Chrissy said. "It was stupid."

"We survived," Liddy said, striding down the beach, her heels sinking deep into the sand. On their left, in the low dunes leading to the cliff, the terns wheeled and cried. "There's nothing more to be said."

This was not true, but Chrissy didn't challenge her. It would never be possible for her to explain that feeling she'd had as she held Liddy's foot between her hands. Liddy would hold tight to her view of the way things were.

They didn't speak again as they made their way up the cliff and climbed onto their bicycles. Along the road and on the bike path Chrissy rode even with Liddy, but on the long hill from the lighthouse she fell back and let Liddy go ahead. It wasn't important for her to be in the lead—that was something Liddy cared far more about. She liked being the one keeping watch, the one who saw things that the person on the lead bicycle never could.

22

When the others had gone to bed, Estella took her flashlight from the top of the refrigerator, called Jenks, and went back to her studio to spend the night. She liked returning to this space she thought of as hers—the space full of the tools of her art so that had she wanted she could have gotten up in the middle of the night and started drawing. The studio was her space; Philip had never occupied it.

And yet she dreaded turning out her light and closing her eyes. During the day she did not think about Philip—engrossed in her work, there was no place for thoughts about him—but at night when the world around her was quiet and she had no distractions, she was sometimes struck by longing. She could see Philip perfectly, the way he had settled himself in bed propped on pillows as he held the newspaper loosely in his hands listening to her talk idly about the day's happenings; she saw the two of them sitting in the kitchen in the middle of the night, their heels braced against the chair rungs as they whispered together over their bacon-and-tomato sandwiches, keeping quiet so they wouldn't wake one of the children. They didn't want to be joined by children just then—it was time they wanted to themselves.

Yet it drove her crazy, that weakness in herself that made her remember those earlier times; what she passionately wanted was to cut Philip out of her life so completely that nothing at all would remain—not even memory—

but it was obvious she couldn't do this. Not always, at least. She tormented herself far more than anyone else could have, and she couldn't stand that self-betraying part of her; she wanted to tear it away and throw it in the garbage can. With all she knew, it was intolerable to still have moments of missing Philip. No wonder that on her narrow cot she turned restlessly and slept poorly, her dreams scattered and vague.

Yet one night she had a dream of great vividness—one that held, she knew from the moment she entered it, great importance.

In the dream she was on the path that led from the village where they'd lived with the Tungi, the path that followed the little brown river before it meandered out into the bush. Over her shoulder there was a foraging bag, and in her hand was the digging stick for roots. And ahead of her and behind her there were the other women talking lazily, laughing, so close to her she could have touched them with a hand if she had lifted it. Only then, when she felt the familiar path under her bare feet—the ground beaten slick and smooth—only when she saw Wausu turn her head and greet her, eyes squeezed almost to slits with her laughter, did she know how terribly she had missed it all. She was full of happiness and wonder to be returned to what she thought she had lost.

There was so much to say she did not know where to begin, but the others must have understood what was in her heart, since it was with joy that the women greeted her. Wausu fell back into step beside her, putting a thin arm so easily and confidently around her waist.

"Wausu," she said, as they walked along where the land was filled with light, "my man has taken another woman."

Wausu tipped her face up to hers (she'd forgotten that way Wausu had of holding her head to one side, cocked and alert the way a bird listens for the movement of worms underground, her eyes as shiny and dark as a crow's), laughter trying to escape the corners of her mouth so that she put up a hand to stop it. And Estella had to laugh too, knowing that Wausu would see it all as a joke. She herself had had many lovers and couldn't consider this any big thing. Quarrels about lovers taken or suspected raged fiercely among the Tungi, but in spite of the quarrels it was common for a woman to leave her husband's side in the middle of the night and join her lover in the bush.

"If it were your man?" Estella said. "What would you do, Wausu?"

"I'd make him sorry," Wausu said. "I'd make him very much sorry."

"How?"

(249)

"Draw him back to me," Wausu said, and her eyes narrowed in what was no laughter.

"Tell me," Estella said, but Wausu kept silent.

There had always been times like that between them when Wausu would fall silent and give her that look which meant it was the end of talk for that time. In spite of how much she liked Wausu, there had been things she hadn't understood, barriers she could not cross.

Now the women were turning away from the path beside the narrow river and heading toward the grove of trees surrounding the spring where even in the driest part of the year the ferns grew lush and the frogs croaked. But in spite of its beauty, it was a place of bad spirits, a place to be avoided. Estella herself had once seen, in that very place, a white lion move silently between the trees surrounding the spring. She had stopped where she was on the path with Chrissy riding on her back, afraid to move, though she had known the lion wasn't flesh and blood. She'd known it was one of the spirits that inhabited the shadows under the grove of trees. "White cat," Chrissy had said, pointing over her shoulder.

In her mind Estella made an obeisance to the lion, thinking that, as spirit, it surely knew what she was thinking. And then had turned and left without looking back.

In her dream there lay the grove of trees under the hot sun. The women had turned from the path and were heading directly for the trees and the haunted spring. "That's a bad place to go," she said uneasily. "No one goes in those shadows by the spring."

But the women were walking fast, and she was caught up among them and was forced to go on too.

They were so near the trees she could see the tendrils of the ferns and the dark shadows that moved across the ground. She tried to free herself, to run away, but the other women were pressed against her too closely and she couldn't move. Wausu's face, inches from hers, smiled, a smile she couldn't read. "Look," Wausu said, pointing. "Look there." But she was terrified to look and shut her eyes tightly, though her feet carried her on, deeper into the haunted grove.

"I don't want to see it, whatever it is," she cried out to Wausu.

And then her eyes, which she had squeezed so tightly shut, opened and she saw the moonlight lying across the floor of her studio, moonlight she saw us uncanny and strange because it was still touched by her dream.

"Make him sorry," she remembered Wausu saying. "Draw him to you."

(250)

She understood then what Wausu meant, and what she intended her to do. Because the dream still seemed more real than the place where she found herself, she got out of bed and planted her feet firmly on the floor, shutting her eyes better to remember the steps of the magic love-charm dance she'd danced so many years before with Wausu and the other women in the circle far beyond the village.

But her feet remembered. All she had to do was to let them move again forward, back, forward, back, and then it came to her too the sway of the hips, the sensuous roll of the knees. She had no red sticks this time, but she raised her index fingers, letting them be the magic instruments. She'd known, when she made the dance the first time, that these movements were important to remember, though she couldn't have guessed then how she would use it. To draw Philip to her. And then? But she didn't know. To draw him was enough. To draw him was revenge. To draw him and then to look on him with contempt. This was what Wausu would do.

For a long time she moved through the moonlight over the floor, swaying back and forth.

But when the moon passed beyond the stand of pine trees and the studio grew dark, she lay back down on the narrow cot and fell into a heavy sleep.

She woke just before dawn, when gray light filled her studio, and got up slowly from her bed, surprised at how sore the muscles of her legs were. Had she really danced in the middle of the night, a magic dance to make a love charm? It seemed, judging by the soreness of her legs and by the tenderness of the soles of her feet, that she had.

As she pulled on her shirt she groaned. She must have been crazy to have done that. What if Jasper had needed her in the night and come looking—what would he have thought to see his mother dancing by herself in the moonlight with her eyes closed?

And yet the dream still left its influence on her, so that when she went outside into the pearly light she felt disoriented—what she looked for was the cooking fires and, in the distance, the narrow river. It seemed strange to see the tent where Jasper lay with his blond hair pressed against the netting, the deck gleaming with dew. And it seemed strange, too, that the only human sounds were those she made herself as she filled the coffeepot with water and turned on the radio that sat beside the toaster. It wasn't the news she wanted to hear especially, but she left it turned on anyway with the sound low. She could still hear the newscaster telling of

(251)

hostilities in the Middle East, of an airplane crash in Madrid, of the approach of the hurricane season. As usual, disaster and the threat of disaster trembled in the air, but it seemed to her on that morning that the dangers recounted by the newscaster were very remote. There were others that pressed on her with greater immediacy.

Wausu, she thought, what has happened to you? Very easily Wausu could be dead, since the Tungi, in spite of the power of their magic, did not live long lives.

Yet, even if she was dead, for a little while Wausu had come alive for her—about that she was certain.

When the coffee was made she took a cup and carried it back to the deck where she could see the sun, that flaming red disk, just above the water, and all she could see trembled in that light, as insubstantial as anything she had seen behind her closed eyelids in the darkness.

23

On the other side of the island, in the house on the moors, Philip had a nightmare. There were no pictures to see, no sounds to hear—there wasn't even pursuit, only blackness and falling. He could not open his eyes...he was helpless...his terror so great that he knew he would die. His only hope lay in making some move for himself. One finger, even, if he could just move that much.

He never knew, later, when this sensation of falling came over him while he was asleep—he couldn't call it a dream—how he managed to free himself. How he was able, suddenly, to open his eyes so that it was ordinary darkness he could see around him as he lay panting, his heart beating madly in his chest. If he understood how he had managed to wake, then the next time he wouldn't be so helpless. Perhaps, even in his terror, he would be able to remember the key, the way out.

If it had been Estella lying beside him, he would have waked her. Not by anything as obvious as shaking her shoulder or calling into her ear, but he would have waked her all the same. He would have gotten out of bed and gone to the bathroom, would have turned on the bedside lamp, dropped a book on the floor, rustled the leaves of the newspaper as he turned them. And Estella would have waked and turned on her light too. They would have talked, made love, gone to the kitchen and heated milk for hot chocolate.

But he wanted to let Jane sleep on. He was touched by her need for sleep—by the way she thrust her hands under the pillow and turned to dig her cheek into it, her face becoming tense with the need to hold to her dreamy state. In the middle of the night she was too dazed to be of much use.

So he moved carefully to his side of the bed, sliding his pillows gingerly along the headboard and raising himself so he was half sitting. It was a relief just to touch the sheet with his fingers, to rub one foot against his leg and to find his body still did what he asked it to.

He didn't want to turn on his bedside lamp, but he also didn't want to get out of bed and go downstairs to read. What he wanted was to lie where he was, looking at the moonlight that lay over the floor, so bright that he could have seen, if he'd chosen to, the objects on top of his dresser.

Clearly he could see the pulse beating in Jane's throat, and he longed to put his thumb against that spot so he could feel the skin rise and subside again, but he was afraid of waking her. So he contented himself with looking. It was only when Jane was asleep that he dared to look at her all he wanted, since when she knew he was looking she turned her face away, embarrassed.

There was a faint quiver of her eyelashes against her cheek—was she dreaming?—and he saw the tiny scar, like a very small star, just at the point where her right eyebrow ended. He had noticed the scar a long time before, but he could never remember to ask how she'd gotten it.

As he bent over her, he realized that the only other time in his life he had looked so intently into a human face was when Liddy was a baby. Because she was the first, he had spent more time leaning over her crib watching her while she slept than he had the others. Never had he seen anything as fine as the perfection of Liddy's eyelashes or the way the baby hair grew in a whorl from her forehead.

But he'd never felt easy holding Liddy in his arms—she was so fragile, it had seemed to him; his arms grew tense with the responsibility when he held her, afraid she might fall. Always he'd marveled at how casually Estella carried Liddy—and later Chrissy and Jasper—on her shoulder, balancing a baby with only one hand, or how she held one in the crook of an arm. He had never been able to be so casual with the children when they were babies. It was from a distance he preferred to look at them— to lean over their cots and watch them sleep or to extend a finger so they could grasp it in their hands, holding on the way a bird wraps its claws around a tree branch.

When he was a young man he'd loved women easily and, it now seemed to him, uncomplicatedly. When he saw a woman who attracted him he wanted to go to bed with her—and he did if he could. That was all. And since he'd been handsome and had an easy charm, he'd usually gotten the women he wanted. Undeniably he'd enjoyed it—that sense he had of his own power—and looking back now, from the vantage point of his middle age, he envied that man he had been, even while he knew it would be utterly impossible for him to ever live that way again.

It was tenderness, he thought, as he looked down at Jane's face, that had been his undoing. It was the tenderness he felt for Jane—as it was the tenderness he had felt for his children—that had bound him.

Not even making love to Jane could altogether ease that ache he felt when he looked into her face—it was still there, no matter how many times he made love, that little nugget of painful tenderness that he could not rid himself of.

There were times when he thought he had been better off as he was before—a kind of barbarian, really, when it came to love. Certainly his life had been easier then. And yet, on the other hand, he looked back on that man he'd been with a kind of pity, too; he had known so little.

Impossible, even if he'd chosen, to go back to being the man he once was. Years of his life stood between himself and that young man he'd been.

But it did seem hard that his children, having aroused all that tenderness in him, had turned away from it when they grew beyond childhood and no longer needed it. As Liddy and even Chrissy grew older, his attention only made that impatient look come to their faces and they had held themselves back.

It was his children, he knew, who had made Jane inevitable in his life.

Though he would never tell her, it was the way Jane looked sometimes with that faraway, sad look in her eyes that wrung his heart. She wasn't even aware that she looked sad and wouldn't have been pleased if he had told her, but he knew that in spite of all her accomplishments there was something in Jane that was still unsure—something of the child sitting in the darkness of her parents' closet, running her hands over their clothes.

"Sweet Jane," he whispered just above her ear as he touched her hair with the tips of his fingers.

But she only pushed her cheek a little more deeply into the pillow and slept on, safe from his love.

(255)

Chrissy's Animal Essays: Bullfrogs

On the other side of the rock wall that separates the yard of the farmhouse from the woods, there is a path I've made through walking that way so often down to a pond where hardly anyone else ever comes. Jasper, sometimes, but he's afraid of things jumping suddenly at his feet, and there are places he would rather play. But I like to walk down the path and through the woods, watching for the sparkle of sunlight between the trees that is the first glimpse I have of the water. The pond is my particular place, and I crouch on my heels on the bank for a long time, for so long that the birds and the dragonflies and the toadfrogs start thinking I'm something as harmless as a bush and ignore me.

When I first walk to the edge of the water, before I settle into my place, I can hear the splashes as the frogs jump from the bank into the water. But after I sit still for a while the frogs climb out of the water and sun themselves on the bank, sitting as still as I am, while they wait for an insect to come close enough for them to grab with their sticky tongues. While they are swimming through the water, or when they are posed on the bank just ready to slide into the water again, the frogs' eyes are bright and gleaming, but when they are waiting for food to come near, the lid settles halfway down over their eyes. They must not appear to be looking if they hope to catch something. I too sit with my eyes half closed and I don't blink very often. I seem barely to be breathing, and if I sit long enough I forget what I am, exactly. I might be one of the frogs myself, waiting for a fly to settle near enough to grab. I like sitting there without thoughts—to be nothing except eyes, fixed on a shiny weed stem or on the surface of the water which slides forward ever so slightly in a breeze.

There are many different kinds of frogs that live around the edges of the pond, but the ones I watch out for most are the bullfrogs, because they are the largest and also the rarest. It's usually in the very early morning that I've seen them sitting in the shallows—frogs as broad as my hand with large flat mouths. They will eat anything they can open their mouths around, and they don't hesitate to eat frogs smaller than they are. In fact, they don't hesitate to eat each other.

Once, when I came to the pond at first light, in the early summer when the frogs had all come out of hibernation and were, I suppose, especially hungry, I saw a frog on the bank of the pond doing what appeared to be a funny dance. It was the back of the frog I could see, and its long back legs were moving from side to side, every once in a while lifting the frog from the ground so that it seemed to be trying to walk upright. A frog, walking like a human being.

I moved toward the frog carefully, not wanting to frighten it away, but it didn't seem to hear me. It went on with its dance, and so I moved much closer. It was only then when I was a few feet away that I could see that this frog had another pair of legs sticking out of its mouth—legs that were also trying to dance. At least they gave a twitch now and then. It made me stop where I was—that frog with two sets of legs. I didn't want to touch it—it gave me the creeps—and I remembered a painting I saw once. There were bird legs holding up the body of a fish and human legs carrying around the head of a bird and I stared and stared because they were so horrible.

I knew all along that what I was seeing was one bullfrog that had swallowed another bullfrog—one too big for him to swallow. He couldn't take it on down and he couldn't regurgitate it. A cannibal choking to death on a frog spawned maybe from eggs he'd fertilized himself a few years before.

If I'd taken hold of both pairs of legs and pulled, I might have separated the two frogs and saved their lives, but I couldn't bear to touch that monster frog. So I suppose both of them died, though I never saw the bodies later. Something else came along, in all probability, and ate them both. At least, they disappeared.

PART III

1

In the A&P, Estella pushed a cart with wonky wheels past the bins of grapefruit, mangoes, avocados, keeping her head down, hurrying, forced to push the cart in its drunken path around the clusters of people gesturing excitedly. She caught snatches of their conversation—"...headed right for ...winds of one hundred and twenty-five miles an hour...added flights..." —but she did not slow down for those people clogging the aisles.

As she was putting a loaf of brown bread into her cart, a woman she'd never seen before, a perfect stranger, put her hand on Estella's arm and said, "Are you leaving the island? I just don't know what to do. The airport will be a madhouse, and I'd be afraid to go by ferry unless I went tonight. Imagine how awful it would be to get caught *out there*..." The woman's eyes looked into Estella's a little wildly—a thin, delicate woman with a sharp, avid nose. Estella knew that others often found her bulk, her gray hair and look of solidity, reassuring; she was the kind of woman that children, lost in a crowd, came up to and told they wanted their mommy. And so she wasn't surprised by the woman's appeal.

"But I'm afraid I don't know what's going on," she said when the woman hesitated.

"You really haven't heard?" the woman said, putting her hand over Estella's arm while their grocery carts glided companionably side by side. "You don't know there's a hurricane headed directly toward Nantucket?

Tomorrow afternoon they think, if it stays on course. A-hundred-and-twenty-five-mile-an-hour winds? You haven't heard anything?"

"I hardly ever turn on the radio," Estella said. "And we don't have a television here. But I wouldn't worry if I were you. I've been through other hurricane scares and nothing ever happened. Rough water, maybe, and some wind."

"You really think it might be nothing?" the woman said. "Oh, I know so much of what you read is alarmist, just journalists trying to sell papers. It's all distorted, probably. I mean, it's impossible to tell, don't you think, the truth about anything? But there're all these reports on the radio and television and photographs of the storm looking like a giant pinwheel."

"The island won't blow away," Estella said. "No matter what they're saying."

The woman let go of Estella's arm. She looked a little annoyed.

"It might be a major disaster," she said. "Lots of people are leaving."

"They haven't lived here as long as I have," Estella said.

She felt perfectly calm as she pushed her cart on down the aisle; a major disaster did not seem imminent to her. But still, if there was even a minor storm heading their way, it wouldn't hurt to take a few precautions. The electricity might go, and she knew they didn't have any candles in the house. She would just sneak over and get some before others thought about doing that too.

But though she searched the aisle where the A&P kept its candles, she couldn't find any. All she was able to find—in the special-foods section, nearly hidden behind the boxes of matzos—were a few Yahrzeit candles. The boxes were dusty and she had to reach behind the matzos to extricate them; clearly there was no great demand for Yahrzeit candles on Nantucket. But she took all they had, not unaware of the irony—Yahrzeit candles for the dead. But Yahrzeit candles were better than nothing.

Then she remembered tape for the windows. If you put masking tape criss-crossed over the windows, didn't that lessen the likelihood of the glass splintering into many dangerous fragments when it fell from the frame? She was sure she had heard that somewhere. But others had apparently thought of tape, too, since there was nothing where the tape should have been but an empty hook. All she could find was some garish yellow stuff used for sealing containers of food before it was put into a freezer; she took the last three rolls of that.

The store was crammed with people piling their carts with food, and she wondered if they saw their houses being surrounded by water so that they would have to wait, like Noah, forty days and forty nights for it to subside.

Estella saw one woman put five loaves of bread into her cart and say to her companion at the same time, "Don't bother with the fresh meat, Rory. If the electricity goes we won't be able to cook it. Run ahead and get canned stuff. You know. Stew, anything like that."

Estella was headed for canned goods herself, elbowing others out of her way.

In the canned-goods aisle there was pandemonium, and Estella took what she could reach from the shelves—three cans of spaghetti and meat-balls, though she knew none of them liked canned spaghetti, and cans of beets and lima beans. Already whole sections of the shelves were bare, and Estella could see that by noon the A&P might be reduced to nothing more than cans of Dutch Cleanser and Lysol. If a house was going to be blown by the wind into a heap of rubble, then it clearly didn't matter whether or not it was clean.

By the time she reached one of the long lines leading to the cash registers, she was breathing heavily from her exertion but her cart was piled as high as most of the others. Her family would eat if anybody's did.

Yet when she emerged from the store she saw that the day had not—as she'd expected—altered while she was in the store. It was still overcast with thin, high clouds that gave a kind of metallic sheen to the sky, and the air was perfectly still. A storm, at least of the catastrophic kind being envisioned by the shoppers in the A&P, seemed remote. And Estella felt embarrassed as she lifted the sacks of groceries from the cart and put them in the trunk of the car. When she thought about it reasonably, she knew they didn't need all those sacks of food. Even if there was a storm that cut them off from the stores for a week—a most unlikely possibility—they had plenty of food in the house to live on for that long.

She wouldn't do that again, she told herself firmly as she climbed into the car. She wouldn't be drawn into that kind of easy panic again— that herd reaction which was not a pleasant aspect of the species she belonged to. After all, she was not one usually drawn in by others' fear.

Though she'd grown up in a place where people tended to look anxiously at every dark cloud, fearing a tornado, her own parents had never built a storm cellar—a refusal which others in the family thought foolhardy. "If I'm blown away, then I'm blown away," her father had been fond of saying, "but I sure won't go down in a hole like a rabbit, down there in the damp like a root of some kind." So while her cousins were waked in the middle of the night at the first flashes of lightning to take their pillows and run for the storm cellar where they would have to breathe musty air and sit on hard little folding cots until the rain passed over, she was left to lie in her comfortable bed and watch the play of purple lightning through her room and later to listen to the drumming of the rain on the roof. As a result, she had always liked storms and was a little sorry to hear of a good one she'd missed.

When she got home, Estella did not go back to her studio to work, but ate lunch with her children, all of them helping to carry the cheese, bread, watercress, and lemonade to the table. It seemed like a holiday of some kind, with all of them in good spirits.

"After we eat," she told them, "we'll have to get ready for the storm." It filled her with gusto—the excitement, the prospect of all of them working together.

"Oh, Mother," Liddy said in disgust. "It's absolutely still. You know that storm will never come here. Wasn't it just two or three years ago they predicted a hurricane and nothing at all happened?"

"Nevertheless, we'll get ready in case it does come," Estella said. It gave her satisfaction to think of taking precautions—of securing all that they could against the storm.

Chrissy sat with her hands in her lap, looking in the direction of the water. "Can you imagine what it would be like?" she said. "A-hundred-and-twenty-five-mile-an-hour winds?"

"What?" Jasper said, alarmed. "What would they be like, Chris?"

"More terrible than anything you've seen before," she told him.

"Would we all be washed out to sea?" Jasper said. "Would we die?"

"Of course not," Estella said, looking hard at Chrissy. "Even if it does come, we'll be ready for it."

"How will we get ready?" Chrissy said. "With that yellow tape you bought? With the candles?"

"Yes," Estella said firmly.

When they had cleared away the food from the table, Estella brought out the rolls of yellow tape and passed them around. They all stood on the deck, barefooted, looking dubiously at the sliding doors.

"I think it's stupid to do this," Liddy said, "but if we're going to, where does it go? Inside or out?"

"Since the windows would be blowing inward, I suppose it should be on the inside," Estella said. "Or maybe both inside and out?"

"There won't be enough tape to do all the windows even on this side of the house," Chrissy said. "And what about the boathouse?"

"I'll move my things out of there," Estella said. She spoke forcefully and with great conviction, though she had not, until that moment, considered what she would do with the pile of drawings in the corner or the collages that lined the walls of her studio. "I'll put my things in Philip's study," she said then. "It's on the sheltered side of the house."

Across the expanse of the sliding door, Liddy and Chrissy put tape running from top to bottom, and Estella and Jasper put theirs from side to side. They kept dropping the rolls of tape, forgetting where they had put the scissors, stepping on each other's bare toes.

"Now the kitchen looks like a cage," Jasper said. He opened the door and stood inside it with his hands outstretched—a lion clawing against bars.

"It's only for a day or two," Estella said absently. "We'll take it off when the danger passes."

"But that's all there is," Chrissy said, holding up her empty cardboard roll. "There's nothing for the other windows."

"If the others shatter it won't matter as much," Estella said. "If there is a storm we'll all go into Liddy and Chrissy's room. It's away from the sea, and the windows won't blow out there."

It gave her an odd feeling when she thought about what she'd just said—the absurdity of it all. Would any room in the house be safe if there really were winds of over a hundred miles an hour racing in from the sea? Maybe the entire house would collapse, for all she knew. And yet she was so sure in her pronouncements.

"Maybe we should leave," Jasper said. "Maybe we shouldn't even stay here."

"We will, Jas, if we need to," she told him. "What do you think? That I'd let you drown? If it sounds bad we'll go to higher ground."

Through the afternoon they worked, rolling up the sleeping bags and taking down the tent, putting the bicycles in the house, moving the furniture away from the windows. When the other work was done, Estella went to her studio and began carrying stacks of her drawings, prints, and collages to the house. She had not been in Philip's study since he left the house, but when she opened the door she saw that it was, as always, extremely neat. His heavy old IBM was sitting on his worktable; doubtless he'd taken his portable typewriter when he left the house. But of course the neat stacks of papers—the manuscript of the book he was working on—were no longer on his table. She set the IBM on the floor and dragged the table to a corner of the room, away from windows. There, covered with a plastic sheet and the tarpaulin they covered the Sunfish with in the winters, her work would be as safe as anything else in the house.

Though she was tempted to look through the collages before she carried them to the house, she resisted this temptation. It would take too long, and anyway, she knew without looking that the series was not complete. It was there, a pressure in her head, or perhaps in her heart, a pressure as definite as that which predicted the storm—the need she had to make more images, to finish what she'd started. But for a day or two she would have to wait.

After she had carried all the prints and collages to the house and had taken, too, the suitcase of family photographs, there was nothing more left to do. Everything that they could do to prepare for a storm had been done.

It was strange, having nothing to do in the middle of the afternoon. Estella walked to the beach and looked out at the water, which was glossy under the sun, swelling and subsiding lazily. Almost it could have been mocking them in their activity of the afternoon; nothing, it seemed, could possibly disturb that calm surface. It was a staid and ordinary day—one of dull light and still air—a kind of Wednesday of the soul.

She was still there, digging her toes in the sand, when her children found her.

"We've been listening to the radio," Jasper said. "The man said that people living on low-lying parts of Nantucket should be prepared to move to higher ground. People should go to the high school."

"But it also said," Liddy added, "that the winds have slowed. Down to ninety or something. It's kind of idling along."

"Cassandra," Jasper said. "That's what its name is."

"And it's still heading for Nantucket, even if it has slowed," Chrissy said.

Estella had always disliked it when all of the children talked at once so she had to turn her attention three ways.

"Tell me again what the man said about low-lying areas," she said.

"To be on the safe side, we should move to higher ground," Liddy said. "But they're always overly cautious. I'll bet people are pouring off the island like rats. The first little thing and they fly into a panic."

"Well, here we are as calm as rocks," Estella said. "And if it does come, you know, we'll have ringside seats."

She found the possibility exciting.

2

The moment Philip opened his eyes, he was full of desolate emptiness. Even before he flung his arm across the side of the bed where Jane slept and found only the sheet, he had known she wasn't in the bed and wasn't in the house, either. He felt its silence, though he listened for the soft tread of Jane's feet across the kitchen floor.

The desolation that came over him was the same he had felt when he was a child, waking in an empty house. No explanation given later ever eased him—his mother saying indignantly, "But Philip, your father and I only went to the bakery for rolls warm from the oven. I supposed you'd sleep on until we got back." His mother had always refused guilt, implying that this was an emotion reserved for lesser and weaker people. He knew that his tears would not do him any good, though that knowledge had not stopped him from crying, all the same, as he sat at his place at the table with his arms around his knees, watching the careful way his mother distributed the rolls in the shallow straw basket.

With heart beating wildly, he leaped from the bed and flung open Jane's closet door. Emptiness was what he expected and had tried to brace himself for, but the sight of her shirts and dresses, still hanging in an orderly line, gave him only momentary relief.

Like a wild man he pulled on his shorts, thrust his feet into sneakers. Jane had gone for a swim without him and been drowned; she had gone for a walk down the narrow road and been hit by a car. Somewhere, hidden behind a dune, he would find her body, mutilated by a madman.

As soon as he came outside, onto the deck of the house, he began calling her name, but he hadn't expected an answer and didn't listen for one. He ran down the driveway to the road, where he hesitated, looking up and down. But it wasn't likely she'd headed in the direction of town—not at least if she was only out for a walk—and so he headed the other way, toward the beach.

He was sprinting, his heart hammering, when some movement in the dunes to his left stopped him—someone's head, perhaps, there against the sky.

"Jane!" he called again, leaving the road and passing through the shallow ditch, climbing up through the coarse grass.

And then he reached higher ground and could see some distance across the low dunes. It was then he saw her, standing with her back to him, looking up at the sky.

At first relief filled him—she was only taking a walk after all, and his fears were groundless—but he didn't understand why she didn't answer him, why she didn't turn to him and wave, summoning him to her.

He slowed to a walk, knowing he shouldn't let her see how afraid he'd been.

"I wondered where you were," he said when he was just behind her. "I couldn't see you from the deck."

"I'm just looking at the sky," she told him, her eyes still fixed on the thin clouds that dulled the morning light. "I heard over the news that a hurricane is headed this way, and I wanted to know if I could see anything. What the sky looked like. But it's ordinary enough."

"Oh, Jane," he said, putting his arm around her shoulders and turning her gently back in the direction of the house, "I can't tell you how many times since we've been coming here that there've been hurricane scares."

"That doesn't mean there couldn't be one."

"No," he was forced to agree. "I suppose it doesn't."

"It won't reach here until tomorrow afternoon. If it does come."

"I was afraid when I woke up and you weren't in the house," he told her.

He thought she would be touched by his solicitude, but instead she frowned.

"What did you think?" she said. "There aren't many places I could be."

The world was full of places she could be—this was what he thought but did not say.

For the first morning since he and Jane had rented the house together, there was nothing he wanted to do. He'd gotten up late, and this had thrown everything out of balance—or something had. By late morning he was getting up from his chair on the deck every few minutes to prowl up and down, looking at the sky, drumming his fingers against his thigh.

"I think I'll go swimming," he said finally. He thought the water might ease him, and the exercise would certainly do him good.

Jane came with him, carrying her towel draped over her shoulders, walking along briskly at his side, but he wasn't sure she was coming because she really wanted to or only to humor him. She walked with her eyes on the ground, lost in thoughts of her own.

Once he was in the water he did feel better. It was calm on that side of the island, and he swam for a long way, parallel to the shore. For a time Jane swam with him and then she went in to the beach, where he could see her lying on a towel, her face turned to the dull sky. Once he knew she was there he found himself looking back at Jane every few minutes, compelled for some reason to make sure she was still all right, though this struck him as a silly thing to do. What could possibly happen to Jane, lying on her towel on a beach where only four or five other people were gathered?

And then he remembered all those years when he had kept his eyes on the children's heads as they played in the waves. Two dark heads and one light. He'd never been able to rid himself of a picture in the back of his mind—there was one of his children lying facedown in the water, hair carried gently forward and back by the ebb and flow of the tide. It was his own private horror.

That remembered fear spoiled his swim, and when he headed for the shore he felt annoyed. If he had been able to swim until he was really tired to the point of exhaustion he might have rid himself of his restlessness, but as it was, he felt the old anxiety waiting for him even before he climbed out of the water.

It was late afternoon, however, before he decided what he wanted to do about it.

All afternoon he kept switching the radio on and, after hearing the usual message about the hurricane, turning it off again. He was a little furtive about this, but he was helpless to stop himself. Each time he turned on the radio, it seemed that he heard the same thing—the people living in low-lying areas near the south coast should move inland to the high school. And of course the house where Estella and the children were was in just such an area.

Finally, by four o'clock, he couldn't stand it any longer.

"I'm going to town," he told Jane. "I've got to telephone Estella and tell her to get the hell out of that house until this hurricane scare dies down."

"I thought you said there wouldn't *be* a hurricane," Jane said.

She looked up at him, and he could see the careful way she studied his face.

There was something about this watchfulness of hers that irritated him, and his irritation made him speak sharply.

"I'm not God, am I, Jane? How can I be one hundred percent sure?"

"If there's danger then *we're* the ones who ought to go to the school," she said. And now he heard it unmistakably in her voice—the child, wanting attention for herself.

"We're in one of the safest places on the entire island," he said. "We're not the ones in danger."

"Oh, of course," she said, and there was bitterness in her voice. "I knew it wasn't us you were concerned about."

"Dammit, Jane," he said, "you're in a safe place. I don't have to worry about you."

"And of course Estella can't take care of herself. She's incapable of coming to her own conclusions and making decisions."

"She has my *children* there with her," he said, his voice rising.

"The children, the children. Don't you think that word has become a broken record around here? And two of them are hardly what I would call children. Anyone would think it was three-year-olds you were talking about."

She looked at him, furious, but it was only surprise he felt. He hadn't known Jane was so bitter about the attention he gave his children.

Without saying another word to her he left the house, went to the tool shed, and took out one of the mopeds. He wouldn't try to talk to Jane when she was being so unreasonable.

* * *

He thought he had braced himself and was prepared for Estella's voice over the telephone, but when he heard it he was flustered and for a moment could say nothing at all. "Estella?" he said finally. "It's me, Philip."

"I *do* know your voice, Philip," Estella said. "Even though I haven't heard it for some time."

"I wondered if you'd heard the news about the hurricane," he said quickly, and felt immediately foolish. Of course she must have heard.

"And I do have a radio, Philip," she said. "Or have you forgotten this house the way you seem to have forgotten a great many other things? There are two radios, as a matter of fact. One in the kitchen and one in the bedroom."

"Then you know what they're saying about the low-lying areas. That you should spend the night in the school."

"I do believe I've heard something about that, too," Estella said. She was toying with him, and he felt both flustered and angry, though now that he'd started the conversation he was determined to say what he had to.

"So you're going to the high school, then? The cottage is certainly in a low-lying area."

"If you know all that," Estella said, her voice deliberate and careful, "then you must know, one, they're saying that even if the storm does come it's not expected before tomorrow afternoon, and, two, that it's starting to veer and might not even brush the island, and, three, why don't you mind your own business?"

"You think it isn't my business?" he said, his voice rising, though he knew even as he spoke that he was throwing away any chance he might have had to get Estella to listen to him. "Has it slipped your notice that it's my children you have there with you? On the most dangerous part of the island?"

The noise Estella made might have been a chuckle. She had just been waiting, he thought, for him to show his anger. "Now it comes clear," Estella said. "Only *Daddy* can take care of his children. Is that right? Are you saying that I don't have the sense to listen to the radio and come to my own conclusions? That I don't know enough to take care of my own children?" It was the *my* she stressed; he heard that clearly.

"What I hear, Estella, is that you'd rather be washed straight out to sea than to listen to anything I might have to tell you. But you've always been so goddam stupidly stubborn."

The noise of the receiver being slammed down sounded in his ear, and all he could hear after that was the dial tone making its flat ugly sound of disconnection.

He was so angry that he was nearly out of town before he thought of something else and turned the little moped around in the middle of the road. If he went as fast as he could he might get to the garage that rented dune buggies and other four-wheel-drive vehicles before it closed.

When he reached the garage, Mike, the owner, was just pulling the door to behind him, clearly leaving for the day. But when he saw Philip waving to him he waited.

"I know it's closing time, Mike," Philip said. "But I need a buggy— anything with four-wheel drive. You're always the person I come to for that," he added, thinking of all the times they had rented buggies for Jasper's birthday.

Mike stood, his hands flat against his back pockets, looking closely at Philip. "Sure, I remember you," he said. "But the thing is, if this hurricane comes the way they say it might, then rescue squads might need some of my buggies."

"I understand that," Philip said, "but I need one very much. I've been a customer of yours for years. And I'd surely appreciate it."

Mike gave him a long, steady look that was supposed to mean he was making up his mind, though Philip was pretty sure he'd already decided; Philip had been coming to the island for so long he had clout; he wasn't a recent arrival.

"I think I have something for you," Mike said. "If you don't mind using an old Land Rover. I keep a couple around to use myself. I still say they're more reliable than those newer things. But you know and I know that storm's not going to ever get here. When was it we had the last one of these scares?"

"Sure, I know," Philip said. "I know it's going to veer out to sea. It's all a big fuss about nothing."

Relief filled him, now that he was going to have the use of a vehicle that would surely get him wherever he needed to go.

Jane was on the deck when he arrived back at the house with the moped in the back of the Land Rover. She lowered her book to watch him put the moped back in the tool shed, but she waited until he climbed the steps, jiggling the key in his hands, before she spoke.

"Planning to make a tour of some beaches, maybe?" she said. "Going out to Great Point, are you?"

He could not meet her eye, though it annoyed him that he couldn't.

"I just thought it might be a useful thing to have around for the next couple of days," he said, heading for the doorway.

"To carry us to safety," she said, and he heard the strain in her voice. "Was that what was in your mind? If the house blows away?"

"If this house *did*," he said. "Sure."

"I know perfectly well why you got it, Philip," she said. "It's more than obvious."

"Then you couldn't possibly object. If you know why I got it."

"Estella wouldn't listen to you, would she?" Jane said, scooping her book from the floor and holding it in front of her. "She told you where to head in, didn't she?"

Philip had the door open, but he didn't step inside. "You have many fields of expertise, Jane," he said. "But Estella and what she will or won't do is not one of them."

"I don't hear you telling me I was wrong, though," she said, propping her book firmly in front of her face.

3

When Jane saw Philip behind the wheel of the Land Rover, driving it up to the house, she knew immediately why he had rented it, and it was the extravagance of the gesture that dismayed and angered her. She understood that Estella was going to remain in the house—Philip's telephone call to her had assured that if nothing else had—and if the storm did come to the island, then, in a cottage in a low-lying area Philip's family might well be stranded. But she saw, too, that help in the form of Philip and the Land Rover would be on its way—Philip, like someone in a movie, coming doggedly through wind and rain—smart Daddy, clever Daddy, to have thought of everything. In that moment she understood very well the story Philip was playing out in his head, like something out of the pages of *The Black Arrow*—a knight galloping to the rescue. Even Estella might have to submit to being rescued by Philip if she didn't want to stay behind all alone in a flooded house.

So now it comes clear, she thought. The story from Philip's point of view. From her own, she had seen it very differently, but now it came to her with perfect clarity—all the time Philip had been with her he had been scheming to get back into the good graces of his children and, for all she knew, of Estella, too. Her own part in this drama was much smaller than she'd realized, and maybe Estella had always held the female lead— a fact that Philip had known all along.

* * *

They hardly spoke to each other during supper, though when they did they were very polite. Jane knew that Philip watched her, hoping to see some sign that she would relent; his own anger had faded quickly after he'd gotten what he wanted.

When they'd finished eating and he'd gone upstairs, she remained below in the kitchen; even after he called down to ask her if she wasn't coming upstairs, she told him no. Not yet. There were some things she wanted to do.

She knew that Philip wanted them to make up their differences; he wanted her to say she was sorry she'd gotten so angry over the Land Rover—that she'd thought about it and understood, and of course now it was all right. Even though she'd acted like a child before, thinking only of herself, she now saw the error of her ways. He was just waiting to forgive her, to show his generosity—she knew that too. From his point of view that would be just fine. But she didn't feel at all like being forgiven.

When she was upset, Jane liked to do something energetic; she could think better when her hands were busy. And since she liked to use her energy in useful ways, she often chose those times when she was angry or disturbed about something to clean house. When other people might have taken a walk or played solitaire, she cleaned the oven and washed spice jars.

So as soon as Philip went upstairs, Jane took a Brillo pad and began scrubbing away the grease around the burners of the stove. She lifted out the trays under the burners and cleaned them under a stream of hot water, spread newspapers on the floor, and, holding her breath, sprayed Easy-Off inside the cavernous oven—a job she ordinarily put off doing as long as possible.

Upstairs, she could hear Philip walking up and down in the bedroom—getting his robe out of the closet, lining up his slippers beside the bed. There was a light thud as one shoe and then the other hit the floor. And she knew that in less than a minute she would hear the door to the bathroom close and then there would be the muted rush of water as Philip stood in the shower.

A pawn, she thought angrily as she thrust her hands into rubber gloves. I've been nothing but a pawn. My use was only to make Estella jealous.

Dipping a sponge into a bucket of hot water, she began washing the grease from the oven, the fumes from the chemicals bringing tears to her eyes.

Surely he must know that she couldn't bear to be left standing on the side, alone and awkward. It was what she always most feared would happen—Jane, by herself, getting more and more odd by the minute. If people expected her to behave well she usually did, but if she was ignored or treated badly she turned strange and didn't know how to defend herself.

Philip's family, it became clear to her as she scrubbed, didn't need rescuing. They were grown-up, intelligent people with a car; they were perfectly capable of making their own decisions. But Philip was treating them like a bunch of three-year-olds who didn't have the sense to get out of the way of a storm.

The story, as it worked itself out in her mind while she emptied the filthy water and ran fresh into her bucket, was altogether different from what she'd thought it was.

The scenario that Philip was busy working out was such an old and mundane one that she couldn't believe she hadn't recognized it before.

In all those years Philip had spent with Estella, resentments had built up. They always did. Estella saw through Philip too well, or maybe she didn't understand him well enough. In any case, she didn't give him his due. And so he wanted to get back at her, to jolt her into seeing him with fresh eyes—he wanted to make her appreciate him more and perhaps to depend on him more too. He wanted attention paid to *him;* he wanted to play a bigger part in Estella's life.

So what was the easiest way for Philip to get Estella's attention? The answer to that was embarrassingly easy. Philip would prove that Estella was more vulnerable than she'd supposed—that she couldn't take him for granted and must work harder to keep his affection. Philip would find another woman.

So it was at that moment, Jane thought bitterly, that she had happened to cross the lobby of the Sheraton Hotel in Boston heading for the registration desk. Just at that moment their paths crossed and Philip saw a woman who reminded him of a lost love and he thought, *That woman there. She's the one. She'll do.*

Angrily Jane wiped her nose on the back of her hand. The fumes from the oven had gotten not only to her eyes but to her nose also. She slammed the oven door shut, got fresh water again, and began mopping the floor.

Why hadn't she talked more to her mother about these matters when she had the chance? Her mother, after all, must have known quite a lot, married as she had been to Jane's father—that difficult, elusive man. But there had always been some reserve that had closed her mother in as though she were perpetually shrouded in dense fog. The truth was that her mother never would have been any use, even if she'd ever gotten up the courage to ask all those questions she'd wanted to ask.

As she mopped the floor, shoving the mop up and down, a kind of jingle began to accompany the movement. Alone, a-lone. The *a* came at the top of her stroke, the *lone* at the bottom. A-lone, a-lone. It stayed in her head so long that the sound slipped away from meaning altogether. A-loooone became a kind of gliding movement, a graceful skating over the floor.

So that was the way it was, and she'd been an idiot not to see it before. It had never been for herself, but because of all those other reasons that Philip had sought her out and had fooled himself into thinking he was in love with her. It had never been anything but a sham, no matter what he said.

Braced by her anger, she went up the stairs when she'd cleaned everything she could see to clean. She would be cold with Philip, she would show him that she'd seen through him and that it was a very banal and cruel little game he was playing out with her.

When she opened the bedroom door and stood with her arms crossed, looking at Philip lying propped on pillows, she was ready for accusations, for recriminations and fury, but when she looked into his face, her heart sank.

There he was with his book opened out over his stomach, smiling at her in a kind of anxious hope. "Jane?" he said. "Are you ready to come to bed now?"

Already she could feel her resolve weakening, her certainty dissolving.

"I don't know," she said, lowering her eyes.

"I kept listening for you to come up the stairs."

Could he possibly look at her with such anxiety if she didn't matter to him—if she was, as she'd convinced herself in the kitchen, nothing more than a pawn in his maneuvers to bind Estella to him more firmly?

She couldn't believe it, not when she was with him. When she looked into his face and saw how anxious he was, then all she'd been so sure of only minutes before seemed uncertain after all.

"I don't want to quarrel with you," Philip said. "Why should we quarrel?"

"We were never quarreling," she said. "It was something else."

"Come on to bed with me, Jane," he said.

His confidence, his certainty, that he was justified in whatever he did stirred her irritation once more, but this time she refused to give in to it. She didn't want to believe what she'd just been thinking about him, after all. She preferred to see him as he was that moment—smiling, waiting for her to come to him.

4

When Estella hung up the receiver on Philip's voice she was trembling with anger. The heat of her rage made her flush, and she could feel it, prickling the roots of her hair.

What did he think? That she was some feather-headed person, incapable of making up her own mind about anything? But no. It wasn't even as simple as that. It wasn't her competence he doubted, exactly; it was that he couldn't resist interfering—he had to be the one in command even when he was no longer there to, as he would think of it, oversee what was going on. It was his way of making his presence known, of remaining a force in their lives. Of course, the storm gave him the excuse to try to worm his way back in; she saw that clearly.

When she came into the kitchen, where Liddy was making a salad and Chrissy and Jasper were setting the table, she was breathing as heavily as she would have if she'd just run several miles.

"That," she told them, "was your father. He felt compelled to inform me that a hurricane was heading this way and that we should go and spend the night in the high school."

"Doesn't he know it's not meant to get here before tomorrow?" Liddy said. "There's not even a breeze blowing."

"That's just what I said," Estella said triumphantly. "If anybody goes to the high school it should be him and his precious Jane. They can lie on the floor all night being stepped on by hordes of people and dogs if he thinks that's such a desirable place to be."

Jasper stood still in the middle of the floor with the spoons in his hands. "If Daddy said we should go to the high school, I think maybe we ought to do it," he said.

"Oh, for heaven's sake, Jasper!" she said, turning on him. "You think your father has some kind of inside information about the storm? Something that only fathers are allowed in on?"

"I don't know," Jasper said, lowering his head, and she felt immediately remorseful for being so fierce with him. He didn't, she knew very well, have the means to defend himself against her. But it *was* the fact that Jasper felt such confidence in Philip in spite of everything Philip had done that made her so annoyed with him. After all, even when they were together, she'd always been better at dealing with crises than Philip had. He had a tendency to hesitate too long, debating between one course of action and another, whereas she simply plunged ahead, acting on instinct that had stood her in very good stead so far. But of course Jasper couldn't be expected to know this.

"Nothing's going to happen, Jasper," she told him. "It's just that your father can't resist being bossy."

She could imagine him very well, on his side of the island, complaining to Jane about how impossible Estella was for not listening to him. But there wasn't anything he could do about it. He could complain all he wanted to, but she was the one who would make the decisions. Since he'd cut himself off from the rest of them, he'd made himself helpless as far as they were concerned. She hoped he knew that and knew, too, that he had worked himself into that hole with no help from her.

For the first time since the beginning of the summer, Estella slept in her old bed—the one in the house, the one she had shared with Philip. Not since she had carried her bedclothes to the studio the morning after Philip told her about Jane had she slept in the house. It wasn't for fear of the storm that she chose to sleep there in the room where the curtains stirred lightly, blowing out from the sill and collapsing against it, but because her studio, after she brought her work to the house, felt barren to her.

Yet she was no longer easy in that bed where she had slept for so long. Even the room felt foreign to her, and she remembered the time when they first started coming to the house, the summer after they were married, when it had still been very much Philip's father's house. His clothes were in the drawers, his pipes were left on the mantelpiece. Though the house was full of his possessions, he did not often come there; after Philip's mother died the house held sad memories for him.

When the house became theirs after the old man died, they did empty the drawers and closets of his clothes and took them to the secondhand shop that raised money for the cottage hospital in town. The pipes they threw away. She had intended, at the time, to replace the chintz chairs and the bamboo tables; the furniture had grown shabby and it had never been to her taste. But, in fact, she had never done any of this. Only when something became unusable did they replace it, and this was less because of economy than because she couldn't be bothered. She'd gotten used to the dishes with their faded pink flowers, to the tarnished brass lamps, and to the ship's sextant hanging beside the living-room door. The house had always seemed to her to belong to Philip and his family, and she hadn't tried to leave her own imprint on it except in minor ways. It hadn't been important to her to do that. And anyway, during all those years of their marriage, she had rather liked having all those reminders of a past that went back beyond a time when they'd known each other. It had pleased her to use the same cooking pots that Philip's mother had used.

But now, as she lay once more in the bedroom where Philip's parents had once slept, she felt for the first time alien. Though she thought of the farmhouse as hers—even though she knew she would not remain in Providence, no longer married to Philip—she knew the cottage had never been hers, and maybe now she no longer belonged there. This was true even though she loved the place—the sea and the pine trees and the white sand—even more than Philip did. The end of all their summers there together—it was hard for her to accept that or even to grasp it. For a moment, as she lay watching the curtain billow and settle, billow and settle, she felt she was on the point of knowing something about the pattern of her life—the way things fell away, changed—but then whatever it was she had almost grasped slipped away from her again and she lay watching the red numerals of the clock radio slowly change from 11:03 to 11:04.

Abruptly she reached over and turned on the radio to hear, as she had so many times during the day, the news about the storm. But it was the same as it had been at suppertime. The winds had slowed to seventy miles an hour and the storm appeared to be veering from the island. If it continued on its present course, it would pass harmlessly out to sea. She clicked the radio off again and lay with her hands under her head, listening to the sea washing forward and back.

Lying in the middle of the bed, she thrust her legs into the far corners. Surely this was a more comfortable way to sleep than to have to make accommodation for another body. Both she and Philip liked to sprawl, and they had carried on struggles with each other even in their sleep.

It was all she held against Philip that kept her awake—her bitterness that contaminated the bedroom for her. All those old struggles between the two of them had nowhere to go now that Philip had left; her anger and accusations had no outlet. It was the way the waves were forced to climb the sheer rock until they broke on Cornwall cliffs—up and up they went, searching for passage that couldn't be given until down they dropped, finally, once more into the sea.

She feared she would be awake all night, shifting from one side to the other, her head more and more full of contention as her body grew more tired.

A door closed softly, there were light footsteps in the hall, and Jasper was suddenly standing beside her bed. "I want to come in with you," he said.

She hesitated only a moment before she held back the sheet for him. Philip wouldn't approve, she knew, but then Philip, after all, was on the other side of the island.

Holding Jasper in the curve of her body, she put up with having his cold feet lying against her legs. When he was quite small he had climbed into their bed often in the middle of the night, but he had been clever about it, slipping so quietly next to her that most of the time she hadn't even waked up. He knew she didn't mind having him there, that she liked feeling his warm body against hers in the night.

"In the dark I could see the eye of the storm watching us," he told her.

"Why should it do that?" she said, putting her arms around him and nuzzling her nose against his hair, which had a faintly sweet smell, like clover. "There are so many people in the world, Jas. Why should it single us out?"

"I don't know," he said. "But Cassandra can see so far she can see our beach and our house. She knows we're here. I can feel her looking. Every time I shut my eyes that's what I see—this big eye, watching."

"You know this house is set far back from the water, Jasper. And there are all those pine trees to protect us. So I don't think you should worry about Cassandra. She couldn't see us under the trees, even if she was looking."

But she could tell by some alertness in his body that his thoughts were far from what she was saying to him. "Jasper?" she said, nudging him gently so she could feel his ribs like tightly strung bows under her hand. His eyes were open, looking out at the dark, and she knew he listened to the sound of the sea as she did.

"Things feel funny."

"In what way funny?"

"Just funny."

In her arms she rocked him. "Nothing's going to happen, Jas," she told him.

"I can still see that eye," he said. "When I close my eyes I can see it and when I open them I can see it. It follows me around."

"It's only in your head."

"I can see it anyway," he told her. "I know it's there."

In just a minute she would take him back to his bed. She would draw the sheet in closely around his shoulders, and she would turn on his nightlight for him. In just a minute. But she might as well let him get his feet warm first. It was no good taking him back until he was nearly asleep.

She was aware that she was sliding into sleep herself, but it wouldn't matter if she dozed a little. It had been so long since she had slept with Jasper that she didn't think it would matter if she did for a little, just this one time. He was getting so big now, perhaps this was the last time he would ever come to her bed, looking for comfort.

5

As soon as Chrissy and Liddy had been put to bed when they were small, in the twin beds under the poster of the Peaceable Kingdom, one of them would whisper across the space that separated their beds, "You want to come to mine or should I come to yours?"

Together, in one of the narrow single beds, they had clung to each other so one wouldn't be edged out onto the floor. They had lain with their arms around each other, hanging on, their faces inches apart on the same pillow, tasting each other's breath on their tongues as they whispered.

"Hush, now, you girls," Estella would say, looking in the doorway at them, and for a little while they had pretended sleep in case she came back and found them still whispering. Sometimes they had not been able to stay awake and had fallen asleep that way, sharing the same pillow.

So Chrissy knew when Liddy was feigning sleep. Although Liddy lay very still, only her shoulders rising and falling gently with her breathing, Chrissy knew that she was awake.

But though Chrissy watched Liddy's breathing rising and falling, she had no idea what she was thinking about, as she'd often been able to tell when they were children. She wondered if Liddy was thinking about the storm and was afraid of it as she was. In the pit of her stomach there was an emptiness—the way she felt when a wave closed over her head; in her head, without even trying to, she could hear the terrible roar of the wind.

It made her frantic being so near Liddy with so many things she wanted to say to her and yet not know where to start, which question it would be safe to ask. She leaned back against the pillows on her bed and Liddy leaned against hers, and neither of them looked at the other.

Chrissy thought that maybe Liddy was also trying to decide what to say; maybe she felt, too, *This time must not be wasted,* but it was impossible to tell. Perhaps Liddy was only bored.

"Do you want to see some photographs?" Liddy said suddenly, and instantly got out of bed without waiting for her answer.

"I guess so," Chrissy said, at once greatly relieved that the silence had been broken and yet terribly disappointed that now it would be impossible to say anything that mattered.

Liddy turned on the light and got out of bed, rummaged across the top shelf of her closet, and came to Chrissy's bed with two fat envelopes in her hand.

Liddy sat on the edge of the bed and passed the photographs to Chrissy one by one. She glanced at them and put them in a stack on her bedside table. The first ones were of buildings—the apartment house where Liddy had stayed, London University, the British Museum—and they held little interest for Chrissy. Even the people, smiling beside bushes, smiling in front of statues and the big gates in front of Buckingham Palace, were dull. "Amy," Liddy said, pointing. "Sara, Tony, Leon, Becky, Colleen." It might have been a list she was ticking off. It was impossible to tell what Liddy thought about any of the people, but there were so many photographs to get through that Chrissy didn't want to interrupt and say, "That one. Tell me more about that one."

"You seemed to go a lot of places," Chrissy said.

They passed through Stratford, Salisbury, Stonehenge, Devon.

"Wait," Chrissy said, rescuing a photograph from the discard stack. "Who're those people?"

In front of a sand-colored house with a white door, flanked by trellises of yellow roses, a middle-aged man and woman and a young man stood in a row, looking somewhat shyly into the camera. The older man was nearly bald, with a round, smiling face, wearing a baggy brown vest-sweater with pockets that sagged. There was something, Chrissy saw, that sagged about all three of them. The woman's dress sagged over her breasts, and the young man's jacket sagged from his shoulders.

"Oh Lord," Liddy said. "I'd forgotten taking that picture. I took it out of guilt, probably, trying to show that I thought this was a special occasion that ought to be preserved for all time, when the truth is the whole thing struck me as being almost unspeakably dreary. Nigel," she said offhandedly, "and his parents. The Sunday I had lunch with them in Leicester. Nigel was somebody I spent quite a lot of time with one way or another."

Liddy looked more closely at Nigel, but it was hard to tell much from the photograph, which was slightly out of focus. He was tall, thin, and had sandy hair that slanted sideways down his forehead. He looked very young in the photograph—but that must have been deceptive; Liddy wouldn't have spent time with someone sixteen years old.

"He looks sort of nice," Chrissy said.

"Oh, he is. But the problem was he hung around too much. If he hadn't done that it might have been fine, but as it was I gradually liked him less and less as he got to bother me more. That day we went to his parents—it was late spring by then and the roses had just come into bloom—he'd been wanting me to come with him for Sunday dinner for ages and I'd put him off. Finally I felt trapped into saying yes. And then when we got there I saw they'd gone to trouble. Roast rack of lamb and apple crumble for dessert, and I wondered what Nigel had told them about me. His mother kept giving me these smiles as if we had some conspiracy together—as if she assumed I thought Nigel was as wonderful as she did. It made me very uncomfortable."

Chrissy felt sorry for Nigel's mother, whoever she was. She could imagine her in the kitchen of her house cutting up the apples for the crumble and worrying about whether this friend of Nigel's liked lamb. And then to have Liddy looking at her across the table with that little half-smile on her face which could have meant anything. No wonder the poor woman kept smiling and smiling, too nervous to stop.

"After we ate, they showed us the garden—they were both very proud of their garden—and when we left his mother insisted on sending some of the roses back to London with us, all bundled up with their stems in a wet cloth. And even a little sack of fresh butter biscuits. I'd forgotten about that. It was awful, though *I* wasn't responsible for whatever it was that Nigel told his parents about me."

"You must have felt bad," Chrissy said.

Liddy shrugged her shoulders. "The whole afternoon depressed me. I hate being sucked into a false position, but I don't like hurting people's feelings, either. I'd much rather not, but I can't stand for people to get little hooks in me. That makes me wild."

(287)

"I wouldn't know how to manage any of that," Chrissy said. It seemed immense—what she didn't know.

"You'd be surprised what you can do in the interest of self-preservation," Liddy said. "You'll manage better than you think you will, Chris. You just don't know yet what you can do."

"How do you know that?" Chrissy wanted to ask, but already Liddy was sticking the photographs back into the envelopes.

"What a bore," Liddy said. "All of that." She got back into bed and turned off the light. "If the hurricane comes in the middle of the night you can wake me," she said.

"In all those photographs, who would you say were your best friends, Liddy?"

Liddy rolled over on her side, away from Chrissy. "I just like to move in a crowd, you know. I like to have fun but I don't want to get...oh, bogged down."

Was that what Liddy considered her to be? Chrissy wondered. A bog? She was acutely aware that if Liddy hadn't been her sister she would probably never look twice at Chrissy. She wouldn't even be one of the people standing in a line smiling for the camera. But, on the other hand, if Liddy weren't her sister, what would she think of *her*? If they met somehow just by chance and all she knew about Liddy was what she saw? The answer to this was simple. If she met Liddy that way, as a stranger, she wouldn't like her. All she'd see in those circumstances would be Liddy's beauty and her certainty. She'd take fright and see nothing else at all, and so of course she wouldn't really see Liddy—only Liddy from the outside, as distant as though she were a piece of sculpture. So whatever she thought about Liddy would be wrong; it was only as Liddy's sister that she could know her as she did. And since she did know her that way, it would never be possible *not* to know Liddy, no matter how much pain Liddy caused her.

"Liddy?" she said. "Is it better to love somebody or to have that person love you? If it can't be both ways?"

"You really want me to answer that?" Liddy said. "You're serious?"

"Yes."

"Then it's not really love you're talking about," Liddy said. "It's something else. It's people getting little hooks in other people."

"I don't think I understand that."

"Oh, you will," Liddy said, and there was a trace of bitterness in her voice. "You do, more than you think."

"Mom and Dad?" Chrissy asked, but as soon as she did, even through the distance that separated them, she could feel Liddy's disgust at being asked this question.

"Don't ask me," Liddy said. "I don't want to know. I don't care."

Even in the darkness, Chrissy could see that Liddy's eyes were squeezed tightly shut.

"But what do you think?" Chrissy asked; it might be the last chance she'd get to ask those questions.

"I don't want to talk about it anymore," Liddy said.

After that there seemed nothing possible for Chrissy to do but to shut her own eyes under the doomed beasts of the Peaceable Kingdom and pretend to sleep.

6

By morning, the storm was still vacillating, and the newscasters were saying that if it stayed on its present course, Nantucket could be spared everything except heavy seas and rain. But hurricanes were erratic, and it was impossible to say with certainty what this one would do; it was still strongly advised that people living in low-lying areas of the island should evacuate.

Estella turned off the radio in impatience. It was the uncertainty that drove her crazy; she'd rather know that the storm was definitely coming to Nantucket than be left in limbo, not knowing what to expect.

Even if she hadn't packed up her studio, she would have been too restless to work in it; until all threat of the storm had passed, she would be able to do nothing.

At midmorning, since she couldn't think of anything else to do, she took a walk to the main road with Jenks following along at her heels. She had noticed that since Philip left, Jenks felt uneasy when she was out of his sight, and he spent most of the day sleeping in her studio, sprawled beside the bed. Evidently he thought she was the most dependable family member left and he didn't want to take a chance of losing her.

There was never more than an occasional car on the narrow road leading to the highway, since people rarely came that way except for the families who had houses there, so Estella wasn't surprised to find that the road was deserted. But just because she saw no cars it didn't mean that everyone had left that part of the island, and anyway, she heard the barking of a dog somewhere in the distance. It seemed unlikely anyone would have left behind the family pet. The fact that she saw no cars on the road meant nothing.

But the main highway, when she reached it, was deserted too. She stood for some minutes without seeing so much as a bicyclist. Yet she told herself that since it was a cloudy day, tending to rain, it was not the kind of day that enticed people to the beaches or the tennis courts. It meant nothing that nobody seemed to be on the roads.

Still, it gave her a slightly eerie feeling as she walked back the way she had come without seeing anyone at all. Even Jenks, she thought, felt uneasy, staying just at her side and not even going once into the bushes sniffing for rabbits.

By afternoon, when there was no further news about the storm and the sky remained cloudy and still, they were all bored. Chrissy and Jasper laid out the pieces of a jigsaw puzzle in a corner of the living-room floor, but their patience with it didn't last long, and Estella noticed that Liddy kept looking up from her book and staring into space. One or another of them got up often to go out on the deck to look around, but there was nothing remarkable to see.

Not until late afternoon did clouds rise dark and threatening in the southeast, but the newscaster, when Estella turned on the radio, was still saying that Nantucket would catch no more than the edge of the storm. Perhaps, she thought, the storm clouds she could see from her window were merely offshoots of the bigger storm; maybe they had little to do with the hurricane.

By four-thirty it was getting dark. Estella looked out at the bank of clouds as she started fixing an early supper and, against her will, imagined the swirling winds that those clouds might conceal, but she refused to dwell on that possibility. After all, she'd always liked the feeling of electricity in the air just before a storm; it woke her up and made her feel alert. It was perfectly understandable to her why horses galloped in front of the wind that came before a rainstorm and why cats bristled their fur and climbed wildly up trees—it was a rush of pure excitement acting directly on the nerves.

So, although the sky turned slate-colored in the rising wind and the sea was full of choppy waves driving into shore, Estella felt better than she had all day. It gave her pleasure to do the tasks necessary to get food ready for cooking—the peeling, chopping, cutting. With care she mixed the lemon juice and a little dill into melted butter as she listened to the voices of the children in the living room and the sound of the wind slapping the end of the clothesline against the house.

The steam rising from the cooking condensed against the windows, blurring all the outside world, and she remembered how it had been when the children were younger and they had all been shut inside the cottage through a rainy day—how peaceful it had been playing Clue or putting together an intricate puzzle. It had been a relief sometimes to be spared the sun and sea, even though they'd had to make an effort to entertain themselves. Those days, when they'd all been confined to the house together, had been some of their best times.

The wind was beating against the house, and soon there would be rain. Already she could smell it in the wind. But the fish would turn golden brown, would crisp at the edges, the white flesh flaky and sweet with the taste of the sea in it still. The bread would come hot from the oven with the crust so dark it would snap between the fingers. She would make a salad using the small tomatoes that could be popped between the teeth, and she would scatter ripe olives and goat cheese over the top. It would be perfect, that dinner, and she hummed to herself as she worked.

By the time they all came into the kitchen and crowded around the little table, it was dark outside and the rain was beating in sheets against the sliding doors. They had just started eating when the lights flickered twice and died and the motor of the refrigerator, which they hadn't been aware of before, coasted into silence like a long sigh.

"Damn," Estella said. "There goes the electricity." She could still see Liddy and Chrissy across the table from her, though in the light that was left, their faces looked pale.

"Go get the hurricane lamp, would you, Liddy?" she said. "It's on top of the bookcase."

"Is this the hurricane then?" Jasper said, sounding alarmed.

"That's just what the lamp is called," Estella said quickly. "It's called that because, I suppose, the idea is that it would stay alight even in a hurricane."

It occurred to her, as Liddy was getting the lamp, that until the electricity came back on it wouldn't be possible to get further news of the storm. But she knew all she needed to anyway. If the storm got worse, she'd bundle them all in the car and go off to spend the night in the high school; she'd decided that the moment the electricity went. Philip accused her of stubbornness, but he accused her unjustly. She wouldn't take chances. She certainly wouldn't remain in the cottage just to spite him.

Liddy set the lamp on the table and leaned over to light it. When she turned up the wick, the light blossomed inside its globe and they all watched it, glowing white. Like cats they watched, Estella thought. Unwilling to turn their gazes away.

How easy it was to be cut off from the world. Nothing seemed to exist except the four of them at the table in the light of the lamp, and around them the sounds of the wind and rain blowing against the house.

Under the table Jenks was lying on top of Estella's feet, and she knew he would have crawled into her lap if she had let him. From the time he was a puppy he had been afraid of storms, pawing at the door to be let in when thunder rumbled in the distance. Obviously he thought that safety lay with humans—a belief Estella found touching. There he was, soothed just because she ran her feet over his back as she ate.

"Where did you park the car, anyway, Liddy?" she asked. "I don't want a tree blowing over on it."

"Where I always park it," Liddy said. "Those trees aren't about to blow over, Mom."

"They've been here for a long time, it's true," Estella said. "They must have survived many storms."

She wasn't afraid, exactly, but some restlessness made it hard for her to sit at the table. What she wanted was to prowl from window to window seeing what could be seen in the flashes of lightning. Nevertheless, because of the children, she forced herself to stay where she was, to appear calm and untroubled.

"If the electricity stays off," she said, "we won't be able to have even coffee for breakfast. So you'd better eat up everything now."

None of them looked up at her, but she felt it all the same—they were all perfectly aware of her nervousness but chose to pretend not to notice. They wouldn't have it—her being afraid—and they were giving her warning.

J ane was beating the eggs with a fork, the tines clanging against the sides
of the metal bowl, when the lights went out; the noise of her beating,
which she continued a second or two more, seemed deafening. In the pale
remaining light all the objects in the room became ghostly and a little
sinister—the white slab of the refrigerator, the shiny surface of the cabinets. Only the ring of fire around the stove burner continued burning—
a blue flame flickering red.

"Philip?" she called. It was disorienting—that eerie light and the
sound of the wind.

Then she heard him in the next room, opening and shutting drawers,
and he was hurrying into the kitchen, his hands full of candles. He took
holders from the cabinet where the wineglasses were kept, stuck candles
in three of them, and set them on the table. One at her place, one at his,
and one in the middle. When he lit the candles the room became friendly
once more.

Jane had always been afraid of storms, and she couldn't help wincing
when a purple flash of lightning filled the kitchen; she was all too aware
of the prominent way the house jutted up from the dunes. Wasn't lightning
attracted to solitary objects? But she tried to hold her hands steady as she
tipped the omelet pan to coat the sides with butter. She didn't approve
of her childish fear of storms.

"The wind's getting up," Philip said as Jane slid his omelet from the pan onto his plate. "Hear that? Just in the last few minutes."

"I don't think so," she said. "You're imagining things."

"But the rain's lashing against the house. Really lashing."

"Eat your omelet while it's hot," she told him.

He picked up his fork, but the distant look in his eyes told her that it was still the wind he was listening to.

As she was emptying the eggs for her omelet onto the hot surface of the pan, another flash of lightning cut through the kitchen; she was startled, and her finger slipped across the edge of the pan.

When she put her fingertip into her mouth trying to ease the burn away, tears suddenly came into her eyes. Philip was paying no attention to her; he hadn't noticed that she'd burned her finger or that she was afraid. She was filled with dismay. Once before, when a storm had risen in the middle of the night, Philip had held her tightly to him, had shielded her so that, as he told her, the lightning would have to stroke him first before it could get to her. She'd felt taken care of and comforted that night. But now Philip sat steadily eating his omelet, unaware of how she felt. It was only the others—the ones on the other side of the island—that he had any thought for now. She saw that. And all her old fears returned, but with a new strength. It couldn't be her imagination that Philip was ignoring her—that his attention was centered elsewhere. It was clear in everything he did, even in the way he sat braced against the table with that faraway look in his eyes. Thoroughly cut off from her, he might have been a man she scarcely knew.

"It's only a little rain," she said. "I don't know why you look so grim."

"It's more than a little rain, and you know it," he said, not looking up.

But she would concede nothing. "You're overreacting, Philip," she told him. "Can't you even admit that's what you're doing?"

"I know you want to pretend I don't have a family on the other side of the island, but it doesn't matter what you want or don't want. I do have a family, and I'm worried about them. All right? Can we end this conversation?"

"And only what you want matters, does it?" she said. "Just don't be surprised if I don't oblige you."

Her lips felt so stiff it seemed an effort to open them for a bite of her omelet, but she forced herself to eat, slowly and methodically, her hand rising and falling mechanically. If he chose to be cold, fine. She could be like ice. He'd never know how painful it was for her to sit there beside him, eating her omelet; she could become like stone if she had to.

8

On the floor of the living room, Estella could see all three of her children in the light of the lamp, their backs humped like turtles' shells, bending over the pieces of the jigsaw puzzle. As far as it was possible to do, they were ignoring the storm beating against the walls of the house—even Liddy was crouched on her knees, searching for the pieces with straight edges, the ones that would make up the border. Clearly they didn't want to be troubled by questions of uncertainty; they'd had enough of uncertainty that summer, and any decisions would have to be made by her. Though she wanted to protect her children, it made her feel lonely, too, being the only one left on guard.

Estella couldn't tell if the wind had risen any or not. If the storm got no worse there was no reason why they shouldn't stay where they were, since it was distinctly unappealing to think of making their way to the car in the rain and spending the night—or hours of it—cooped up with a mob of other people with crying babies and barking dogs. And perhaps an even worse possibility would be to arrive at the high school and find only a handful of other people had bothered to take refuge there; she would feel foolish if that was the case.

While the children hunched over the puzzle, she walked through the rest of the house, Jenks at her heels, looking out the windows. The sea was rough—there were whitecaps driving into the shore—and the wind was strong, but it was not a worse storm than many they had waited out in the cottage. She was sure it was no worse. But she was also aware that she might be seeing what she wanted to see. Each time the lightning revealed the world outside the windows, she was struck by how isolated they were, after all. Their privacy, which had seemed so sweet at other times, now was frightening. Sheltered as the house was by trees and dunes, it was impossible to see another from their windows; the world beyond the farthest line of trees might as well not have existed.

If Philip had been there, the decision would have been much easier to make; they would have passed the question back and forth between them until somehow, in a moment, it would have come clear to both of them what they should do.

But it was a mistake to think about Philip; she saw that immediately. As soon as she thought about Philip she imagined him and Jane in their house high on the dunes, so secure they could even be smug about it; no flood could reach them in that house, not unless the entire island was inundated.

"Damn you, Philip," she said, resting her forehead against the sliding doors where the water streamed just in front of her face. She had not admitted, until that moment, how alone she was.

Though she wasn't aware of making the decision, when she came back into the living room where the children were huddled around the lamp, she knew what she would do.

"I'm just going to move the car closer to the house," she told the children as she took her slicker from the closet and her car keys from her purse. "I don't like where you've left it, Liddy, out there under the trees."

"There're trees anywhere I might have left it," Liddy said. "But I'll move it if you want me to."

"No, I'll do it," Estella said as she tied the strings of her hood and pushed open the door. It wasn't because of where Liddy had parked the car that she was moving it but because if the storm worsened and they did have to leave the house later on, she wanted the car right beside the back deck.

The rain was heavy beating on her shoulders, and the wind was so strong she needed both hands to keep the hood from being blown from her head; the strength of the wind forced her to make her way to the car in an odd zigzag fashion, blown forward by the gusts and staggering backward to get her balance, though she reached the car without real difficulty.

When she turned the key in the ignition the engine sputtered into life; the sound filled her with relief. As long as the car would start and she knew it was waiting for them just beside the steps, she didn't think they had anything more to worry about; she was certain she could get them to a place of safety if she had to. Carefully she turned the car around and backed to the side door just outside Philip's study so that it would be headed in the right direction; she was pleased with what she'd done.

"The car's ready to go," she called out as she slipped off her dripping slicker just inside the door. "If we need to leave, we can. So listen, you kids. I want you to get off the floor and find the sleeping bags. Collect your pillows and books and anything else you'd want to take with you if we do leave in the night and stack all that stuff right by the door. I'll get the toothbrushes and soap."

"If we're going to gather up all these things, then maybe we should just go on to the school," Liddy said. "Go on and be done with it."

"We'll be more comfortable here in our beds," Estella said. "We can leave anytime we need to. But if the storm does get worse I don't want to have to take time finding the sleeping bags. I want us to be able to leave fast."

"I'm not sure it would be like that," Chrissy said. "Neat. Remembering to grab your toothbrush. You wouldn't be able to *think* if it really did come."

"That's why I want everything ready," Estella said.

It gave her pleasure to see how efficient she was being. While the others were getting the spare pillows from the linen closet, she put cheese, boxes of crackers and cookies, tea bags, and mugs into a small picnic bag. They would even have something to eat if they needed it.

When everything else had been put beside the door, she remembered Jenks's leash and draped it over the sleeping bags.

"Jasper, you and I are going to sleep in Liddy and Chrissy's room tonight," she told him. "I'll sleep with you in one bed and Chrissy and Liddy can share the other. That room is the most sheltered, away from the sea."

"Can I go to bed just the way I am?" he said. "No pajamas?"

"Pull off your jeans," she told him. "You'll be more comfortable. But leave on your shirt."

By the time she set the lantern on Liddy's chest of drawers, Jasper was in bed with the sheet pulled to his chin. "I wish it was a storm every night," he said. "All of us in the same room. I love it."

"Well, naturally you do," Liddy said. "You're small and Mom will give you most of the bed anyhow. But Chris and I won't be able to turn over unless we both do."

But they all liked it, Estella saw—the excitement of the unusual. It was the way it had been when they'd gone camping together, all of them in a tent like pioneers, she'd always thought, in a one-room cabin. But of course this wasn't the same, after all. It wasn't all of them together in the room where the hurricane lamp made a white glow.

"I'll leave the lamp turned on low," Estella said. "So if we wake up in the night we won't be in the dark."

It was just rain, she told herself as she lay down beside Jasper. Only rain and a little wind that would probably pass long before morning.

9

Perhaps in spite of the fact that he thought he was awake the entire time, Philip did fall asleep after he and Jane lay down on the bed side by side, their faces to the ceiling. With the electricity out and the only light in the house from candles and a flashlight whose batteries had grown weak, there didn't seem much to do except to lie down and wait for the storm to pass and the electricity to come back on.

But suddenly Philip came fully alert, as though some part of his mind, keeping guard, had decided that this was the moment to wake him. It was the wind he heard even before he opened his eyes, and he knew when he heard it that this wind was of an altogether different quality from the wind he'd fallen asleep to.

This is the real thing. That was what he opened his eyes thinking.

As soon as he woke, he sat up on the bed and grabbed his jeans from the chair and his flashlight from the bedside table.

When he moved, Jane sat up too.

"It's the storm," he told her, leaning over to shout in her ear, but of course it wasn't necessary to say even that much. The room was full of the shrieking of the wind. Philip saw fear leap into Jane's face, and though he knew it was a petty thing to think at such a moment, he couldn't help feel satisfaction that Jane could no longer deny the seriousness of the storm. All along he'd been right and she'd been wrong.

The flashlight cast a pale circle of light, flickered once, and nearly went out. Only when he gave it a hard shake did it burn more brightly.

"Philip!" Jane called, and he could see her running across the floor behind him. "Wait!"

On the stairs the flashlight failed again, and he rapped it against the wall to shake more light from it. He could feel Jane just behind him, but he didn't turn or try to speak. Not until he'd reached the bottom of the stairs and crouched beside the open closet door did he try to make himself heard over the noise of the wind.

She'd knelt beside him, and he turned his face to hers. "Listen to me, Jane," he said. "I have to go out there to make sure they're all right. To take them to the high school, maybe."

He ran the light over the floor of the closet, trying to find his rubber boots, the ones he used for clamming.

"But Estella has a car," Jane said, and he could hear a desperate note in her voice. "She can do what she has to. It's crazy for you to go out there."

"You know I have to, Jane. Be reasonable."

He tried to speak calmly, but it was impossible for him to keep the irritation from his voice. There wasn't time for the quarrel that had been building between him and Jane, not when he was so frantic to leave the house; all he wanted of Jane just then was for her to let him go easily.

He found his boots in the back of the closet, thrust his feet into them, and stood up. In a moment he'd pulled his poncho from the hanger and put his head through the opening. But as he did so, Jane pushed past him and started searching frantically through the jackets for her own slicker.

"If you're leaving then I'm coming with you," she said.

"But you're much better off here, Jane," he told her. "This house won't be flooded. It'll be miserable coming with me. I might get stuck by the side of the road. Anything could happen."

Jane found her slicker and put it on.

"Don't you know I'd be scared out of my mind to stay here alone?" she said. "Don't you know that?"

"I've got to go," he said; he could see the waves lapping against the side of the cottage. "It wouldn't hurt you to think of somebody besides yourself for once."

Even in the feeble light, he could see how much he'd shocked her, and if it had been possible he would have retracted his words. But of course it was too late for that.

"Who are you to accuse me of selfishness?" she said. "The white knight charging out there to save everyone. I know what you're doing whether you do or not. It's not even them you care about, it's how *clever* you are. The figure you cut. Don't you think I know that?"

In spite of his urgency to leave the house, her words held him utterly still, all knowledge of movement having seemingly left him. So this was what Jane thought about him; this was Jane saying exactly what she believed. The knowledge astounded and sickened him.

She was beating his shoulders with her fists, crying tears of anger and frustration, but when he stepped back from her she dropped her fists to her sides. He knew that she was alarmed because of what she'd just said, but he felt nothing for her in that moment—not even anger.

"Go and gather up a couple of blankets," he told her then in a calm voice. "I'll take you to the high school on my way through town."

He handed her the flashlight, and she took it without speaking. He was left in darkness while she went upstairs. The noise of the storm was so great that he could not hear her in the bedroom above him; he just stood leaning against the wall with his eyes shut trying to make his mind blank. But after a time he saw the wavering light in the kitchen and there was Jane, holding a bulky garbage bag in her hand.

She kept her head lowered and would have walked past him without looking up, but when he reached out his hand for the bag she let him take it. She was just behind him when he reached the front door.

The house faced north, the sheltered side of the island, and he'd parked the Land Rover just beside the steps leading to the deck; he didn't think it would be too difficult to reach it.

But when he tried to open the door of the house, he found he had to push hard, so that when it did open suddenly he was flung back against the outside wall of the house. The wind took his breath and doubled him over; he just managed to make a wild grab for Jane's hand, pulling her beside him. He thought she cried out, but he couldn't be sure; the wind whipped not only sounds but the very breath from their mouths.

The flashlight was useless, and it was by feel that he managed to get his shoulder behind the door and force it shut behind him. And then the wind was pushing them across the deck; they were sliding over the wet boards the way they would have slid across the deck of a ship in a high gale.

He dropped Jane's bag, managed to grab it again, and found the stair railing with three fingers. Then they were scrambling down the steps, and when he reached out, his hand came to rest on the slick side of the Land Rover. He slid his hand to the door handle and opened it, pushed Jane and her bag in front of him, and climbed inside himself.

Rain blew around the opening of the door, there was water on the floor, and he doubted the engine would start. But as soon as he turned the key, the motor turned over. When he turned on the lights they cut a thin beam through the driving rain.

Going down the driveway, the Land Rover bucked under him like a wild horse, and he would not have been surprised if they had been lifted into the air and carried off into the dunes. But sliding from side to side, shuddering, the Land Rover reached the road and he was able to turn into it. And as soon as he did there was an immediate improvement in their situation. The road was lower than the banks on both sides, and the Land Rover was somewhat sheltered from the wind.

They moved slowly, the headlights picking out a bush, a fencepost, a driveway—clues that allowed him to determine where they were. But it took great concentration to do this, and he strained forward, looking for anything that might help him. He was aware of Jane sitting very still, holding tightly to the edge of the seat, but he could not turn his attention from the road to speak to her. And anyway he didn't know what he would have said. Nothing she could do would retract what she'd said to him, since what she'd said was clearly the way she saw him—a self-deceiving man. That was her view of him, and he couldn't forget it or pretend she hadn't spoken those words.

10

It was the sensation of noise that Liddy felt before she actually heard the sound—the house rocking—and she was lifted from the bed as a wave would lift her. She thought it *was* a wave, and the house a boat shuddering in the crash of the water. Even as she woke she struggled to swim, her lungs straining. It was only then, when the bed rose to meet her and she knew she wasn't falling after all, that she heard the terrible splintering crash that had already raised her off the bed—the ripping of boards and nails giving way and the tearing of the wind, a roaring that filled the house.

If she cried out she couldn't hear her own voice. She didn't know, until she felt a fine spray of water across her cheeks and opened her eyes, that she was holding Chrissy tightly in her arms and that Chrissy was holding her. Chrissy's eyes were looking straight into hers; the lamp, amazingly, still burned on the chest of drawers, through unaccountably a part of the ceiling above it was gone, and rain was pouring through the jagged hole.

She could feel the childish boniness of Chrissy's ribs under her arms, but Chrissy's eyes looked back into hers unwavering—not the eyes of a child anymore. "The house has fallen in," Chrissy said, her lips barely moving, and Liddy saw fear leap into Chrissy's eyes at the moment she knew, by the lurch of her heart, it had also leaped into her own. All she could see then was those black pupils of Chrissy's eyes grown big with fear, all she could feel was her arms holding tight. United in their fear, they were together the way they'd been when they were children, sleeping together in the same bed. For a moment it was the way it had been then.

"Girls?" Estella said, and Liddy sat up on the bed with the rain blowing on her face.

"Part of the roof must have blown off," Estella said. She was pulling on her jeans, and Liddy grabbed hers and tossed Chrissy's to her. Jasper was hunched on the bed with the blanket making a hood around his face, and Jenks had climbed up too and was lying across Jasper's feet.

"Stay here," Estella was saying. "Let me go and look." But Liddy was pushing her feet into sneakers as quickly as she could and she saw that Chrissy was doing the same thing. Liddy had the sense that everything they did was done in speeded-up time, and yet it was grotesquely slow, how her fingers struggled to make ties of her shoelaces. She was five again, making each careful loop.

Estella grabbed the lantern and ran to the door, but Liddy was just behind her.

In the hallway, where rain whipped into their faces, they seemed to have stepped from the door into the outside world, though the wall on their left was still intact and it was from above their heads that the rain whipped in.

Ahead, suddenly Estella came to an abrupt stop with the lantern swinging in her hand. "Good lord, look at that," she said.

A tree had sprung up in the middle of the house, its dark branches drooping with water, the sharp smell of pine clear even in the rain.

"Blown over," Estella said, looking up at the hole in the roof. "One of those old trees."

Liddy stepped past Estella and tried to push her way past the tree. Eyes squinted, arms outstretched in front of her, she would have forced her way through if the tree had yielded. But whenever she moved she felt branches wet with water and sap, branches as big around as her leg that would not let her pass.

"It's blocking the hallway completely," she told Estella. "We can't get to the sleeping bags and the car."

She felt it draw tight in her throat—fear at being trapped. It would be horrible to be trapped inside the house while the wind tore it away from them, piece by piece—mice in a burrow that a dog is clawing its way to.

"The bedroom window," Estella said then, and they ran back the way they'd come.

Liddy forced back the curtains and braced her arm to raise the window. The wood had swelled with the rain, but her desperation gave her strength; the window slowly opened, and she took out the screen and flung it to the floor behind her.

She had one leg through the window and was sitting on the sill before Estella said, "Wait! You'll be drowned out there, Liddy. Wear a slicker."

But she couldn't wait and she didn't know what good a slicker would do anyway in that rain and wind. She hung on to the sill then with both hands, her feet braced against the wall, and then she pushed off and jumped. It would not have surprised her to have fallen into water, but it was in sand that she landed.

Behind her Estella shouted, and she saw Chrissy climbing out of the window behind her, but she didn't stop to wait. She found the side of the house and, touching the boards with her fingers, made her way along it.

She'd found the softness of pine needles, her hands were deep in them, when Chrissy grabbed her shoulder.

"Mother wanted me to take the lantern, but I knew it'd get washed out," Chrissy said in her ear. She caught Chrissy's hand in hers and pulled her along behind.

The house protected them from the full onslaught of the wind, but the rain so engulfed them it was like being under a waterfall.

"The tree's here," Liddy said, pressing Chrissy's hand to the needles. "We'll have to work our way around it to find the car. It must be on the other side somewhere."

With one hand holding Chrissy's and grabbing the pine boughs with the other, she inched her way. Now that her eyes were used to the dimness, she could tell that the darkness wasn't total—where the tree was looked darker than anything else around her—and yet she couldn't *see* exactly. Only when she turned her head could she see the glow the lamp made in the window, a blurred light like one seen underwater.

The boughs brushed her legs, and she knew if she held on to them she would eventually come to the trunk of the tree. Then she could climb over to the other side, where the car would be.

When her leg touched something hard and solid she thought it was the trunk and reached out her hand to touch it. But she knew with sickening certainty as her fingers ran over a surface like ice that it wasn't the trunk of the tree she was touching.

She turned loose of Chrissy's hand and pushed aside pine needles, forcing her arms as far as she could along the body of the car before she came to branches, trunk; she could feel the bent metal of the roof caved in, pinned down, under that weight.

Chrissy was beside her then, touching where she had touched. "It's the car," Liddy told her. "It's under the tree."

She could feel the tears swelling her throat and burning her eyes, but she forced them back. What good would crying do?

It was easy finding their way back to the place where the fuzzy light of the lantern shone. Liddy boosted Chrissy through the window and then climbed up herself.

"The car's smashed under the tree," she told Estella, feeling the water stream from her clothes. "We have to walk out now, before we're flooded."

"In this wind?" Estella said. "It's no good, Liddy. We wouldn't be able to walk in that wind. And we wouldn't have any protection from falling tree branches, from anything being whipped through the air. Where could we go that would be better? We have to stay here."

"If that tree had hit this part of the house we'd be dead."

"If a tree blows over on you in the road you're dead, too, you know."

"I'd rather take that chance than be cooped up here, just waiting. We're trapped in this place."

"If there's a flood we can climb on top of the house. We'd manage that if we had to."

"We'd be blown right off," Liddy said. "If you don't think we can walk through this wind, what makes you think we could hang on to the slippery roof of a house?"

"Nevertheless," Estella said, "I'm certain we're safer here."

It was Estella's certainty that drove Liddy wild. She didn't understand how Estella could sound so sure when evidence of her fallibility lay all around them.

"The way you made us safer by moving the car from under the trees?" Liddy said. "If you'd left it where I parked it we'd still have a car."

"Nobody could have known that, Liddy," Estella said, her patience wearing thin. "You know that perfectly well."

Pulling Chrissy behind her, Liddy began stripping off her soaking clothes with her back to the room.

"The way nobody could have known a lot of other things, I suppose," Liddy said, without turning around. She dried herself on an old sweatshirt and passed it over to Chrissy. The noise of the storm filled her with giddiness; she could say anything and not care—that was the feeling she had.

Behind her, Liddy knew that Estella was rising on the balls of her feet in indignation. "Just what do you mean by that?" Estella said. "What other things? I'd like to know, Liddy."

"I mean if we'd left last night we wouldn't be in this mess. That's what I mean."

"And if we had left last night, you know what you'd have done? You'd have griped, griped, griped the entire time. So just what is it you're blaming me for, anyway, Liddy? Say it and be done with it."

Liddy's jeans fell to the floor behind her, and her hair flicked like a horse's mane. "Not one thing," Liddy said. "I don't blame you for one goddam thing. You're blameless."

"You think," Estella said with the kind of finality that let Liddy know this was something she'd held back from saying for a long time, "I shouldn't have let Philip go. That *somehow* I could have stopped him if I'd just put my mind to it. I know that's what you think and what you blame me for, but your thinking it doesn't make it so."

Liddy, pulling on dry shorts, looked around at Estella in surprise and dismay. Even if what Estella said was true—and she didn't think it was—it was beside the point. Here their lives were in danger and there Estella was still stuck in that old rut. What should she have done about Philip? Estella didn't understand that none of that mattered anymore.

"Here's some dry sneakers," Chrissy said, handing them to her from the closet, and she quickly forced her feet into them. She defied the house to fall on her—she defied it. If she had to she'd make her escape all alone out the window; if she needed to she'd go by herself down the road, inching her way along. She refused to be crushed and she refused to be drowned and that was all there was to it.

11

If Philip had not known the roads and streets of Nantucket as well as he did—knowledge that had accumulated over the years—he would have become hopelessly lost as soon as he reached town and entered those mazelike streets and lanes which might have been laid out by a drunk. But there was more protection from the wind once they reached the town, and he made his way steadily, without a mistake.

Now that they'd gotten that far without any trouble, he looked over at Jane, who sat beside him hunched miserably in her slicker. All that he could see of her face was one cheek and a few strands of hair that had worked their way out of her hood and lay wet and limp against her raincoat.

He wished he could forget what she'd said to him in the house, but he remembered every word.

It filled him with indignation that although she didn't have any difficulty in ascribing deceit to him, she was blind to deceit in herself. She seemed to have no notion of how much the spoiled child she'd acted, demanding attention for herself when it was clear that he must be worried about Estella and the children. The injustice of it still rankled.

And yet, even against his will, the sight of Jane sitting so miserably with her head turned away from him made his heart squeeze in pain. Evidently, loving her had become a habit that he was reluctant to give up.

If his attention had not been held so closely to the road—in spite of everything—he would have put a hand on her thigh.

At the high school there was a great confusion of cars, and since he intended to leave again as soon as he got Jane inside, Philip didn't want to take the Land Rover into the parking lot, which was a mad jumble of cars and trucks. People had been unable to see in the driving rain and had left cars wherever they could. So Philip parked at the edge of the lot where he wouldn't be hemmed in, even though he saw it would be a long walk in that wind and rain to the door of the school.

"I'm sorry, Jane," he told her. "But I'm afraid to get any closer. We'll get soaked, but maybe you can dry off inside."

She didn't say anything to him. But as soon as he brought the Land Rover to a stop she opened the door, pulled the bag containing her blankets out with her, and was lost in the rain.

"Dammit, Jane, wait!" he shouted at her, though he knew she couldn't hear. He was so annoyed with her for going off like that he could have slapped her. What did she think? That he could possibly let her go alone? She couldn't possibly think him that cruel. And if she didn't, then what did her act of independence aim to show him? That she didn't need him? That she was so angry with him she would rather die than let him help her? Whatever she thought, he was sure her intent was to hurt him.

He climbed out of the Land Rover and made his way slowly around it, feeling he was being crushed by the weight of the wind and rain. "Jane!" he called to her again, but of course the wind tore the word from his mouth and swallowed it up in its own noise.

He saw her then, a few yards away, being blown forward with such force that she fell to her knees as he watched. But long before he could reach her she was up again and struggling forward.

When he did reach her he grabbed her arm tightly—it was anger, partly, that made him grip so hard, but he was also afraid of being torn from her by the force of the wind. It was all he could do to guide them between the cars as they weaved from side to side, hanging on to each other.

Just inside the doorway of the high school they leaned against the wall, catching their breath. Philip felt beaten, scoured by the wind-driven rain so that his skin felt tender when he touched his cheek with his fingers. Jane, he saw, might have been a drowned person, with her hair plastered to her head and the water streaming down her face. Almost miraculously he was still holding her bag of bedding.

As he handed the bag to her his hand brushed her cheek, but she turned her head away and he let his hand fall.

They were surrounded by a confusion of people—children, dogs, the frightened yowling of cats confined to boxes. The hallway of the high school and the gym, where, Philip could see, people were clustered around piles of bedding, were lighted with battery-powered lamps, so that the far reaches of the gym were lost in darkness, and so was the high vault of the ceiling. People moved through that space as though they were in a huge cavern, and he thought of prehistoric times and little groups of people taking refuge in caves against the terrors of the night.

Jane, he saw, looked as dazed as he was sure he did. She dragged her sack of bedding a little way from the door, and there she sat, uncertain what else to do.

Philip motioned for Jane to stay where she was while he went to a table at the gymnasium doorway where a Red Cross volunteer was trying to get the names of the people as they came in. In front of the table, men and women with babies and small children were shouting and gesticulating, and Philip was sorry for the woman trying to cope with the chaos, but he had needs of his own. He pushed to the table and leaned over it to shout that he needed to see her lists. That he was looking for a family by the name of Sloan.

She waved him away, a look of great annoyance on her face, and he saw that it would be hopeless trying to get her attention long enough to get what he needed. Instead he made his way to the back of the table, and while the woman leaned forward, getting the names of one of the families standing in front of her, he slipped the stack of papers from beside her arm and carried them over to a lamp hanging from the wall. The woman shouted angrily at him, but he made calming gestures and she was too harassed to leave her post and come after him. He stood under the lantern and read the names.

But Estella's wasn't there, which was exactly what he'd expected. Estella and his children were where he'd known they would be—in a house on the part of the island most vulnerable in this storm.

Before he gave the lists back to the woman, he wrote Jane's name at the bottom of a sheet. Then he made his way back to where she was sitting on her sack of bedding, just as he'd left her.

He crouched so that he could see her face.

"They aren't here, Jane," he told her. "I have to go out to the cottage to see what I can do."

(312)

Her hands were lying in her lap, only inches away, and he wanted to put his hands over them, but she gave him no encouragement, sitting hunched up, shut in on herself.

"Then I'll come back here," he told her.

"No you won't," she said. "Once you're with them again."

If she'd sounded angry he would have set himself against her, but it was the desolation in her voice that made him want to put his arms around her. Yet the way she sat with her hands helt tightly in her lap, cut off from him, made it impossible for him to do this.

"The whole point," he said, "is to bring them back here."

"Even if you do..." she said, her voice trailing off.

Even if you do, she meant, you'll be with them and there'll be no place for me.

He held her hands—it seemed the only gesture he could make—but they lay cold between his.

"I have to go," he told her, getting to his feet.

"Then go," she said.

Only when he reached the door did he look back. She was watching him, but when she saw his head turn in her direction she quickly dropped her eyes and there was nothing for him to do except push the door open and once more go out into the storm.

12

The blanket made a kind of tent over Jasper's head and he was squeezed so close to his mother's side that, with his ear pressed against her ribs, he could hear her breathing, the air going in and out of her lungs. Jenks lay across his feet with his head down between his paws. If it weren't for the noise the wind was making—tearing at the house, making the house moan and wail, trying to get at them where they sat in a row on the bed—he wouldn't have minded it. It would have been almost fun if it hadn't been for the wind. But Cassandra knew where they were. She could see through the roof of the house as if it weren't even there, and she wanted to get at them and carry them away with her. The waves rose in a frenzy—higher and higher—and the water would come after them because it didn't have anywhere else to go. Higher and higher it would rise until it forced them all out of the window; they'd have to go out there where it was dark and the water swirled.

But when he had to go out there into the water, he would grab somebody and not let go. He would hang on so tight that nothing could pry him loose, and so he would be saved. His mother, he thought, was the strongest swimmer; he'd seen her lots of times out beyond the place where the waves broke, her head bobbing up and down, just sitting there in the water like a cork in a bottle, so he never worried about her being able to get to the shore again. He knew she could do it.

So when he had to climb out the window and jump into the water, she would be the one he would grab. Chrissy was too light. Chrissy couldn't hold him up and maybe they would both drown. Jenks would probably drown too, because he was old and he would get tired of making his legs paddle up and down for a long, long time. Liddy wouldn't drown, he thought, but she wasn't as strong as his mother.

For a long time they'd have to swim around in the dark, but he had it all figured out—the way it would be. They'd have to swim and swim but since they wouldn't be able to see anything and since the rain would be pounding down on their heads, this would be hard to do. In fact, they'd be down to their very last bit of strength—his arms would feel like they were dropping off. And his head would keep slipping under the water so he'd barely be able to hold on to his mother.

But then, finally, he'd see a light up ahead—a light that would come closer and closer. And there would be a noise, too—that creaking noise that oars make in the locks—he'd hear that distinctly—and then his father would say, "Hey, Jas, I'm here. Give me your hand and I'll pull you into the boat."

He and his mother would climb into the boat and lie there getting their breath back. They'd be saved.

He'd come, his father would, but not until the very last moment. Not until they'd given up hope.

Into the warm place at his mother's side he curled up and pulled the blanket right over his head. With his whole head covered the noise wasn't quite so bad. It was warm in there under the blanket, and just for then he felt safe. Maybe it would be a long time before they'd have to go out into the water.

13

When Philip turned from her and hurried out the door of the school into the storm once more, such a terrible desolation came over Jane that if she had not been surrounded by other people she would have cried out with it. Instead she bit the fleshy part of her thumb until the pain brought tears to her eyes.

If she'd done what she wanted she would have run after him, would have grabbed his poncho so he could not have left without her, and told him that if he was going into the storm she was coming with him. But she'd seen it in his eyes—that distance—and she knew he'd turned against her. He thought she was jealous and childish, and she couldn't defend herself against what he thought. In the face of his disapproval she was helpless—desolation had come over her when she saw that she did not come first with him; when real difficulty came it was easy to see where his loyalties lay.

And yet she knew that what she'd said to him was the truth. It *was* absurd, this game of rescue he'd worked out for himself, tearing off into the storm to earn the gratitude and love of his family once more. How much he would like driving down the narrow lane to the cottage, riding the Land Rover like a bucking horse, coming through the doorway shouting to Estella and his children. She understood exactly what it was he wanted—to be in the center, directing the action. He hadn't known how much of *that* he would sacrifice, living with her.

Dragging her sack of bedding behind her, she entered the gym, where families had established themselves in little clusters all over the floor, each family occupying an island of blankets and pillows, surrounded by ice chests and portable carry-cots. As she made her way between the clusters, as if crossing a crowded beach, she saw babies being given bottles and small children chewing on arrowroot biscuits. Some people were playing cards, sitting in a circle beside a camping lantern.

It was amazing to her how quickly other people set up cozy little home bases for themselves, how they were able, even in the middle of the night, to think of all the things to bring with them that would make them more comfortable. She didn't understand how they were able to do this— how other people knew what was necessary to make their lives easy— since it was something she'd never been able to do herself.

All those evidences of care being taken—of people giving thought to one another—made her even more aware of her forlorn and outcast state. She knew she was bereft and exposed, knew no one would call out to her, "Over here, Jane! Let's set ourselves up over here!"

But Philip would soon be together with his wife and children and dog; the circle would open for him and he would slide in as easily as if he had never left—that was the way she saw it—though only the outsider, the one forever excluded, could know what it meant to sit so casually in that circle. None of them, not even Philip, would give any thought to her, the ghost at their backs, though Philip might feel the draft coming from the cold where she stood and turned up the collar of his jacket.

He'd made his choice. When he left her at the school and went out into the storm again, she'd known well enough what it meant. And so had Philip, though he might not admit it. If he hadn't known, he wouldn't have left her the way he had, glancing back only once to see her sitting on her sack of blankets. Not even a fool could deny such evidence, and she was no fool.

As she made her way uncertainly across the floor of the gym, a man wearing earphones suddenly jerked them from his ears and for some reason singled her out to be the recipient of his information. "Guess what I just heard," he said to her triumphantly. "Winds of *only* eighty miles an hour— *only*, get that!—are slamming into Nantucket from a hurricane they all thought would do nothing more than graze the island. Did you ever hear anything like that? Like some kind of Ping-Pong ball this thing went back and forth..."

She would have stayed to talk to him, but he was off, telling someone else his opinions about the storm, and she was left turning around and around, surrounded by crying babies and small children, by the dogs that seemed to be everywhere. There was no place for her; she was left in confusion not knowing where to go.

Then she looked up and saw, in the bleachers, dark shapes moving in the glow of flashlights like fireflies in a deep field, and she knew that this was the place for her to go, up there as far away from the chaos as she could get.

And so she made her uncertain way upward, dragging her sack behind her. She didn't have a flashlight and she grazed her shins on the bleachers more than once—the light that illuminated the gym was fitful and uncertain.

But she finally found a place near the wall where she would be by herself, and she took off her slicker and wrapped one of the blankets from her sack around her back. By some miracle it had remained dry inside the heavy plastic, and she was grateful she would not have to sit shivering with cold.

From her perch, she looked down at the milling groups of people, and the murky light and the shrieking of the wind combined to fill her with confusion. She didn't understand how she'd come to find herself there, looking down at that churning mass of people. It made her dizzy just to contemplate.

Yet she knew that if she'd been down there among them, if she'd been part of one of those clusters, it would no doubt have felt very different to her. Then she'd have been engaged and might have felt benevolence, even love, for all of those people in their ordinary and even simple humanity—those people ready to flee danger and establish anywhere their little comforts: light, warmth, milk for the baby. It might have seemed simple, if she'd been a part of it all.

But the vision she had from her high vantage point, watching from a distance was a very different one. Jane alone, divorced from it all, with nothing but the wind to keep her company.

14

They'd pushed the beds against the south wall of Liddy and Chrissy's room—as far away from the hole in the roof as they could get. Estella had turned the lantern low, but had been reluctant to extinguish the light; it was important, she told herself, that they be able to see if the water started rising in the house. And in that light she could see, if she chose to, Chrissy leaning against her shoulder, Jasper in the hollow of her side, Liddy within reach of her outstretched hand.

She could tell by the stiff way Liddy sat keeping herself a little apart from the rest of them that she still blamed Estella for allowing them to be trapped, refusing to see that what had happened to the car was just bad luck or depended on things neither Estella nor anybody else could have been expected to know. She was certain this was the way Liddy felt, but how could she defend herself against such a charge? It was impossible. There were reasons why that particular tree was blown over and not another—the angle of the wind or roots weakened by age or disease—who knew?

Yet there *were* reasons—in that Liddy was right. One thing did lead to another and, inexorably, to the next. A decision taken years ago proliferated such necessary happenings that a structure incredibly intricate and complex inevitably developed, boggling the mind. No one could explain it, though Liddy wanted something clear-cut. Liddy wanted it to be simple. If Estella hadn't left the car where she did, it would have been safe and they could have carried their sleeping bags to it, gotten inside, and driven off. Or

Estella could have told them all the night before, "We're leaving. Now. Grab your toothbrushes." That's all Liddy wanted to know. She wouldn't see—perhaps she couldn't—that beyond all those decisions there had been not just Estella but also Philip. After all, in the years they'd been together a structure so elaborate had been formed between them that it constituted an entire little world impossible to understand except a little here, a little there.

Even now, as she sat looking into the dim glow of the lantern, she could not say surely, "Philip is this," or "Philip is that." Oh, she could see him for an instant, hunched over his typewriter, his eyes half shut, or walking fast through the sand with his hands in his pockets, or his face, lowered over hers, his lips drawn back...in a smile was it? And yet he seemed very remote—memory was like a dream, after all, fitful flashes very apt to change into something else even while you watched.

She could not even imagine Philip there with them on the bed, taking up the space beyond Chrissy against the wall. Though she knew he had altered her forever, even in ways she couldn't guess, she could no longer see him there with them. Nothing except what she could see in the dim light of the lamp, could touch and hear, held importance for her. Only she herself, her children, Jenks lying across her feet, the shrieking of the wind and the lashing of the rain. Those were the things she believed in.

"What are you thinking?" she said. "Chrissy? Liddy? Have you gone to sleep?"

"Just waiting for the wind to stop," Chrissy said. "All I can do is listen to the wind."

"Jasper's gone to sleep, I think," Liddy said. "Isn't that something? Not even Jenks can sleep in this noise."

But in spite of what they said, Estella knew that what they were really thinking was how afraid they were. She knew this because their fear was a reflection of her own.

Her arms were around them, but she was well aware she couldn't comfort them as she had when they were children. They weren't like Jasper, who still believed she could save him. They knew she couldn't, though they were still young enough to blame her for not being able to.

"You could go to sleep," she told them. "I'll watch, in case anything happens."

But Liddy shook her head. "I have to watch for myself," she said.

And there was nothing Estella could say to that. She knew Liddy was right to depend on herself, no argument was possible, but it saddened her all the same.

15

The moment the door of the school closed behind Philip and he was engulfed once more by the wind and rain, his breath snatched from his mouth, he knew he should turn around and grab the door handle again. He should go directly back inside and sit with Jane, waiting for the wind to die. Nothing could be accomplished by what he was trying to do, and he knew that the second the door closed behind him, exiling him once more to the storm.

But having closed the door behind him, he hated to open it again; he didn't want to return to Jane and say, "I've changed my mind." He believed in his steadiness. He was dependable—the one who would not fail the people who needed him. Battered, half drowned, he would somehow, miraculously, battle his way to the cottage and carry them all to safety.

And so he fought his way into the wind, stumbling against cars, holding his arm in front of his face to break the wind, to give him a little space to breathe. The flashes of lightning showed him the confusion of the place—cars and trucks parked in a jumble so it was impossible to tell if he was going straight or in a circle. Since he could see only a few feet ahead, there were no landmarks. But then he saw a stream at his feet and realized it was the ditch between schoolyard and road; somewhere near was the Land Rover.

Though the prospect of finding shelter from the rain relieved him, he was aware at the same time that he'd half hoped he would not be able to find the Land Rover after all—that he could honorably return to the school and take refuge. It was with some dismay that he saw it there, in front of him, and knew there was nothing to do except climb inside.

It occurred to him, as he made his slow way from the school, that there might be a roadblock at the rotary leading out of town preventing travel to other parts of the island. But when he reached the rotary he saw it was not blocked, and so he felt fated to go ahead. His bluff, if that was what it was, had been called.

And so, with the town behind him, he went out into what felt like emptiness. No cars, no house lights. For some way after he left the rotary, the road was, Philip knew, sheltered by trees and hills, though he could see nothing beyond the highway.

But eventually he reached the part of the road where the trees and houses gave way to open stretches of dune covered with bushes and stunted trees. He knew when he reached the open stretch because the wind rocked the Land Rover more furiously than before and the windshield wipers faltered and staggered in their labor to clean the glass. He strained his eyes for a glimpse of the white strip down the middle of the highway which showed him the way to go; he knew how easy it would be to slip off the pavement and into a ditch.

Even though he knew he was a long way from a beach, he feared being swept away, out into an invisible ocean. It was the fact that he could see nothing that panicked him, surrounded as he was by noise that his confused mind told him was the sea crashing over his head.

He drove for what seemed hours, creeping along, watching the white line that led him on to a destination he could no longer imagine—into darkness, that was all he knew. Once he looked at his watch and saw it was a little after two o'clock, but this knowledge had little meaning for him. He had been traveling forever, it seemed, and would go on forever; it was a long time until daylight.

It was just then, when his attention had been taken from the road, that he lost sight of the white line—all he could see was the headlights making tunnels through the driving rain, and he did not know which way to go as the lights turned left, right, searching for something familiar. And then he felt the wheels sliding over the pavement and into something soft so that he couldn't turn the wheel, sliding until the Land Rover was tipped on its side and came to rest against what he realized could only be a bank. He could tell by his position that two of the wheels were in a ditch.

Though he knew it was no use, he tried to extricate himself, but when he heard one wheel spinning free he knew that even with four-wheel drive his situation was hopeless and he cut the motor.

He turned off the lights and managed, with difficulty, to climb over the seat and into the back, but when he groped there he could feel that the floor was wet. Instead he chose the front seat, the passenger's side, where, by bending his knees around the gearshift, he was able to half lie with his shoulders against the door. To conserve heat he brought his poncho over his head, and there he was, brought to a halt, cramped, cold, in the middle of nowhere. Impossible to know where he was, on the side of which hill he was stuck. All he was certain about was that he was somewhere between the cottage and the school, between one woman and the other.

Pride—he admitted it—had something to do with his situation. And even what Jane had said about him as a rescuing knight—he supposed there was a little truth in that. But he was certain it was only a small part, of little consequence, and he wouldn't accept Jane's view of him as a manipulating conniver. He wanted to save his family—what was so terrible about that? The flood that he feared, that he could see rising foot by foot if he let himself—nobody could deny the danger of that now.

He put his hands over his ears to dull the noise, but he could still hear the tearing of the wind, the crashing of the waves, and he knew he was cast off, adrift.

He opened his eyes and pulled aside the poncho, welcoming even the green glow of his digital watch. The darkness he feared lay behind his own eyelids.

He would not think of any of them—not his children, not Estella, not Jane. Where he was now they were all remote, and in his present condition there was nothing he could do for any of them. He wasn't responsible; he could do nothing.

Loving Estella, loving his children, loving Jane—how could he be blamed for that? For *loving*? It was clear to him that he couldn't be. No one could attach any blame to him. And at least he was a man who could love. Wasn't that what everyone aspired to? That state which he came into so easily?

His panic eased as he stared down at his watch, the seconds dissolving in such an orderly way, and he settled back once more, trying to find a comfortable position for his legs. He was too large a man to be cramped in so small a space, trapped in such a frail shelter. But until daylight he would have to endure. He would have to close his eyes and think of simple pleasures—of stretching out on a bed with a clean, taut sheet under him, of fish grilling under the flames. He would rest easy knowing he had done what he could; he was certain he had pushed himself far beyond what others would have done. And he was sure nobody could have succeeded any better.

16

It was Liddy's eye Chrissy wanted to catch as she sat forward, looking across Estella and the top of Jasper's head, but Liddy, leaning back against the wall, had closed her eyes. Perhaps she was dozing. Estella too had shut her eyes, though she stirred when Chrissy shifted her weight. What did Liddy think? That was what she wanted to know. She wanted to trade the question back and forth with Liddy, neither of them saying a word, the way they had traded questions in the back of the station wagon when they were children listening to the grown-up talk—the way Liddy had looked at her when they heard the crash of the tree splintering the roof, each of them holding the other so tightly they could hardly breathe, each of them knowing what the other was thinking. But if Liddy was dozing, she didn't want to wake her.

Carefully Chrissy settled back against Estella's arm, looking up to see if there was any hint of daylight coming through the hole in the roof where the water fell. Perhaps if she lowered the lamp a little more she could tell. Leaning forward across the bed, reaching for the lamp, she could see the floor clearly, the door on her right, and what she saw made her stop where she was, with her fingers reaching for the lamp.

Under the door two trickles of water were flowing, two dark snakes that rippled across the floor.

"Mom," she said softly, "there's water coming in under the door."

Instantly Estella and Liddy opened their eyes and bent down to look. But it was Liddy who sprang up first. "The house is flooding," she said.

"I'm not so sure, Liddy," Estella said, taking the lamp and opening the door into the hallway, with Liddy and Chrissy pushing behind her.

"I think it's just water from the rain," Estella said, holding the lamp high as though to point out the hole in the ceiling.

"It could just as well be water from the sea," Liddy said. "What makes you think it isn't?"

"Taste it," Chrissy said. She dipped her hand in the water and licked her palm, but she couldn't be sure. Perhaps there was a slightly salty taste, or maybe it was just the saltiness of skin under her tongue. It was impossible to tell.

"We're crazy if we stay," Liddy said. "What do you want? To wait until the water lifts the house and washes it out to sea?"

"I don't think that will happen," Estella said, going back into the bedroom and setting the lamp on top of the chest of drawers. "We're going to sit down and talk about this, Liddy," she said then. "We're not going to run around like chickens with their heads cut off."

"You can do what you want to," Liddy said, standing in front of her closet and searching for a slicker along the rack of clothes. "I'm going to go."

"Nobody is doing anything alone. We all go or we all stay. There's no question about that."

"We listened to you before," Liddy said. "Where did that get us?"

"That was one decision, this is another," Estella said firmly. "Now come sit, Liddy."

"You can't force me to do something I don't want to do."

"No," Estella agreed. "But we're going to decide this together, nevertheless."

"Wake up, Jasper," Chrissy said, bending down to his ear. "You have to wake up now."

He opened his eyes so immediately that she was sure he hadn't been asleep anyway. He'd only been pretending.

"What is it?" he said, letting his eyes take on the cloudy surprise of someone just waking, but she was sure it was all an act.

"There's water coming in the house and we have to decide what to do."

"Dad's going to come with a boat," Jasper said. "That's what I think."

"No, he's not," Chrissy said. "It's just us, Jas. We're going to be the ones who have to decide."

"You can talk all you want to," Liddy said. "I won't necessarily listen."

"All right," Estella said. They were back on the bed, sitting in a circle. "I'm ready to hear you, Liddy. Say what it is you think we ought to do."

"If the house is flooding it should be obvious to anybody that it gets more dangerous to stay here all the time. There's no reason not to go now, before we're stranded."

"Nothing's changed that much," Estella said. "There's still the wind and the danger of being hit by tree limbs. There's no shelter and it would be impossible to walk far. I can't see any reason to go tearing off. We can always get out later if we have to."

"Exactly what you said last night about going to the school," Liddy said in a tight voice. "According to you, we'd have plenty of time. Well, we didn't."

"It's not at all the same thing, and you know it. What do you think we should do, Chris?"

Chrissy looked at her hands resting in her lap, avoiding looking at Liddy. She would have liked to agree with Liddy, but she couldn't.

"It isn't too long until daylight," she said. "I think if we can we should wait until then to do anything. I don't want to be out there in the dark."

"I think we should wait, too," Jasper said. "Somebody will come by with a boat. Sooner or later they will."

"I knew what you'd say anyway," Liddy said bitterly. "I've listened to you and now I'm going to go."

Liddy turned to climb off the bed, but Estella grabbed her arm. "Just why do you want to leave so much?" she said. "Just why are you in such a hurry?"

"I don't want to be *trapped!*" Liddy said, trying to tear her arm from Estella's grasp. "Can't you understand something as simple as that? I can't stand feeling trapped."

"You can leave if you want to," Estella said. "But if you do, we'll all come with you. I won't have us separated."

"I can't even move without the rest of you hanging on, and you don't call that being trapped? You won't even let me *breathe!* Did it ever occur to you that I don't want to have the responsibility for everybody else dumped on top of me? All I want is to go by myself."

"And I won't let you. Carry on all you care to, but *I won't let you.*"

Liddy yanked her arm free from Estella's hold and slammed it, fist doubled, into the bed. "Goddammit," Liddy said, putting her head down on her knees.

"Hush," Estella said, brushing her hair back from Liddy's forehead with the palm of her hand.

"Goddammit to hell," Liddy said.

Chrissy felt Jasper's hand working its way into hers the way he had done sometimes when he was very small, his fingers and thumb taking little bites in the air as he used to do when he'd played being an alligator. When his hand had worked its way into hers she closed her fingers over it and held on.

It was the way they had sat together around the dinner table under the pink sky, holding hands, making a circle against danger—that was what she thought. An old strategy, she knew—the circling of the wolf pack, the phalanx of the elephant herd, but a fragile stratagem all the same, since the circle could so easily be breached.

17

So all right, Liddy thought, her forehead pressing against her knees. Estella could keep her against her will, she could force her to stay there and be drowned with the rest of them if that was what she wanted, but it wouldn't change the way she felt.

"Why do you want to go out by yourself, Liddy?" Jasper said in her ear. He was crouched down with his hands, cupped, making sure she couldn't fail to hear him.

"Don't bother Liddy," Estella said.

"I wasn't bothering her," Jasper said. "I was just asking a question."

Liddy sat up and pushed her hair back from her face.

"I'll tell you in the morning," she said. "If we survive until morning,"

"I won't want to know then," Jasper said.

"Do you wish Dad were here?" Chrissy said, turning her head and looking her so intently in the face that Liddy was startled. It wasn't a question she would have expected Chrissy to ask in front of Estella.

"Do you?" she said.

"Sure. I wish it was all of us together."

"But he isn't," Liddy said. "And that's that."

"I think you wish he were here all the same," Chrissy said. "Whatever you say."

"And even if I did?" Liddy said. "What difference would it make?"

Liddy saw the sharp look that Estella turned on her, but Estella managed to hold her tongue.

Still, she knew exactly what it was Estella wanted to ask. She knew it even though reticence kept her from telling Estella what she wanted to know. If she hadn't felt that reluctance to speak about it, she could have told Estella that she was on her side far more than she was on Philip's. After all, Philip had deserted her, too, when he left Estella—a fact that was inescapable whatever he might say to the contrary.

"You care more than you act like you do," Chrissy said. "You've always been like that, Lid."

"Nobody would know better than you, then," Liddy said. "You've studied me enough."

She leaned back against the wall and closed her eyes. For a few minutes she'd half forgotten about the wind, but now she heard it again. Yet it was an odd thing about fear; she'd come to realize that it was impossible to be afraid all the time, even in the worst situations. Fear, too, came in waves, just as the wind did, there were times when you grew tired even of fear and it couldn't touch you.

18

Slowly Estella raised her head.

It was gray sky she saw through the rent in the ceiling. Light rain fell on her upturned face, but the wind had stopped—it was the silence she had felt in the half-sleep she'd fallen into. The only thing that stirred was the water under the bed, sliding slowly forward and back—a movement that showed it was still a part of the ebb and flow of the tide.

Even that unlovely portion of cloud she could see through the hole in the ceiling—a ragged strip—was amazing to her. A sprig of pine needles caught in the splintering wood when the tree fell stirred against the sky, and she kept her eyes on it for a long time, studying it as though it were an omen with something of importance to tell her. It was hard to believe it was all still there—that world of sky and light and air.

The bulky chests of drawers, the lamp on the dresser—even these objects seemed worthy of being looked at for a long time, and she knew there was nothing she could pass over lightly, nothing she could see except with wonder. She was astonished that her eyes still worked, that her lungs still took in air and released it. Those simple marvels should be enough to content for her for the rest of her life.

Lying against each other, curled together to make accommodation, her children slept. Jasper had slipped down between Liddy and Chrissy with his hand on Jenks's neck. Sleeping heavily, in exhaustion, their mouths turned to the mattress, they looked so young and helpless that for a moment she was frightened. But she could see their shoulders unmistakably rising and falling with their breathing, and though she longed to wake them, to share with them the wonder of ordinary light, she let them sleep.

Carefully she eased from the bed and sloshed her way across the floor to pull back the curtains.

Under the windows water lapped against the side of the house as it would have lapped against the pilings of a pier, but behind the house where the land rose steeply to the narrow little road, she could see trees with the lower portions of their trunks in the water, and beyond the trees, bushes. So it wasn't so far they would have to swim after all. It wasn't as she'd imagined in the night when she had feared they were surrounded by water.

And yet, how much everything had changed in the night! The battered pine trees showed yellow gashes where limbs had been torn from their sides; a lake of water obliterated the yard and driveway.

Clearly the world they had left at nightfall was not the one they were returned to at first light. It was a landscape altered utterly—a world in which nothing was the same as it had been.

As Estella leaned out of the window, lifting her head to that ragged sky, a gull flew just above the treetops—the only living creature she could see—and she watched until it disappeared to the west, reluctant to let it go.

When Estella clambered out of the window and dropped into the water, she held her breath, prepared to swim. But her feet touched bottom and her head remained clear of the water. "It's cold," she told the others watching her from the window. "But we can more or less walk to higher ground."

Jasper climbed out next, and she took him on her back. Liddy followed.

Estella had to help pull Jenks through the window where Chrissy was trying to push him. He'd always been afraid of water over his head. But once Estella pulled him free and dropped him into the water, he swam with his neck stretched out, his nose pointing to safety even while his legs paddled wildly. He was the first of them to reach the pine trees, to struggle out to high ground. Estella could see him there, shaking an arc of water from his fur.

(332)

With their arms held high, they plodded through the water and climbed out beside the trees.

It was only then, when they stood shivering in their wet clothes, that Estella turned around and looked back.

Half the house was gone, she saw then, caved in under the large, heavy pine tree. The top part of the branches had come to rest on the roof of the house, and under the trunk the back bumper of the car was visible; beyond it the south wall of Philip's study was crushed.

It was then she remembered that her drawings and collages—her summer's work—were in that room. So much effort for nothing. And it would be impossible, she knew, to work her way through the series again—she could never recapture the time in which she'd done them. They were gone as surely as those days spent under the summer sky. And for the first time that morning she felt loss. She hadn't cared, really, about the house or car, but she grieved for the drawings and the collages made from the family photographs.

She turned away from the house and made her way with the others, climbing over the fallen pine branches to the upper part of the lane, where it rose to meet the narrow road. From that vantage point, when she stopped to look back, she could see only the ocean with the house rising from it like a boat, flooded nearly to the windows.

"Mom!" Jasper said. "Your studio! It isn't there anymore."

"So it isn't," she said.

Where it had stood there was nothing but an expanse of water. Somewhere down the beach her studio had come to rest tilted on its side, she supposed, her brushes and paints left floating.

It was hard to believe that she would never again sit in that studio listening to the waves break on the beach, absorbed in what was emerging on paper or on canvas.

And the house, though it had not floated away, was ruined too, and would have to be rebuilt. Furniture would have to be replaced, and the rugs and curtains. So much would have to be done—so much work— and yet no matter what they did it would never be the way it had been before.

But then she realized. *She* would not be the one to do that work. Philip would have to, or Philip and Jane, but she would not. The cottage had always been Philip's in a way it had not been hers, and now, after this summer, she would never come back there again.

The children were leaving her, making their way up the lane to the road, but she lingered, looking at the water and the pine trees. It was a place she had loved—a place she had supposed it would give her the greatest pain to give up. And yet, as she looked out over the water and the house emerging from it, she felt nothing at all. It was an alien landscape—all she had cared for wiped away in one night. She was surprised that she felt so little, and yet this knowledge freed her, so that she felt as though a weight had been lifted from her as she hurried to catch up with the others. It was gone—all that she had known of that place—and it now existed nowhere except in her mind, where, after all, she might make use of it someday.

The others were already to the road, picking their way around fallen branches and debris. She shivered in her wet clothes and wished they could run to generate a little warmth for themselves, but the road was too littered with branches.

"Swing your arms as you walk," she called to the others. "Get the circulation going." She could see them then swinging their arms and stamping their feet as they went—a kind of ragged army they looked, survivors of a battle.

It was only then, for a moment, that the sensation came to her—of walking down that road with Philip as she had done so many times in the past, taking a rest from children and their demands, just the two of them walking idly along, talking, enjoying a few minutes of late-afternoon peace. For a moment she felt again the way it had been, and then that too slid away. It was gone as so many things in their common world were gone. A memory easily slipping into something else.

It was curious, but she found she was staggering as she walked along the road, and she realized it was manifested in her as physical sensation— that sudden cessation of the tension she and Philip had held between them so long. For the moment she lost her balance. She knew—she could feel it in the dizziness of her head—that the connection between them was broken, as an anchor rope can be snapped in a high sea.

19

At daylight Philip opened his eyes, though he doubted that he had ever slept; he was certain there had never been a time when he lost awareness of the ache in his legs and the stiffness in his shoulders, and if he had dreamed at all it had been of lying with his knees pressed under the steering wheel. Certainly he had heard, while it was still dark, the wind starting to slacken. But it was only when it died that he opened his eyes, knowing he had been let go, turned loose. All night he'd had the sensation of being shaken like a rat in a dog's teeth and knew very well when he was freed. The dull thudding of his heart and the lightness of his head told him that he was exhausted; surely he was too tired to get up and struggle with the difficulties the day would bring. For a few minutes more he put his arm over his eyes and tried to forget it was daylight.

What he longed for most intensely was rescue—for a truck to stop on the road, and for some stranger to tap on the window and offer him a warm cab, a hot cup of coffee. But of course that was absurd. He might lie there for hours more before anyone found him. And he was not, in any case, lost.

He groaned as he sat up, pushing the poncho away from his face.

What he saw first through the rain still washing over the windows was the muddy bank the Land Rover had come to rest against. Gray, billowy clouds lying close to the ground, and, in the road a few feet from the Land Rover, a metal barrel lying on its side, blown to that unlikely resting place by the storm. Of course, there was nobody to be seen and no rescuing truck climbing the hill behind him; what lay beyond the crest of the hill he couldn't tell.

Though it was an unwelcoming landscape, once he sat up he did not want to slide back into his old cramped position. There was nothing to do but open the door and climb out.

Though he knew from the way the Land Rover had settled against the bank that it would be impossible to extricate it, he nevertheless walked over to the side and had a look. A glance was enough to show him that his position was hopeless; he would never be able to free the Land Rover from the ditch by himself.

And so he left it in the ditch, made his way through the mud to the pavement, and started walking south in the direction of the cottage. Near the crest of the hill there was a house, but since the windows had been crudely boarded up and it appeared deserted, he passed it by.

The hill, he realized when he reached what he thought was the top, was deceptive, since he could then see that after a dip in the road there was another, higher crest beyond; he would have to reach the top of that one in order to have a view. But time was all he had; he was well aware that he would be too late to be of much use at the cottage—whatever had happened there in the night had long since occurred.

With his head down he could see little except his boots striding along, and he was glad enough to shut out the world around him, choosing not to see and not to think; he preferred looking down at his boots and listening to their dull clumping on the pavement.

But when he reached the top of the second crest, he lifted his head. From there he had a view of the ocean on his left and, in front of him, of the road dipping and then rising again. But where there were ordinarily marshes and a narrow channel at the foot of the hill where the water rose and fell with the tides, there was now only a flat expanse of water that submerged the highway and extended into the marshes on the other side. He came to a halt, looking at that sheet of water, uncertain what to do.

Trying to get a better view, he turned off the road and made his way through bushes, climbing to a spot several yards above it. From there he could see a wider expanse of ocean and, beyond the water that had submerged the highway, the dark strip of highway rising on the other side. A house sat on a point of land extending into the water—a house, as far as he could tell, undamaged by the storm.

But farther than that he couldn't see.

There was a small tree on the hill he had climbed, and he leaned back against the trunk, looking out over the water, trying to decide what to do. As his father had been fond of saying, he was between the devil and the deep blue sea. Forward or back? He didn't know, and so he stood where he was, balancing one possibility against the other. All he was certain about was that both choices were thoroughly unappealing to him.

20

Up ahead, Chrissy could see the others plodding through the rain with their heads down. Since they were soaked, it didn't matter anymore. They were like monkeys sitting glumly in the trees in the wet season, hunching their shoulders against the rain. Chrissy saw that along the way somewhere Estella had picked up a stick from one of the broken tree limbs and was using it as a walking staff as she strode along—a chunky, determined figure, looking straight ahead.

Maybe it was because that staff reminded Chrissy of the digging sticks the women used to carry as they went into the bush, but she had a sudden vision of a line of women with their foraging bags on their backs walking along the worn path that led around the haunted spring. She'd seen them as she looked over Estella's shoulder while she rode piggyback, that wavering line of women with digging sticks in their hands, heading into the bush. It was uncertain, that picture in her mind, as unreliable as trying to remember a dream, because beyond a certain point in the path the line of women seemed to just disappear; she couldn't remember any more of the scene. They had walked down the path and then . . . they were gone.

But Estella, with the stick thumping firmly on the ground in front of her, appeared to know where she was going, what she was heading for, even though all they could see was the desolation of sodden bushes and broken trees under a gray sky. For all they knew, they could have been the only people left alive on the island.

Up ahead she could see Jasper lifting his face to the sky, his hair bright even in the dull light, and Liddy with her shoulders hunched, her hands in her pockets—they were so far ahead of her that she suddenly felt afraid. They would go around the bend in the road and she would lose them altogether; they would disappear the way the string of women with digging sticks in their hands had disappeared, and she might never see them again.

"Liddy!" she called. "Wait, Lid!"

Liddy walked more slowly and then stopped, waiting, as Chrissy ran, her sneakers slipping up and down on her heels and her wet hair swinging back and forth like a rope across her shoulders.

There were dark circles under Liddy's eyes, and she'd turned pale with the cold. Her shirt clung to her back and her wet shorts made a swishing sound, rubbing back and forth as she walked.

"What will happen now?" Chrissy said. "Where will we go?"

"Oh, there must be emergency shelter," Liddy said vaguely. "Before long planes will be flying out."

Chrissy fell into step beside Liddy; they had walk fast to keep up with Estella.

"The cottage is ruined," Chrissy said.

"It can be rebuilt."

"Next summer..." she said.

Liddy shrugged her shoulders. "Oh, next summer. That's practically a lifetime away, Chris."

"I know it is," Chrissy said.

At the highway they came to a stop and stood uncertainly.

"'Sconset is nearer," Liddy said. "That's where we should go. It's too far to walk to town."

"But that's where we're going to need to go eventually," Estella said. "Maybe we should head in that direction."

"It would be crazy not to go to 'Sconset," Liddy said. "How much longer can we stand to be in these wet clothes?"

"Look," Jasper said.

Around the curve, coming from the south, a van approached slowly. They stood watching it, not even speaking as it drew closer; it was amazing to see any evidence of human life.

Long before it reached them, the van slowed; beside them it stopped and a man leaned across the seat to open the door. "Looks like you could do with a ride," he said. "Where're you heading?"

"Wherever you can go," Estella said. "We're soaked, though, and we have a dog with us."

"I wouldn't care on a morning like this if you had a horse," the man said. "Climb on in. Get out of the rain."

Estella climbed into the front and the rest of them got into the back.

Chrissy sat gingerly in the seat beside Liddy; it was more uncomfortable sitting in wet clothes than it had been walking in them. But still, the van was warm, and she thought that perhaps they would dry out a little. Almost immediately, with all those wet bodies inside the van, the windows steamed up so that Chrissy had to keep wiping the glass with her hand in order to see out.

It seemed astounding to be transported so immediately into warmth and ordinary concerns. It had happened so quickly that it felt dizzying.

"Our house is flooded," Estella told the driver of the van who whistled through his teeth.

"Up in 'Sconset it wasn't too bad at all," he said. "Some trees down and roofs damaged. Things like that. Not nearly as bad as it might have been if it'd hit us the way they thought at first it was going to. Lucky, I guess. It just gave us a good swipe in the end."

"It seemed worse than that where we were."

"Oh well," he said. "I suppose some of those houses right along the water were bound to get flooded. But it could have been a lot worse, that's all I'm saying. I work for the telephone company, I'm a line man, and I can tell you there're plenty of lines down all over the island."

"A tree blew over on our house," Jasper said. "It got the car too."

"Lucky it didn't get you," the man said, but his main attention was for the road. What had happened in the night was clearly of less interest to him than what he could see outside his windows.

The van crested a low hill and came to an abrupt stop. "Would you look at that," the man said. "Highway washed right out."

Chrissy leaned forward to look through the front windshield, and she could see the sheet of water that lay in front of them at the foot of the hill where the marsh had been.

The man backed into someone's driveway and turned around. From the side window they could see the hill rising on the other side of the water, as cut off from them as if it were part of an island.

"We'll have to go back through 'Sconset," the man said.

"Look," Jasper said, pointing. "There's somebody standing on the hill over there under a tree."

"Where?" Chrissy said, but then she could see the man too, someone wearing a gray poncho.

"I think that's Dad," Jasper said. "He has a poncho like that."

"So do lots of other people," Liddy said. "Why would Dad be standing over there under a tree?"

"It's him, anyhow," Jasper said.

"Somebody you know over there?" the man asked.

"I can't see anybody," Estella said, twisting her head to look. "Which tree are you talking about?"

"Whoever he is, he's going to have to go back the way he came," the man said. "He won't be getting through that flood."

Chrissy looked out the back window as they pulled onto the highway. "Do you think it's Dad?" she asked, turning so she could see Liddy's face. But that wasn't the question she wanted to ask, after all. Will it be all right?

"I don't know," Liddy said."

"It *is* him," Chrissy said. "You know it is, Liddy."

"You can see as well as I can," Liddy said. "Maybe better, for all I know."

Their heads touching as they pressed against the glass, they watched together while the figure under the tree grew smaller and smaller and finally disappeared altogether as the truck passed the crest of the hill and continued back the way they had come, searching for a safe road into town.

Mary Elsie Robertson is the author of three pre-
vious novels, *After Freud, The Clearing,* and *Speak,
Angel,* and was the recipient of a 1983 NEA Fel-
lowship in Fiction. She teaches in the Warren Wil-
son M.F.A. Program for Writers, and lives in upstate
New York.